Who turned up the heat?

* * *

TIMUR
The modern rebel who took the name of
an ancient conqueror.

* * *

FAST EDDIE
Part American. Part Russian. All
commando.

* * *

JACQUI
Roving journalist. She covered all the big wars.
And started a few herself.

* * *

KARPONIN
The legendary Russian general whose worst
enemy was his own government.

* * *

SHIH
Beautiful professor. Reluctant spy.
And an even more reluctant killer.

* * *

MARRON
American agent. He found the vision of a
lifetime in a desert hotter than hell.

RED SANDS

**VICTOR
MILÁN**

WARNER BOOKS

A Time Warner Company

For Joseph Reichert

WARNER BOOKS EDITION

Cover design by Tony Greco
Cover illustration by Don Brautigam

Warner Books, Inc.
1271 Avenue of the Americas
New York, NY 10020

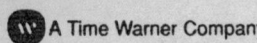 A Time Warner Company

Printed in the United States of America

First Printing: January, 1993

10 9 8 7 6 5 4 3 2 1

ACKNOWLEDGEMENTS

Any number of people offered moral and technical support during the writing of this book. I'd specifically like to thank Rob Pruden, Raina Robison, Melinda Snodgrass, Mike Weaver, my agent Ricia Mainhardt, and my long-suffering editor Brian Thomsen.

*A nation that enslaves other nations
forges its own chains.*

—**Karl Marx**

*There are some things you ignore at your peril, but
you pay attention to Central Asia at the risk of your life.*

—P. J. O'Rourke, *A Parliament of Whores*

PROLOGUE

From jigging veins of rhyming mother-wits
And such conceits as clownage keeps in pay,
We'll lead you to the stately tent of War,
Where you shall hear the Scythian Tamburlaine
Threat'ning the world with high astounding terms
And scourging kingdoms with his conquering sword.
View but his picture in this tragic glass
And then applaud his fortunes as you please.

—Christopher Marlowe,
Tamburlaine the Great, Part I
Prologue

Like a figure out of dream, the white goshawk exploded from the old man's hand. It sprinted forward, wingtips almost brushing the straight white boles of the closely set birches.

The apprentice could barely follow its flight through the green morning, busy as he was trying to keep his startled horse from dumping him into the underbrush. Not for the first time he wondered why he had apprenticed himself as a *manaschi*, a singer of the great Kirghiz epic poem of a quarter million lines.

The master singer sat his chestnut mare and watched the bird weave in and out among the trees, serene in his gabardine suit and skullcap with the rolled-up brim. At the last moment a hare darted out from beneath a fallen log. The goshawk dropped. With a sudden impact it was done.

The apprentice felt his stomach turn over.

He must have moaned. "How can one of such a tender stomach hope to do justice to a song of heroes?" the master singer asked mildly. "To concentrate your mind, recite to me, from the Third Song, the battle between Manas and Er Kökchö the Kalmyk."

He nudged his horse forward, to get to the prey before the goshawk had a chance to begin to eat.

Tashkent, Uzbek Republic
The late 1990s

As long as he could remember these high narrow hallways, they had smelled of varnish. Now they smelled of burned powder and lubricant, and fresh-spilled blood.

In an office to his right he saw a skinny, bearded youth in an embroidered skullcap, white shirt, and loose duck trousers playing the white breath of a fire extinguisher into a green metal wastebasket. Almost, the man smiled behind his turban; unlikely that any important documents were being destroyed there. Still, it was good to see the youth, his AKS-74 slung jauntily over one shoulder, following instructions so assiduously.

The men who had seized the Uzbek Republic headquarters of League internal security—still known by the initials *KGB*—an hour before dawn all had detailed instructions, and they had all been carefully chosen. That was what made this day different from a typical civil disturbance in the vast commonwealth which had succeeded the Union of Soviet Socialist Republics.

The glass had been shattered from the front doors and windows. It lay on the scuffed linoleum floor like crystal snow. The mob noise came rushing in like a flood. He paused. Without being aware of it he breathed a single word: *Gulistan*.

He raised his hands, reassuring himself by feel that the tail of his plain gray turban hid all of his face except the eyes; a safety pin discreetly tucked inside a fold ensured it held. He allowed himself a flicker of amusement: *Allow us messianic leaders our little parlor tricks*.

He glanced left and right at his two escorts. They gripped their Advanced Kalashnikovs and looked grim.

They disapprove of my exposing myself, he thought. *If only they knew how little I was risking*.

And how much.

"How can I lead, if I fear to show myself to our

people?'' he asked. He drew a short breath, surrendered himself to fate, or Allah, or random chance, and stepped outside.

It was still cool and umbral; the sun had not clambered over the rugged wall of the Tien Shan Mountains. His first thought was how much the scene resembled an early-morning meadow in the lush Fergana Valley that ran into the Tien Shans east of Tashkent. Thousands of men and women filled Navaaiy Prospekt and Teatralnaya Square and the broad steps of the Opera beyond, their *tyubeteyka* skullcaps bright and various as summer flowers, their body motions stirring the white dust that overlay all Tashkent so that it flowed among them like the mists of dawn.

Someone stepped up to him, reaching for the lapel of his ill-fitting suit coat. His guards didn't react; this was the technician Yilderim the Tadzhik, pimpled, earnest, and scarcely twenty, who made sure the small microphone was clipped securely in place. He nodded, smiled shyly, and faded back into the crowd, blinking rapidly behind the thick lenses of his wire-rimmed spectacles.

The man cleared his throat. Thunder answered. It was time.

''*People of Turkestan,*'' he said, ''*I am Timur. I have been a prisoner of the League. As you have all been prisoners.*''

He paused. ''*Today we are free.*''

The crowd screamed until its voice began to fail. Wolf howls rose above the roar, orchestrated by youths wearing pale blue *tyubeteyka*, symbolizing *Kok-Bori*, ''the Sky-Blue Wolf,'' legendary progenitor of the Turks and Mongols. The man who named himself after the greatest of all Turkic conquerors was grateful that his turban hid any reaction. *They strengthen us today,* he thought, *but will their fanaticism get out of hand?*

He raised his hands. The crowd quieted. Dotted here and there he could see video cameras trained on him by foreign telejournalists—yes, and Leaguers too, Great Russians and Balts.

So much the better—let all the peoples of the League see

that we bear them no ill will, that all we desire is our freedom—though censorship was likely due to rear up again, so that only those citizens who owned satellite receivers would hear his words unedited.

That mattered little. Later—if there was a later—he would address the world. Today he was speaking to his people, captive remnants of the great Turko-Iranian-Mongol *Millet* that had once ruled a sixth of the world. Speakers borrowed from the Alisher Navaaiy Opera and Ballet Theater carried his words to the multitude gathered in the Tashkent's dusty heart.

From the roar of the crowd, turbulence caught his eye. People were running into the square from Pravda Vostoka. Running as if away from something. Screaming.

Dar ul-Harb, they called it, "the World of War." It meant, strictly, the non-Muslim world—but when a Central Asian used it, he or she meant the USSR or, now, the League. And either, of course, meant Russia, when the masks were stripped away. As English permeated Turkestan with the advent of satellite TV, the fad was to translate the phrase as "the World of Hurt." In truth, that caught the spirit better.

The *Dar ul-Harb* came out of Eastern Truth Street incarnated as a T-72, twelve diesel cylinders growling, its fat smoothbore cannon elevated like the trunk of an angry elephant bull, the tricolor of the League snapping from its whip antenna. It skidded, treads tearing chunks from pavement, and crumpled a faded blue Daewoo subcompact with its portside mudguards.

For a moment it hunkered there, low and wide and ominous. The crowd flowed away from it like mercury from a fingertip. Its engine farted. The treads sucked the trunk lid and fender panel off the Daewoo and wadded them like Kleenex as it lunged ahead.

Timur's guards seized his arms to drag him back inside. He shrugged them off with a glare so furious they backed away despite themselves. The tank shouldered aside a young plane tree with a splintering crack. The mob started to fray, come apart before the tank, people trampling one another in their frenzy to get away from the mottle-painted monster. It elevated its coaxial machine gun and fired.

7.62mm bullets jackhammered the front of the KGB building. Flecks of grit stung the back of Timur's neck, and for a moment he was hidden in billows of cement dust like smoke.

The dust cleared. Timur stood there, erect, unmoving. One guard lay decapitated, blood spurting in diminuendoing pulses from his stump of neck, making red mud of the white dust. The other crouched beside Timur, aiming his Kalashnikov with bared-teeth defiance at the steel beast.

The tank lowered its main gun to bear on the lonely figure. Two teenage boys in light blue skullcaps raced from the steps of the opera house and scaled the rear of the tank like monkeys. A third ran after them, tossed up two small metal cylinders, and darted back into the crowd like a minnow into its school.

The videocams turned, zoomed in to show the viewers back home what marvels of high-tech weaponscraft emboldened mere boys to challenge the forty-ton monster. The boys shook the devices vigorously as one scrambled over the top of the low turret and the other worked his way around its side.

Then they began to spray over the armored-glass vision blocks with black paint.

With a furious mechanical whine the turret cast left and right, trying to dislodge these impertinent insects. Yipping shrilly, more coyote than wolf, the boy in front ducked under the 125mm cannon and went on spraying over the driver's periscope.

The tank was a killing machine of awesome power. It could shrug off shells that would level a house. Its sophisticated night-vision and laser sighting devices enabled it to detect and destroy rival behemoths at two kilometers and beyond.

Blind, it was a paperweight. Worse, it was a *target*. A giant can stuffed with thousands of kilograms of fuel and high explosives.

A Pepsi bottle rose from the crowd in a tumbling arc to smash on the tank's rear deck. It was empty, as was the next, and the next. *But there was no way for the tankers within to know that.* They could only crouch helplessly behind their weapons and levers and instruments and wait for the first telltale *whoomp* of a gasoline bomb.

The T-72 was supposed to be proof against chemical and biological attack and radioactive fallout. Its metal plate wouldn't burn; its air intakes were baffled and filtered. But enough Molotov cocktails would exhaust its air; a protracted enough bonfire would heat the metric tons of metal until the occupants inexorably roasted—unless the ammunition cooked off first.

With vision obscured, it couldn't even escape. The buildings of Teatralnaya Square were either Russian colonial, dating from after the conquest in 1865, or had been built after the 1966 quake. In either case they were massive, and overbuilt. Powerful as it was, the T-72 had no hope of bulling its way blindly through them. It would get stuck or throw a tread. Then it would be blind *and* immobile.

The driver broke first. He came rearing out of the overhead escape hatch like a sounding whale. The youth on the front glacis, who was performing a sort of hunkered-down arm-waving victory dance and ignoring the glass shrapnel bursting around him, howled and sprayed the tanker in the face with his paint can.

The tanker screamed as stinging paint filled his eyes. He threw his hands to his face and rolled off onto the cracked cement of the square. The commander and gunner emerged from the top of the turret, arms upraised in surrender.

The mob bellowed like a soccer crowd greeting a tie-breaking goal, came surging forward to engulf the tank. Commander and gunner were roughly dragged down. The driver, still groveling, convinced some hideous acid was eating away his face, was kicked and pummeled to his feet.

An ugly, animal moan rose from the crowd. Timur heard voices crying for the League soldiers' heads.

He held up his hands. In response to the gesture—or to the urgings of the blue-cap cadre salted among them—the crowd thrust the tankers forward.

Timur looked down upon the captives. The commander faced him with head raised, defiant and scared white. The gunner just looked glum. The driver, eyes staring red-rimmed from his raccoon mask of spray paint, was turning foolishly this way and that, touching his comrades and captors on the arm and muttering in Russian, "I can see, I can *see*," like a man who'd just been faith-healed on some American TV revival.

Though less than half the crowd packed in between the *faux*-European buildings around the square were likely to be practicing Muslims the blood-feud tradition still ran strong as Tien Shan runoff. Timur felt the hatred boiling within the crowd.

The same hatred surged up suddenly within him: *They have much to answer for, these Nikolays. The blood of a hundred years. The blood of innocents. The blood of—*

He moistened lips, which were dry as the desolate heart of *Qizil Qum*, "the Red Sands." From the corner of his eye he glimpsed Yilderim, eyeglasses askew, gamely bellycrawling toward him, unsure that the danger was past but suspecting he might be needed.

Miraculously the microphone still worked. *"Release them,"* Timur said.

The square was silent but for the wind off the Tien Shan, the Heavenly Mountains. A moment blew away in that wind. A youth in a blue skullcap threw down the tank commander's arm as if tossing a piece of spoiled fruit in the street before a vendor's stall. He stepped back.

One by one the others who gripped the Russians followed his example. The tank commander stared up at Timur as if unsure what manner of being this was. The Russian was young—a child, really—blond and snub-nosed, an angry bruise already spreading across one cheek. With unthinking reflex he slowly brushed the white dust of Tashkent from his black uniform.

The gunner pulled the driver's arm over his shoulder. After a last glance at Timur, the young commander took the other arm. The crowd parted noiselessly to permit them to pass, and so they made their way unhindered up Navaaiy— once Lenin Prospekt—until they passed out of sight.

"Let the people of the League of Affiliated Republics see," he called, as if calling after the stumbling tankers, "that we bear them no ill will. It is the League itself, which claims to be voluntary but which sends its tanks to crush those who wish to claim true sovereignty, that we fight!"

A voice soared high: *"Temir, haqiqatan Turkestaan aatasi-siz!"*—"Timur, truly you are the father of Turkestan." The crowd began to chant his name: *"Te-mir, Te-mir!"*

The Red Sands Rebellion had begun.

PART I

The World
of Hurt

There is a powerful craving in most of us to see ourselves as instruments in the hands of others and, thus, free ourselves from responsibility for acts which are prompted by our own questionable inclinations and impulses. Both the strong and the weak grasp at this alibi. The latter hide their malevolence under the virtue of obedience. The strong, too, claim absolution by proclaiming themselves the chosen instruments of a higher power—God, history, fate, nation or humanity.

—Bruce Lee, The Tao of Jeet Kune Do

Chapter
ONE

Oh-dark-thirty. Jesus, isn't it time to move?

Little Alex let go of the pistol grip of his CAR-15, made himself scratch his nose instead of checking his watch again. He glanced to the side, where Delgado hunched over his own weapon behind a tuft of feather-dry grass. Texas Team's light weapons specialist gave no sign of noticing. Alex had a tendency to overamp before action, to the point that the nerves seemed to stand through his skin like wires. Controlled frenzy had served him well in the past, but right now he needed *optimal cool.*

An old GAZ-69 truck, marooned on a concrete slab to serve as a generator, pounded the night like a garage-band bass, monotonous but not entirely regular. He let it throb up into him out of the ground, concentrated on it, on breathing crisp Caucasus air that smelled of soil and summer-dry vegetation. *I refuse to fidget, dammit. I can trust my internal clock.*

Inside the wire the League SIGINT station slept: a mal-formed circle about two hundred meters across slapped down on a comparatively flat patch of mountainside. A shallow arroyo cut a chord across the western perimeter near where Alex and Delgado lay belly-down in the scrub. Beyond it were prefab barracks for the thirty-man security platoon, and just downslope the mess tent and kitchen, a latrine and shower block. Alex smelled soapy water, grease, and spices. Further confirmation that most of the security detachment was ethnically Georgian—Great Russians would get the running shits from hot local fare. It also confirmed a fringe benefit of being a KGB Border Guard instead of a League Army grunt: better food. Or at least livelier.

Upslope of the barracks lay the CO's trailer. A commo van was parked next door. The water tower loomed right behind like a quiescent Martian death machine. In the compound's center stood a watchtower equipped with a powerful searchlight, a PKM machine gun whose full-sized 7.62mm ammunition gave it a lot more range and authority than the current generation of 5.45mm support weapons, and two sentries who, if the last three nights were any indication, were stone asleep.

Beyond the watchtower lay the reason everybody was out playing in this godforsaken spur of the Caucasus Range: a huge white parabolic antenna aimed at Turkey. The generator bebopped away behind it.

Except for red glints filtering from the black van where the graveyard shift technician monitored the big dish ear, and yellow light spilling out the windows and door of the on-duty squad's ready shack by the solitary gate across the compound, the camp was dark. Apparently the commandant disliked the idea of spotlighting the facility to the NATO troops it was spying on, southwest across the line in the black mountains near Ardahan.

The League seemed to be trying to keep the station seriously unobtrusive: just a single course of fence, three meters high and topped with razor tape coils; no minefield; no cleared kill zone around the perimeter, though the scrubby mountainside offered damned little cover to intruders less skilled at snooping and pooping than Texas Team. Lights were spaced around the perimeter, but they were unlit, keyed to motion sensors sown outside the wire.

Alex was unimpressed. The Georgian-weighted ethnic mix was too risky. Georgia was perpetually pissed off at the League for preventing it from liquidating its Muslim Azeri minority, and made constant noises about pulling out of the

League, as it had from the old Soviet Union. That was noise; Georgia could no more get by without the League than a horse could run without one of its legs, any more than any republic—except maybe Russia herself, central and eternal. But truculence didn't make the Georgians reliable troops for the Leagues' internal security *apparat*.

Also, I'd *light the place so bright the lizards would be out trying to sun themselves*. Did the Greenstripers of the Border Guard think the Turks and their American allies didn't know they were there?

The sorry truth was, anybody who gave a good goddamn knew about the station. Forget military satellites; the SIGINT post was big enough to be seen by the private and quasiprivate weather satellites that blanketed the whole damn planet, to the endless annoyance of the superpowers. Like the French SPOT weather satellite that discovered back in 1986 that the big radioactive plume that was giving Western Europe the fits pointed like a finger to a place called Chernobyl—only the new ones were a lot more sophisticated.

He sensed Delgado stirring. It was a subliminal sensation; you didn't actually *hear* the Cat, unless he wanted you to. He glanced over. Delgado had his face turned toward Alex. Alex was so dialed in to the darkness that by starlight alone he could see the bored expression on Delgado's handsome face, the heavy eyelids at half mast, even through the coating of black and dark grey camo stick.

The sleepy look was pure *dezinformatsiya*—now a good American word, if illegal for Americans to use. Delgado was always alert.

Alex scoped the compound one last time with a folded-optics ambient-light enhancer—starlight scope—the size of a pair of opera glasses. Nothing stirring but the three sentry pairs, drifting like sleepy green ghosts inside the wire.

He let himself peel back the Cordura flap that hid his watch, with a slight Velcro rasp. Everyone in Texas Team wore old-fashioned dial jobs. The hands were easier to read in a quick Gestalt flicker than LCDs.

Time. He popped a stick of gum, looked at Delgado. Delgado nodded, raised his CAR-15 with the thick-barreled M203 grenade launcher slung underneath it like an elephant cock. He held up a magazine, showing Alex the open end to confirm it was empty, then slid it home in the CAR's well with only the faintest click as it caught.

Little Alex slid an empty magazine into his own un-adorned CAR. He flowed to his feet. The time had come to express the dancing energy within as action. This was what he lived for, pushing it to the edge—*testing the envelope*, as the fighter jocks said.

Even if it was just *coitus interruptus*. It was their first in months, and he planned to enjoy it.

Enough time had elapsed for the four who had gone in ahead—Pete with Tex, Georgie, and Buddy—to neutralize the four sentries close enough to interfere. If they hadn't . . .

Alex shrugged and grinned into the darkness. They carried communicators small enough to button into the breast pockets of their cammie battle dress, with smart phased-array antennas that enabled them to link directly to low-orbit communications satellites with a minute expenditure of power. Virtually undetectable—but *virtually* wasn't good enough, here in the shadow of a few million rubles of radio direction finding gear. RDF was one area where League high-tech, still well behind the West, actually delivered as advertised. Texas Team was moving in complete radio silence.

Their first clue that they'd failed would be the shit hitting the fan.

Fyodor Vasiliyevich knew what was happening right away. His mother had raised no fools. When he felt that hard cold pressure on the side of his neck and swiveled his eyes down to see the glint of starlight on a huge tapered blade, he knew: *Rambo had his chunky ass.*

The Rambo character was hopelessly passé in the sensitive, caring West, but Cold War habits died hard, and anyway the League tended to run about twenty years behind the rest of the world. The old Sly Stallone films hadn't *exactly* been shown to troops in indoctrination during the Soviet years, but everyone saw them. Even more than an earlier generation's John Wayne, Rambo continued to personalize the Threat: arrogant, psychopathetic, invisible killers in green berets. And they all had *big knives*.

"*I surrender,*" Fyodor squeaked. He cursed himself for not having paid more attention in English class. But at the moment it was all he could do to remember to speak in *Russian*.

Pressing his Arkansas toothpick tight up under the sentry's jaw, Georgie relieved him of his AKS-74. The rifle was slung— slovenly, but that was the way of sentries, God bless 'em.

"Hands behind you," he hissed, using the worst *Amerikanskiy* accent he could muster. Emphasizing your alienness emphasized your menace; it was all part of the psywar game. Just like the big knives.

Drawing the sentry's wrists's together behind his back, Georgie wrapped them tightly with West German *Bundespolizei* nylon restraints. He took a rolled pair of cheap Polish athletic ankle socks—unused; there were supposed to be no atrocities on this mission—and stuffed them in the sentry's mouth, then took a turn of Taiwanese duct tape around his head to hold the socks in.

Texas Team's equipment was vintage global village. Their battle dress was made by Basques, boots in Croatia, and their rucks hailed from New Zealand. All stuff that could be bought at any K-mart from Beijing to Budapest. Of course, their knives and CAR-15s would mark them as U.S. Special Forces in the minds of anyone they encountered, despite the fact their short assault rifles were mounted with British-made SUSAT night-and-day optical sights instead of American issue. But maintaining deniability was intrinsic to the "work," even when futile.

For good measure Georgie taped over the sentry's eyes,

just to keep him disoriented. Then with the muzzle brake of his CAR he urged the man to his knees and on down to his belly.

Then he noticed that Buddy was still dangling the other sentry by the neck.

"What the hell do you think you're doing, you idiot?" he hissed.

Buddy showed him a grin, shocking white teeth set in the midst of a great dark-mottled jack-o'lantern face hovering over the sentry, whose struggles were gradually diminishing.

"For God's sake, put him *down*." Georgie's eyes darted like small caged animals. His knuckles were white on the grips of his carbine.

Buddy let the Border Guard collapse into a little pool of humanity on the hardpan at his feet. He unlooped his garrote and held it up wordlessly. A two-centimeter-wide leather strap dangled from ivory handles polished by skin oil and friction, in place of the usual fine wire. The strap sufficed to choke a man into unconsciousness. The wire, tightened by a twist of Buddy's massive wrist, would have severed the neck to the spine.

"Just havin' me a little fun," Buddy said sotto voce. It was supposed to be less detectable than a whisper.

Georgie grimaced and squatted down to watch the distant guard shack while Buddy secured his victim.

Alex slid over the lip and down the meter and a half cut into the arroyo. Delgado flowed after him. Here they were hidden from view of the buildings.

Civilians were required to keep their distance from military installations, even ones far less sensitive than this. But the local Georgian hillmen, surly and semiliterate, figured the laws only applied if you got caught. They ran their sheep where they damned well pleased; if the border pigs caught them, that was just the Black Mother's will. The penalty was usually just a beating anyway, though occasionally the *Komitet* got a hair up its butt and capped a few offenders to encourage the rest.

During the three days the team had spent scoping out the place, Alex and Pete had come up with an excellent little skit to put on for the Border Guards. Before they began bellycrawling around to test the motion sensors, they'd swiped a few sheep. When the lights went on, they'd chase the sheep into the illuminated zone. If the security boys got itchy and opened up, they had a spare sheep hog-tied in another gully that they could shoot and leave for the Border Guards to find. The scheme would show them just how comprehensive sensor coverage was, and with luck would irritate the guards into disregarding or even turning off the gear with repeated false alarms.

It hadn't been necessary. The first probe brought guards running to the wire to yell and wave at the spotlit sheep.

The second brought nothing at all.

Weeds and trash had gathered at the base of the wire, where it extended down into the arroyo. The first infiltrators had carefully replaced it. Alex and Delgado scooped it aside again. At the bottom the mesh was pulled loose.

Alex lay on his back, pulled the wire out, slid through the half-meter gap between fence and sandy bottom. He drew his rifle after him and crouched to cover while Delgado followed.

They duckwalked up the arroyo. Their objective was the CO's trailer. The stars overhead were as bright as glass nail heads. Alex kept making faces at the night; he'd gotten sand inside his cammie blouse. He hated the way it sloshed around and coated his skin. At Fort Bragg they said he was too fastidious for SF. Then again, they'd also said he was too short. He made them eat that too.

As they crept up past the barracks, a dark figure scrambled over the edge of the arroyo and dropped to the bed. He took a step and stopped dead, his face an elongate moon with a dark astonished crater in the center of it.

Alex pounced. He locked his hand over the man's mouth

and drove the CAR-15's barrel into his solar plexus, doubling him over and turning any nascent cry for help into a grunt.

Three more forms dropped into the arroyo with sandbag sounds.

Delgado sidestepped, covering the newcomers with his CAR-203. Alex slammed his man against the bank with enough force to knock what breath he'd collected out of him again. He screwed the muzzle brake under the man's chin.

For a moment they held that tableau. Alex could read the Border Guards' minds: They were trying to decide whether they were more afraid of the dreaded Green Berets or their own superiors. If the facility was captured, maybe the brass would overlook the fact that they'd been caught sneaking out to score some booze or dope or a little local talent through the hole they'd carefully left in the sensor screen.

On the other hand, if they could give the alarm and somehow survive, they'd be heroes. . . .

Motion behind the dithering squaddies. The rearmost started to turn.

"Enough."

The voice was quiet, but cracked like a near miss. It spoke Russian. Its tone spoke of counting trees or mining gold, or getting shot in the back of your head. It was a tone every Russian was schooled from birth to obey.

"Put your hands behind your necks and drop to your knees. *Now.*"

The Border Guards complied. With a quietness that belied his enormous bulk, Buddy's identical twin Tex dropped into the arroyo and quickly secured them with nylon restraints.

Alex pushed the one he'd caught at Delgado. The interloper stood casually covering the prisoners with his CAR. The floppy downbrim boonie hat all the world's Special Forces wore when their butts were actually on the firing line shadowed his poster-boy features. His name was Pete, but behind his back most of Texas Team called him Mr. P: *P* for *Perfect.*

Heart in his throat, Alex moved to the bank. The hardpacked earth was cool and fragrant. He risked a three-second look over.

Nothing showed from the bunkhouse. He let himself feel a moderated rush of relief. The brief scuffle hadn't given them away.

He jerked his head at Delgado and moved silently up the arroyo.

"Glad we could help," Pete murmured to his back.

"All *right*, damn you," the major shouted, sitting on the edge of the bed while his feet scrabbled in search of his slippers. As cold as it got up here in the heights at night, even in high summer, he wasn't about to put his bare feet on the linoleum floor. "No need to pound the door down."

He found the slippers, slid his feet into them, got up and pulled a robe around him. For a moment he paused, contemplating the Makarov in its holster lying on the nightstand.

No. No alarm had been given. And if as he suspected it was some manner of bungle that had dragged him from sound sleep, he did not need a pistol to make whoever was responsible regret that his parents hadn't aborted him. These Georgians were flighty and irresponsible as so many teenage girls. But he was Great Russian as well as KGB. He knew how to keep their kind in line.

He opened the door. For a moment he wondered how a journalist had managed to penetrate a secured facility. A shocking degree of license permeated the League; the nationalists had claimed that devolution of the Union would lead to decadence, and they had been right. Still, anyone, League or foreign, who got into such a secret installation without permission had bought himself a one-way ticket to a room with soundproofed walls and drains in the floor.

Almost, he smiled. *Some* things hadn't changed.

. . . He realized that the cylindrical object in his face didn't have the rounded foam contours of a microphone after all, but the hard edges of blackened metal. A suppressor. Of the sort screwed onto . . . handguns.

"Trick or treat, motherfucker," a voice said in English.

The door to the commandant's trailer opened. A tech from the black van slouched in at the point of Georgie's CAR.

"This one seemed to be in charge," Georgie said, subconsciously smoothing his mustache with his thumb.

The technician wore a food-stained white T-shirt pouched out at the waist to hold a goodly roll of flab, rumpled pants, outrageously bogus Hong Kong Reebok rip-offs. He seemed to have made a gesture at sweeping his curly black hair up and back in approved Old Bolshevik style. Mostly it looked as if somebody had been at his head with a Garden Weasel.

With a lazy wave of his Glock 23, Alex gestured him over next to the bunk, where the major and his morale officer sat stiffly. Georgie slipped out the door in a hurry, as if the tech's sloppiness might be catching.

The technician sized Alex up through Coke bottle glasses and nodded.

"Good," he said, "*Amerikanyets*. Maybe they'll have some decent cigarettes."

"Fool," the morale officer said. "Americans can't possess cigarettes."

The tech sneered. "They're *Spetsnaz*. Of course they have cigarettes. They can have anything they want, and they're stationed in Turkey, for the Black Mother's sweet fucking sake."

Delgado's eyes widened infinitesimally at the mention of *Spetsnaz*. Alex flicked him lightly with his own. The tech had used the word in the archaic, *Soviet Military Encyclopedia* sense, that no one ever used anymore: *Spetsnaz* originally meant *Western* "bandit" formations, like SAS and Special Forces. The American media had latched on to it to signify Soviet commando types, and that usage had come filtering back into the Motherland with all the other Western corruption the Rad-Trads were so pissed off about.

With the CO secured, the rest went swiftly. Pete, Georgia, and the twins caught the two off-duty squads asleep—the ones who hadn't tried sneaking out for the night—secured them without any fuss, and locked them in their barracks. League barracks were designed for locking troops in, even prefab ones in the boondocks. A field-phone call from the commandant himself woke up the pair in the gun tower and brought them blinking in to join their comrades.

A shit-scared NCO was sent off with Tex to troll in the final pair of perimeter guards and the two on duty at the gate. They went into the barracks too.

The facility belonged to Texas Team.

"Not a bad little gig," Alex said to Delgado.

The major, who had been sitting there turning red, abruptly found his voice. "You won't get away with this."

"Show a little originality," Alex said.

The commandant was just getting rolling. He sputtered something about bandits. The morale officer quelled him with a look.

Little Alex laughed and unscrewed the suppressor from his Glock. If there was trouble now a little noise more or less would make no difference.

As the major watched with cocktail-onion eyes, Alex unbuttoned a breast pocket of his cammie blouse, pulled out a magazine. He glanced at it quickly to confirm that the numbered holes on the left side of the staggered magazine showed .40-caliber silvertips, the right the rubbery blue tips of Glaser-type "safety slugs." Unlike the rest of Texas Team he didn't have much faith in knives, however big.

Beside him Delgado dropped the empty magazine from his CAR, stuffed it into a back pocket of his pants, then drove a full box into the well with the heel of his hand. He worked the bolt and grinned.

"What on earth are you doing?" the major asked.

"Making sure you don't go anywhere," Little Alex said

in Russian. "You and your men are under arrest, my very fine Chekist. For negligence of such a nature as to endanger League and Motherland."

The captives stared at him as if he'd stepped out of a flying saucer.

"Isn't it fortunate," he went on, "that we *are Spetsnaz*—Diversionary Troops of the Chief Intelligence Directorate of the League General Staff, instead of real American Special Forces?"

He rammed the magazine home.

"I guess that means no cigarettes," the technician said.

Chapter
TWO

The sun was falling into the Rockies. To the north Pikes Peak had taken on a red glow, like an iron pyramid heated in a forge. The light on the treeless finger of ridge the two horses and three riders were following was golden, lending the scene an unreal, cinematographic quality. It was warm, and warmth beat up from the sun-warmed ground, but the restless wind had a cool undertone.

"It's going to be dark soon," Elinor Marron said. "We should have headed back earlier."

Francis Marron glanced back over his shoulder at his wife. "Probably. But Becky seemed to be having such a good time."

His bay gelding tossed its head up and down. "Look, Daddy!" five-year-old Rebecca chirped. She was mounted in front of her father, and didn't seem to mind at all being whipped by the horse's long black mane. "Lindsay's nodding. He had a good time too."

Marron steadied her with his free hand. "No, honey. He just knows we're headed home."

"He's hungry and tired, that's all," Elinor said. Her tone suggested the beast wasn't the only one who was eager to get back to the barn at the Broadmoor after a day in Bear Creek Canyon Park.

The trail led into a grove of aspen whose leaves rattled with a cicada sound in the breeze, then wound down among Ponderosa pines, the horses' hooves churning up dark soil and long three-needle clusters.

The path crossed Gold Camp Road before leading into Cheyenne Mountain Park. Despite the fact that there wasn't much traffic up here these days—*anymore*, as they said in the Colorado vernacular Marron had grown up with—they sat and waited, watching, for a full thirty seconds before crossing the road.

A few tendrils of the formaldehyde-rich smog, emitted by the methanol-burning auto engines state and federal law mandated, that overlay Colorado Springs had just begun to sting Marron's eyes when they hit the picnic area. It was no more than a widening at the end of a little cul-de-sac that led off Gold Camp, with some cement picnic tables and a good view out over the Springs.

There was a surprising amount of activity, Marron noted, at least a dozen men moving around. The gravel-covered parking area was dominated by a giant white RV, stream-lined in a whale sort of way, that everybody of Marron's generation—the tag end of the Baby Boom—knew automatically as a *land barge*. Though she was riding behind and to his right, outside the periphery of his vision, Marron could see in his mind the way his wife's mouth and eyes tightened in disapproval.

They rode skirting the artificial clearing. Something tugged at the corner of Marron's eye; he looked more closely at the land barge, noticed a discreet logo painted on its gleaming flank: a stylized eagle head and white star in a badge-shaped shield, surrounded by the words DEPARTMENT OF ENFORCE-

MENT AFFAIRS/FEDERAL POLICE AGENCY. Beneath that in block capitals was painted the legend PIU 92.

He was just beginning to feel his heart dropping in his chest when Elinor screamed.

He tore his eyes from the vehicle, saw what had made her scream. A man lay sprawled across one of the weathered gray railroad ties that edged the gravel. The front of his T-shirt was soaked black with blood. Beyond lay other bodies, fallen in that rag-doll way death has with you when it comes quick and violent. He'd seen that look often enough before, in Central America and the Middle East. He'd hoped never to see it in America—and not because he was squeamish.

A man had been squatting over the body, dropping something beside it. He straightened, staring gape-mouthed at Marron. Marron's instinct was to turn the horse's head to the trees and dig his heels in hard. He quelled it. It was too late already: somebody shouted, and then there were men running toward them. Men bulky in white jumpsuits. Men with guns in gauntleted hands.

"Frank," Elinor said, voice shrill. "Frank, what's happening?"

He didn't say anything. He was busy holding one hand over his squirming daughter's eyes and fighting to keep control of the sidestepping, eye-rolling gelding with the other. Horses feared the scent of fresh-spilled blood. They weren't as stupid as everyone thought.

A white-gloved hand grabbed Lindsay's reins. Fat suppressors screwed on the muzzles of stubby machine pistols ringed Marron in.

"Who are these men?" Elinor demanded.

"Federal Police, ma'am," one of the jumpsuits said. "Public Information Unit."

In the background someone was yelling, "You fucking call that keeping a lookout?" Rough hands grabbed Rebecca, dragged her out of Marron's arms.

"Daddy!" she screamed, kicking and clawing for him.

He started out of the saddle after her. The machine pistols held him back.

"Yeah," one of his captors said, "come down off of there. But slowly, motherfucker."

Deliberately Marron swung down. A Public Information Unit man was helping Elinor off her mare Stevie's back, gingerly but none too gently.

Two flanking, one behind, a trio of agents prodded Marron forward toward the RV. He was ultraconscious of his surroundings: a few clouds rushing overhead, seemingly just out of reach of the talon trees; the gravel squeaking beneath the soles of his cowboy boots; the manic chatter of a mountain jay; the shadows clustering, ominous and cool; the smell of blood, raw copper, and that staling of the air that comes with the nearness of death.

The object the man had been dropping next to the body—*replacing*, Marron dutiful corrected himself—was an ungainly little firearm, handgun-sized, with the box magazine placed in front of the grip. He recognized it at once: a "zipper" machine pistol in .22 short or long rifle, a home-brewed knockoff of the 9mm Scorpions the FedPols had trained on him. American ingenuity at work.

"Frank," he heard Elinor call, "Frank, *tell them who you are!*"

One of his flank escorts glanced sidelong at the other as they herded him around the vehicle. Both chuckled.

They stopped him near the vents toward the rear. Elinor was on the other side, out of sight. Rebecca had been carried inside. If she was still protesting, the vehicle's soundproofing masked the sound.

One FedPol patted him down expertly while the other two covered, relieving him of his wallet and the Buck knife at his belt. Then he swept Marron with the wand of a metal detector.

All day long Marron had been nagged by guilt at not wearing a pistol. It was a violation of procedure, and Marron was a man who believed in the book. But Elinor hated and feared firearms. And she could always tell, even when he was carrying a tiny Walther TPH concealed in an inside-the-belt holster.

Now he was glad for Elinor's sensibilities. If the FedPols had found a piece on him, at the very least he would have been battered semiconscious. Owning a gun was a serious offense. Carrying one opened season on you.

The agent disappeared into the RV with Marron's billfold. The other two stood nearby, apparently ignoring him.

Marron looked around. He could see eight bodies strewn around the picnic area: four men, two women, two he couldn't tell. Or maybe *boys* and *girls* would be more accurate. Of those in condition to identify, none seemed older than twenty. Some of their jeans had the holes in the knee that were obligatory for trend-conscious youths who didn't buy into the future-Puritan Serious look, but their clothes looked well kept. They had all been shot.

The deaths were obviously recent. He wondered why he and his family hadn't heard anything. Zippers were fairly noisy, and sound carried in the mountains.

There were perhaps a dozen agents in the Public Information Unit, stalking among the bodies, examining them, taking samples. It was their job to get to a site where a potentially controversial event had taken place, ensure that nothing on hand would damage national security or the public before clearing the press to cover it. *Decontam squads*, they were called within the Federal Police Agency, or *containment teams*. They were young, tall, athletic, crop-haired. One of the two standing guard on him now was a black; his was the only non-white face Marron had seen in the unit.

A folded piece of paper skittered past Marron's foot: a leaflet, with a prominent block L in a circle displayed on the front. It was the symbol of the *Libertas* terrorist underground.

A couple of jumpsuited agents with slung Scorpions stood near the front of the RV, chatting and laughing, occasionally glancing Marron's way. A word drifted down a gust of breeze to him: *desparecido*.

His blood turned to liquid helium. A civilian who used that word could be arrested and fined or even sent to a work camp for slandering the government's war on crime. And these men didn't seem to care whether he heard them use it or not.

"Frank?" Elinor's voice came from the far side of the beached-whale machine. "Frank, what's happening? What are they going to do with us?"

He heard something harsh said—what, he couldn't make out. He hoped they wouldn't strike her. Ellie wasn't used to that sort of treatment.

Dear God, he thought. He wasn't a religious man, but he prayed now: *Don't let them do anything hasty.*

An agent emerged from the van. He was shorter than average for this crew, stocky, his blond hair cut short enough to show a silvery plush sheen. He shouldered past the two who were standing and telling dangerous jokes and marched straight to Marron. The pair glared after him, then quickly away.

He handed Marron his billfold with his photographic SmartCard ID clipped to it with his thumb. "My apologies for the inconvenience, Mr. Marron," he said. "You should have told us you were with the National Security Agency."

The two escorts exchanged looks and fell back. The black let a long breath escape through flared nostrils. Marron moistened his lips, nodded, then slipped the ID back into the billfold and returned it to his hip pocket. Another agent brought Rebecca down the metal steps. She broke away from his grip as soon as her running shoes hit gravel, raced to her daddy. He knelt to gather her in his arms.

Two agents brought Elinor around the rear of the RV. She was maintaining a look of patrician calm, but spots of pink glowed on her high cheekbones, and her blue eyes had a hunted animal light. A strand of dark blond hair had pulled free from her ponytail and hung unnoticed across her face.

"Ms. Marron," the stocky agent said with a nod. "We regret having alarmed you. But we have a youth-gang incident on our hands here, and it's very serious, as you can see. We couldn't take any chances."

She said nothing, only compressed her lips. Her husband handed Becky off to her. The girl tearfully wrapped her arms around her neck.

The short agent looked at the agents standing nearby. "You all have jobs to do, am I right?" They turned away and started looking busy.

"We're not sure exactly what went down here," he explained as he walked the Marrons over to where their horses stood under guard with their reins tied to tree boles. "It might have been some kind of a faction fight—these middle-class revolutionary wanna-be's breed splinter groups like rabbits. Or it might have been a deal that went bad with some other gang. Drugs, guns, porno, illicit data—people who deal in that stuff play heavy." Fat, shiny brass 9mm casings crunched into the gravel beneath his combat boots.

Marron helped Elinor into her saddle. Her mouth tightened slightly when Rebecca refused to climb up with her, choosing to ride with her father instead.

"You understand the need to be discreet about this, of course, sir," the agent in charge said as he handed Becky up. For the first time he showed something other than complete self-confidence.

Marron nodded and, after a moment, found his voice. "Of course." He settled his daughter in before him and hugged her close.

"And one more thing, sir," the agent said. He gestured at the bodies cooling beneath the high blue sky. "You should always wear your sidearm. Crime isn't staying in the streets anymore."

Chapter
THREE

"The point of power is to exercise it," the handsome young general said as the videocam zoomed in on his face. He turned his head subtly to present his best angle, emphasizing the shell-splinter scar that ran from hairline to chin. Many of his fellow veterans of the Afghan War were shy about the marks the conflict had left on them—ashamed, even; not him. That scar was his trademark. It had helped him become the contemporary poster boy for *Homo sovieticus,* "the New Soviet Man," back when there were Soviet men. It had likewise helped make him the most famous officer in the League Armed Forces. "We are the executive; we are the League's strong right arm."

A pair of Su-25s swept by, so low over the sparsely covered steppe that their cockpits, glinting in the harsh sun of the Russian Republic's Rostov Oblast east of Novocherkassk, were on almost the same level as the hilltop regimental command group.

"It's rare to encounter a man so forthright," the reporter breathed when the surf-roar of their passage had dwindled enough for speech. "Even among military leaders."

"The concept of *decadence* is overdue to be rehabilitated, don't you think?" he asked, and reached for a microphone.

At his command came a sound as if strips were being torn from the cloudless blue sky. The ridgeline half a kilometer away flashed into flame.

The reporter gasped, clasped her lower lip in her teeth. But she didn't flinch. As the two BRDM-2 scout cars streaked forward in advance of the dun cloud raised by the T-80s spearheading the assault, and the armored personnel carriers behind to give it mass, the general studied her with frank interest. The maneuver was developing nicely and for a moment or two would not require his attention. He was not a sidelong man by nature.

He liked what he saw. Her straight hair was pageboy short, a striking orange shade of auburn he'd never seen before, but which appeared natural. Her face was feline, flat and wide, almost as if she were Central Asian herself. Her nose was snubbed. Her eyes were invisible behind flamboyant domed mirror shades. She was above average height for a modern Western woman, 176 centimeters or so. By traditional Russian standards she was skinny.

But General Major Anatoliy Karponin had cosmopolitan tastes. That was not necessarily a compliment in the society he had sprung from; for years "cosmopolitanism" meant decadent Western tastes. Yet Karponin was a vocal exponent of a return to classic Russian values of discipline and duty. It was just such contradictions—like an acknowledged Great Russian chauvinist bandying fluent French with a woman telejournalist, to show he was *kulturnyy*—that made the Radical-Traditionalists such a magnet for the world media. And that made the charismatic Afghan War hero an ideal symbol and spokesman for that movement. *Point man*, as he liked to think of it.

He held the scrutiny long enough to note a pink flush blossoming on those wide cheekbones, beneath the sunscreen. Then he turned his attention back to the exercise.

Explosions drew a solid chestnut curtain of dirt across the ridgeline. Helicopters hovered in dead ground to either flank, out of the flight path of shells and 122mm rockets. The four-wheeled BRDMs turned back shy of the crest, thirty meters from the flame-shot earth curtain.

"So close," the reporter murmured. "So bold. Magnificent."

But Karponin's face had gone white, except for the scar: That burned bright red.

He grabbed the microphone from a subordinate who had begun to quiver like a poplar leaf. *"Cease fire!"* he bellowed in Russian. "Stop the assault."

The storm of noise was subsumed by ringing in the ears; the dust cloud settled in heavy folds. Out on the flats, tanks and APCs began to mill around aimlessly as the orders were passed down.

"General, what's going on?" the reporter asked. "What's wrong?"

He waved her off. "Return to the assembly point. Anyone who's not in jump-off position in one hour's time will be mining gold within the week."

As the vehicles began to stream back toward their original positions, he turned back to the reporter, all calm personality again.

"The League is a world power," he said in a voice like the well-tuned turbine engines of his forty-two-ton tanks. "But much remains to be done."

"What went wrong with the assault, General Karponin?"

He smiled. "Wait a few minutes. Will you have tea? You can tell me what you think of this new opera by Nguyen that opened in Paris last week, the one I've heard such controversy about."

When the regiment was back at its starting line, he had himself, the reporter, and her videocam crew driven down in his command car. It was a camouflage-painted Liga four-wheel drive, which meant it was actually a Toyota, assembled at the giant license-built plant outside of Tashkent to avoid American and EuroCom restrictions on Japanese imports. Cashing in on the raging trade war was a very Russian scam.

Seasoned though she was, the reporter had visibly had difficulty containing her anticipation during the hour's wait for the regiment to reassemble. League military maneuvers were as exquisitely rehearsed as any Bolshoi ballet—and consequently bore about as much resemblance to real war. In the rigidly hierarchical Soviet scheme of command, which the League had inherited along with most of the Soviet armed forces, an officer was absolutely answerable for the performance of his men. A career was far too important to entrust to the whims of chance.

But not for General Major Karponin. He was on the golden road to a marshal's baton, a fighting soldier in a peacetime army, and regarded obstacles as something to be overcome, not wished away.

She sat beside him, one hip pressed not disagreeably to his, whispering to herself. Actually she was subvocalizing for the benefit of the flesh-tone microphone taped over her larynx. He caught the words "Desert Fox" and "Scarface." He smiled.

Being mentioned in the same breath as Rommel, Guderian, and, most glorious of all, George Patton, did not bother Anatoliy Karponin in the least. Any serious student of history knew they were the best, not their Soviet rivals, who relied on mass alone. That was what being a Rad-Trad was all about: taking the best of what was foreign and making it Russian. Assimilating it, like those clever little monkeys, the Japanese.

As for the other name . . . Anatoliy Karponin was a man who was consciously building—and living—his own legend. The Afghan resistance had given him the nickname "Al Capone" after one of their mortars laid his face open in the Zhawar assault in 1986. He had to pretend disapproval of his men calling him that or Scarface. But he was far too self-directed to be sensitive in fact about anything that was such splendid media.

His driver stopped the car facing the front rank of vehicles. Karponin stepped down on hot dry ground which had already been churned up and denuded by hundreds of treads and cleated wheels. Drivers and commanders stood up in open hatches, catching a breath of hot, diesel-fouled air that was still fresher than inside their cramped armored cans.

For a moment Karponin studied them, hands on hips. He was a tall man, athletic, with the kind of presence that drew attention.

"In modern war, he who sees first, kills first," he said. A mike discreetly clipped to his battle-dress lapel picked up the words and ran them through a loudspeaker in his command car. Since it also broadcast them to the armored vehicles' radios, that was merely a gesture—only the first few rows were in position to hear him anyway. But it was gestures of that kind that made him what he was.

"Do the *dushmans* not have cannon-launched guided projectiles to kill our tanks from kilometers away, if we cede their spotters the high ground for even a moment?" There were some grins at that, only halfheartedly hidden. *Dushman* was an Afghan word that meant, literally, "enemy" though the connotation was "bandit." It was what the Afghan Army and Group of Soviet Forces, Afghanistan, had called the Resistance. Its subtext here implied that the *mujahidin* had only managed to hold out by a massive influx of high-tech from the U.S. and People's Republic of China.

"We have helicopters, General, sir," someone called out.

The reporter tensed, as if waiting for an explosion. Karponin smiled thinly. He accepted, even encouraged, input from his officers and NCOs. As long as it stayed within bounds. Old and new: flexibility within a steel framework of discipline.

"Have the Threat forces broken their own helicopters down to make riding lawn mowers out of, then? Do they not have antiaircraft artillery and backpack SAMs? Our helicopters can help us, comrades, but only if we help them. Tanks and infantry, working in combination with artillery: that's the *real* battle. The war on the ground. We need our spotters in place first, to mark down targets for our comrades in Frontal Aviation and the artillery."

"But to drive right into the shellfire—" began a youthful sergeant-commander of a BRDM, who had taken off his helmet to let the air cool his plush of white-blond hair.

Karponin frowned. He recognized the lead vehicle that had turned back first from the barrage. "Sergeant, what is your name?"

"Peters, sir."

He scowled. "What kind of a name is that?"

"R-russian, sir."

It wasn't, of course; it was German. Karponin notoriously disdained non-Russians. But he commanded a League division, not a Russian Republican one. Besides, many ethnic Germans lived in Russia and played at assimilation.

"Well, now, my good Russian sergeant, we rely upon the initial artillery barrage to suppress both enemy observers and missile infantry, allowing our tanks to charge ahead, as tanks ought do. You are familiar with this doctrine, at least?" His voice was silken with menace.

"Yes, sir!" The boy was stiff and quivering like an arrow in a target now.

"How long do you expect them to cower in their holes?" Karponin thundered. "We shall be fighting *men*, not marmots! Every second you delay costs the Russian blood of your comrades!"

Peters swayed as if about to pass out. "Great stuff," murmured the reporter's Moroccan videocam man, as he zoomed in on the youth's face.

"The artillery bombardment is precisely timed. We must trust our comrades to know when to lift it. Now we will try again, and we will do it right," Karponin said. He gazed at the ranks for half a minute.

"And I shall lead."

Through startled silence he strode to the other BRDM, the one not commanded by Peters, clambered aboard using the handholds welded to the hull in front of the side firing port. From the top he glanced back. Without awaiting permission, the Frenchwoman was climbing up after him. Her cameraman waited for her to get out of the way, visibly unhappy with the prospect of riding into an artillery barrage in a lightly armored vehicle.

Karponin smiled and signaled for the assault to begin.

Again came the tearing cloth sound of incoming artillery. Havoc assault choppers lifted off in a swirl of khaki dust, to jitter a meter or two above the ground, waiting to sweep forward to engage targets beyond the ridge. As the crestline erupted, the regiment began to move.

Karponin rode in the open in the cupola behind the 14.5mm gun. He disdained a helmet. The hot wind ruffled his short dark hair.

He glanced back. The reporter rode half out of one of the rear hatches, hanging on against the violent jolting with practiced aplomb. In the other rear hatch rode her Arab cameraman, doggedly recording the whole scene in digitized images.

The car lunged for the crest, fishtailing as the tires skidded in the arid dust. Karponin felt his pulse quicken. At any moment a shell fragment might slice the top from his skull. He felt fear, but it was a wild, pulsing fear, not a small, cold thing to turn the guts to water. It *exhilarated*.

Again he looked at the reporter. Her lips were peeled back in what seemed a grimace of sheer terror. Then he realized she was *laughing*, the sound completely masked by the bone-shaking noise of the shells.

Shell bursts buffeted him with dragon's breath. Overpressure threatened to implode his eardrums. The telejournalist pointed, lips moving in a soundless shout.

A car roared past them, wheels tearing chunks from the short tough grass. It was Peters's BRDM. Riding like his general with his head and upper torso sticking up from the cupola, the young ethnic German plunged into the maelstrom of explosions. He beat Karponin's car to the crest by thirty meters, then started over it.

A 152mm shell landed directly on top of it, just aft of the cupola. The entire top of the armored car erupted in a yellow and black ball of flame.

The barrage lifted, a heartbeat late. The telejournalist screamed. Karponin still couldn't hear her.

The assault went with textbook perfection. The spotters deployed from the scout cars, illuminated dummy tanks with their laser flashlights. The Havocs popped up and blew them to pieces with rockets guiding on the dots, invisible to human eyes. The attacking tanks took position hull-down behind the crest, and the infantry spilled from their BMPs as the tracked carriers raked the steppe with their light automatic cannon. Karponin watched with satisfaction.

He stood up and signaled that the exercise was at an end. The telejournalist was right beside him.

"Those men—everyone in that car—they were killed." She pointed to the BRDM, still burning fiercely. The stink of burned flesh and rubber and diesel fuel overpowered even the reek of spent explosives.

"We strive for realism in our exercises. Those men died regrettably, but heroically, in carrying out their orders. Though the Motherland is not now at war, they died to defend her and will be recognized."

"Do you realize what the media would do to you if you were an *American* officer who had men killed on an exercise like this? They'd crucify you!"

He snorted and turned away. "Perhaps America is no longer fit for world leadership. The League is young, and vigorous."

She took off her insect-eye glasses. Her eyes were hazel, luminous and large.

It seems I've conquered more than a barren patch of steppe this afternoon, he thought. It was no great surprise.

Chapter
FOUR

"Daddy, are we almost home?"

Francis Marron glanced across the top of his daughter's

head, caught his wife's eye. The three of them were sitting in the front seat of the Ford station wagon, huddled together like animals seeking warmth, though the evening wasn't particularly cool.

Elinor tousled Becky's hair. "Sure, honey." She leaned her head on her daughter's. Marron slipped his right arm around them.

Down in the Springs the lights were coming on, by law. In this privileged suburb on the flank of Cheyenne Mountain, you still got to have night, without being required to fill the yard with artificial daylight.

Francis Marron was looking forward to an evening sitting on his redwood deck, watching night come down. He had sweated, had risked his life to earn the privileges his family enjoyed. This was among the ones he cherished most.

He particularly needed it tonight.

"Maybe we should have another child," Marron said. "Would you like that, Rebecca, honey? Your own little brother or sister?"

Becky started bouncing up and down as enthusiastically as her seat belt would allow. Instantly Elinor drew away from him, straightening, stiffening.

"Don't get started on that Norman Rockwell two-point-five-children-a-family routine again, Frank." She pulled down the sun visor and checked her hair in the mirror on its backside.

"No, it's not that. It's—I just think we'd find it so rewarding, you and I. And Becky. . . ."

He was floundering, and knew it. *Some shadow diplomat you are. You can't have a conversation with your wife without some misunderstanding.*

Though he kept fit, ate lots of fiber, and kept his serum cholesterol low, he was at an age when the foreshocks of mortality came more frequently, more intensely. The incident at the picnic ground had intensified them.

Am I really so conventional, to grasp at such a banal and obvious life-affirming straw? He didn't like to think of himself that way. He was a mover, a shaker. A take-charge guy.

Elinor didn't notice his bemusement; she had her own agenda. "Sometimes I think barefoot and pregnant would just about fit your image of me. Somehow I never did manage to follow my career, did I?" A brittle little laugh. "I know how it goes with a he-man type like you: 'No wife of *mine* is going to work for a living.' "

His mouth compressed. "Ellie, that simply isn't true. Nothing would have made me happier than for you to pursue your studies."

"But it was always your career first, wasn't it? And then Rebecca came along, and you were gone all the time on your mysterious missions."

They had been married three years before Rebecca was conceived, but he did not remind her. Odd to think that their original goal in having a child was to draw them together. And it had, in that both of them felt the same fierce, exhilarating love for their daughter. But otherwise . . .

"You have your work," he reminded his wife. He had almost said *causes*, but she would have accused him of patronizing her.

She leaned against the door with her elbow propped on the windowsill. "You've never been exactly supportive of my activism, now, have you? You've always thought I was something of a bleeding heart."

He shook his head, feeling futile, feeling helpless. He knew this was her way of coping with the horror they'd seen, coping with the brush with the containment team. Still, this wasn't what he needed.

"I respect what you do," he said weakly. Fortuitously the turn onto their street came up. That enabled him to pretend making the corner took a great deal of concentration. At least it broke the argument's rhythm.

He turned into a driveway covered in red lava gravel. Their house was a passive solar design, south-facing, glass fronting an adobe Tromb wall. Two stories high in front, the roofline swept back and down to a single story.

Before Elinor was all the way out, Becky popped out the door, dashed up the gravel path edged with railroad ties that ran between the flower and cactus gardens to the door. The crowded blossoms, red and gold and blue, that usually filled the yard had mostly closed up shop for the night. Marron's rank rated a water allotment for a lawn, but he and Ellie both preferred playing in the garden. And having a garden, ostensibly less ecologically burdensome than a lawn, did make them look properly communitarian.

While Ellie was watching their daughter, he snagged his compact Walther from the holster beneath the driver's seat and tucked it in a back pocket of his jeans.

When he straightened, Elinor was leaning with her arms on the car roof, a knowing look in her eye. When she was like this—no makeup, cheeks pink with wind and the sun that inevitably managed to get through the blocker, the strand of honey and ash hair escaped again and trailing across her face like seaweed—she looked in truth rather plain. Yet somehow she never looked more beautiful to him.

"Frank," she said, and her tone was different than before: softer, almost cajoling. "That—that stuff this afternoon. It had to do with your work, didn't it?"

He started to laugh it off: *Hey, I'm just a money manager.* What he saw in her eyes stopped him.

"No," he said. *My work is what got us away from there, made it end where it did, rather than . . .* "No dear. It didn't."

If they'd listened to me, League General Vorontsov thought, *this never would have happened.*

On-screen heads covered with embroidered skullcaps bobbed up and down and fists struck the air. It was a French satcast of rioting in Tashkent city center, twenty kilometers away. It was getting near time to call his divisional intelligence chief in for a magisterial ass-chewing. He understood perfectly well that his intelligence officer could have done little more than he had: GRU had given him nothing, and KGB permitted him no assets of his own, claiming domestic surveillance was their bailiwick, no amateurs allowed. But League doctrine held that somebody had to be to blame, and the intelligence officer was convenient.

Actually, the League General Staff was to blame. Or rather, the self-obsessed politicians who gave them their orders; STAVKA was comprised of army officers selflessly serving the state just as he himself was, shackled and betrayed at every turn by their civilian masters. *That* was a better way to think of it.

Tashkent had once been a major military nerve center. Headquarters for the Turkestan Military District, it had served as the main mustering point for men and matériel fighting the imperialist and Zionist-backed bandits in Afghanistan.

Then the Politburo betrayed the army and treacherously ordered withdrawal, though Soviet forces were clearly seeing the light at the end of the tunnel. Union gave way to Commonwealth, Commonwealth to League; the Iranian threat heated up. With the shift in policy from prosecuting the Great Game to discouraging an unruly neighbor from exporting disorder along with radical Islam, Turkestan District HQ moved to Ashkabad, capital of the Turkmen Republic. In army terms, Tashkent was a hollow shell, its once great bases now military ghost towns.

And so the black-asses are free to riot against the civilization we've brought them. I must rely for my intelligence on the capitalist news media—and I have a bare regiment of Class B troops to deal with the problem.

When Andropov seized power from the dotard Brezhnev—to all intents and purposes in the late seventies, though his titular accession had to wait until the 1980s—his KGB seized power with him. In the League the *Komitet* still held great power, though patriots and traitors alike had chipped away at it. KGB was riddled with Jews, mongrelizers, those

whose only concern was their own power and influence. The
Rad-Trads had it right.

Vorontsov was not a Rad-Trad. STAVKA discouraged
officers from taking sides politically. The army stood for the
League.

But Vorontsov knew the cost of a pound of evil. The
Rad-Trads were gaining influence by means of the very
elections they despised. Someday soon, it might be hoped,
real discipline would be restored to the Motherland—and
the League.

Vorontsov frowned. The voice was Lithuanian, as were
most of his troops. The Lithuanians were every bit as
turbulent and ungrateful as the black-asses, but it was
assumed that in case of trouble the Balts would feel no
kinship with the locals, who were at least as alien to them as
to Great Russians. Vorontsov never liked that either. The
Lithuanians were lax. Even their *accents* were lax.

That Turkestan District had had the League Army cham-
pionship basketball team the last three years running was
small consolation. With Patrice Lumumba University openly
recruiting Africans for its athletic programs, military teams
were scarcely competitive anymore. For his part, Vorontsov
wished the Baltic states had never been cajoled into joining
the League.

The telephone rang. "General Vorontsov? Command Center. We've lost touch with Colonel Klyavin. Perhaps you
should come down here."

He clicked off the TV by remote control, rose, and set off
down the corridor for his Command Communications Center. When the cry for help came from the Tashkent civil
authorities he had dispatched a motorized rifle battalion and
a tank platoon under Klyavin. He'd held back his artillery.
God knew what the media would make of him shelling a
city of three million people. President Fyodorin would have
his nuts if he made the Motherland look *nyekulturnyy* by
overreacting in full view of the TV cameras. Those traitors

at *Buducsheye* had it in for the army. They'd blow everything out of proportion.

Terrible to know just how the Americans felt.

Maybe I should have stayed in Command Center right along, he thought. Current doctrine was to permit subordinates to carry out orders without jogging their elbows, to maintain some degree of flexibility, the academicians said: *bah.* To Vorontsov it was just another example of the laxity creeping into society at every level in every republic.

The problem was, Klyavin was a nitwit. He would have been over his head commanding a labor-formation platoon on a particularly challenging roadside trash-clearing project; as a young company commander in the Ukraine, he'd fucked up bringing in the *harvest,* for God's sake. His only visible talent lay in cataloging the plants of the desert-mountain transition zone, his main interest in life. But his father-in-law was a wheel in Ryazan' Oblast who'd just been appointed a Russian Republic junior secretary for Mining, and you couldn't dislodge the clown with plastic explosives.

That didn't necessarily mean Vorontsov had to give him a field command. In the last decade, first the Soviet and then the League Army had attempted to bring promotion and responsibility more in line with ability and less with *klass* and influence, one of the few reforms Vorontsov was in sympathy with. But enter the fucking KGB again. In the last three months they had purged every officer above the rank of captain in the entire Turkestan District who had the sense to pour piss out of a boot with instructions printed on the heel. He had been left with dolts, Balts, and political appointees. The only man left with any talent was a shifty little brown man in charge of his artillery regiment, almost a black-ass himself, though neither Turk nor Tadzhik. Vorontsov never really trusted him, though he had the most impressive collection of medals of any man on base. At least he wasn't lax.

Dim unshielded bulbs swept over Vorontsov's bald head like spirits of the impenitent dead in a Spielberg scene. He turned and entered the red-shot womb dimness of Command.

"What's going on?" he barked.

"Colonel Klyavin's communications operator reported running into heavy small arms fire near Teatralnaya Square, General. Then he went off the air."

Small arms? Where did the black-asses get small arms? From the Uzbek Republican Army, no doubt. He felt as if he'd swallowed a lump of anthracite. If the Uzbek Army was in on a plot to bolt the League, he was well and truly fucked.

He could not let himself contemplate the possibility. Introspection led to inaction, a cardinal military sin. *So the fool Klyavin got himself ambushed. I should have led the attack myself.* But no, his place was here—

"General," another operator said, turning from his console with two fingers pressed to his headset. "Moscow. General Staff wants to know if you have authorized calling up the republican reserves."

Vorontsov laughed out loud. "Arm *more* black-asses? Does Staff have its head firmly wedged—"

A third man said, "Sir, Divisional Artillery respectfully requests your surrender."

"I— What?" He turned to the man. A vein beat on the side of his forehead. He couldn't have heard that correctly. This lax Balt swine had to know that if he was making a joke, Vorontsov would have him beaten to death with rifle butts, and hang every journalist in Turkestan if *Budushcheye* complained.

"What did you say?"

"I have a call from the officer commanding Divisional Artillery," the operator said, enunciating very carefully, as if to a deaf person or particularly slow child. "He asks that we surrender in the name of Free Turkestan, or he will be compelled to fire on us."

"*Yob tvoyu mat'*," Vorontsov breathed.

"He says to fuck your mother," the commo man relayed.
"Wait, you idiot, that was an expression—"

The rising whistle of 122mm rockets in flight cut through the soundproofing like a knife.

The house felt wrong. Nothing he could put his finger on—a strange touch of scent, an air current out of place. Something that woke up all his field instincts. Something that screamed *intrusion*!

"Honey," he said in a low, clipped voice. "Take Rebecca and get back in the car."

"Where do you get off ordering me ar—" She saw him standing there with the TPH held before his chin with both hands, like a man at prayer, and stopped. "Frank, what is it?"

"Just do it."

Becky was starting to skip down the linoleum-tiled foyer to the living room. Elinor caught her up and ran out the front door.

Marron ducked sideways into the kitchen. Bent low beneath the counter that communicated with the dining area, he duckwalked through the kitchen to the door. Straightening, he stepped out and sideways, arms extending—right arm locked, left elbow bent and slightly dropped—into the isosceles triangle of a perfect Weaver stance.

The sliding glass door to the rear deck was open. A lanky black-haired man lay on one of the redwood chaise longues.

"Yo, Frankie. Thought you'd never get back." He gestured with a bottle of Wild Turkey. "I brought some of the bad stuff. Come on out and set a spell."

Marron let the three fat white dots of the sight drop away from his line of vision. "Dick? Dick Torrance!"

"The Original Swinging Richard himself." Torrance got to his feet, a process that always reminded Marron of one of those Taiwanese wooden snake toys that folded in all different directions, first this way, then that. He came forward and caught the shorter Marron in a Latin-style *abrazo*, endangering the back of his head with the bottle.

"How the hell have you been?" he demanded, tousling Marron's hair.

"Fine. Hey, just fine." Marron drew back. Torrance knew playing with his hair like that made him nuts. That was the kind of guy Torrance was.

Torrance stepped back and gestured at the small black pistol. "That how you greet an old comrade-in-arms? Or is that always how you come into your house these days?" He shook his head and laughed. "And people say us FedPols have too much power. You know what we always say—'You don't like the Federal Police, next time you're in trouble, call a hurt-pusher.' "

He laughed again. From the front door came Elinor's voice: "Frank, are you all right? What's happening in there?"

Marron grimaced. "Come on back, Ms. Thompson," Torrance called. "It's just old home week in here. Don't mind the bottle; I'm a FedPol, and you know we can do no wrong."

Chapter
FIVE

National Security Adviser Sondra Mohn arranged her features in her trademark faint patrician smile and tried not to wonder if there was rain in her hair. Almost all the members of the National Security Council's Crisis Management Unit were on hand. Time to make sure her game face was in place.

Rain still fell on 17th Street, outside the Executive Office

Building. Traffic hissed sporadically past. Curfew was in effect. At this time of night only those on official business and commercial and service people with appropriate stamps on their internal passports—newspaper delivery trucks, night-time janitorial staff, and the like—were permitted on the streets of the nation's capital.

Despite the lack of traffic, it was an inconvenient time for most members of the National Security Council's Crisis Unit. On the other hand, the limousine ride through eerily deserted streets enhanced their sense of *being special*, their awareness of playing a vital role in the shaping and preserving of their country's destiny.

In other words, it made them feel more important than they were. Just the way Sondra Mohn had planned it.

The door opened. The representative from Enforcement Affairs flew in with a swirl of the London Fog thrown over his shoulders, inevitably late. With his racquetball build, longish slicked-back hair, and cover-boy looks—thrust of forehead hanging like a cliff over brooding blue eyes—he was widely considered to be on the fast track to power. Not least by himself.

He had bolted a high-visibility prosecutorial job with Justice for the sexier enforcement end, though the move entailed a nominal demotion. It paid dividends: he was the Secretary's head hatchetman already. And a thoroughgoing young snake who bore close watching.

Pentagon and DIA looked at each other. Defense Intelligence rolled her eyes. Pentagon let his lips peel slightly back from his teeth. Though both were serving military, they seldom agreed on anything. They did on this.

"Excuse it," the latecomer said. "I was with the Secretary in Detroit when I got the call. Complications came up."

Someone snickered. Secretary Doyle was filming a Public Service Announcement in the inner city for the kick-off of Operation Clean Sweep, dressed as McGruff the Crime Dog. There had been complications, some too overt to gloss over.

At least the hard-pressed containment teams had managed to keep the mortar fire off the *CBS Evening News*.

"Since Mr. Serafin has at last seen fit to honor us with his presence," Mohn said in her finest spoon-tapping-crystal voice, "perhaps we can begin consideration of the events of the last twenty-four hours in Central Asia. Mr. Chamorro, if you'd care to brief those of us who have not had a chance to familiarize ourselves..." She let the sentence die. She had little use for those who had trouble catching the drift—or, rather, she had little brief for them; they could be *use*ful indeed.

Henry Chamorro dithered briefly with his face with both hands, a process that ended with the hands' simultaneous discovery of his heavy-rimmed glasses. They grasped the glasses, briefly, as if he were peering through binoculars, and lit at last on the keyboard inset in the table in front of him.

"What, ah, what has happened," he said, "is a series of revolts that seem to be spreading rapidly throughout Central Asia."

"Civil disobedience, you mean," barked Major General der Hagen, the Pentagon man. His wattles shook and his gray crew cut bristled; he seemed to take slights against the League's military capabilities personally.

"I mean *revolt*, General," Chamorro said, exasperated. "Rebellion. As nearly as we can ascertain, it seems to have originated in Tashkent, capital of the Uzbek Republic—"

Mohn cut him off. "Before you continue, Henry, perhaps Francine can give us a *concise* background on the region in question."

The representative from State looked at Mohn with a tentative blinking smile. Dr. Francine Wollstonecraft was an incredibly ingenue Yalie, young for her job and highly photogenic. She was beginning to entertain vague suspicions that the National Security Adviser didn't like her.

"Well," she said, "Central Asia, also called Russian Turkestan—"

The room was a power room, but an *old-fashioned* power room; Mohn liked her people to be reminded of their roots. Discreet, elegant sculpted molding and dark oak paneling, a smell of age and rain. It wasn't hopelessly out of date: Francine pressed buttons on the keypad before her own chair, and an apparent expanse of dark-stained hardwood paneling turned into a four-foot-square color LCD screen showing a map. The Adviser liked to think of it as appropriate technology.

"—is generally considered to extend from the Caspian Sea to the vast mountain ranges, the Tien Shan and the Pamirs, which form the border with China. To the south the region is bounded by Iran and Afghanistan. Its northern boundary is less distinct, roughly a line running from the northern tip of the Aral Sea to Alma-Ata, capital of the Kazakh Republic. The people of Turkestan are predominantly Altaic, of Turkish or Mongol stock. There is a large Persian-speaking minority, the Tadzhiks, centered in Tadzikstan.

"The Russians conquered most of the region in the last century, under the Tsars. The assimilation wasn't, however, completed until the 1920s. The population of the region has been expanding, while population levels are stable or even receding in the predominantly European areas of the League. As a result—"

"Thank you ever so much, Francine," Mohn said. "Henry."

Chamorro gouged his thumbs at the purplish bags beneath his eyes. "The League has simply lost communications with military and civil authorities in the major Uzbek cities of Bukhara, Samarkand, Tashkent, and the Kirghiz capital Khokand. Dushanbe, which is the capital of the Tadzhik Republic, reports severe street fighting, with air strikes on the city center. Strikes and massive demonstrations are reported in Alma-Ata, though the participants seem to be ethnic Russians, Ukrainians, and Germans protesting *against* the revolt."

He glanced at Mohn. She nodded, once. He touched a key. The map gave way to a view of street fighting between the crumbling facades of giant housing blocks, with an IndoNews/English logo in the lower left-hand corner of the screen.

It was a view forbidden to private citizens—unauthorized access—but still available to anyone who could afford a modern toaster-sized phased-array satellite antenna on the black market. Even with restrictions on the availability of technology, stiff penalties, and extensive informer programs sponsored by government and legitimate media alike, the Federal Police Agency—executive arm of Serafin's Department of Enforcement Affairs—estimated between twenty-five and thirty million homes had them.

A failure of the will, Sondra Mohn thought. The state could offer all the technical training and access necessary through its own channels, and squeeze intrinsically anarchic private endeavor completely out of existence. Therefore the state had the responsibility to do so.

The screen flared, fire splashing across the rear deck of a BMP-2 armored personnel carrier as a Molotov cocktail shattered. Francine gasped and covered her eyes. Mohn's lips curled.

Here we see what happens when a state begins to lose its nerve, begins to fear to fulfill its responsibilities she thought. *And here's where we shove it up their asses.*

Chamorro was rolling his eyes around at random in their dark sunken sockets. Mohn felt the overpowering urge to grab him and shake him, but squelched it. He was always that way.

"Your 'civil disobedience,' General," Chamorro said at last. "It seems to bear a startling resemblance to a violent—and very well orchestrated—uprising."

"Crap," Pentagon said. "It's all fortuitous, copycat stuff. Nobody revolts against the League. System's too interdependent. Each of the republics is afraid of anything that might give its neighbors the jump on it, and most of 'em hate the ragheads more than the Great Russians do. If the

Central Asians did try to break away, the rest of the League would dogpile 'em in a hurry.''

Seated in his usual position off to the side—his Gray Eminence chair, he called it—NSA's Ward Archer had been stoking his pipe and ignoring Mohn's occasional dagger gaze. A tall, donnish man in late middle age, he was a registered addict, entitled to receive prescriptions for his tobacco habit. Because he had acknowledged his problem, Mohn couldn't use it as a dodge to get the press to ratpack him; that would be insensitivity. She hated not having a handle on people this close to the throttles of power.

"The other republics have condemned the uprising," he said through a cloud of reeking blue smoke. "But *somebody* over there takes it seriously. Namely League internal security—our old friends the KGB."

Der Hagen turned a bulbous bulldog glare at him. "What do you mean?"

"We have skim-offs from their Molniya satellite network indicating that State Security regards the uprisings as linked. Moreover, they don't think either the League or republican armies can contain them."

Pentagon snorted disbelief. "That's the largest army on earth you're talking about, guy. They've squashed dissidence in the republics before. When are you people gonna realize that the threat we all grew up with hasn't just withered up and blown away?"

"Oh, grow up, Ernie," Brigadier General Wofford of the Defense Intelligence Agency said. A black, bespectacled Marine with shoulders like a defensive lineman, she knew full well that she was a token. That she was also good at her job—analysis and evaluation—was incidental. Her status meant she was fireproof. She did not exactly bend over backward to be diplomatic.

"I find it curious," Serafin said, half reclining in his seat in that languid panther way of his, "that No Such Agency manages to infiltrate possibly the most secure satellite network in the world, and can't get a handle on unauthorized access in our own country."

Archer puffed furiously. "That's a different matter entirely. You're talking there about millions of Americans—your estimate—tapping into a network of several hundred private and government-owned communications satellites, many of them launched from countries which make not even a pretense of regulating the uses to which they're put. They log on and off at random, along a variety of pathways so numerous as to be functionally infinite. Opposed to that, we are monitoring throughput of a known and carefully restricted system. The League refuses to trust its secure traffic to the global commercial network, which they feel, quite correctly, to be anarchic." *Puff.* "But then, you couldn't be expected to know that. Intelligence stuff. Quite outside your realm of competence."

Serafin colored to his hairline, which he hoped people would not notice was receding.

Mohn contained a smile. "Thank you, gentlemen," she said. "Henry." Chamorro blinked and belatedly cut the feed.

"What is State's assessment, Francine?"

"Over the last few years Central Asia has become increasingly vital to the League economy. The Uzbek Republic, in particular, has become a major world source of cotton—an increasingly valuable commodity, as you know, because environmentally aware legislation has restricted both supply and demand for synthetic fabrics in the developed world. The area also supplies a disproportionate amount of other agricultural products, particularly fruits and vegetables. Petrochemical reserves beneath the Red Sands and Black Sands deserts are now estimated to be among the largest remaining in the world."

"And it all gets piped straight into the Russian Republic," Wofford said. "The League still treats Central Asia like a colony. That's a big part of what turned your Russian in the street off to the idea of total devolution. All that old-style imperial tribute started drying up.''

"Well, we have to understand that most of the League's population lives outside the Central Asian republics—"

"For now," Wofford said.

"And the League is a very *caring* polity, very concerned to put the needs of the many before the selfish desire of the few."

"Jesus," der Hagen said. Wofford made a jack-off gesture below the table's edge, out of Wollstonecraft's view but not Mohn's. Behind hands at State, they called Wollstonecraft "Francinestein."

Wollstonecraft produced a frown. It made her look like a petulant flower. "Certain parties, who are apparently unable to let go of the Cold War even after ten years, appear to mistake the League as merely a successor to the Union of Soviet Socialist Republics. Nothing could be further from the truth. The League is a commonwealth, a voluntary bonding together of the former constituent republics of the USSR, similar to the model of Unified Europe."

"If it's voluntary, why are there APCs in the streets?" Wofford asked.

" 'Voluntary' as in our income tax system, General," Archer said.

"The League *does* perform certain functions of a government; I'm sure no one here would prefer the same sort of anarchy that wrecked Yugoslavia and Canada to affect such a widespread area. The League's police department—the once-feared KGB, now playing a role analogous to our own Federal Police Agency—was instrumental in putting an end to systematic and violent persecution of minority groups in Moldava, the Ukraine, and Armenia, to mention a few. Additionally, the League administers those formerly Soviet assets fair ownership of which was impossible to apportion, such as power plants, the Baykonur Space Complex—"

"—the nukes," der Hagen said.

"Perhaps *most important* to understand is that the League

is dominated neither by Russia nor by Russians,'' Francine said tartly. "It's in their charter.''

"Francine,'' Wofford said, "get real. Russia has three times the land mass of all the other republics combined. It's far and away the biggest country on Earth yet, twice as big as the U.S. It has half the League's people, and most of its trained professionals. All by its lonesome, it's a superpower.

"Beyond all that, Great Russians form pluralities or even majorities in other republics—Kazakhstan, for instance, which is apparently what's kept it from flashing off with the rest of Central Asia. Just who do you *think* really runs that show?''

Der Hagen barked a laugh. "The League is just the old Soviet empire on the cheap. They ditched communism because it didn't work for squat. They ditched the Soviet Union because the Russian people saw it as a means of sticking them for the operating expenses of a bunch of tributary republics they think are half-civilized anyway, stuff like welfare, infrastructure, administration. This way the money all comes *in* toward the center: everybody pays for League protection from big, bad neighbors like China and Germany and the raghead countries; everybody pays the League for being the life-support system that keeps the republics' one-lung economies going. They get the bennies of empire without the cost.'' He shook his head, grinning a lizard grin of reluctant admiration. "It's a Russian empire for the New World Order.''

"Ernest,'' Wollstonecraft said scathingly, "*nobody* uses that phrase anymore.''

Der Hagen slammed his palm on the table. "Dammit, doesn't anybody get the picture?''

Mohn gave him a look. He licked his lips and said, "With all due respect, Madam Adviser, those who forget history are doomed to repeat it, and dammit, some people here are being pretty forgetful. Everybody counted the Sovs out after the phony coup in '91. I say they've risen from the grave.''

"Like Joan Crawford,'' Wofford muttered.

"What?"

"You wouldn't get it."

"I wouldn't think a serving military *person* would find much to laugh about here, General. This wonderful League of Francine's took every cent of the hundred billion we sent them, everything the Japs and the EuroWeenies sent, and they *rearmed*. Bootstrapped themselves right back into a goddamn superpower at our expense. Sure, they tossed some bones to the republics, and you know what? *They* spent the loot on arms too. Henry has the figures for you, if anybody's goddamn interested. You can't deny it."

"No," Mohn said, "we can't, Ernie, and thank you so much for pointing that out. But we are concerned with the *present*." She looked around. "Appreciations?"

"It's not worth fiddle-futzing around with," der Hagen said. "The League Army will give these ragheads a whiff of the grape, and that'll be that."

"General!" Wollstonecraft exclaimed, scandalized.

"Other opinions?" Mohn asked.

"Like Henry said," Wofford said, "KGB thinks differently. In-house assessment say it'll take a major push, probably by the League Army with major commitment of republican forces."

"League has half a million men in Turkmenia," der Hagen said. "That's Central Asia, isn't it?"

"They're going to stay there too, Ernie. That's the border with Iran. The Shi'ites have been giving the Russian fits for years, and if the Russians take their eye off them they're liable to come swarming in to liberate their Muslim brothers themselves."

Chamorro was trying to scour his philtrum with his tongue. "They have forty divisions on the Chinese frontier too, General. And they, uh, they're stuck too."

"But the League has settled its differences with the People's Republic," Wollstonecraft objected.

"They've been doing that for years," Wofford said. "And they're still shooting at each other across the Amur."

"And let's not forget Germany," Archer said. "The League doesn't. As the Soviets did, it imagines itself to be surrounded by enemies." He chuckled. "Of course, it *is*."

He turned the polished wood bowl of his pipe around as if he'd just unearthed it on an archaeological dig. "General der Hagen does make one telling point: we do seem to be in the habit of forgetting to ask questions. In 1990, nobody thought to ask what reason we had to believe a reunited Germany—without the Soviet threat to bind her to us— would be our friend. Now here they are, eying Danzig and Silesia and licking their chops. In 1992, we forgot to ask why a non-Soviet Russia would be our friend. The League took our money and treats us as a rival."

Henry Chamorro touched the bone-conduction phone taped to the mastoid process behind his right ear and cleared his throat apologetically.

"Excuse, ah, excuse me, but we have information coming in now. A weather satellite out of Kiribati is showing explosions inside the perimeter at the military base outside Tashkent."

"And what does all this imply for American policy?" Mohn asked. She made herself sit with her customary ramrod erectness. This was a test of the skill with which she'd stacked this deck. She had a definite answer in mind. But it took points off if *she* supplied it.

Pentagon shifted in his chair, grunting softly. "Maybe it shows what a damned old dinosaur I am," he said, "but say this revolt thing is for real, just for grins. I think that gives us a perfect opportunity to stick it to the bastards."

Wollstonecraft gasped. Chamarro blinked like a semaphorist on speed.

"You're talking covert involvement?"

"Sure. I'm not crazy enough to propose direct confrontation with the League. They still have all those ICBMs— hell, Russia still has a few of her own, if you believe Ward and Henry and their little gnomes. But like it or not, it's still *us* and *them*. And this is an ideal opportunity to put some points on our side of the board." He patted his high forehead with a handkerchief. "They sure made us look like monkeys over that aid thing."

Chamorro scraped lower lip with upper teeth. "We're stretched pretty thin right now. The U.S. has its own military situation right now in Central and South America, don't forget, and the boys—and girls, to be sure—need all the intelligence we can feed them. Plus we're keeping our fingers on brushfire conflicts all over the world. It's, ah, it's tough keeping up with the Europeans these days."

Archer took his pipe out and produced a colorless smile. "We have one of your boys working for us now. We could lend him back to you, if you were nice enough to us."

"I don't believe what I'm hearing," Wollstonecraft said. "The League is committed to peace and coexistence. We and they are growing together, and my department is unalterably opposed to taking any action which might prejudice the process. Also—" She hesitated. Outrage was practically choking her, Mohn was pleased to note. "Also, it is an affront to the concept of unity. Communities aren't made to be split up on the—the whim of a bunch of malcontents!"

"Enforcement Affairs concurs," Serafin said. "Hardly wise to promote ideas like secession. We're just holding our own in the fight for community as it is."

"I thought Clean Sweep was going to put an end to anticommunitarianism, Justin," Wofford said sweetly, "along with crime, masturbation, and tooth decay."

"I think sentiment's running against you, Justin," Mohn said. "We have an unprecedented opportunity to enhance our position vis-à-vis the League—which like it or not is a superpower, and like it or not is our rival—with virtually zero downside."

"I don't know, Madam Adviser," Wofford said. "This game is complicated, and the stakes could be pretty high. I don't think we should jump in without knowing all the ground rules. And I'm not sure we *can*."

"Isolationism, General?" Mohn raised an eyebrow. The National Security Adviser's raised eyebrow was internationally famous. "I wouldn't have thought you would advise us to stick our heads in the sand."

Before Wofford could say more, Mohn rose. "Well. We have our consensus, I believe: we keep open the option of low-level intervention to work this situation for what leverage we can without risking dangerous exposure. I shall so inform the President."

Nobody contradicted her, though Francine and Serafin looked sulky, in markedly different ways, and Wofford grumpily dubious. Mohn had spent a good deal of time studying Japanese management techniques—including how their consensus system actually worked.

"Just a minute, Madam Adviser," der Hagen said. "Do you actually think this revolt is going to succeed?"

Mohn allowed herself to laugh. "Not a chance in hell."

Chapter SIX

Beside the great fortified hill called the Ark that rises from the center of Bukhara, behind the Kalyan Mosque with its turquoise-covered dome and the glazed ocher brick minaret from whose top malefactors—meaning anyone who irritated the emir, who was unusually easy to irritate—used to be thrown, the streets are a hopelessly tangled skein. Narrow, potholed, and irrational, squeezed tight by one-story adobe houses from whose flat roofs spring a gleaming forest of television aerials, they look just like the streets of any barrio in northern Mexico.

The skein was knotted with rioters. This street, clear of

the not so civilly disobedient, had looked like an attractive route to the center of trouble for the Uzbek Republic MVD—Internal Security—platoon. And unfortunately it was.

They had almost reached a bazaar, deserted in the stunning midday heat, when a mud-brick wall slumped into the street in front of the lead BTR-80 armored car. As its brakes keened, a Molotov cocktail burst on the front glacis with a crack, a tinkle, and a *whomp*.

The MVD lieutenant catapulted from his cupola with the sleeve of his camouflaged tunic alight. Beating at the flames with one hand, he dropped to the pothole-pitted street.

"Zasada!" he screamed in Russian. "Ambush! Out of the cars, now, now!"

The bright reek of gasoline joined the smells of stale cooking oil, garlic, and hot mud. Gunfire popped full-automatic. Tears of fury mingling with the sweat that glazed his young Slavic face, the lieutenant drew his sidearm. "Those traitors in KGB! They said the rebels had no arms!"

A man stood up from behind the low parapet of the house behind him and fired a burst from an AKS-74 into his back. The boy screamed, more in the frustration of duty unfulfilled than pain or fear, and fell.

The second vehicle's commander fired the 14.5mm gun in the cupola. The weapon would not elevate high enough to rake the rooftop. In frustration he blasted the house to the left, raising clouds of dust from the foot-thick adobe brick, shattering a faded blue-painted door, exploding windows into a glittering snowstorm of glass powder. The muzzle flare set cheap yellowed curtains alight.

A single shot hit him in the back of the neck, below his padded helmet. He slumped behind the gun, blood gushing from his throat.

Uzbeks in doorways and on the rooflines were slaughtering troopers frantically trying to bail out of the burning lead car before it exploded. Thinking fast, the commander of the last car had already ordered his driver to reverse. A wooden telephone pole toppled, bounced on the rear deck. He breathed thanks to the *tengri* that the rebels hadn't thought to drop a live power line on them.

The telephone pole slid off with a screeching of wood on metal. Bullets struck sparks off armor around the sergeant commanding the second car. He crouched as low as he could in the cupola and waited.

Thirty meters back down the street and his machine-cannon would finally train. He triggered a burst. The upper torso of the man who had butchered the young lieutenant vanished in a black and scarlet spray.

"Withdraw!" the sergeant shouted over the vehicle's loudspeaker—fortunately the MVD vehicles were outfitted for crowd control.

Ambushers dove away from his fire as he lashed both sides of the street. With the surviving occupants of the lead car clinging like baby opossums to its armored back, the second BTR began backing out of the killing ground.

"—understand the sacrifices Russia has made in the name of civilization," said the man on the big screen in the wall of the Marrons' den. The camera switched to show the woman interviewing him, dressed all in white and leaning forward like a pointing dog. "For centuries we shielded Western civilization from the onslaughts of the East. More recently we have brought the benefits of the modern era to much of the East itself, in the process ending the bloody and arbitrary rule of the native emirs."

He steepled his hands before him. "This confers upon the Russian people certain messianic rights."

The woman turned toward the camera. "I'm Leslee Howe, and I'm speaking with noted Russian novelist and Radical-Traditionalist activist Yevgeniy Glazunov about the current crisis in Central Asia. We'll return after these words from your local stations."

A wan young woman with lank blond hair, in her teens or early twenties, appeared in front of the Advertising Council logo. "I want someone to make decisions for me," she said, big-eyed. "Free to choose, free to lose."

"*Fu*-uck," Richard Torrance said. He clicked the remote control as if command-detonating a claymore.

This time it was a male ingenue in a woolly sweater, wandering in front of generic public service announcement trees with hands in pockets: "I used to feel access to information should be open and free. Then I found out how often it's abused—how some people encourage others to do things that aren't right for their community or themselves, or actively pass along knowledge of how to disobey the law. I found out that researchers might accidentally or even on purpose create some new life-form capable of wiping out all life on earth in hours. I didn't used to believe 'a little knowledge is a dangerous thing.' Now I know better."

Click. "—not since Saddam Hussein has an upstart Islamic tyrant produced such a profound impact—"

Click. "—Miracle Network report: 'Millennium's End: Getting Ready for the Rapture.' "

Click. "When we come back, our Eye-of-the-Lord Investigative Team will show us shocking evidence of how local and federal police authority turn blind eyes to the Satanic activities of illegal role-playing gaming groups, but first, let Brother Jimmy—"

"Jesus," Torrance said. "Jesus. Fuck this. Aren't you on the Net?"

Elinor had left before dinner, pleading an early meeting of her regional Greenpeace executive committee and taking a balky Rebecca with her; she disapproved of Torrance. Richard insisted on fixing dinner, whipping up a fast stir-fry from ingredients on hand. It was excellent. He was vain about his cooking, and not without reason. Since then he and Marron had been male bonding, with alcohol for adhesive.

Marron raised his head from his chest. He was sunk well down in his favorite leather chair, his legs propped on a footstool from about the lower thighs down.

"No," he said muzzily. "Just cable." His old friend of Agency days had brought more than one bottle. Like the earlier Prohibition, current alcohol control laws failed to proscribe possession of liquor, just manufacture, sale, or transportation. "Just don't ask where it came from," Torrance had said with a grin.

Now Torrance glowered at his host. "Don't be a weenie. You can trust me. We're comrades-in-arms, aren't we?"

"No. Seriously. I don't have a satellite link. Ellie wouldn't hear of it, even if I was into that sort of thing."

"Yeah, you were always Captain fucking America, weren't you? Gave up smoking in the seventies, wore condoms in the eighties, and now you don't eat meat. What are you going to give up when the end of the Double Cross rolls around? Air?"

"I have my heart to think about," Marron said. "I'm not a kid anymore." Dick Torrance had always had a nasty streak, and it didn't only show when he had a load on. It was one of the reasons they had drifted apart, after Marron switched from CIA to NSA. You just had to be ready to ride it out.

"Maybe your show will be on soon," Marron said placatingly.

Torrance snorted. "No such luck. Not tonight." *Federal Police* was the most popular show on the air. Since a congressional compromise had defined violence as pornographic, leading to passage of a comprehensive bipartisan anti-porn package, television ran to carefully edited current events, nature shows, end-of-the-world evangelism, and white-bread sitcoms. On TV as in the courts and in the streets, the FedPols got to play by their own rules; *Federal Police* showed more skin and gunplay than all other legal shows rolled together.

Or maybe, as Enforcement Secretary Doyle claimed, it reflected all-but-unanimous public approval of its subject.

Marron gazed at his friend. "So, what brings you out here to the Front Range, anyway?"

"The Biz. What else?"

"I figured you'd be back in Washington, hip deep in planning for Operation Clean Sweep."

Torrance jutted his chin and nodded. Clean Sweep was Department of Enforcement's and the FedPols' ambitious plan to carry out a systematic search of every dwelling and workplace in America. Approaching kickoff, it was all over the media—at least, had been until this Central Asian thing hit.

"I am well and truly involved in the Big Broom, and it shall be *righteous*, have no fear," Torrance said. "But this is an iron I've been keeping hot, lo these many months." He gave Marron a lopsided grin. "Understand you had a little run-in with our boys this afternoon."

"News travels fast."

"We know everything. It's our fucking job." He took a deliberate pull and laughed out loud. "Wish I'd been there to see your face. You've faced down Sandinista patrols and death squads in Guatemala, and Amal militiamen in fucking Beirut. And there you were, sweating bullets with nothing to say in practically your own backyard."

"I knew it wouldn't do any good."

Torrance laughed again, visibly swelling with pleasure. "Fucking-A, *fucking-A*. We are incorruptible, indestructible, and we can do no wrong." He tipped the bottle up and killed it while TV light danced on the glass.

"So you had something to do with that?" Marron had his head up and was watching his old friend very closely.

"Been following the case for months, just say. Kind of a pet project, in fact."

"You must be disappointed with the way things turned out. "No trial."

Torrance shrugged. "Hey. Street justice, you know?" He laughed softly to himself.

He met Marron's eyes. "I could tell you some stories, my man. But you aren't *on-line*, if you know what I mean. Need to know, all like that."

Marron sipped at his own bottle with suddenly diminished interest.

"You really should have come over with us instead of going to No Such Agency," Torrance said softly. "We're where the action is. We're remaking this fucking country; we are stone what's happening."

On the screen the Russian tipped his huge round head to one side. "Be perfectly clear about this one thing, Ms. Howe," he said. "We will never surrender so much as one square centimeter of Russian soil."

"I like it where I am, Richard," Marron said.

Chapter
S E V E N

Nikolay Stepanovich Kuliyev watched the heliostat flash of muzzle blasts winking at them from the small boat. He showed teeth beneath the sweep of his magnificent red mustache.

"Do you *believe* these guys?" he asked, and banked the chopper right.

He was back in Hinds again. That was the NATO name for them; Russians called them *Gorbach*, hunchback, or sometimes drew the obvious pun and called them *Gorbachev*, after the man who betrayed the army in Afghanistan. Actually, Kolya and most of his squad mates just called it "Hind," as often as not.

As he saw it, your Hind series of attack helicopters had three big advantages:

A. They were fast.
B. They were well armored.

C. They were the *baddest*-looking aircraft in the history of man. Or at least since the German Stuka.

They were also huge. And loud. In modern combat, to be detected was to die, and the dragonfly-on-steroids Hind was hard to miss. It could not hope to survive either a high-tech Western air-defense environment or an old-fashioned Warsaw Pact—a name that was starting to be whispered again, with the Germans acting like that—lead sky.

In short, the Hind was designed to impress the natives. Like the Stuka, or the Americans' vaunted missile-magnet battleships.

And the Hind had impressed in Afghanistan: the rebels—Kolya was never complacent enough to think of them as "bandits," which was indicative of why he was back in goddam Hinds—were afraid of the Mi-24, which they called the "flying tank," and of *Spetsnaz*. The rest of the Soviet/Afghan fraternal forces they regarded the way Geronimo felt about the Mexican Army: "We only need cartridges for Americans," the Apache leader said, at least according to a book Kolya had read. "Mexicans we kill with rocks."

But the Afghans did have cartridges, including the immense 12.7mm ones digested by what they called the *Dashaka*. That is, the Soviet DShK heavy machine gun. The Russians provided these to their noble socialist allies in the DRA Army. Their noble socialist allies took them along with them when they deserted, so the *mujahidin* wouldn't kill them.

The Mi-24 and its kin, the M-25 and Mi-35, really were armored, and their titanium plate was supposed to be invulnerable to *Dashaka*—a claim young Warrant Officer Kuliyev had been intensely skeptical of, even if he was a *Komsomol* brown-nose in those days. On the other hand, if they got *above* you, and fired down into your fuck-your-mother *rotors* as you made an attack run, they could dump your white ass right into the Panjsher, armor or no.

Which was why he wore a weight lifter's belt to this very day when flying. And why he wore a Ruger Super Redhawk

.44 Magnum with a 75mm barrel in a sweat-stained holster beneath his left armpit.

In a way it was also why he was still in Hinds. And still a warrant officer, for that matter. Ever since that choking hot red-dust afternoon in 1986, he'd had an attitude.

Morale officers hated him. But they couldn't dislodge him. He was as good a rotary-wing jock as Frontal Aviation had. And he was that rarity of rarities in the League armed forces: a man who'd reenlisted after time on civilian street.

He belonged in modern high-performance choppers, Hokums or the sexy, savage little Havocs. Actually, he should have been helping develop tilt-rotor attack vertis, hybrids of fixed and rotary-wing aircraft, that combined the speed and endurance of airplanes with the hover and maneuver capability of helicopters. They had already proven successful as utility and assault transports. The new racing-shell breed promised to be primo tank and chopper killers. The kind of work the Cowboy had been born for.

But no. Hunchbacks it was. And doing the Azerbaijani National Guard's job for it. Cooperating with LeagueFleet out of Baku, worst of all, unappreciative bastards that they were.

"Call in on these nutcakes, Ivan," Kolya said to the flight-systems and communication man beside him. Ivan nodded his helmeted head. He was busy craning out, trying to see the funny people who were impertinent enough to be shooting at them. He was a young, impressionable sort, who believed everything his superiors and the design bureaus told him about the superiority of modern League matériel. The thought that even a little 5.45 or 5.56mm round might conceivably get lucky and drop them into the Caspian would have shocked him to the bone.

"Viktor," Kolya said, leveling out to increase separation and set up his run.

"Yo, Cowboy."

Kolya the Cowboy winced. Ivan secretly disapproved of his pilot-commander and his call sign. The gunner hero-worshipped him, and tried to emulate him, which was probably worse. He was even trying to grow a handlebar like Kolya's. He wasn't succeeding.

"Did the ground crew remember to load bullets for your Gatling this morning?" He bantered, but there were things you didn't take for granted in this man's air force.

"I'm ready to come on command," Viktor answered. He'd checked all the systems in the "greenhouse" cockpit up front himself before lift-off, as Kolya insisted. The Cowboy was short on formality and Party pietisms, but he ran a tight damn ship.

Kolya banked again, heard a high-pitched hail clatter hard by his head.

"What was that, sir?" Ivan asked.

"One of the ragheads got lucky and bounced a couple rounds off the canopy. Nothing serious."

Ivan paled. You felt very naked when somebody shot at you for real for the very first itme. Somehow all that armor didn't seem so invincible.

The dinghy was veering for an inlet now, churning up a white vee of foam in a futile effort to beat the speeding Hind.

"Wh-what do you think they are?" Ivan asked, obviously trying to show he wasn't rattled. "Terrorists?"

"Can't tell." Kolya grunted. "More likely they're just smugglers. But they might be both, running guns or explosives in to Azeri separatists."

The big chopper was crossing a bare gray stone knuckle that jutted into the greenish water. "Would they shoot at us if they were only smugglers?" Viktor asked.

"Who can tell? They're Shi'ites. Even other Muslims think they're nuts. I mean, these boys are Turks who want to be part of *Iran*. What does that tell you?"

"We should teach the Iranians a sharp lesson," Ivan said through gritted teeth.

"Shall I fire a warning shot?" Viktor asked.

"Nope. They fired us up first. Fuck 'em."

The first burst from the 12.7mm Gatling gouged a raw white gash in the water ten meters beyond the boat, which was running almost perpendicular to the Hind's approach. The boat rocked wildly and turned as one occupant, more timid or realistic than the rest, stood up and dove over the gunwales.

Viktor fired again. The boat vanished in a splash of spray, shattered planks, and assorted sundered parts. A moment later yellow flame fountained as the gas tank went.

"We should just invade," Ivan said. Spots of color glowed on his cheeks, right beneath his tinted visor. "Teach the black-assed barbarians to trifle with us."

Kolya worked his tongue around the inside of his stubbled cheeks as he orbited the chopper widdershins around the wreck. "Tried that before. It was called 'Afghanistan.'"

"I didn't mean that. I meant Iran. We could defeat them easily, and the West would never dare intervene."

"They said that about Afghanistan too," Viktor said. His voice sounded funny, constricted, as if he was having trouble holding in his breakfast. He'd never used his shiny multibarreled gun on humans before.

Ivan started to sputter.

"Leave that sort of thing to me, boy," Kolya told the gunner. "You've still got a career ahead of you. Don't damage it running your mouth."

Kolya glanced sidelong at his youthful instrument man. There was a time for even the Cowboy to hold his tongue. As far as things had come in the League, you could still take for granted that, out of a three-man air crew, one would be an informer. The League had to keep up with the rest of the world, after all.

Still, Viktor had it right. League and republic were running fairly regular air strikes and KDB—punitive airmobile—missions across the border against Azeri Party of God guerrilla bases and the *Pasdaran*—"Revolutionary Guard" —units that covertly trained and supported them. The Iranian government just blandly denied involvement with Hezbollah terrorism and filed another protest with the U.N. A lot of the League Army's more vocal traditionalists were screaming for more decisive action.

But as Kolya knew, the USSR had sent troops into Iran on a 1,300-kilometer sweep through Seistan back in 1981. A retributive raid for Iranian revolutionary support of their rebellious upland cousins, a warning, or a reconnaissance for a future strike to the Persian Gulf—depending on whom you believed—it had been claimed as a success by Group of Soviet Forces, Afghanistan. But they're never gone back for anything more ambitious than in-and-out border crossings. And the Iranians kept backing the *muj*.

Ivan tapped the side of his helmet. "Base says to try to take them prisoner. KGB wants to interrogate."

Kolya glanced down. A few smoldering planks were all that remained visible of boat or crew.

"Oh, *well*," he said, and plugged a tape into the player he'd illicitly installed beside his seat. Time for some good Hank Williams.

Shih Tai-Yu froze with her hand on the knob of her apartment door. Thoughts of the essays weighing down her backpack evaporated. *There are voices inside!*

The hallway was like a greenhouse from a day of intense Beijing summer. The smell of paint seemed to beat off the sickly green walls like heat from a stove. The fumes cramped her, crowded her, made her feel claustrophobic.

Tai-Yu felt her legs turn the consistency of boiled squid. Her heart seemed to beat right behind her solar plexus as she shuffled possibilities rapid-fire through her mind—haste making her spill cards, or flash them by without being able to assimilate them.

Who it could be had many potential answers: the Ministry of Public Security's secret police, the Party Discipline Inspecting Committee, army internal security; the players in the game changed from week to week, like the policies of the government of the People's Republic. Like the rules of the game.

That man eyeing me at the market? she wondered. *Could he have been following me?* It was an open-air market near the university, where peasants were allowed to come and offer produce grown on the small private plots some of them were allowed. She preferred them to the supermarkets, Western-style but state-owned, dotted around Beijing. In the open-air markets fresh fruits and vegetables were more likely to be available, and of better quality when they were.

The man had been pretending to peruse a bin of stumpy dead-white *daikon* radishes with the earth still on them, but he kept looking at her. It did not occur to her that he might have had other motives for staring than surveillance.

Or could the block cadre have called the authorities down on me? Her apartment block was maintained by the university for its middle ranks, lesser administrators and instructors, like herself, of no great tenure. The block leader was an old woman, a former custodian who ran sullen and shrill by turns. She disapproved of the young professor of Altaic Studies, thought her too unconventional, intellectual, and foreign. She was an ethnic Mongol, after all. Any good Han knew they weren't to be trusted.

Perhaps it was nothing; perhaps after all it was De, her lover, the disheveled poet and university hanger-on. He had a key . . . but then who might he be talking to?

Do they know? she wondered, a big black ball of fear rolling up into her throat. She remembered the father she hadn't known till she was seven, recalled his tales of arrest, abuse, and years of imprisonment during the Cultural Revolution. She recalled the terror of the Beijing spring, shots and screams and bodies falling as if in slow motion through air thick with heat and the smell of filth, as this neat hallway was filled with the stink of layer upon layer of paint.

She recalled her childhood friend Hua, always optimistic and pretty as a spring flower, who had fallen sick and not been present that terrible day in Gate of Heavenly Peace

Square, but who nonetheless had been called from the elementary school class she was teaching just two months ago. She had not been seen since. Her friends and relatives had heard nothing of her. Her husband had been arrested for growing demonstrative when he went to the police to ask after her, had been systematically beaten and released—all without acknowledgment that the authorities had any knowledge of what had happened to his wife.

Such disappearances still befell the Tiananmen "criminals." Some of Tai-Yu's friends theorized that the government knew who all of them were, but trolled them in gradually, rationing the arrests, as it were, in order to maximize the effect.

I should turn, she thought. *I should simply walk away.*

Instantly she derided herself for the notion: *Where would you go? You're a cloistered academic, not a revolutionary. Helpless. They'd pick you up within hours, days at the most. And even if they didn't, you'd only starve.*

She took a breath: *Best, then, to seek a quick resolution.* She flipped her single glossy black braid back over the shoulder of her blue proletarian tunic and opened the door.

The television set was on. The screen showed a map of Russian Turkestan, shaped like a dentist's chair, with Kirghizstan and Tadzhikstan as the back, Uzbekistan and Turkemenia the seat, and the Kazakh Republic as the bloated headless occupant. One of the voices she had heard was saying, "—continues at this hour in Alma-Ata. An air of tension still prevails in the Turkmen Republic, though no outbreaks are reported—"

She sagged against the doorframe of her tiny apartment. She should have felt relief. Instead she was nauseous.

When she felt reasonably confident she wouldn't throw up, she pushed off and carried her bundle of vegetables the few steps into the kitchen. As she put them away, she noticed that De had eaten the last of her eggs before leaving this morning—not to mention leaving the TV on. She made a small, irritable sound.

Perhaps it's time I threw him out for good, she thought, stripping off a stalk of celery and washing it in the sink. She thought about how easily the notion that he was a police informer had fit itself into her mind. The state didn't approve of those on the fringe, of those without a visible and steady means of support. Perhaps he provided services in return for indulgence of his Bohemian life-style.

"I should be honest," she said aloud. "I'm getting bored with him anyway."

Gobi Desert sand crunched between the floorboards and the soles of her black slippers—the desert was creeping closer, year by year, like her ancestors' final revenge. She took her celery into the other room and sat in the one cheap chair with the upholstery that was beginning to rupture terminally despite her dogged efforts at repair. It was seldom that anything on television interested her. And here was her specialty erupting all over the news.

The Turkestanis want to go it alone, she thought. *Don't they know that the world will never let them?*

Chapter
EIGHT

"Timing is everything, my children," Sher Khan said. "Timing and the love of Allah."

He glanced around at the students clustered around him in the meadow overlooking the deep gorge. Sunken-chested city youths, pale in their Western street clothes and *tyubeteyka*. They did not, praise Allah, look like much.

They looked like librarians, convenience store clerks, and the sort of students who belong to clubs devoted to some esoteric hobby, like stamp collecting, science fiction, or home electronics. Pushtuns thought all Tadzhiks *were* librarians, clerks, and besotted hobbyists. But Sher Khan was bound by the three precepts of *Pushtunwali*, the hillman's iron code: hospitality, safe conduct, and "exchange."

"Exchange" had the Old Testament sense: an eye for an eye. The Nikolays still owed Afghans a lot of eyes. Sher Khan knew it was not God's responsibility to make collecting easy for him. It was Allah's way to cast obstructions in the path of His chosen people. Tadzhiks, for example.

In the distance a train's air horn sounded. One of his listeners jumped as if a bee had stung him. Trying not to shake his head, he bent once again over the transmitter he had carefully propped on a sandbag.

"When we fought the Nikolays," he said, "one might detonate a charge with a burning fuse, or with a well-placed shot from an *inglisi* rifle. Do not look dubious, O beardless ones; I did this thing myself.

"But in His compassion and His mercy, Allah has seen fit that my eyes should no longer be as keen as once they were, to rival a mountain eagle's. So now I make use of *this*."

"So all we need to be *mujahidin* is Western technology?" one of his pupils asked.

"By my beard!" Sher Khan roared. The Tadzhik youngsters quailed. Almost two meters tall in his baggy dust-colored *kameez* pajamas, hook-nosed and bearded like an ill-trimmed hedge, Sher Khan looked the perfect image of an Afghan *mujahid* hillman right off the *CBS Evening News*. "To be a struggler one needs the heart of a lion and the wisdom of a Sufi sage, not toys! Ten years we fought the *Rus*, and only at the end did we have any of this technology you speak of."

He fixed one of the youths with ferocious gray-green eyes. The boy tried to retract his head inside his Satanta T-shirt like a turtle.

"If Western technology was all it took, you would be the mightiest of warriors, with your video games and television cartoons! Do you then think yourself the better of Sher Khan, the Tiger Lord?''

No, now, old fool, keep a tighter rein on your tongue. His charges looked as if they were about to take flight down the mountainside. As it happened, he had a powerful taste for video games himself, but this didn't seem a propitious time to mention it.

The train's horn sounded again. ''Behold, it comes 'round the mountain now. Watch in silence, that you may learn wisdom.''

Air horns bellowing like a frightened calf, the lead engine charged off the broken track, pulling the other two engines and the first ten cars of the hundred-car train off with it. The Tadzhik youths stared in openmouthed amazement, half ecstatic, half horrified at what they'd helped to do.

''Observe,'' Sher Khan said with only a trace of smugness. ''The train was just coming off a curve, and momentum was still drawing it outward, ensuring it would jump the track where our explosive cut it. And it had slowed for the curve—very important when ambushing a munitions train, lest your valuable prize vanish before your eyes in a single brilliant flash.''

Small figures had appeared among the bases of the tall pines perched above the railroad cut. The popcorn sound of distant small-arms fire drifted across the valley. Sher Khan picked up his ancient Lee Enfield sniper's rifle from the rock on which he'd leaned it.

''Come,'' he said, ''we must hurry. The Sukhois will soon be on their way, and the flying tanks not far behind.''

He set off down the hillside at a gangly run, tails of the coat he wore over his *kameez* flapping, lending him the appearance of a great ungainly crane. The Tadzhik youths exchanged glances and followed. The three fortunate enough to have Kalashnikovs moved self-importantly into the lead.

League labor-formation *Starshina* Bulgachev staggered along the metaled right-of-way with smoke in his nostrils and blood streaming into his eyes. Men were screaming, guns were shooting.

"*Basmachi!*" somebody yelled: *bandits.*

His youthful charges clustered around him. "Senior Sergeant! We're under attack! The train will blow up! What can we do?"

He wiped his eyes. Some of the understrength League MVD platoon guarding the train had thrown their weapons away and started bounding down toward the stream that ran along the valley below, probably more afraid of the train's blowing up than the attackers. Others were crouching on this side of the train, leaning around the cars to snap shots upslope. Even as Bulgachev glanced toward them, he saw one crumple and the others turn in horror as they were taken under fire from behind, across the narrow valley.

"What are we going to do?" asked a burr-headed boy with tears streaming down his face. He was holding his arm; a white spear of bone jutted through the blood-soaked sleeve of his tunic. In his panic he spoke his native Uzbek.

"The only thing we can do." Senior Sergeant Bulgachev tore the red, white, and blue League patch from his sleeve, tossed it down, and ground it into the dust with his bootheel.

"We've been pack animals for the *Rusyalar* for too long. Now it's time to live or die as men. As *Ozbeklar.*" He ripped open his tunic and began to tear a strip from his undershirt to serve as a surrender flag.

There were advantages to being old, Sher Khan decided as he threaded his way up the slope between pines, the astringent smell of their sap burning in his flared nostrils. Well, *senior,* and serving as teacher to these eager but naive Tadzhiks. Even his bare-cheeked young cadre of would-be saboteurs were bent under the weight of boxes of rifles and rocket-propelled grenades, or hauling on the tethers of horses made nervous and balky by the smells of burned powder and spilled blood.

He caught the eye of the stocky Uzbek *Starshina* who had come over to the rebels. He rode a horse bareback, at the insistence of his troops—Lord Tiger had seldom seen Nikolays so solicitous of one of their noncoms. But then, these weren't exactly Nikolays, though what they truly were remained to be seen.

The *Starshina* grinned and nodded, seeming happy as if he were going off to a goat-polo game with all his friends. Sher Khan was slow to trust a Turk, a city man, or a man who had worn the greenish brown coat of the League, and the senior sergeant was at least two of those three. But the Tiger Lord had seen enough defections in his time to feel this one was probably sincere.

There was always the chance he was a KGB or GRU plant. Sher Khan shrugged. What would be, would be. Certainly the Uzbek had already served the young rebellion well: his labor company had at least doubled the amount of loot Sher Khan and his group were able to carry off, the infinitely valuable arms, ammunition, and explosives. Even as it was, they had barely made a dent in the train's cargo.

One of his students caught sight of him and waved enthusiastically. "*Shabash*, Sher Khan, bravo! Are we not now truly *mujahidin*?"

The horse the boy was leading shied from his waving arm, dragging him off his feet and making its hastily secured burden slip alarmingly to the side.

"You pup!" Sher Khan roared as the boy's comrades broke up laughing. "You are young fools, barely *badmashi*, bandits. You may laugh in Nikolay's face when you've heard the thunder of his guns!"

The valley filled with a whistling roar.

Scurry like ants, you black-assed bastards! the flight leader exulted. There were dozens of the traitors swarming around the derailed train, many of them carrying crates of loot on their heads—very much like ants, in point of fact.

At the sound of the approaching Su-25 attack planes, many of them threw away their burdens and began to run.

He glanced to the side. His wingman was out of sight, behind and to the right. The valley was too narrow for them to maintain much lateral separation, especially since the leader was bringing his four-plane flight in low to make sure they got the best possible run on the bandits.

"Flight Udarnik, this is Udarnik One," he called. "We'll make the first pass with cluster bombs, then come back and finish this with rockets and cannons." As acknowledgments crackled in his ears he triggered two cluster bomb pods. They fell away from his squatty attack plane, spinning slowly, then breaking apart to scatter dozens of one-kilogram bombs like so many lethal eggs.

When the first strike plane appeared, the Tadzhiks started to scatter. "Wait!" Sher Khan shouted, his voice rising above the scream of jet engines. "They're not after us! It's the train they'll strike."

The Tadzhik youths stared back down into the valley in horror. Several score of the ambushers were still down there looting. Their cousins, their brothers, their friends.

Sher Khan had time to think, *So now you learn the bitterest lesson of war.* Then he saw the two 500-kilogram CBUs drop from the Su-25's belly.

"Down!" he screamed, and threw himself flat.

The train went up in a giant white flash.

The flight leader's wingman and the lead ship of the second element simply vanished. Udarnik Four came wobbling out of the black mushroom cloud rolling up into the sky, but it had been FOD'd: *foreign object damage,* debris thrown up by the blast, had crippled it. Within five hundred meters its pilot punched out.

As the rebels raised faces streaked with tears of terror and grief and triumph, the Sukhoi drove into a mountainside at five hundred knots. The chute on the zero-altitude ejection seat never deployed.

Chapter
NINE

Ah, civilization, Little Alex thought, in parody of an O'Neill play he'd never read but whose title had always intrigued him. The humid warehouse district air was full of the smells of diesel fuel and the salt waters of the Black Sea, stinking polluted despite the League's shamefaced efforts to clean it up. That was all fine with Alex. He was a city boy at heart, content to leave the mountains to the goats and eagles.

It had been a tense wait for the choppers. If they pulled off the SIGINT grab, Texas Team was bulletproof: they would have the bulk of GRU between them and Komitet payback. If not . . .

Alex grinned. *Fuck that shit,* he thought. *They came. We're golden. It's time to party.*

Dusk was falling onto Sochi like dusty theatrical curtains, settling between tokens of the League's fitfully increasing prosperity, stripped and abandoned cars parked to either side of the narrow, rutted street. Somewhere a radio tuned to the Georgian state channel was playing mariachi music.

Georgie stopped on the curb with his hands in the pockets of his fashionably baggy trousers and took a deep breath. "Ah. Vicente Fernández. The good stuff." He bounced up and down on his toes a few times.

"Gesundheit," Alex said, a little sourly. Mariachi was too close to the salsa music he'd hated so much as a teenager in New York. The Georgians had been hooked on the stuff since the mid-seventies.

Georgie gave him a reproachful look. He owed his

nickname to the republic of his birth, and the perverse whim of his unit leader. His real name was Vissarion Vitaliyevich Mzhavanadze. His father had taken him to America as a child, then brought him back to the USSR, as the song had it, as a teenager when Mzhavanadze, Sr., finally decided he couldn't handle living in a society he found anarchic and confusing.

Texas Team, minus Pete but including Simms—Simonov, the thin and nervous Canadian who'd come to the *Soyuz* as a student in search of his Dukhobor roots—was on the prowl for nightlife. That was a commodity Georgia had more of than even Moscow, province or not.

They weren't interested in the usual attractions of the League's largest resort town, the sanatoria and the promenade down tree-lined Kurortniy Prospekt. Tourist fare was too thin for *Spetsnaz* blood, unless you counted some of the more recent, less licit attractions. The underground nightclub known as the Western World had all by itself brought Sochi a reputation as the Hamburg of the Black Sea, without a bit of help from Intourist.

From somewhere to the north came a series of quick pops, like a finger being tapped on a tabletop hard. Another set responded, faster and higher pitched, like somebody touch-typing on an old-style manual typewriter. Texas Team stiffened in unison. You didn't have to be *Spetsnaz* to identify *that* sound: somebody using modern-issue weapons was slugging it out with parties armed with old 7.62mm pieces, AKMs or even ancient AK-47s. It was a sound that had been increasingly familiar in the Black Sea ports for twenty years—and was gradually becoming known all across the country.

"Street gangs versus *militsiya*," Georgie guessed, relaxing as much as he ever did. The shooting was too far away to involve them.

"Yeah." Buddy snickered. "And three guesses who's got the muzzle-loaders." The police had a reputation for being poorly armed, poorly trained, and generally fucked.

Tex cranked his white straw Stetson back on his head—it would have fetched a month's pay from any self-respecting worker on the "left" or black market—and punched his brother in the biceps hard enough to send him lurching off the buckled sidewalk and into a pool of water left by a late afternoon shower.

"Let's get a move on," he said, fending off Buddy's efforts to retaliate by knocking his hat off. "We spent too damn much time bellycrawlin' around them mountains, and I'm half-past ready to howl."

The Ponderosa was another triumph of League modernization. There was no air-conditioning, and not much air period coming in the saloon-style doors, as the afternoon breezes died with the sunset. Mucky dampish sand crunched underfoot and drifted around the peeling veneer at the base of the bar. Fat blue flies hung suspended in the heavy air as if it were amber.

By Western standards it was too dim to be a restaurant and too bright to be a bar, but it in fact was a hell of an improvement over drinking establishments in the classic Russian mode, which were mainly places you stood while blotting up as much vodka as it took to get you blind in a hell of a hurry. It wasn't really *legal*, what with the League in the throes of yet another anti-alcohol campaign, but that had never been of much concern to anybody. Especially here in Georgia, where they specialized in getting by by getting by.

First through the swinging doors was Alex. For this stand-down sortie he wore high paramilitary drag: Russian republican gray and white camo paratroop trousers, a U.S. Army tunic with GORSUNOV stenciled in black over the breast pocket, open after the fashion of League walking-out dress, but worn over a black T with a Green Beret clad skull and the legend *Living by Chance, Loving by Choice, Killing by Profession*. Topping it all was his own Green Beanie, complete with Fifth Group insignia, worn American-style, lopped to the side instead of standing up the way the Russians did it. After him came Georgie in his baggies and black bolero jacket, an elaborate earring hanging from his pierced right lobe, Delgado in black shirt and white jacket and pants, and finally the Lynko brothers in regulation walking-out VDV dress, if you overlooked the cowboy hats and the stiletto-toe sharkskin goat-roper boots.

The bartender sized them up with sleepy eyes and a slow nod. They were either a particularly nasty street gang or Special Operations. Either was welcome, as long as they paid.

The bar was not yet crowded. It wasn't a proletarian hangout, and the night people who were its normal clientele were just crawling out of bed. Alex picked a round table not too near the bar, and as far as possible from both the jukebox, which was blaring out a George Strait song, or the big-screen TV, where a local with stains on the lapels of his lime-green leisure suit was staring with slack blue jaws at the end of *Dallas*.

A couple of nondescripts, after eying the new arrivals surreptitiously for a moment, went back to a heated discussion in Georgian, with lots of hand motions. Alex glanced at Georgie, who showed no reaction, meaning the two weren't saying anything controversial.

Alex caught the word *chornyiyzhopa*, "black ass," which was the standard Russian slur for Central Asians. Georgians hated ragheads worse than the Rad-Trads. Alex gathered the Asian nationalities were up to something. Again. It wasn't his problem.

The waitress had peroxide hair and coal-black roots, and Alex couldn't tell if the dark around her eyes was makeup or contusions. She wore a cowboy hat, blue bare-midriff top and short skirt, fringed white vest and cowboy boots. Alex took note that she had nice legs, and had eaten garlic for lunch.

The waitress swayed away. Tex leaned over the table and flicked Georgie's earring with a stubby forefinger.

"Who-*ee*. You gonna get some tonight for *sure*. Got your old Mepps trout lure and ever'thing."

Georgie's eyes flared, but he only winced and pulled away without batting at Tex's hand. You didn't get physical with either of the Texas-born twins without being ready to carry through. In all of the full twelve-man agent detachment, only Little Alex and Pete were generally willing to take it that far.

Delgado grinned and jerked his head after the waitress. "Hey, maybe you hook her. She sure smells right, you know?" He waved a hand in front of his nose, in case anyone hadn't gotten it.

Tex slammed a slab hand down on the table. "Hey, now, I think the greaseball just made a pussy joke. Shit, all you Cubans know about eatin' pussy is when you catch cats in coon traps up on the roofs of your huts and stew 'em up for dinner."

Buddy bobbed his head and laughed his *hur-hur* laugh. He had trouble keeping up with this kind of repartee, but he liked to show he was following right along.

Alex sank down in his own wood-backed chair, sipping his apple juice. He neither smoked nor drank. In fact, except for one small detail, he was almost as perfect a League man as Mr. P the poster boy.

The after-action let-downs had him. He was subject to mood swings anyway, and he didn't have any taste for the kind of thigh-slapping jock releases the others were indulging in. He wouldn't have come at all, except as unit leader he had to at least show the flag when it came to carousing. But when he returned from a mission, he was filled with energy, even if he was drained of purpose; he couldn't stand to hang around the detachment's barracks, although by League Armed Forces standards—or anybody's, for that matter—they were fine quarters indeed.

He watched the waitress go by with her fringe swinging. A little mouthwash and she'd be quite acceptable. As soon as the rest of the team got a load on, they'd undoubtedly want to sail off looking for professional companionship, and that was always when he got off the boat. There was something about paying for it that made him feel funny. Of course, with his silver tongue, he generally didn't have to.

He leaned back, trying to shift emotional gears to start sweet-talking the waitress. The flying doors opened. Tex lifted his head, sniffed, and said, "Who farted?"

The four men standing in the doorway wore beards, dark blue berets, and jumpsuits with indigo-striped T-shirts underneath: *Morskaya Pekhota,* naval infantry from LeagueFleet/Black Sea. Elite enough to rate leave—unlike, say, the green-stripe squaddies from the Araks, who had to crawl through the wire for a night on what passed for a town—and elite enough not to give a good fuck-your-mother that the Ponderosa was off-limits even to them. The fact they were marines was enough to make them instant enemies of Texas Team, who all had trained as VDV—paratroops.

But the ill will ran deeper than that. These boys belonged to Black Sea Fleet's attached *Spetsnaz* brigade. Like Texas Team, with whom they sometimes carried out maneuvers, they were *vysotniki,* the cream of special ops. Officers and extended-service NCOs instead of the conscripts that made up most of *Spetsnaz, vysotniki* were trained along the lines of U.S. Special Forces to undertake sensitive small-unit missions, true snoop-and-poop stuff. This bunch was deployed on anti-smuggling duty on the Black Sea, a job akin to trying to hold back the tide.

Their leader was a petty officer named Derezhov, who had a head shaped like a cinder block. He stood, arms akimbo, scanning the dubious types who'd begun to fill up the bar. His eye lit when it hit Texas Team. "Well, if it isn't Moscow's own sweet bun boys."

Alex smiled sweetly. "In your dreams, Popeye."

"Have a good day?" Georgie asked. "You catch anybody trying to smuggle in nonbiodegradable laundry soap?"

"If anybody's running short on dope," Alex said, "the Black Sea sales force is here."

"Got any samples?" Delgado asked, drawing spilled-vodka circles on the scarred tabletop.

Berzin, the biggest naval infantryman—to Alex he looked just like Bluto from the old Popeye cartoons—growled and started for their table. His two nameless buddies held him back, looking like dogs baiting a bear. Derezhov sneered again and shook his head. He said something sidelong, and Berzin allowed himself to be pacified and led to one of the stools that had suddenly become available at the bar.

Tex cracked his knuckles loudly. Berzin made a guttural sound and started to turn. The bartender hastily slammed an open bottle of export-grade Stolichnaya in front of him, distracting him.

Bored with the byplay, Alex glanced at the television. A *blondinka* only slightly more convincing than the plastic-buckskin-vested waitress was seated in front of a giant logo for *Budushcheye,* the Russian Republic's leading private TV network, reading the news.

He focused, trying to hear her over "Six Days on the Road," for God's sake. He wondered why all the music he'd really hated in America had to follow him back to the Motherland. Worst of all, Serious and Dutyrock were making big inroads in Moscow. *Why can't they play some Santana?* He was a committed airhead, hard outlaw rocker to the core.

"—racial incident involving Yusuf 'Pat' Baraka, the first American high school athlete to sign with Moscow University's athletic program," the blonde was saying. The viewpoint switched to a scene of a lot of pale-skinned youths who obviously ate a lot of starch jostling a skinny black kid who towered over them like a radio mast. A hatless *militsioner* waded in with his nightstick, not looking too pleased at having to go to bat for a black, but painfully conscious that racist outbursts made the Motherland look uncultured, and withal always happy to bust *khuligany* heads.

"The latest incident arose over Baraka's alleged relationship with top Bolshoi School student ballerina Irina Pavlova."

The scene returned to the anchorwoman, then pulled back and panned as she turned to a freckled little man in a red vest and immense bow tie who looked like a drunk cartoonist's caricature of a leprechaun.

"And speaking of sports, here's Dzhonniy Davidov to tell us about the Moscow Stars coming home to face the St. Petersburg Defenders in a showdown series for the All-League Baseball Federation's Northern Division pennant. . . ."

One of the naval infantryman turned and spat on the stained linoleum. "'Dzhonniy,'" he repeated. "*Johnny.* What kind of name is that for a Russian?"

Derezhov looked deliberately back at Little Alex before replying. "Better you should ask, 'What kind of name is Davidov?'"

Berzin thought that was funny. He snorted vodka through his nose and all over the bartender.

"Who do we know who is one of *them,* Lieutenant?" asked another naval infantryman, catching the game.

"No one we can trust. Even though *they* might affect to be brothers in arms. You know the old saying: 'no matter how well you feed a wolf, it keeps looking back toward the woods.'"

"You mean Americans?" the fourth one asked ingenuously, though he knew perfectly well what the saying meant, and to whom "*they,*" emphasized in that particular way, invariably referred.

"Not even those imperialist swine. After all, just because our comrades were exposed to the disease of decadence doesn't mean they were infected. But when the sickness runs in the blood . . ."

It was quiet in the bar. Suddenly Dzhonniy Davidov's voice seemed to be coming from far away, another planet maybe. Alex pushed back his chair and looked at his teammates. None of them met his eye.

He rose and walked deliberately to the bar, leaned on it, almost brushing Derezhov's sleeve, but not looking at him.

"You interest me. What is this blood sickness you are talking about? It isn't *white*, is it?"

Derezhov showed teeth stained brown by tobacco and tea. He wasn't big, but he had a good ten centimeters on Alex, and maybe ten kilos. "What would it say under nationality on your internal passport, if your father had not pulled strings in the Party?" he asked.

Alex turned to him, smiled, and said, *"Yevrey."* Then he kicked the stool out from under him.

The back of Derezhov's head hit the hardwood edge of the bar with a sound like a gunshot. The naval infantry lieutenant landed flat on his back, with his head rolling from side to side like a boat rocked by ocean swells and strange creaking sounds coming out of his mouth.

Alex was astride him, hauling him up by a fistful of undershirt. "It would saw 'Jew,' you shit, you bastard. And what would it say on yours if you weren't spreading your cheeks for all of Black Sea Fleet?"

Derezhov groaned. Alex heard the scrape of barstool legs as the other naval infantry boys pushed back and cleared for action.

Another fine mess you've gotten us into, a voice said somewhere in the cheap seats of Alex's mind. He was going to have to do something about his temper.

He risked a quick glance back at his table. His heroic comrades were just sitting there.

No backing down now. "Well? What would it say, you sow?"

A semblance of intelligence was coming back into Derezhov's eyes, which was about as much as he could muster anyway. Alex became aware of the redwood trunks of Berzin's legs rising up out of the linoleum right in front of him. He heard a crash, and glass and clear pungent fluid cascaded over him as the giant broke a Stoli bottle on the bar.

Alex's hand dove under the skirt of his U.S. Army jacket, snaked his Glock out of the inside-the-pants holster at the small of his back, and jammed its blunt muzzle into Berzin's nuts.

"I'll tell you what it would read," he yelled into Derezhov's face without ever taking eyes off him. "It would read *nyekulturnyy.* Am I right? Am I?"

Nyekulturnyy was the worst there was. It meant "uncultured," but what it really meant was you were an ignorant sheep-fucking, booger-eating, vodka-swilling, illiterate gap-toothed cross-eyed hillbilly with lice in your hair and pig shit between your toes. It would've meant you spent all your time at bear-baiting and tractor pulls, if they had tractor pulls in the *higa* yet, and if there were any bears left. Peter the Great killed all kinds of people in the seventeenth century to make Russia quit being *nyekulturnyy,* and they still loved him for it.

Derezhov mouthed something. Still keeping his pistol shoved into Berzin's crotch, Alex grabbed the lieutenant by the face and slammed his head against the floor. "Say it!" he screamed, "Say, I'm a *nyekulturnyy* motherfucker.' "

I could use some backup, guys, he sent telepathically to his teammates.

"Mrm mm nrmfy mrf'mr," Derezhov said.

"I can't hear you." *Crack!* "What are you?" He banged Derezhov's head a third time for good measure. Meanwhile he sensed his buddies doing lots of nothing. He'd never had any faith in ESP anyway.

"I-I'm a *nyekulturnyy* motherfucker," Derezhov enunciated very clearly, trying to burn holes in Alex with his eyes.

Alex snapped off him and upright in half a heartbeat, thankful once again for high-school gymnastics.

"There," he said, covering the four with his pistol and backing toward the door, "don't you feel better? Confession's good for the soul."

"—turn you over to Mikhayl Sergeiyevich Rakov for a half-hour special report on the crisis in Uzbekistan. For those who missed our top story of the hour, communications have been cut between Tashkent and the rest of the League in the wake of two days of rioting in the capital of the Uzbek Republic—''

His butt hit the swinging doors. The rest of Texas Team rose and slid shame-faced past him as he kept his Glock on the naval infantrymen.

''Hey,'' he said from the side of his mouth, ''thanks for the help.''

''Anytime, little partner,'' Tex said.

The light pinned his head to the pillow, right through his eyes. He started to reach for his Glock, wedged between the mattress and the cold stucco wall, realized it was way too late.

''Senior Lieutenant Aleksandr Pavlovich Gorsunov?'' a voice asked from somewhere behind the light.

He tore his head loose from the light and made himself sit up, rubbing at his hair. ''Yeah. That's me.''

The light switched off. ''Lieutenant Shadrin, *Komitet Gosudarstvennoy Bezopasnosti*. Come with me, please. You are summoned to Moscow immediately.''

Chapter
TEN

Feeling eerie, Little Alex leafed through last week's *Time*. The cover story was WHILE AMERICA SLEPT, about something called *sleep abuse*, for God's sake: ''It's incredible that an activity which takes up so much of our lives—as much as a third—has gone unregulated for so long.'' After a decade in the U.S. he'd come home during the upheavals of *glasnost'* and *perestroika*, and it felt as if he were entering a country he'd never visited before. Now, after nearly another decade, his second homeland seemed from a distance almost unrecognizable. He felt as if he were in the Twilight Zone.

Or maybe the overbright, jittery fluorescent overheads were conspiring with stress and travel to disorient him. They certainly made it impossible to relax. On the other hand, relaxation wasn't something you expected to do in a waiting room in the nerve center of the KGB.

"Come *on*," he muttered. "Let's get it over with." It was all he could do to keep from jumping to his feet and marching up and down the waiting room. But he wouldn't give the *Chekists* at their hidden-camera monitors the satisfaction of seeing him pace like a caged beast.

He popped a stale half stick of Doublemint into his mouth; he didn't remember having spit one out two minutes before. He knew when he was well off. He hadn't been escorted to the cellars—yet. And while the sterile chrome and vinyl and pale olive walls were more reminiscent of a dentist's waiting rooms than the gloomy, grimy hallways of the legendary KGB redoubt on 2 Dzerzhinskiy Square—now headquarters for the Russian Republic's secret police—at least they were reminiscent of a *Western* dentist's office.

He had good reason for the nerves. The KGB had undergone a serious image upgrade since the Union fell apart. There had even been a movie, a joint American/ Russian production, glorifying the K's campaign against persecution of minority groups in the republics and drawing parallels with the FBI's war against the KKK in the 1960s South. What the movie never mentioned was that that particular Good War was fought by shots in the neck, running dissidents' cars off icy roads, and wiring people's dicks to electric train transformers from Toys 'Я' Us—*Toys Ya Us*, the way it read to the Russians.

That was no skin off any part of Alex's anatomy; he'd been brought up a New York Jewboy, and he didn't have much use for crackers from either Georgia. But Military Intelligence and State Security had hated each other like owls and crows since the surrealistic thirties, when their death squads hunted each other across the world at Stalin's behest. Their names had changed, and even the country they served, but the grudge endured. Alex was one of GRU's fairest-haired boys, and he had peed in the K's pool big-time. And he knew for a fact that *KGB* didn't stand for "Kinder, Gentler Boys."

Just about the time the sun should be coming up out of the woods of the Moscow Oblast, the door opened. A receptionist stood there, leggy and lean in a medium gray suit, with a shock of ice-blond hair and meltwater eyes.

"Senior Lieutenant Gorsunov? Follow me, please." She looked as fresh as midmorning. The Big K liked to give the impression, like the old Pinkertons, that they were an eye that never slept.

Here's another thing they didn't have at Dzerzhinskiy Square. He flashed a grin as she held a heavy oak door for him—putting something on it, ninety-five miles per hour with plenty of movement. Those no-color eyes looked right through him. *Tight-assed Slav bitch.*

A lot had changed in the almost thirty years of Alex's life, in the *Rodina*, in the army, even in the KGB. But some things never changed. The man behind the desk was clearly one of them.

A Western executive would no doubt have received a visitor while seated behind the enormous gleaming oaken desk, a modern monarch enthroned in his dark hardwood and green baize audience chamber. This man clearly preferred to stand, beating down visitors by sheer bulk in the classic Russian manner.

He had a lot of bulk to beat with: he looked like a shaved bear, and an indifferently shaved one at that. His vast body was stuffed into one of those lumpy awful Soviet-style suits that no self-respecting member of the *nomenklatura* had had to settle for since the seventies. The tie knotted around what neck he had was askew. He had a pugilist's nose with a thumbtip-sized mole beside it, hairy ears that stuck out, a few gray hairs combed straight back from his liver-spotted forehead. Despite the sparseness of his hair, his eyebrows were like two wolf tails, magnificent disheveled plumes. He looked as if he owed his position less to the Central Committee than to Central Casting.

Alex clicked his heels and came to a beautiful attention. Having qualified for membership in two of the world's most elite military formations, he was an expert in attention. He could hold it buck naked in Arctic weather while a fire hose played icy salt water over him. He *had*, during the hazing he'd gotten from instructors during his early *Spetsnaz* training days, when they still through of him as a product of a hated rival system who had to be broken down for honor's sake.

He didn't salute. The huge man wore civilian clothes.

The big man nodded, in that glacial Russian way that could connote either deliberation or genuine slow-wittedness. Either was a real possibility, Alex reminded himself. Intellectuals who flashed their wit on the upper slopes of the Soviet power pyramid tended to wind up, like Trotsky, in some flyblown Third World hospital with ice axes buried in their egg heads. On the other hand, true dimwits like poor Kostya Chernyenko, who poured the mineral water at Helsinki in '76 and got to pretend to be General Secretary for a few months in the eighties before he dropped dead, could sometimes rise to the top simply by being gopher to the right man.

But people who had gone all the way by seeming to be nothing more than simpleminded drudges, bumpkins, or glad-handing yes-men had names like Stalin, Khrushchev, and Gorbachev. From where Alex stood, there was no way to judge which category his host fell into.

"Senior Lieutenant Aleksandr Pavlovich Gorsunov," the bear said in a voice which had achieved the texture of the average Russian road through lifelong intake of *makhorka* and raw alcohol.

"That is correct, sir." Alex kept eyes-front.

The man paused to draw on a cigarette. "Do you know who I am?"

"No, sir." Alex lied. No matter what GRU liked to believe, the League's KGB was not the *Cheka*. Its higher officials were public figures, though most of them tried to keep their profiles low. Alex had seen this man caricatured in *Ogonyok*—still not the brightest thing in the world to do, but *Ogonyok* was like that—not two months ago. He was determined to concede not one damned thing.

"I am Arkady Arbatov. I am head of the Fifth Chief Directorate of the League State Security Committee."

Might as well be hanged for a sheep as a lamb, Alex thought, *whatever that means.*

"I am surprised, Chief Director. I should think it would be the Chief Director of Border Guards who wished to conduct this interview."

Arbatov dropped a scarred hand to his tabletop and stared at Alex through a cloud of smoke. His brows almost hid his tiny boar's eyes.

"What in God's name are you talking about?" he demanded.

"The seizure of your SIGINT station in the Arak Mountains by a half complement of Agent Detachment *Tekhas,* GRU Diversionary Troops, under my command."

Arbatov went the color of boiled beets. *"You insolent young pup!"* he roared. "The world is falling into ruin, and you think we're concerned with your silly Young Pioneer games?"

Alex tucked his head back on his neck and blinked. *What the fuck, over?*

The director lowered himself into his chair, slowly, as if arthritis was chewing at his joints with sharp rat teeth.

"Enough of these dominance games," he said. "Sit. You are a sufficiently worldly young man to realize that, should it be my design, I could snuff your life like a candle flame, with a pinch of my fingers." He made the appropriate gesture.

Alex started to answer back. He sat instead. At close

range, the director smelled of cheap soap and sweat as well as smoke.

"Are you aware of what has gone on in the last twenty-four hours?"

Alex shook his head.

Arbatov's fingers fell like bludgeons on a thick folder on the desk before him. "Six weeks ago, KGB-Samarkand arrested an agitator known only as Timur." He raised his eyebrows. "Does that name suggest anything to you, Senior Lieutenant?"

"No, sir."

The big man sighed. "The American influence. And not just you, nor is it indeed the time you have spent in America. It affects all our youth: in looking heedlessly toward tomorrow, they forget the past."

Where Alex had spent the second ten years of his life was classified a League secret. But if naval-infantry *Spetsnaz* lieutenants were aware of his background, Alex couldn't very well be surprised that a top man in the K knew.

"It is a Turkic word meaning 'iron.' It was borne by a fourteenth-century conqueror who claimed to be the grandson of Chingis Khan and made pyramids of his enemies' skulls. A man whose armies twice occupied Moscow."

"Oh, Tamerlane," Alex said.

"The man the West calls Tamerlane. Of course, Americanized as you are, you've never heard of him."

Alex commenced a slow burn. Arbatov went on. "Much of Central Asia is in revolt."

"I did hear something about that on the news," Alex admitted.

"We have reason to believe this Timur is at the heart of the rebellion."

A knot was slowly unwinding in Alex's belly. He had finally caught on that if Arbatov *didn't* have him here to strangle him on a meat hook, he must need young Alex very badly indeed—though for what, Alex had no clue. Heads of Chief Directorates of the mighty *Komitet* did not pass their dawns chewing the fat with snot-nosed Special Designation lieutenants, no matter how elite they thought they were.

Which gave him at least a measure of the privilege the GRU walk-on-water passports conferred on Texas Team, the ones that allowed them to go crawling through all kinds of off-limits dives without the *militsiya*, Georgian Republic MPs, or even low-level KGB types daring to fuck with them.

"So the rebels are trying to grab for a little faded barbarian glory, calling their main man after the Iron Limper." *So there, you fat old fuck, I even know what Tamerlane's name* means.

Arbatov glowered at him through the hedges of his brows. "Young man, you talk like a beer commercial. But you are correct."

"So what's this got to do with me?"

"Young man!" Arbatov thundered. Alex snapped like a spring out of the chair to full attention. "You have obviously ascertained that your Motherland has dire need of you. Being Russian, you are eager to make use of the advantage this confers. But remember: however badly I may need you, I know many ways of making your life miserable while making use of you! Understood?"

"Yes, sir!"

"Then sit, and show respect."

"Yes, sir."

"Yesterday a mob seized KGB headquarters in Tashkent and freed Timur. They acclaimed him their leader. Intelligence indicates the rebels are doing likewise all across Turkestan."

"What about the army, sir?" Alex burst out. He knew Arbatov could carry out his threat if he took exception to the young man's daring to ask a question. He couldn't help himself. There was nothing he hated worse than *not knowing*.

"The army has the responsibility, as they never tire of reminding us, of securing the League's boundaries against the savages and irredentists who ring us in on every side."

Irredentists was current Kremlin-speak for the Germans. "While the armed forces claim great successes, it is apparent that they have been unable to suppress the bandits."

There was a real obvious question here, and Alex's jaw ached with the effort it took not to ask it.

"I see you trying to hold your tongue, young man," Arbatov said. "Yes. It was in all truth the KGB's responsibility to foresee and prevent the outbreak—and the Fifth Chief Directorate's. Something has gone very wrong in Turkestan."

He pushed the thick dossier across to Alex. Alex hesitated, then picked it up. It was thick gray-green card stock. He paged quickly through the printouts. They were mostly fragmentary accounts of specific incidents—the surrender of the League base at Tashkent, the ambush of a munitions train outside Dushanbe, fighting in Bukhara's narrow streets.

"There's not much here about Timur."

"Indeed. We first learned of him during the troubles between the Meskhetians and the Uzbeks, ten years back. He was urging tolerance for the Meskhetians, who are a Turkish group deported by Stalin from the very part of Georgia in which you played your little prank upon the Border Guards. At the time, we dismissed him as what your American friends would term a 'bleeding heart.' It appears instead that his idea was to promote Turkish unity. He envisions nothing less grandiose than a Turko-Iranian nation-state, a 'liberated' Turkestan."

"He's crazy," Alex said.

"He is paranoid, at least, and cunning as the black devil himself. In all this time we have not managed to obtain even a single undisputable photograph of the man. He is a man of almost total mystery." Arbatov looked at Alex. "The mystery that interests us most at the moment, however, is how he managed to orchestrate what appears to have been a carefully planned and precisely timed uprising while *captive in the most secure cell beneath KGB-Tashkent.*"

Alex pursed his lips in a soundless whistle. *Somebody*

screwed the pooch big time, he thought. His GRU soul rejoiced. *But what the hell does this have to do with* me?

Arbatov picked up a second folder, thinner than the first. He perched a ridiculously tiny pair of reading glasses on his nose and began leafing through it. "'Agent Detachment *Tekhas*,'" he read. "What do we see? The son of a Georgian defector who changed his mind. An idealistic Canadian in search of his roots, in emulation of American Negroes, of all things. And the Old Bolsheviks thought *jazz* was decadent. A Cuban. The son of a scientist whose family Gorbachev permitted to live abroad with him." The last referred to Pyotr Yermakov. Mr. P.

"Now, here's a delightful pair. Gleb Lynko, American born, American given name Gavin. Given the choice of the army or jail after beating a student from a rival high school almost to death after a football game. After basic training, he joined the Rangers.

"His brother Boris, a marine guard at the American Embassy here in Moscow. Caught by GRU in a simple honey trap and turned. Detected by his own side and arrested. Strangled his armed escort in a men's room at Domedovo Airport while awaiting a flight to New York and escaped. When word of his exploit reached the American media, his brother also deserted and defected."

Arbatov shook his head. "A colorful set of *khuligany*, to be sure. Cowboys indeed. This agent detachment is well named, don't you think?"

Alex said nothing. He was fighting not to fidget.

"Ah, dossiers. They are more vivid than any novel, to those who know how to read them. They encompass a man's life: the beginning, the meat of the middle, and, in time, the end.

"But here—here we have the most fascinating story of all. A young son, only child of a minor Party official in Smolensk. An extraordinary boy, the tests revealed, a natural gymnast with a talent for languages, though sadly deficient in mathematics. What to do with such a one? His physical gifts are not of Olympic caliber, but in combination with his mental abilities still make him a potential treasure to the Motherland.

"Our esteemed colleagues in GRU have an idea. The father is loyal to the point of folly, a man who sent away his very beautiful wife when their son was seven, because it was unfitting that an ambitious servant of the Party should be married to a Jew."

He looked out beneath his eyebrows at Alex, whose hands were fisted so tight his knuckles cracked.

"Or perhaps he is merely expedient. But a willing tool, withal. So the clever GRU will wait until our boy is ten, and had plenty of time to learn to be a Russian. Then arrange for his father to 'defect,' during the great exodus of the late seventies. The Americans welcome them with open arms, as they welcomed all the fools and traitors and weaklings we pawned off on them. Father and son become good Americans.

"In due course the boy grows up. He graduates high school with honors. An adventurous lad, he joins the army. He applies for training in the Special Forces. Of course, they snap him up; he is mentally and physically superb, being of strong Russian fiber. And he can think like a Russian, speak like a Russian, because he *is* a Russian. Who better to infiltrate the *Rodina* and carry out acts of sabotage and terrorism? Is he not a fugitive from oppression? Who could be a more loyal American?"

Arbatov shut the dossier. "And so we have the ideal sleeper, the perfect mole, in place in the heart of the American covert-warfare machine. What went wrong, Aleksandr Pavlovich?"

Alex's teeth peeled back from his lips. "I don't know. I made it through training without a hitch, got sent to Germany for an advanced course." It occurred to him that Arbatov did not know the beginning of this story without knowing how it ended, but it was coming out in a lanced-boil rush of bitterness. "The CID bastards made me. Somehow." *And I was a good troop, dammit. I earned my beret.*

"So you forced a window in a second-story bathroom in Bad Tolzburg, jumped down eight meters to the ground, and managed to make your way to the frontier of the Democratic Republic. It appears that sanitary facilities have served the men of Agent Detachment Texas well."

He spent the next twenty-seven months in solitary, reading, perfecting his Arabic and Persian, practicing tae kwon do *kata*, dry-firing his Glock, and watching Desert Storm on satellite TV while GRU debated whether to trust him, whether he'd been tainted by his protracted taste of Western life, or whether he might already have been caught and redoubled. Toward the end, his gut began to tell him they were fixing to say *fuck it* and just shoot him in the head.

Then KGB-run *agents provocateurs* sprang the phony coup, to smoke anti-reform reactionaries out of Gorbachev's charmed circle. In the ensuing purges of suspected hardliners, Alex's keepers decided the most survival-positive course was to let him go, just to show what liberal guys they were.

Arbatov removed something from the dossier, slid it to Alex. It was a small packet covered in green leather. He picked it up with fingertips that had already started to go numb.

He opened it. His stomach did a slow somersault. His own face was staring back at him through a stamp on the Great Seal of the United States. RANDOLPH, the passport read, EDWIN ARTHUR.

He looked at Arbatov. This *was* a State secret. *If the K has* this—

"Are you truly surprised, Alyosha? Lenin himself provided that the Chief Intelligence Directorate of the General Staff should be a separate entity from the Committee for State Security. Yet he also provided that the *Komitet* should retain the ultimate say in the doings of Military Intelligence. It is our right to claim you, and we have."

"What do you want of me?"

"It has become clear that the rebellion will not be

suppressed until the League mounts a major offensive. To do this without fatally weakening our frontiers will take time. During that time, adventurers from around the world will flock to Central Asia to offer their services to the traitors.

"One of them will be the American mercenary who calls himself Fast Eddie."

Arkady Arbatov sat slumped in his chair, staring unseeing at the door through a screen of *makhorka* smoke.

It opened. His assistant entered, a gaunt gray man, tall, though shorter than the chief director.

"Ah, Leosha," Arbatov greeted him. "Things were so much simpler in the old days, when all we had to do was arrange that political rivals of Yuriy Vladimirovich should drive off icy roads and break their necks."

Leonid Leosha sat in the chair recently vacated by the young lieutenant. "Do you really wish those days back, Arkasha?"

Arbatov sighed explosively. "If wishes were gruel, none should go hungry. But no, I do not." He reached in a drawer. "Vodka?"

"Arkady Semyonovich, you forget my ulcer."

"Your health again," Arbatov grumbled. "You're as bad as an American." He poured himself a glass and tossed it off as his old friend watched.

"Do you think he bought it?" Leonid asked.

Arbatov set the glass down and wiped his mouth with the hairy back of his hand. "He must, Leosha. Or the Motherland is lost."

Chapter
ELEVEN

Keeping his head elevated while Yilderim the Tadzhik made fussy final adjustments to the special microphone clipped to the lapel of the Western-style jacket he wore under a striped Uzbek robe, Timur waved away a flock of overzealous studio techs.

"My turban obscures my face," he said. "Why then do I need makeup?"

It was festival time in the studios of Television Tashkent, crowded with warriors and youths in blue caps and townspeople who had attached themselves to the celebration. The uprising was succeeding far beyond anyone's expectations. Even his.

League military might was structured and deployed primarily to defend against outside aggression. The KGB's anti-intolerance campaign had been a convenient pretext for squashing such separatist sentiment as devolution had not co-opted. The League had grown complacent.

The League maintained three enormous peacekeeping—coercive—mechanisms: the army, the KGB, and the Interior Ministry's MVD. Each of the republics had its own army or National Guard, and most had MVD and/or State Security agencies as well. They all came with their own command structure, bureaucracy, and hostile attitudes toward other services. When the hammer came down, C^3I—command, control, communications, and intelligence, not to mention coordination—simply fell apart.

"Bukhaara! Samarqan! Dushambe! Aalma-Aata!" In the

background voices were chanting the Uzbek names of great Central Asian cities where the revolt had succeeded. Tadzhikstan and Kirghizia were almost entirely in rebellion, as was Uzbekistan and southern Kazakhstan from the mountains to the Aral Sea, except for the vast and well-defended Baykonur Space Complex north of the Red Sands and east of the Aral. Of all of ancient Turkestan, only the Turkmen Republic—occupied by ninety percent of the Central Asian Military District's forty-division strength—remained firmly under League control.

"Quiet! Enough! In the name of Allah, *gapirmang,* don't speak!" Timur's bodyguards and the television techs were trying to hush the jubilant mob. A few of his men began to raise rifle butts to club the recalcitrant into submission.

He raised a hand. The Kalashnikovs were lowered. The noise ceased. He took his place on the stool set in a flood of light, white and mean-souled. Facing the glass video eyes, he began to speak in English.

"People of the world, of the League, and of Free Turkestan, I greet you. I am Timur."

"Jesus fucking Roosevelt Christ," said the tech at the console deep in the guts of the Federal Police Agency's Media Compliance Monitoring Facility in downtown Washington, D.C. "The guy's declaring independence from the League? I thought those damned countries *were* independent. What the fuck, over?"

He glanced up at Justin Serafin. The youthful undersecretary for Enforcement Affairs was wearing black tails, but the bib front of his shirt hung unbuttoned and his white tie was wadded in a pocket. Officially he had been called out of a banquet his department was sponsoring for the U.S. Conference of Mayors to help launch Operation Clean Sweep. Since it was two in the morning Washington time, most of the night shift assumed he'd been summoned by beeper from some hotel room to which he'd lured a young mayoral wife. Now he had a headset pressed to his ear beneath the slicked-back hair. He nodded curtly; the transmission was still okay to go out over America's legal airwaves.

In Sochi it was ten in the morning. The Ponderosa Saloon never closed. The blonde waitress leaned her elbows on the bar and gazed into space. She was thinking about the young VDV trooper—Special Designation, though of course you weren't supposed to know that—who'd gotten in the scrape with the Naval Infantry night before last. He was quite handsome, with an acrobat's build and green eyes and blond hair and a devilish grin when he looked at her. She wished he'd stayed long enough to ask her out. It didn't matter that he was shorter than her. It didn't even matter if he was really Jewish, as those horrible *Morskaya Pekhota* bullies said when they were picking on him. He didn't *look* Jewish. And she loved the way he had dealt with *them*.

A couple of early birds down the bar were staring at the TV set with fumes coming out their ears. *Budushcheye* was showing a press conference. A man with a cloth wrapped around his head, a turban or something. He had nice eyes, brown and a bit Asiatic. Maybe he was Jewish too. Idly, she tuned in to what he was saying:

"*—no desire to conquer. We wish only what is ours, and to live at peace with our neighbors—*"

"*Bullshit!*" exploded the older of the two men at the end of the bar, spraying sunflower-seed shrapnel from his lips. "It's the Mongol yoke all over again. It goes to show how useless the Russians are: they take our youths as conscripts and all our money as taxes, and still their League cannot keep the black-asses in line!"

His friend shook his head. "These Tatar animals will never rest until we're all their slaves once more."

"But all he wants is to be left alone," she heard herself saying. "Is there anything so wrong with that?"

They both turned and glared at her so fiercely she pulled away and looked around for the sawed-off baseball bat the night shift bartender kept under the counter.

The older one shrugged. "What does she know? She's only a waitress."

"Though we are predominantly Muslim, we adhere to the ancient and honorable Islamic tradition of sufferance. It is not to impose our ways on others that we have taken up arms, it is only to prevent others' imposing on us. We shall respect the rights of our nonbelieving brothers and sisters, as we shall respect the rights of women, and all those not of Turkic or Iranian blood who dwell among us."

The words fell like drops of lead from the speaker mounted on the wall of the anechoic chamber beneath KGB Central. An operator tore his headset off and threw it to the floor.

"*Yob tvoyu mat'!* The damned nigger's running his voice through a speech synthesizer. We haven't got one hope in hell of identifying him!"

The water greeted her like old friends—it embraced her immediately, eagerly even, but it was cold as ice.

She swam a pool length underwater, feeling the silk caress of water on her naked skin, feeling the blood begin to flow again through her travel-fatigued body. *This is better than sleep, after a night on that wretched airplane.*

She reached the far end. Then, though it felt as if steel straps were tightening around her chest, she made herself do a racer's flip-turn, swam the return lap with strong confident strokes, never breaking the surface. Just to show that *she* was in control.

She returned to the world of air just under the diving board, clung there to the cold cement. The sky before dawn was banded in lavender and honey. The sun hadn't cleared the Mont Alban headland in nearby Nice yet, hadn't truly touched the villa. The villa did not belong to her; she disdained wealth, and bragged that she owned little but an admittedly extensive wardrobe. Still, the villa was hers on extended loan, from an old friend, as she put it.

The "old friend" was the government-owned Dassault/

Groupement Industriel des Armementes Terrestres arms manu-
facturing combine. After all, her relationship with it had lasted
longer on cordial terms than her relations with any individual.

She ducked her head under briefly, shook back her hair,
relished the way it felt cascading wet and icy down her
back. It was *vivid*. That was the way she liked life.

She breast-stroked to the side of the pool where coffee and a
basket full of chunks of steaming fresh bread awaited. Marcel,
her huge, gay Senegalese caretaker, had propped a flatscreen
plasma LCD television the size and shape of a breadboard on
an easel next to the pool. She could not stand to linger long
away from a set; being *in touch*, keyed in to the constant
electric flux of events around the world, was her drug.

In America she'd have been called a Nethead, an access
addict, although she lacked the interest in computers per se
that that implied: she cared only for *video*. Pictures, images,
bright and mordant as fragments of broken stained glass.
Members of EuroCom had considerable leeway as to what
they could allow their citizens to view—or at least France
insisted she had such latitude, and permitted her people to
see anything. Not, of course, that that mattered to Jacqui
Gendron.

The image that met her as she propped herself on pool's
edge with her elbows and reached for the beaten-silver
coffeepot was a face intriguingly concealed behind the tail
of a turban. What skin showed was a bit brown for a
Chinese or Southeast Asian, and the eyes displayed only a
hint of epicanthic fold. A Pakistani, perhaps, or a Turk of
some type. From the skin around the eyes and subtle clues
in the way his head moved as he spoke, she guessed he was
middle aged.

Text at the lower left-hand corner of the screen informed
her he was Timur, leader of the Central Asian rebels,
speaking from Tashkent.

*"—left alone, we shall not attack. Attacked, we shall not
surrender."*

She eeled out of the water, twisted lithely to rest her bare rump on the lip of the pool. She crammed a piece of bread in her mouth without being aware she was doing so.

Merde, she thought. She wondered briefly and maliciously what her proud League general made of *this*. Like many great men, he was ahead of his time. Unfortunately that also applied in bed.

"Marcel," she called, still chewing her bread.

"Madame." He appeared from the sliding glass doors, a mountain of gleaming black muscle in his customary striped sailor's T-shirt and white duck trousers. It was a waste, really, and she liked to titillate herself with the notion of getting him drunk sometime and seducing him—that sort of thing was feasible again, thanks to gene-tailored contraviruses. Unfortunately, he was a Muslim, which complicated the project.

"Don't call me that," she said, as she inevitably did. "It makes me sound like a dowager or a whorehouse proprietor."

She jumped up and began vigorously toweling off, before the delicious edge of morning cool turned to chill. She was vain about the racing-lean lines of her body, the firmness of her small breasts. She was forty, and while you couldn't say she looked younger, she knew she looked damned good.

As always, Marcel failed to rise to the bait. That was why he survived in her employ. "You wished something?"

"Yes. I must go to Tashkent at once. Call TéléFrance and tell them to begin making arrangements."

She began to walk toward the house, whose pitched red-tile roof was beginning to catch fire from the rays of the sun breaking like surf over the knob of Mont Alban. Her bare feet slapped terra-cotta tiles liberated from a Roman villa recently excavated nearby. Accords of the early nineties forbidding traffic in such antiquities had of course increased demand for them tenfold.

"What we believe has already been well expressed, two centuries ago, in what may be the most revolutionary document ever written. With your kind indulgence, I shall in closing quote it:

"'*When in the course of human Events, it becomes necessary for one People to dissolve the Political Bands which have connected them with another . . .*'"

"Shit," she said, speaking to the air, as she frequently did when a microphone wasn't handy. "Back to Russia."

Still, she reflected, it was better than the trip she had planned, to Belgrade to cover the Shining Path terrorist international, now centered there. Serbia was so dreary this time of year.

"Answer, damn you," Sondra Mohn said to the telephone clipped between one cheek and a nightgowned shoulder. On the TV inset in her bedroom wall, the man who called himself Timur was saying, "'—*among these are Life, Liberty, and the Pursuit of Happiness—That to secure these Rights, Governments are instituted among men—*'"

"Jesus Christ," she said to the screen. "What's next, a papier-mâché replica of the Statue of goddam Liberty?"

The voice that answered sounded wide awake, though she would have sworn the man she was calling was seldom in bed later than ten. "Ward? Sondra Mohn—oh, I see. You're watching it too, of course.

"That man you were telling me about, the one who used to be with Central Intelligence—" she took a deep breath, "I *think* we are going to have a use for him."

"—*that whenever any Form of Government becomes destructive to these Ends, it is the right of the People to alter or abol—*"

Justin Serafin snapped his fingers and drew his forefinger across his throat. "Cut! *Cut,* goddam it! That's enough." The technician hit a button, breaking the connection that fed the news conference to America's TV and radio networks.

Serafin sighed and smoothed back his hair. "That was close. We can't have shit like *that* going out over the air."

* * *

"Sir! Do you think it's wise to expose yourself like that?"

Wearily, the general shook his head and waved a hand at his aide. It wasn't wise, but he didn't care if a Tadzhik sniper picked him off through the ostensibly bulletproof glass of Dushanbe airfield's control tower.

It would greatly simplify matters if one did.

Who would have thought a mere mob could overrun a Soviet Air Force base? Yet they had.

Although perhaps *mere mob* was incorrect, though the hundreds, perhaps thousands, of Tadzhiks that had overwhelmed his perimeter defenses in minutes surely seemed to qualify. The two MiGs still burning on the runway, caught at the moment of landing by a rocket barrage, attested to that. So did the smoke and flames billowing out of the hemicylindrical shelters that housed most of the rest of the Frontal Aviation regiment's planes. Sappers had done that, teams of infiltrators with demolition charges.

Mobs didn't have rockets or demo charges. Nor did they have automatic weapons, including the latest-model bullpup Advanced Kalashnikovs. Not even weapons looted yesterday from the ammo train from Ashkhabad, which the leader and sole survivor of the attack flight scrambled from the base had falsely claimed to have destroyed before the bandits got to it, could account for the variety and concentration of weapons the defenders were facing.

He sighed raggedly and faced his aide. "Broadcast a cease-fire to all units. Order a white flag run up the pole. Use a bed sheet if you can find nothing else."

The aide turned pale and opened his mouth soundlessly. Perhaps he was shocked by the notion of surrender. Or maybe he just feared for his elderly parents back in Minsk. The use of hostages was a Russian tradition Western inroads had done little to weaken.

"Do not be afraid," the general said. "I am the commander. I alone am responsible."

The general's life, of course, was forfeit. *And what of that?* He had no fear of hostage-taking himself; his wife and two college-age daughters had all been struck down in Kiev during the pandemic outbreak of the intensely infectious retrovirus called *white* two years ago. Died even as the American C-17 carrying the genetically engineered cure was touching down on the runway.

His command was all the family he had now. He would secure their welfare as best he could. Whatever the cost.

"But what will they do to us?" a traffic controller asked, voice breaking in fear.

"This Timur has promised decent treatment of prisoners." The general shrugged. "And surely our comrades in the League will not force us to wait long for rescue."

He folded the crumpled paper on his lap. The floodlights died.

"Slovo nye vorobey," a *Budushcheye* crewman said, *"viletit nye poymayesh'." A word is not a sparrow; if it takes flight, you can't catch it.*

The studio erupted in celebration, people clinging to each other, weeping, shouting the name of God, kissing one another on the cheek and tossing skullcaps in the air. The foreign correspondents huddled on the sidelines, shouting into microphones to beat the din.

Timur smiled sadly. A small, neat man appeared beside him. He wore a League uniform from which all insignia and medals had been stripped except the gold crossed-cannon collar flashes of the artillery.

"'This, too, shall pass,'" he murmured in Timur's ear.

"You are erudite, Ali, my friend." Timur smiled sadly. "Let them enjoy while they can. The time of trial begins now. As the Japanese admiral Yamamoto realized after Pearl Harbor, all we have done as yet is awaken a sleeping giant. Whether we can do more remains to be seen.

"And may God have mercy on us all."

PART II
Red Sands

In war, numbers alone confer no advantage.
Do not advance relying on sheer military power.

—Sun Tzu, *The Art of War*; IX, 45

Chapter
TWELVE

The two Americans wore identical mustaches, cammie head rags, olive drab T-shirts with the sleeves torn out, and paratrooper pants. They locked fingers and butted heads and chanted, "War on *drugs*, war on *drugs*."

Standing with arms folded and his back to the hot concrete wall of the vocational high school, Fast Eddie shook his head. *Assholes*.

So this was the mighty Karakoram Brigade, at least as much of it as had assembled to date. *If we're getting FedPol rejects, we are in one world of hurt*.

The Big K had the spastic colon big time over the "Gentleman Adventurer On-line" recruiting ad, even though it had been their ticket for infiltrating Eddie into the rebel army. In that marvelous simple-minded yet paranoid way of theirs, they were mortally convinced that all of Turkestan was going in short order to be crawling with mail-order Rambos, CIA trained and lusting for Russian blood. And all, needless to say, with Big Knives in their teeth.

Well, here they were, herded together in a chain-link-fenced schoolyard with sweat pouring down them and white dust starting to cake on their faces: a couple of TV-movie heroes who probably fucked each other in the shower. Couch potatoes in camouflage sacks. Five guys with wild dark hair who spoke no English except to say, "We American *Green Beret*!" in some unidentifiable accent. A smattering of Desert Storm retreads with regulation flattops and

111

retired-NCO potguts. An enormous black adolescent with a neck wider than his head who looked like he'd been recruited as a lineman for Tashkent University and was wondering how he'd wound up *here*. Tower snipers, goofballs, boozers, losers, Cold War nostalgia buffs, and a couple—three at most—dudes who looked as if they knew their shit and had gotten bored with civilian life, and for some reason hadn't felt like upping in American's current War on Everything.

And one KGB spy and former New York State High School All-Star second baseman, standing to the side wishing he were anywhere else. *Oh,* yeah.

Somebody wandered his way, with his face all full of that dopey American good-old-boy buddy glow. Eddie gave him a flat hate stare until he faltered and went away. He was not here to pick up any new best friends. The less interaction he had with real live Americans, the less stress was going to be put on the secret ID the GRU spiders had spun him, within the Americans' computers.

He should have felt good about the turn-out, of course. This was *the enemy*. The problem was, he was supposed to go into *action* with these clowns. And Karponin's Operation *Sukhovey* was rumored to be getting ready to roll at any moment. Getting wasted by that butthole Al Capone did not form part of his game plan.

He had to admit old Scarface was cute, very cute. *Sukhovey* was the hardass southwest wind that blew out of the Red Sands into the Steppes. The official translation League spin control was promulgating was "Desert Wind." Any similarity to Desert *Storm* was purely intentional.

Vendors wandered through the crowd crying their wares in Uzbek, Russian, and a weird sort of advertising English they'd picked up from TV: "Grab for the gusto. Grapes? Here grapes. Cigarettes, new, improved, menthol and regular."

Eddie bought a handful of almonds and a big red bunch of grapes. Tashkent didn't do much for him so far, but he did love the grapes. The city was renowned for them; everyone kept telling him so.

He spat his gum into the wrapper, rolled it up, and stuck it in his pocket. Not leaving sign behind had long since been programmed into him, and some of these dildos looked seriously unmoored enough to tee off on you if your damned gum stuck to the soles of their iron-toed Mad Max boots.

There was an interesting stratification in the people buying cigarettes, he noticed. They were either among the few volunteers older than he was, or the even fewer in their early twenties, who'd come to adolescence after cigarettes' declining popularity was rescued by the U.S. outlawing them.

He moved away from the mob, steering around a couple of green turd-apples dropped on the weed-cracked asphalt by a little dun ass who'd inexplicably wandered into the compound and was being fed grapes by the black kid jock. He wanted to crawl out of his skin from the need to be *doing* something, but he put the nervous tension down hard, pushed it away. At this stage there was no action to take. He put his back against a wall and slid down to a sitting position to wait for whatever was going to happen.

This part of town looked almost depressingly like the outskirts of any other city in the world. There was a strip mall a few hundred meters away across a field of scrubby savage weeds, a high-rise apartment box stuck off of the middle of nowhere—a taste of place here, since the block was made of that Soviet Wonder Concrete that started to crumble before it dried—a factory in the background adding to the khaki haze that overhung the city. The only discordant note was the pair of shaggy Bactrian camels grazing on the embankment of the overpass on the superhighway that led southwest to Samarkand, under the sleepy eye of an adolescent in white shorts.

Traffic seemed about right for a city this size, not inner-city congested this far out, but brisk with the nearing midday rush where everybody was hurrying to get back from wherever they'd been in time for the two-hour downtime Eddie couldn't help thinking of as siesta. If all was chaos in the rebel-held region, as ITAR-TASS claimed, you couldn't prove it by Eddie. It was chaotic, certainly; but that was *normal* chaos.

He let his eyes fall shut. The best cure for his tendency to go hyper was to give into the natural soldier tropism for sleep in any time and place. The baking heat of midday made drowsiness as easy as sweating. . . .

"At the turn of the century," the driver said over his shoulder, "Tashkent was the only truly large city of Central Asia. It is today still the very largest. This does refute those who claim Samarkand is our first city." He wore a blue skullcap and a happy Chamber of Commerce smile.

Jacqui Gendron sat turned around in the backseat with a knee, watching the line of cars, trucks, and vans that trailed behind, past the ruins of the League KGB headquarters, which had been shattered by a mysterious blast within hours of Timur's liberation from its cells. Every vehicle was packed with press. Timur was reputed to be personally accessible to the Turkestanis, and his aides would indefatigably answer reporters' questions at any hour, but he tended to shy from direct contact with the media.

"At least we're in front this time," she said, with a smile of sour satisfaction. She had been trying to get an interview with the rebel chieftain for three days. It was an almost unprecedented delay for her.

"Keep close to him," she directed the driver as she turned to face forward. "If you lose him this time, I shall strangle you."

"*Jacqui,*" her cameraman said in alarm. "We're almost in the trunk of that limo already."

She smoothed back her orange hair and mopped her forehead with a towel Tewfik sullenly handed her. The car had no air-conditioning, of course.

"Oh, pay no mind to him, Hassan," she said. "Tank battles and terrorists are nothing to him, but get him in traffic and he loses control of his bladder."

The videocam man hunched himself down behind his shifting polychromatic oil-film sunglasses and pouted. The driver gave Jacqui a wounded glance.

"I have asked you please to call me Eric," he said. "That is the name I wish to go by."

"It says 'Hassan' on your work permit."

"It doesn't matter. We don't use work permits anymore; we are free."

"No work permits?" You mean, you can get a job or leave it anytime you want?"

The driver nodded proudly.

"What a way to run a country—look, they're moving! Don't dare lose him!"

The young Uzbek stomped on the gas. The shoe-box Moskvich wheezed asthmatically and lurched forward a beat late. Not even the strings Jacqui was able to pull—in Tashkent or anywhere—had enabled her to get a better rental car.

"Now here we are passing the beautiful Alisher Navaaiy Opera House—" Eric/Hassan said with relentless good cheer.

Jacqui pounded on the back of his seat and yelled in his ear, "Bugger the Opera House! Catch him, you fool, he's getting away!"

The driver leaned well forward, either to urge the car on or escape the noise. The engine whined protest as the subcompact picked up speed.

Almost at once Hassan rammed down the brakes. Tewfik the cameraman yipped as he slid into the back of the passenger seat. Jacqui was able to catch herself in time.

"And now we must stop for the light," the driver said in tones of wounded righteousness.

"What kind of world leader is this, who must stop for traffic lights?" Jacqui asked.

"Ours."

The light changed. The three vehicles of Timur's caval-cade pulled away. Hassan was goading the Moskvich in pursuit when the street filled up with little girls in school uniforms, sky-blue ribbons in their hair and sky-blue Free Turkestan flags in their chubby hands. In front, behind—everywhere, jamming them tight.

"*Khuda ozing meni asragin!*" Hassan exclaimed, hitting the brakes again, *God help me*. He leaned on the horn. The little girls gave him the raspberry and waved their flags defiantly.

Jacqui put her forehead on the back of Hassan's seat and pounded the backseat with her fist. "*Merde. Merde, merde, merde, merde*, merde."

Behind them horns blew. Journalists yelled curses in English, French, Russian, a dozen other languages.

"Jacqui, tell him to drive on," Tewfik said.

Hassan spun in his seat, ready to give the Moroccan what for. "No, Tewfik," Jacqui said regretfully. "Not in this car. The schoolgirls would only turn it over and set fire to it." She leaned out the window to shoot the finger at the procession of angry journalists behind.

Commotion called him back to consciousness flavored with sweat, diesel, and that damned white dust. The male-bonded FedPol types were trying to feed beer to the donkey. You wouldn't think they would sell beer here in the heart of Rebel Ragheadistan, but Timur seemed to take his crazy free-market rap altogether seriously. The FedPols were beginning to lay some heavy hassle on the black kid, who didn't think beer would be good for his new friend, and their banter was taking a nasty edge. All the secret cops he'd known were mean drunks, on either side of the Atlantic.

Eddie stood up slowly. The black kid was huge, but way out of his depth, and the mustache boys knew it.

Eddie smiled and dusted off the seat of his pants. He *liked* bullies.

The taller and rangier of the pair was backing the black kid up, banging him with hard heel-of-the-hand shots to the sternum while the black kid shook his head and looked like he was about to cry.

"You don't want me giving beer to the fucking donkey? Well, make me stop. Aren't you man enough, homeboy?"

An arm grabbed his. "Try me."

There was this little blond fuck standing there grinning at him. He cocked an arm. "Listen, Short Shit, if—"

He had a long, straight Anglo-Saxon nose he was probably real proud of. Fast Eddie broke it for him with a quick vertical punch.

As the man doubled over, spurting through his fingers, Eddie felt a hand grab his own shoulder. *Right on schedule*.

He let the chunkier FedPol's pull spin him, giving him impetus. This was great. A spinning back kick mustered as many foot-pounds as your body could deliver, but they were generally too slow for real-world use. But with the guy going back on his own heels from turning Eddie around . . .

The heel of Eddie's Asic caught the man right in the solar plexus, blasting the air out of him. He ran the FedPol backward till his heel hit a cement parking barrier and he went sprawling on the carefully tended lawn, scattering the audience.

Eddie turned and started toward the first FedPol, who was standing now with both hands pressed over his face, bleeding down his shirt. He began backing away as Eddie approached.

"What's the matter, Sparky?" Eddie asked. "You afraid of me? Shit, I'm half the size of the kid you were picking on. You should be able to handle me by yourself."

"Look out!" the black kid yelled.

He'd started a turn when the one he'd kicked hit him from behind.

Chapter
THIRTEEN

Momentum carried them forward until *they* ran into the damned donkey, which kicked Eddie in the upper thigh. The FedPol hauled him to his feet in a full nelson and his pal slugged him in the stomach.

He missed the solar plexus. Eddie kicked him in the crotch.

The FedPol grimaced, took a step back. Slowly he straightened. He smiled.

"I should've known," Eddie said. "FedPol. No balls."

The smile vanished. The mustached man whipped something small and gleaming-hard in a glittering arabesque. Butterfly knife: of course a FedPol would carry something like that.

The man who had him from behind had the sense to bury his face in the angle of Eddie's shoulder and neck, so Eddie couldn't crack his nose with his skull, and was bent forward to prevent Eddie from going for his groin, knee, or instep with a heel. These two were smarter than they looked.

Oh, Aleksandr Pavlovich, you've gone and stepped in it again. His intuitive flash had been that this was an ideal opportunity to stand out, as a fighter and a tough son of a bitch. He relied a lot on his intuition, and it served him in good stead.

Usually.

From the corner of his eye he saw the black kid, eyes wide, visibly nerving himself to jump on the knife boy, who would promptly stab him in the gut. . . .

The crowd melted *way* back. Eddie heard the sliding clatter of steel on steel. Guns being cocked.

The knife man knew that sound too. He stopped, then dropped the balisong and put both hands on top of his head.

"What is going on here?" a voice asked in clear but accented English.

As the hands slackened on the back of his neck, Eddie looked around. A huge open Toyota—no, *Liga*—four-wheeler had pulled into the compound. It had a padded roll bar with a bullpup Advanced RPK machine gun mounted to it by some kind of jury-rig. A half dozen rough boys in blue skullcaps who had evidently arrived in it had ringed the contestants in and were leveling Kalashnikovs at them from the waist.

A couple of sedans were parked behind the four-wheeler, a Mercedes and whatever *Liga* called their version of the Cressida, with smoked windows and the foot-long arched housings of smart-satlink phased-array antennas on the trunks. A group of less casually dressed men were climbing out and approaching.

The man in the lead was clearly the one who had spoken. He was medium-sized, maybe a little thick in the middle, in a Western-style suit. A white turban was wrapped Tuareg-style around his head and face, so only his eyes showed.

Eddie stared. When the FedPol behind him let him go to step back, urged by the men with assault rifles, his knees almost gave. *Timur!*

For a moment he was tempted. The man was obviously just as crazy as KGB Central was convinced he was, to hang himself out like this in front of half a hundred foreigners, half of whom could be KGB plants, for all he knew—hell, for all Fast Eddie knew.

Most of all, he was exposing himself to Fast Eddie, who *was* a KGB plant, and whom nobody had bothered to relieve of the Glock in its inside-the-pants holster at the small of his back, hidden beneath the untucked tail of his shirt. A quick draw, a quick shot—fuck it; the whole magazine, just to be sure. That would be it for this new-model Scythian Tamerlane.

Of course, that would also be it for Aleksandr Gorsunov, doing business as Fast Eddie Randolph. But under whatever name, he hadn't joined *Spetsnaz* intending to live forever. A score like this was worth life itself to a Special Designation trooper of any nationality, easy.

But Arbatov's orders were clear: "Until you receive contrary instructions, under no circumstances are you to harm Timur. If he comes at you with a knife, let him stab you. Further, do not through inaction permit any harm to come to him." It made Fast Eddie feel like one of Isaac Asimov's robots.

The order made small sense to him. In the movies, Special Forces troopies are always disregarding orders when they disagree with them, just as cops are always throwing away whatever civil rights guarantees still survive in order to just go ahead and fuck up anybody they think deserves it. In truth, Special Forces troops are supposed to exercise a degree of initiative, even in the League Armed Forces, where *initsiyativa* was still a dirty word, and sometimes that can mean constructive disobedience.

But a Special Forces soldier is still a soldier, and soldiers follow orders. The KGB chief director had every legal right to give him orders, and he was bound on his honor to obey to the best of his ability.

Besides, there was his father in America, land of *desaparecido* and Operation Clean Sweep. The KGB had never been known to rely on mere patriotism or sense of duty when they had other handles to hand.

The masked man—*Timur, fuck me, it has to be!*—was standing right in front of him now. "What happened here?" he asked. His voice was quiet, but it cut right through the restless wind off the desert.

The two mustache boys pushed forward. "He went crazy. He *attacked* us. He must be on angel dust—"

The black kid was saying, "No, wait, he was just trying to help me out." Eddie gave him a quick appreciative glance. Having somebody actually back him up came close to being a whole new experience.

Timur held up a hand. Eddie noticed it was soft, the hand of a middle manager, an intellectual, not a worker or peasant. No surprise there; who'd ever seen calluses on Lenin's hands, or Mao's?

"Enough."

The FedPols looked resentful, as if they were unused to being cut off in mid-denunciation. But at that point the shadow of a two-meter *Military Encyclopedic Dictionary* illustration of an Afghan *dushman* fell across them, scowling over a splendid beard. They shut up.

For a moment longer Timur's eyes held Eddie's. Eddie felt his mouth go dry. They were slanted eyes, with a touch of epicanthic fold—Chinese eyes, like so many of these Central Asian Turks had. They seemed to open up all the doors in his head and take a quick look around. Irrationally, he wondered if this was where the false ID the GRU specialists had painstakingly built for him in the American computer network would spring a lethal leak. . . .

Timur turned away. "We Turkestanis appreciate the sacrifices you've all made, the risks you've all taken, to come here and offer your help," he said, pitching his voice for the whole compound. "Yet we must not fight each other. Fighting the Russians will take all the strength we have."

He gave Eddie a final, penetrating look, then began to make his way around the compound.

The interior of the long *Liga* smelled of horse manure, gun oil, sweat, and strong tobacco. Unpatriotic as it may have been, Francis Marron was devoutly glad the car had really been made by the Japanese. He'd hate to rely on League air-conditioning; in the brain-drilling Tashkent sun, a mixture of industrial-strength pollutants like that could turn the confines of a car lethal in a hurry.

He had barely sat down in the back when the other rear door opened and Timur leaned in. "Mr. Marron," he said, fastidiously holding the tail of his turban before his face, as if afraid he'd catch something. He held out his free hand. "I am sorry I have not had time to speak with you before this. So good of you to accompany me here."

Marron shook the rebel leader's hand. Timur sat down. One of his aides slammed the door and slid into the front passenger's seat. The other two aides who had ridden to the school with Timur, the outsized Pushtun and the small, neat, dark man in the League artillery officer's uniform, got into the Mercedes.

"The honor's mine, sir. I must say, I admire the way you ditched the gentlemen and ladies of the press downtown."

Timur laughed. "I must dissuade them as gently as I can. Otherwise they will eat up all my time."

"Well, sir, I'm grateful for any time you're able to spare me, as crowded as your schedule must be. I confess to being intrigued at the chance to see some of the men who've traveled here to join you."

"It seemed only appropriate," Timur said, as the gold-toothed driver put the car in gear with a slight buck. He fishtailed pulling into the street, then headed for Timur's residence downtown. "These are your countrymen, though we have volunteers coming from all over the world."

"I must say I'm impressed with the way you dealt with them, sir." Marron told the plain truth, a rare enough opportunity on a shadow-diplomacy mission like this. Timur had an excellent command voice, firm without being strident, and an apparent knack for saying just enough without running over the line into what his undoubtedly cynical audience would regard as the Bullshit Zone.

His fellow analysts at No Such Agency—the effort of will it took not to think of them as his *former* fellows distressed him—had Timur sized up as insane. Certainly it took an excess of self-confidence to take on the League in open rebellion. But NSA tended to psychological dogmatism, echoing the American Psychiatric Association line that defiance of authority in any form was pathological. Inasmuch as he had spent a good deal of his career pre-NSA in fostering just such defiance, Marron had a hard time buying that.

The more so when he got to Timur in action. The man was smooth and solid as a supertanker in calm water. *They say Ted Bundy was a Republican party worker at one time, too.*

"It is my good luck," Timur said, "that you caught me addressing men who speak a language with which I have some familiarity. It is difficult to make much impression through an interpreter."

"My parents always used to say Hitler made quite an impression on them, listening to him on the radio, and they didn't understand a word of German."

The aide in front gave Marron a hard look. It was a calculated impertinence on Marron's part. He wasn't a cookie pusher from State, after all, Georgetown-trained to accommodate every whim of cannibal dictators. When he was with Central Intelligence, he learned that it was necessary, ever so occasionally, to take a high hand with clients, actual and prospective. He had apologies and fallbacks slotted in place in his mind, ready for launch if he had overstepped.

Timur just flicked him with anthracite eyes. "I have no ambition to resemble Hitler to any great degree. Come, Daoud, can you give me a run-down on our American volunteers? Do any of them show promise?"

His aide turned around in his seat and fussed open a laptop computer. He began to scroll through dossiers. "Here is one named DeVaughan; he has experience with chemical weapons—"

Timur listened for a few minutes as the great white building-block apartments of New Tashkent passed slowly to either side, like matte icebergs. Then he waved his hand. "What about the small one who was fighting with the two others?" What does his résumé say?"

"He is Randolph, Edwin," Daoud said, squinting at the russet plasma screen. "Former master sergeant, United

States Army Special Forces. He speaks Russian, Persian, and some Arabic.''

The aide looked back at his boss. ''The American Special Forces emphasize cadre work, as you know, Timur. As great as our need for training is, he could be a most valuable addition. If what he claims is true, as I fear half the claims these volunteers make are not.''

''I have contacts within our Department of Enforcement Affairs,'' Marron said. ''Friends—the old boy network. I'd be glad to use what influence I have to see if I could get background checks run on any or all of these men.''

''I appreciate the offer, Mr. Marron. Nonetheless, it strikes me that if I begin checking every American who wishes to join us with your Federal Police, we might soon find ourselves running short of volunteers.''

''Oh, I don't really think there's much danger of that, Mr. Timur. That situation is exaggerated by malcontents and professional sensation-mongers abroad. The Federal Police Agency's approval rating with the American public is very high.''

''Indeed. Perhaps you could give me some idea of what brings you to Turkestan yourself, Mr. Marron?''

''As you know, I'm an investment counselor. I represent a group of American investors who have come together for the purpose of making use of what they perceive as a window of opportunity here in Central Asia. After an extraordinarily promising start, economic reform in the League has proceeded painfully slowly. . . .''

But Timur was laughing at him. Marron seated his glasses more firmly on the bridge of his nose, striving for an expression that suggested both willingness to join in a joke and readiness to show steel if American dignity needed to be stood upon. ''Sir?''

''Forgive me. It is a violation of our rather rigid code of hospitality to laugh at a guest. As it is to lead him on—as I have been doing to you. But surely, Mr. Marron, is it not rather insulting of your Central Intelligence Agency to send one of their better-known operatives to me without even bothering to give him a false name?''

Marron swallowed. *Think fast*, he told himself. Blanket denial was clearly out of the question, so—

''Sir, I'm afraid you're working under a misapprehension. I was in fact an employee of the Central Intelligence Agency at one time, it's no cosmic secret. But it has been several years—''

''Working for the so-secret National Security Agency. Come, Mr. Marron, give me a bit of credit. I have my sources too. The United States of America wishes for its own reasons that its approaches be secret, and I am willing to accept that. But I wonder at what I think your jargon calls the *subtext*.''

He settled back against the door and looked at Marron. ''Is your government trying to suggest that, should I not be a good little boy, you will terminate me as you did Acevedo in Costa Rica?''

Chapter
FOURTEEN

''Where are you from, soldier?''

The boy had fat cheeks and biceps that bulged like Polish hams. He seemed on the verge of sneering; then his eyes flicked aside to where, Anatoliy Karponin knew, the regimental *starshina* was regarding him with a look of undoubted hatred. A newly promoted general colonel commanding a Front composed of League troops as well as contingents from all the republics was a being so remote from any reality this miserable muscle-bound conscript understood that he had no idea how to react.

Features writhed beneath pallid skin that shone with greasy-looking sweat, arranged themselves in a set no-look, eyes fixed on the scatter of clouds rolling like dustballs above the distant horizon. He knew enough to fear his noncoms. Good.

"The General Colonel asked a question!" the Russian republican sergeant major snapped. He didn't say *shitbag*, but everybody heard it.

"Moscow, sir," the boy stammered.

"Ah. What district?"

The boy stared into space a moment before he felt the fury radiating off the sergeant major behind Karponin's left shoulder. "L-lyubertsy. Sir."

"A good working-class address." Karponin nodded. "So. You are a Lyuber. I suppose you belonged to one of those so-famous gangs, who wander the Moscow streets assaulting those who don't conform to our traditional Russian values."

The boy was quivering now, it having penetrated one of his brains—either the one in his dumpling-shaped skull or the one at the base of the tail Karponin was certain he'd find if he looked for it—that he could be in serious trouble. He started to nod, then said, "Yes, sir!" He looked hopeful again.

Karponin smiled. "And you are very strong? You can bench press two hundred kilos?"

"Yes. Yes, General, sir." The youth bobbed his head, practically beaming with pride.

Karponin had his mouth near the young man's ear. "And will your fine muscles protect you when a Mussulman's bullet has turned your guts to red jelly?" he asked. His voice was low, but it cut like a whip, and every man for twenty meters heard him clearly.

The boy crumpled as if he'd been hit in the solar plexus. Karponin turned away and, to no surprise, found a youth with long lank blond hair smirking at the working-class tough from several places down.

"And what do you find humorous, soldier?"

The blond boy snapped upright. He could manage a good attention when he had to. "Nothing, sir!" he snapped, all Young League business.

Karponin raised his heavy dramatic eyebrows. "Indeed? Those who grin at nothing are mentally disturbed. Perhaps I should notify your Morale & Development Officer." He tipped his head back, pretending to consider.

Sweat crept from beneath the tan service cap, matting the blond hair further. "Let me guess, my lad. You weren't really smirking at nothing. You were smirking to see a proletarian lout put in his place."

Blondie's lips quivered with the desire, the *need* to deny, but he knew better than to speak. There might be hope for him too.

"So your father is a New State Capitalist, then? Or an administrator for the republic Environmental Bureau? No, you need not answer. You are sick, my boy. Contempt for the working classes which are the backbone of our League is a symptom of mental disease. But we need not trouble your M&D officer. Here in Central Asian Front, we are very conscious of medical progress, and understand that exercise is a specific for many illnesses of mind and body."

He turned. "Therefore, you will don full kit and run down to the right-of-way for the Central Asian Railway. It's only ten kilometers round trip, but that should suffice to help you with your problem. Sergeant Major, send a *yefreytor* along in a jeep to monitor the progress of his therapy."

"Yes, *sir*."

The New Class kid was sent staggering off beneath pack and helmet and the horrible southern-steppe sun. Anatoliy Karponin stepped back to address the formation as a whole. His face was very tan, so that his white trademark scar gave him a dashing, almost piratical look.

"You are not soldiers. You are *khuligany* and spoiled sons of privilege who have slouched and shirked through those years of civil-defense training which were meant to ready you to fulfill your military obligation to your Motherland. A seasoned veteran might quail before the task of turning you into soldiers." *Which is why I selected you.*

"But I am the man they call Al Capone. I am a mean bastard. Central Asian Front is the finest fighting formation in the League, and *you will do* your parts.

"At the beginning of this decade *Rodina Mat'* was disgraced by the fat, sloppy, long-haired weaklings turned out to quell the savages and traitors. Those imitation soldiers gave the politicians the excuse they needed to give the Union away.

"Your noncommissioned officers are all picked men— picked by me. They are combat veterans, hard men, men who know how to take a life. If you do not now fear them more than you fear Timur, then wait. But they and they alone can teach you what you must know to face the desert, and the fanatical hordes who wait beyond.

"If you are attentive, and work hard, and then harder, you may survive. But understand your survival is not necessary; it is a matter of least importance. The Motherland is all. You shall not fail her."

All his life he had transacted business from behind a desk. To do it instead from the midst of a splendid Bukhara carpet from the days before chemical dyes—to do without his accustomed defenses was an oddly exhilarating, riding-the-edge sort of experience. It reminded him, briefly, of the inevitable, indeed the necessary end to this adventure. Yet that knowledge did nothing to diminish the pleasure. If anything, the opposite.

"Ah, Khaalis," he said. "You are well?"

The republic official was a podgy Uzbek with Mongol eyes gotten from his Kirghiz mother, and dark bags under them gotten from overwork, worry, or debauchery, depending on your estimate of his character. Khaalis was not the *head* of his department; that honor had belonged to a European Russian. Of course, being boss made you a prime target of the periodic drives against corruption. Nailing rivals for corruption was a traditional road to power for the ambitious young Party man, and was especially popular now that the Party's successors had to worry both about world opinion and voters.

The European Russian department head—last seen weeping with gratitude as Sons of the Sky-Blue Wolf escorted him aboard the first jetliner out of Tashkent after the revolt—got the title and the heat. It was Khaalis—and his family connections—who got things done, Khaalis and his family connections who held the actual power. That was political reality in Central Asia. As it always had been, even before the Nikolays.

"All my needs have been most graciously provided for, great Timur." The fixer shifted his weight for the third time in less than a minute.

"Would you like a chair? I understand that, from your years as a devoted Marxist, you are unaccustomed to going on your knees five times a day to face Mecca in prayer."

"You misunderstand, Timur *Agbar.* It's merely that my arthritis is acting up. It's the air-conditioning—"

Timur held up a hand. "Be at ease. And please, don't call me 'great Timur.' It makes me sound like some huge unwieldy statue, like the five-hundred-foot reclining Buddhas they pray to in Sri Lanka."

Khaalis's mouth writhed under his mustache. As Timur well knew, his lack of religious observance sprang from laziness, not old-days Party piety. He retained a fundamentalist Muslim's reflexive horror of idolatry.

The functionary covered quickly enough, bowing his head to the parquetry floor of what had been the ballroom of the Russian Colonial house. His *tyubeteyka* was pale green, with violet flowers embroidered on it. "I await your pleasure . . . Timur-*jaan,*" he said, lighting after the briefest hesitation on the polite form "dear Timur."

"I wish to know if you will continue to serve the people of the republic as selflessly as in the past."

Khaalis froze in his genuflection. Only his eyes moved, rolling up like obsidian marbles to stare at the rebel leader.

"I understood you intended to dismantle the political structure."

"And so I do, Khaalis-*jaan*." Inflected that way, *jaan* could also signify either extreme affection or casual contempt. "I also know that you—or rather, your *yurt*—control most of the essential services for the city and much of Uzbekistan."

"You give me too much credit."

"I give you precisely enough. You have a hand in all republic-provided services: water, power, sewage, garbage collection. Your brother-in-law is head of the Transit Workers' Union. Your second cousin controls the issuance of all business licenses. Your uncle is highly placed in housing allocation. Little happens in Tashkent without your extended family having a share in it. Will you take tea?"

Naturally Khaalis would. A youth in sky-blue skullcap attended them, a grin of pleasure at being able to serve Timur himself threatening at any moment to crack his severe composure. Timur was not yet used to being waited on. He hoped he never got too used to it.

The tea was just right, thickened almost to the point of syrup with sugar and dosed with so much mint that the steam rising off the wide *piyaala*, the handleless Uzbek cups, brought tears to their eyes. Timur held his cup up under the facecloth of his turban to drink.

"I will dismantle that system, as I have promised, and permit the market to provide what the people need. I understand quite well that your *yurt* could bring the city and much of the republic to a stop if they wished to obstruct, in a way the Nikolays could never do. I don't want that to happen." *Which is why you've been under house arrest since the revolt began. A brigand band like your clan understands hostage-taking in their bones.*

"Stipulating that my *yurt* possesses such power—and I would suffer my tongue to be torn out before I would contradict the Father of Turkestan—why would it consent to cooperate in the diminution of that power? Speaking hypothetically, of course."

"Of course." Timur sipped. "First of all, there would be compensation. For example, no inconvenient questions would be asked about the wealth your family has already amassed. And while you would lose your monopoly status, you would still be well placed to compete in the open market in a number of areas. You come of resourceful stock, Khaalisjaan. There is no reason your *yurt* could not do as well as before, or even better."

He drained his *piyaala* and set it on the geometrically figured carpet before him with scrupulous care.

"Also, we are fighting a revolution to free our people of the official depredations of the state, which we will treat as the banditry it is. Should anyone whom we permit to continue in office think to abuse his position—" He shrugged. "Are we Turkestanis not called *Sarts*, merchants? I'm sure a progressive *yurt*—your own, for example—could see its way clear to accepting a reasonable blood-price for such a malefactor.

"Dear Khaalis, I bid you good day."

"Kolya," the voice cried, rousing him from his fuzzed fugue state. "*Nick!*"

He sighed. Reba McEntire was singing her little heart out from his box, trying to compete with the throb of helicopter engines on the flight line right behind his folding chaise longue. He really needed earphones, but he refused to cut himself off from the world so completely this close to the firing line. They weren't right up against it, of course; they were in the midst of Operation Desert Wind, Anatoliy Karponin commanding. They also had the well-defended expanse of the giant Baykonur Cosmodrome—so near they could practically feel the heat on their faces when the huge yellow boosters hurled themselves into orbit—between them and the rebels. But they were still on the rebel side of the

Aral, north of Syr Darya, and that meant taking nothing for granted. At least to Kolya Kuliyev. Afghanistan was thirteen years behind him, but he hadn't forgotten the lessons learned there.

"Look!" a younger voice cried. "It's him! Cowboy!"

"Warrant Officer Kuliyev," a second young voice corrected.

The fishy reek of the flats, which had been Aral Sea floor until irrigation of the vast Uzbekistan cotton plantations shrank the inland sea, surrounded him in an oddly comforting embrace, insulating him from the pulsing noise and diesel stink and hot hard metal of the flight line. Time to leave that dubious shelter. He adjusted the mirrorized mylar-over-cardboard reflector he'd improvised beneath his chin.

"That's Junior Lieutenant Kuliyev to you," he said. "And probably the oldest junior lieutenant in Frontal Av."

Reluctantly he opened his eyes. Yuriy, chief of his ground crew, was standing there with the wind off the Red Sands Desert ruffling the sparse white bristles of his hair, grinning an old-fashioned Soviet steel grin.

"These two young bastards were driving everyone crazy trying to find you. At last I relented and brought them, so we might keep our ships in the air and keep the rebels from sneaking in and slitting our throats. Did I do right, or should I have taken them on a flight to Kandahār?"

Kolya winced. A "flight to Kandahār" was about a thousand meters up, then out of the ship without a parachute, a lesson the Soviets in Afghanistan had gotten from the Americans in Vietnam—maybe the only one, on the evidence. Good old Yuriy had very different memories of his Afghan experience than Kolya, had drawn different conclusions.

"That would be too good for them. They must be made to live and face the beast Timur." He slid his sunglasses down his squashed pugilist's nose. "Where did you two drop from?"

"We've been transferred to Desert Wind too," Viktor said eagerly. His square jaw and American-style aviator glasses made him look like an underfed Marlon Brando. Russian Republic TV-Moscow had been showing *The Wild Ones* twice a month late-night since roughly the beginning of time. Apparently some Cold War recidivist had an idea about showing how bad and *khuligan*-ridden America was. Obviously nobody'd gotten around to clueing him that the modern reality was much worse.

"At last we'll see some real action," Ivan added. Kolya's former electronics operator still reminded him vaguely of a celery stalk. "Isn't it exciting? They say General Karponin really knows how to make things happen."

"Al Capone's a prize horse's ass," Kuliyev said.

"He's not so bad," Yuriy said hurriedly. The grizzled NCO lifer so common in Western armed forces was a rarity yet in League or republican armies. You didn't get to be one without certain awarenesses heightened. Yuriy had instantly sized up Ivan as a Youth League hero with a ramrod up his butt, a potential informer.

Kolya waved him off. "Karponin thinks the sun rises and sets on League Army armor. He's not big on the vertical battle and *desant*-type penetrations and the other things that worked for us in Afghanistan, to the extent anything did. We're here for recon and flying artillery.

"The good news is, I'm out of Hinds, anyway. I get to fly Hokums now, which is fun, although flying an anti-helicopter ship would make more sense if the rebels had helicopters."

He rubbed his cheeks. "You still flying Hunchbacks?"

The two looked at each other and nodded. "Sergeant Portynagin is our pilot now," Ivan said. "He's very proficient."

"He's not as good as you," Viktor said at almost the same time.

Kolya laughed and shut off the flip player with his big toe, then settled back in his folding chaise longue. "Care for some fruit juice? I've got a couple different kinds in the cooler."

Viktor looked crestfallen. "No vodka? Not even beer?"

"Not even beer. I'm not the party ape I was at your age. I take care of myself for Marina, now."

Yuriy shook his head in mock reproof. "I can't believe you're talking that way." He looked at the two younger men, who were rooting in the red plastic cooler. "You should have seen him back in Jalalabad in the old days! The rebels had two prices on his head, one for his prowess in the sky, one for his prowess with their women! The Pushtuns don't have much use for women, you see, but they're mighty jealous of them, and our Kolya was always ready to lend them more than fraternal assistance."

He clucked as Ivan diffidently handed him a bottle of orange juice. "*Kolya Kola* we called him then: Nick the Prick. Hard to believe such a lusty cock confines himself to treading a single hen these days. Gah, this stuff isn't fit to drink without good vodka in it."

Kolya shut his eyes and clung to his homemade reflector as a pair of Mi-28s swept low overhead on a recon sweep to the southeast.

"If my attention did stray, Marina wouldn't care. She'd hope I had a good time," he said absently. "That's one of the reasons I never stray. Also, she's all I can handle."

"You are a lucky man, Kolya," Yuriy said.

"I am that."

"You shouldn't be out here in the sun," Ivan said reprovingly, brushing sand from his brief blond hair and taking a sip of apple juice.

"I need to get a bit of a tan if I'm going to work this damned desert. With my redhead's complexion, it's the best protection against a burn."

"Youth League On-line just carried a reminder that direct exposure to sunlight brings risk of cancer," Ivan said primly. "You should wear sunscreen at all times, and not lie out like this."

"Nikolai Stepanovich is a Leningrader," Yuriy said. "Leningraders know the value of a little sun."

"St. Petersburg," Kolya corrected. "If I get cancer, the

bastards can cure it. The purpose of medicine is to cure, not to tell us how to live our lives.'' He pulled out a big cigar and stuck it beneath his mustache, wagging his red eyebrows Groucho-style at Ivan's look of disgust. ''Besides, I want my hide an attractive shade in case I auger in and the rebels lift it for me.''

''Does Timur really skin his prisoners?'' Viktor asked, half scandalized, half titillated.

''Probably not.''

''The Youth League BBS—''

''Give your bulletin board a rest, Vanya,'' Kuliyev said. ''You pay too much attention to it. You want the squadron M&D counselor to think you're a Nethead?'' They didn't have political officers in the army anymore. They had morale and development counselors, which was worse.

Ivan stood to attention. ''There are well-documented reports of atrocities in rebel-held areas.''

''No damned doubt about it. Every group's got its complement of detached assholes. But I think our friend Timur's more the idealistic dreamer type; probably means it when he says he doesn't go in for playing rough.''

''The Shi'ites are idealists too,'' Viktor said.

Kolya laughed, licked a fingertip, and held it up in the poisoned breeze off the sea: *score one*. He popped the top on a bottle of juice. He pulled the tab a little too hard and a seam split, leaking melon/grapefruit all over his hand. ''Shit. Fuck the Greens anyway, for talking the government into making this damned quick-degrading plastic crap mandatory. If they want to do something for the environment, let them first do a better job cleaning up poor old Aral.'' He licked his hand, then slammed the ruptured bottle's contents.

He gazed off across the sea. ''Idealists or not, we've got to fight them,'' he said. With the hard sun glinting off it, the water looked almost blue. Hovercraft milled around raising yellowish wakes, preparing, rumor had it, for a possible advance up the Syr Darya. ''It's our job. Besides, the League's worth fighting for.''

* * *

"Those conscripts," the red-faced Russian captain said, pouring vodka. "Dogs, the lot of them."

"Too gentle," a Ukrainian major said, biting into a cucumber. "*Swine*. Hopeless. Completely hopeless."

Anatoliy Karponin gazed over his staff with half a smile. A colorful flock, these popinjays, plumed in all the hues of the League and the sundry republican armed forces. A man who generally deplored waste in any form, he didn't know in all truth what half these people *did*.

But he was a vain man, who knew how to use his vanity as a tool, as his idol Patton did. STAVKA, the press, the public were all impressed by the size and magnificence of Al Capone's retinue. If only a handful of the lurid hangers-on punishing the lunch buffet in the artificial chill of the command trailer actually had useful jobs, and knew how to perform them—well, Anatoliy Karponin knew which ones they were. The rest were but peacocks, a potentate's display.

And potentate he was. Let the black-assed rebel bastard parade about under the name *Timur*. Anatoliy Karponin would show him a *réal* Tamerlane.

He sipped coffee tart with lemon. "They are precisely what I wanted."

The air-conditioning made the sudden silence remind Karponin of that stillness that lies between low clouds and new-fallen snows of an early December morning. Only the wooden-legged polka thumping of the little two-stroke alky-fired generator disturbed the quiet. Karponin enjoyed the effect.

"The League General Staff in its wisdom was less generous with seasoned troops than one would wish, even though most of our 'veterans' have known no combat more intense than border skirmishes with the Iranians or the Chinese. So I requested the most recent drafts from large urban areas."

"But sir, those are the most disaffected of our conscripts," protested Captain Rybalko, Karponin's operations officer, who was young and looked younger. An officer in the Russian Republican Guard, Rybalko was not among the peacocks. "The proletarians resent their lives; the, uh, the sons of administrators resent being taken from theirs."

"Precisely." Karponin sipped. "They have *anger*. We will give them someone to vent it on."

He set down the fine china cup. "Now, gentlemen, let me urge you to drink and eat but lightly."

They stared at him. "The treatment I prescribed that young man today set me thinking. We all could use what the Americans term an 'attitude adjustment.' Therefore, as soon as luncheon is over, we're all going for an invigorating run down to the railroad line."

Chapter
FIFTEEN

"Astakhfirullaa," Timur breathed. "By God!"

The functionary let the tarp's corner drop. "By God, certainly. And also by Khaalis, my Khan."

His words raced like squirrels between the rows of big, boxy, canvas-muffled shapes and up to the steel rafters of the giant warehouse on the outskirts of *Eski-Tashkent*, Tashkent Old Town. Timur was so startled he forgot to take the man to task for using the title.

The man in the League artillery officer's uniform put his neat head back and laughed. "BM-13s," he roared. "Stalin Organs, almost sixty years old if they're a day! Truly, the Nikolays never throw anything away."

"Their habits of thrift serve us well," Timur said. "How many?"

"In this warehouse alone? *Allaa* knows. In all of Tashkent, to my knowledge—one thousand."

"One thousand?" The giant Afghan's eyes bulged on either side of his eagle-beak nose. "One thousand multiple rocket-launcher trucks? God is truly to be praised."

"Naturally and always, my Lord Tiger," said Khaalis smugly. It was always prudent to show these southern hillbillies that you and God were like *that*.

The smaller one, the Arab, smoothed his Arab Legion-style mustache and looked at Khaalis altogether too intently. "What are they doing here?"

"It is even as you said, Colonel Ali: the Nikolays throw nothing away. These were assembled from all over the Union back during the war of lib—that is, the intervention in Afghanistan. Tashkent was a major mustering point, you know. Did you know it, in 1979 when Babrak Karmal broadcast his appeal for Russian aid, he was really here in the city? My maternal cousin Mahmud was a technician in the studio at the time."

The Pushtun's crack-nailed hand brushed the hilt of his Khyber knife. "You sound proud, little man."

"Do I? An infinity of pardons, Sher Khan! It is a shame upon my *yurt*—one which I hope my little revelation will do much to erase."

"That seems likely," Timur said. "Please proceed with your tale."

"*Ha*, well. It's really quite simple. The Nikolays brought the Stalin Organs here to send on to the army of the Democratic Republic. Then the war ended. What then to do with them? It was certainly not worth the effort sending them back where they came from. The Russians could never bring themselves to break them up for scrap. The only thing to do was drive them into warehouses, throw tarps over them, and lose them from the inventories."

"How do you come to know about them?" Ali asked. Suspicious bastard.

"As the great Timur knows, my *yurt* is spread wide. My kinfolk include drivers and warehousemen."

"Why didn't you find some way to sell them to the DRA yourself?" Sher Khan growled.

Khaalis shrugged. "Dr. Najib did not want them; they were too outmoded, and he was a man who cared only for the best, may the devils turn his spit slowly in hell. So they remained untouched until this day, and I joyfully present them, a present from my *yurt* to my Khan."

"Enough of the traditional obsequies, Khaalis," Timur said. He hesitated. "I have no wish to count the teeth of a tribute mare—"

"Your namesake never balked at that," Ali said.

"I am not my namesake, Colonel. As I was saying, these weapons are most impressive in their numbers, but they are also sadly out of date. Can they truly be of help to us?"

Ali smiled. "More than you can imagine, Timur."

The tent was full of small nervous rustling, clearings of throats, diesel fumes, sweaty uniforms, and the reek of vast fetid *Aral'skoye More* slogging pollutedly nearby. From beyond the low hills came the rumble of a test-bed firing of a new rocket engine. Scraps of tinny music from bivouacked troops and arc-welder sputters from the armories and vehicle parks in the false noon of floodlight towers rolled by like tumbleweeds on the heavy breeze.

Colonel General Anatoliy Karponin stood at the head of the tent, facing the commanders of Operation Desert Wind. Central Asia was a "Front" by sole virtue of the fact that STAVKA said it was. A Front comprised on paper at least four land armies, two combined-arms and two tank, plus a tactical air army. Desert Wind was more a single reinforced combined-arms army at this stage: six motor-rifle divisions, six tank; call it an army and a half. As air assets he had a weak fighter/ground attack division, no dedicated fighters—which made sense, admittedly, inasmuch as the rebels had no airplanes for them to *fight*—a strike regiment of Sukhois that had been flown until the wings were about to come off, and assorted recon and transport units.

The League held out small hope for more. There were borders to be held. Worse, though the republics of the League had unanimously condemned the uprising—including naturally the governments-in-exile of the Uzbek, Kirghiz, and Tadzhik republics—malcontents were beginning to stir. League and republican reserves could not be overcommitted to Turkestan.

Anatoliy Karponin concurred. What he had was more than sufficient to the task at hand.

He gazed about the tent, knowing the kerosene lanterns would throw dramatic highlights across the heavy handsome face. That was why he didn't use generators to light the briefing tent—for theatrical effect. Morale was as important a factor in battle as tactics and logistics—more so, in fact; he felt it deserved its own place with the three accepted elements of military art: strategy, operations, and tactics. As holder of a rare and coveted doctorate of military art, he was entitled to such radical views.

"Gentlemen," he said. "The time has come. Tomorrow we move."

The applause was loud and prolonged. It was a pity the foreign news crews could not be on hand for this, but security and his own sense of propriety forbade. Besides, League Armed Forces archive and publicity units were out in force, camcorders whirring. All the newsnets would get a suitably edited version of this, after the fact.

He rode the response, half smiling, until it began to subside. Then he nodded. The portable two-meter screen beside him glowed to life with a map of the Turanian Lowlands of Kazakhstan east of the Aral and north of the Syr Darya. It was a self-luminous color-LCD unit. Karponin was a believer in modernization with discipline, and it influenced his taste in stage design.

"We will be making a preliminary strike *here*," he said, and as he spoke, a dot expanded to fill the screen. "This is a fortified bandit village. Taking it will give our young men a chance to blood themselves in an easy victory. It will also serve to send a message to the world.''

He raised his head. Lantern fire danced in his dark eyes.

"Let there be no mistake here.'' His voice rang like a long-rod penetrator striking a turret. He was speaking to history now. ''This is a fight for the values of civilization against those of barbarism. Against the new Mongol hordes.

''As of this moment, the initiative passes to the hand of civilization.''

"Damn,'' Kolya said, easing off the collective. ''It makes my dick hard, the way this babe just leaps into the air.''

No response from the gunner's seat, stepped before and below the pilot's spot. Young *Yefreytor* Popel' could only cope with the complexities of combat flying in a volatile little racing-shell Havoc by hiding from the rest of reality behind a wall of existential denial. On the ground, only incessant browbeating by senior NCOs got him to involve himself to the extent of showering and brushing his teeth. There was *no way* he was going to attempt to deal with the mad whims of his pilot. He didn't communicate with Kolya at all except for what duty required.

Given what an introverted little spud he was, that suited Kolya fine. He was his own best audience anyway—he and Marina. But seeing Vanya and Viktor again reminded him how he missed the easy camaraderie of Black Sea days. Ivan was an uptight little prick, but there was a real human in there somewhere, trying to burrow through the Youth League bullshit to daylight.

The eastern sky was muzzy gray with false dawn. Kolya loved getting up early, loved flying early; that was one reason he was widely considered crazy. There was a purity to the predawn hours. The feel of the chopper, the whippet tremble and muted snarl of power held barely under control, only augmented the sensation. Serenity and hysteria at once: the ancient samurai must have felt this way, the morning of battle.

He chuckled. Adrenaline was getting to him. As a pup he'd had his nose rubbed in reality too damned hard to stay wrapped in that warrior-mystic robe too long. War wasn't a game, and it sure as Satan wasn't transcendental meditation.

But it was still the one thing he was truly consummate at.

"It's the real thing, kid," he said, for his own benefit, really. "Stay awake."

"Yes, Junior Lieutenant." The boy gave *literal-minded* a bad name.

Kolya nudged the hypersensitive joystick controlling the cyclic rate, banking the helicopter left, then shooting it forward, above the heads of the cheering ground crew, to join on the stub wing of the squadron leader.

"Cowboy present and accounted for," he said, nodding through the tough polymer canopy. "What's the destination, *Krasnaya Molniya*?"

A gloved finger touched the crimson lightning bolt painted on the front of the other pilot's flight helmet. Captain Derevyanko was neither as big a fire-eater nor as fevered a Rad-Trad as the "Red Lightning" handle might indicate. He was a shrewd, decent leader. He wasn't as proficient as the Cowboy, though, and he knew it.

"Listen up, everybody," Red Lightning said, leading the flight northwest. "We're going to be overflying the Tyuratam missile farm, so don't accidentally jettison any munitions or we'll all be having breakfast with the Holy Mother of Kazan."

Well disciplined, the pilots kept their laughter off the air. If there was any. After all the years of talking peace, the ICBMs, held in stewardship by the League, still drowsed in their silos beneath the bitter Central Asian soil, each tipped with miniature suns.

"I'm transmitting the sequence to release flight profiles . . . *now*."

Kolya's navigational display lit. Kolya studied it with eyebrows lowered in concentration. As he studied it, they got closer together, like two red caterpillars bumping heads.

"Our target is a rebel strongpoint in a collective—strike that, *cooperative*—farm called Ak Tepe. It's approximately—"

"Red Lightning, I don't copy."

"It's on your *screen,* Cowboy, how can you not copy?"

"I have a negative on that rebel strongpoint. Ak Tepe shows negative rebel activity. I repeat, Ak Tepe's no more a rebel *opornyy punkt* than the Volgograd Garden Club."

"That's not what our briefing from General Karponin's intelligence officer said, Cowboy. Ak Tepe is a major mustering point and supply dump—"

"Sod Al Capone and his S-2! Military intelligence is a contradiction in terms. Ak Tepe's in my area of responsibility, Red Lightning. I've been over there every night for two weeks, watching on IR and low-light TV, not to mention my own bloodshot eyes. The place is drowsier than a study hall full of students reading Marx."

"Negative on that, Cowboy." Pause. "Besides, our orders are clear."

"God damn it, we're attacking a peaceful village. These people are *ours.*"

"We have our orders, Cowboy."

Kolya stared at the leader's ship. Red Lightning kept his helmet faced forward. Kolya felt a strange, sour humming in his veins, like a come-down from a high.

"So did the Germans," he said softly.

"Say again, Cowboy."

"I'm calling an abort, Red Lightning." He spun the little ship on its rotor shaft and accelerated back to the flight line.

"What? Cowboy, I didn't—Cowboy? Where the hell are you going?"

"Is everything in order, Junior Lieutenant?" the ruminant voice of Popel' asked in his headset.

"No."

"Cowboy, wait! Come back! Jesus, Nikolay Stepanovich, they'll shoot you for this!"

"Then I'll see you in hell, Red Lightning. Cowboy out."

Chapter
SIXTEEN

Dr. Karolina Ivanovna Rossopovskiy was not a revolutionary. She regretted that, sometimes.

"Ya, Kalima!" The sun had not yet cleared the sea-swell hills of this southern reach of the Kazakh Folded Land, but the doctor from the League Health Service was already out doing her jogging along the irrigation canals. Little Horde Kazakh women with their long braids and brightly colored vests were already coming down the alkali slope of the hill that gave their little village its name to begin the daily work in the fields.

She grinned and waved back; *Kalima* was the closest they could come to her name, or cared to. Some of them turned aside among the small plots surrounding the hill's base. They knew she would not inform on them for spending the day working their private vegetable patches instead of the cooperative's fields.

She pulled lightweight stereo headphones over her ears and punched on the flip player on the elastic band around her narrow waist. She had just downloaded a recording of the League's latest musical prodigy, twenty-year-old Stepan Porotov, son of Nganasan seal hunters from the frigid Taymyr Peninsula, conducting the Rio de Janeiro orchestra in his own *Millennium Symphony*.

As the music filled her head, she turned west along one of the main canals, way from the sixty-house village and *koopkhoz* called Ak Tepe, "white hill." She wanted to get in her six kilometers before the *garmsil* wind blew up out of the Red Sands, sucking the water from the canals and the moisture through the very pores of your skin. Despite the dawn chill, she wore russet shorts and a pale blue sleeveless top; the heat would be thunderous by the time she got back.

She had started off being very circumspect and body-modest. The cultural briefing the League Health gave her before packing her off to spend the final year of her residency bringing modern health and hygiene to the Central Asians had emphasized that these were Muslims, and radical Shi'ite missionaries out of Iran were known to have penetrated much farther north than this. But the Kazakhs, while modest themselves, were Muslims of recent vintage; they had been converted to Islam by the Tsarist government during the nineteenth century, an eccentric move even by the standards of Russian colonialism. A lot of the old Mongol animism survived.

And while women were subordinate, they enjoyed considerably more status among the steppe people than they did, say, in mountainous and puritanical Tadzhikstan, say, where last year a Health Ministry worker got chased and severely beaten by a mob for appearing dressed the way Karolina was now.

The men of White Hill were rather overt in their admiration of her height and long, slim legs; the Kazakhs were on the short side. Instead of resenting the glamorous Great Russian, with her auburn hair and long, fine features, the Kazakh women had made a pet of her. She was there to help them, after all.

She began to wind it out a little, pushing herself. To her right wind played like invisible imps in a field of wheat. To her left the cotton plants grew, with their heavy leaves and swelling green bolls.

She hated them. *Tsar Khlopok*, "King Cotton." The reason for it all: for the overirrigation that was drying the Aral and wasting the entire Turkestani watershed of the *Bam-i-Dunya*, for the promiscuous use of pesticides that turned the soil yellow and left swirls of thick scum on the canals. For the servitude of the people, her friends and charges in Ak Tepe.

They didn't call them *kolkhozy*, for "collective farms," anymore. The new tag was *koopkhoz*: "cooperative farm." Odd how hard the difference was to see.

Odd how it had worked that way with so many of the reforms with which the millennium's last decade began. That was why the privileged daughter of a high government economist, a certified member of the *nomenklatura*, often wished she were a revolutionary.

She had been a *glasnost'* baby, sent to the Sorbonne in the first hot flush of "openness." Soviet disdain for foreign poseurs steered her away from the hard-left students; her circle of friends were true EuroModerns, devout social democrats. She had been sent to the West because the West was *kulturnyy*, and Paris was the theoretic optimum of *kulturnyy*, so it was natural she absorbed the political and economic views of her friends.

Karolina had hit the streets of Moscow with a hundred thousand others to cheer on Boris Yel'tsin and defy the hard-liners. She had spoken out—and voted—to steer republic and League away from the harsh dictates of free-market capitalism and onto the kinder, gentler course of social democracy.

Still the League was locked in perpetual depression. Still a Third World country. The League blamed covert hard-line obstruction and the black market, still booming after all these years.

Except she didn't buy it. It wasn't the fault of Rad-Trads and what the government, American-fashion, liked to call pushers. *It was hers.*

Her role models had gone haggard and vicious. In Sweden, the Promised Land of social democracy, mobs of white youths attacked Iraqi guest workers imported to do scutwork jobs they would not do themselves, for wanting to go on the dole too, for wanting to date pure Swedish women. The nations of the EuroCom fought each other constantly and covertly for domination, even as they sank together into a tar pit of strikes, shortages, and stagnation under the weight of grand social programs. Meanwhile, young men from Oslo fought young men from the polderlands of Holland in East Timor, Portuguese boys killed Bristol lads in Zimbabwe, Poles exhorted the Quechua to fall upon the Guaraní and their French advisers, all because the sole commodity a heavily socialized economy can consistently export that people will willingly pay for is *war.*

In America, the greatest role model of all, you could not change jobs without government permission. You had to carry an internal passport; travel was forbidden without government permission. The police could detain you indefinitely without pressing charges. Just as it was in the pre*perestroika* USSR.

Union was transformed to League, despite the hard-liners' efforts. Social consciousness prevailed. *She* prevailed.

Large corporations were inherently soulless and exploitative; had they not proven this in America and the European Community? So while the farms of Central Asia were no longer state collectives, they were owned by a cartel of giant corporations in each of which republic and League were majority shareholders. Activist, progressive government demanded that everyone contribute his share—and so half the people of Ak Tepe lost the private plots communism had permitted them, seized for taxes. Regulations were needed to keep the sharp practices of a market economy in check, licenses must be applied for. Poor people—farmers trying to wring subsistence from the fringes of a desert, for example—could not afford the effort to keep the paperwork current.

So they lived as virtual serfs of the cooperative. In the big cities, editorial writers inveighed against the coldness that "capitalism" had brought to Russia.

She had helped bring these conditions on, with her naive EuroIdealism. Worse, she was helping perpetuate them.

She ran a general medicine clinic out of the one-room adobe house the villagers had lent her, but her specialization was gynecology. She knew that her work was truly helping these people, but she also knew that the real reason she was here was to help stem the tide of black-asses that threatened to swamp the League's Great Russian masters. The Motherland would not let go of their land—nor their cotton, nor their coal, nor their oil, nor their labor. But God forbid there should be too many of them.

She could almost sympathize with the Turkestani rebels—almost. She remembered the nationalist excesses of devolution's early days, and especially feared what a fanatical Islamic regime would do to its people. She was glad Ak Tepe's folk were apolitical, concerned with tending their own gardens and raising their own brown children—the ones they could choose to have, now, thanks to her, instead of getting by nature and default.

She reached the end of the wheat field. *Funny how quickly the roadwork goes when I'm off on one of my internal tirades,* she thought with a wry smile. She turned south, between the wheat and another field of green-boll tyrants.

The music was by turns bittersweet and brash, jubilant now, then oddly wistful, and finally apprehensive. It was the young composer's farewell to the century about to end, with its unprecedented achievements and unprecedented crimes, and of greeting the new millennium—confident it would bring great things, uncertain whether they would be good or ill.

She did not hear death approaching on a warm desert wind.

The first she knew was when shadows flashed across the ditchbank before her; first one, so quick she thought it was illusion, a trick of wind and vision. Then another, a pulse of shade.

As she looked up she *felt* them, the heat and pressure of their passing: two squat shapes, light below, mottled above, a flash of the new sun on canopies. Knowing nothing of war, she knew at once they were warplanes. She stopped and stared after them, frowning through a haze of fuel fumes. *Should they fly so low? They'll break all the glass in the village.*

Something fell from the belly of the left-hand plane. Yellow flame unfolded on the flank of the White Hill itself, like a monstrous cotton boll breaking open in the Kazakhstan sun. An instant later another flameflower bloomed on the village's far side.

Napalm! My God, there's been some horrible mistake! She could not see if any of the villagers had been splashed with the sticky burning mixture. Some of the Kazakh men and women were running away from the village, others toward it. Others just stood and gaped.

Long legs flashing, the doctor ran desperately for Ak Tepe. She had to reach her people, help them however she could. There was a satlink in her clinic; she could somehow get in touch with the military, make them call off this insane attack . . . . The bandanna slipped off the heavy auburn hair that she refused to cut despite the summer heat.

Two more shadows, low. She screamed in fury and frustration. Noise smashed through her symphony, staccato cracks like a string of firecrackers at a Chinese festival, horribly magnified. Clouds of tan earth pelted her from lines of small explosions marching down the fields to either side. Pebbles and dirt stung bare cheeks and legs. She put her head between her hands, staggered sideways, overcome by sensory overload and fear.

I should lie down, an oddly rational part of her thought. She rejected it. She had to get to the satlink. She had no time to waste groveling in the dust. She ran.

She felt a strange percussion on her skin. The orchestra yammered in her ears like idiot children. She tore the headphones off and let them dangle; their sounds made no sense to her now.

Drumming surrounded her. She glanced aside. A helicopter was sliding past, a hideous thing, huge, striped black and yellow like the locusts who ravaged the fields year after year. Its mate swept by on her other hand. As it flew by the white hill, the gun slung beneath its chin swiveled, spat yellow flame. Dust puffed where the shells hit home.

The helicopters vanished beyond the hill. She had the sense they were landing, for what purpose she had no idea. She could hear screaming now, the ragged edge of agony on the voices. She saw a stout woman sitting between two furrows staring at the blood pumping from her leg, which ended at the knee. She could not tell who it was.

For a moment she slowed, puffing as though she'd run a marathon. The Kazakh woman was bleeding to death. Should she try to help her?

But the children were in the village. *The children.* And the satellite communicator. The woman was probably past help; please God, the children weren't.

It occurred to her Ak Tepe wasn't the safest place in the Motherland to be. It didn't matter. She ran.

Borne on a whistling scream, the first rockets reached Ak Tepe the same instant she did.

Frontal Aviation and the boys from Special Designation thought Al Capone was a dick, but to his tankers he was God. Tanks were the shield of the Motherland—and her mailed fist. The other elements of the air/land battle had their places, to be sure. But the true glory belonged to the men in the black coveralls.

The lead company of the motorized rifle battalion attacked from the west in a classic wedge formation, tanks to the fore, *Bronyirovannaya Mashina Pekhoty* tracked personnel carriers bringing up the rear. The armored vehicles kept the minimum allowed interval of twenty-five meters to maximize impact, and they drove full-out. Concentration was the force multiplier, Karponin liked to say in professorial mode, what made *speed* and *mass*—Soviet shibboleths inherited by the League—into a truly irresistible onslaught.

Of course, it helped that Karponin knew the objective's occupants possessed neither the anti-tank rockets to punish excessive speed nor the artillery that could make concentration fatal.

While BM-22 multiple-rocket launchers pummeled the village, obscuring the hilltop in a cloud of alkaline dust, the BMP-2s stopped a klick away. Desert-camouflaged fire teams spilled out. At a signal from the lead company commander, the battalion's towed and tracked artillery began a rolling barrage, moving across the field toward the hilltop. Stumbling a little across the furrows, the motorized infantrymen began to push through the wheat and cotton—*hugging the barrage*, as their general insisted.

All in all, it was a textbook exercise.

"What are you doing?" she screamed at the well-armed boy.

He turned to stare at her, bringing up the can in his hand like one of the weapons hung from his harness. His uniform and camouflaged-covered helmet seemed two sizes too large for him.

His mouth dropped open at what he saw: a tall woman, hair awry, face blackened but undeniably European beneath ash and grime. He shook the can once or twice as if to accompany words that did not actually emerge. Finally he said, "Painting *'ura pobyeda'* on the wall," as if that should have been self-evident. He had a city-kid accent, Moscow street-tough.

"Why?" she demanded.

"Well—'hail victory,' you know. We—we won, didn't we?"

At the look in her eye he fell back a step, hand moving to the pistolgrip of his slung Kalashnikov.

Comrades' voices, from up the street. Looking relieved, he turned and ran, vaulting a sprawled body without a glance.

She stared after him, wondering if the remote *possibility* occurred to him that the sad bag of meat, leaking now and surrounded by a pulsing cloud of flies, had been the grandmother of half a dozen, including a boy about his own age serving with a labor battalion in the Ukraine. When the Motor Rifle troops had hauled Karolina roughly from the ruins of the clinic, the elderly woman thought they were attacking the doctor, and threw herself at them tooth and claw. They had shot her down, casually, as if she were a gopher in a *koopkhoz* truck garden.

Altynjan, her name had been: "Golden Soul."

The doctor wandered. The invaders hadn't known what to do with her, a League official and Great Russian, to boot. Eventually she was shoved to one side and told to stand there under the eye of a pair of teenaged sentries. But they had been exalted, taking pictures of the glorious desolation they'd wrought, with camera that reduced the scene to data on a floppy chip, and had themselves drifted away.

The stench swaddled her like blankets: fuel and burned styrofoam and roasted meat and dust and the smell of death, thick and sweet and stale. Too bad they couldn't capture that smell, release it in the theaters when they showed movies of the glorious war.

She trailed a finger along a wall. Amazing how much abuse a cluster of dirt huts can take. Low walls of brick, thick mud stabilized with straw, directed the forces of explosions around them. Unless one took a direct hit, of course. The way her clinic had, just before she'd gotten there.

On the theory that lightning never strikes twice in the same place, she had sheltered in the gutted hut with half a dozen villagers. During the bombardment she'd had plenty of time to recall reading that lightning in fact strikes *repeatedly* in the same spot, but by idiot luck she'd survived.

The sound of a helicopter caught the hem of her attention. Swiping absently at a burn on her face, then shaking her fingers to rid them of napalm-residue strings from her hair, she moved toward the village edge.

She knew the man walking up the white shell-churned slope. That handsome face crossed by that scar was familiar to every TV viewer in the League, if not the world. General Colonel Anatoliy Karponin courted publicity as Third World tycoons courted Western film stars.

She blinked at him as he walked by, oblivious to her existence. *Maybe I'm invisible*, she thought. *Maybe I died in the attack, and I'm just a wraith*.

She had left her dilettante/debutante life-style, the dacha near Sochi, the apartments in Moscow and Paris, because at core she really did want to help people; she wanted to *heal*. She was a person who had gotten everything she really wanted, first through her daddy's influence, later through her own talent and unstinting effort.

Now she wanted something she had never wanted before. Something she never thought she *could* want.

She wanted to kill someone.

The videocams followed Karponin through the village like acolytes. The doctor turned and walked into the desert.

Chapter
SEVENTEEN

Day died hard in the desert. The land had long gone dark, but the sky was a weird luminous white-yellow-blue, except for just above the horizon. There it looked as if somebody had dipped two fingers in blood and drawn them across the sky.

From thirty meters along the hip of the escarpment came the reedy just-post-adolescent voice of the apprentice cantor, or whatever the fuck he was. *Poor kid*, Eddie thought, shaking his head to drive away the swarming no-see-'ems who seemed to ooze out of the sandstone. *He'd rather be out cruising, listening to some tunes, and trying to dip his wick. Instead he's got to learn a quarter million lines of poetry about some guy who's always getting his ass hauled out of cracks by his horse.* He wondered how the Kirghiz kid had gotten roped into the apprenticeship in the first place. Probably was doing it to please his dad. God alone knew what had gotten him and the old guy, Aliyev, mixed up with rebellion.

And speaking of horses . . . *horse troopers, for Christ's sake. Here we are on the bubble of the twenty-first century, a new millennium, no less, and I'm in the by God cavalry. What'll these rebels think up next, the crossbow?*

Fast Eddie turned up the volume on the tune he was humming to drown out the droning and shook sweat from his eyes. In a mere couple of hours, he knew, they'd all be grateful for the residual heat baking up out of the hardpan and sand. The humidity in the broad valley of Syr Dar'ya trapped heat, but the weather reports said that around midnight it was going to get cold. By that time they should just be settling into position for their attack on the Operation Desert Wind forward supply dump, one of many dotted along Karponin's projected line of advance upriver.

The slab boulder was hot on Eddie's butt. He was sitting in the open, out from under the tough sandstone overhang where they'd passed the day, in a groove wind had worn in the softer stone below the caprock, and human hands had deepened. This was away from the track usually beaten by caravans, and while the odds were astronomical against anybody monitoring real-time satellite imaging of precisely this stretch of escarpment between the Muyun Qum—the "Camel's Neck Sands"—and the river at a scale that would even show them, they were not going to beat the League Army by taking avoidable risks.

Eddie smiled humorlessly for his own benefit. They weren't *going* to beat the League Army, in the long run. In the short run, they had to; there was the mission, and the incidental matter of his own personal ass.

Immediately speaking, they were *damned well going to*. The fix was in.

He tapped at the keyboard of his notebook-sized satlink computer, being amused at just how easy espionage was in the modern world. The rebels weren't just *permitting* him to haul the computer with him, they *ordered* him to. Timur had very high-tech ideas about how to run a Third World revolution.

Actually, what Eddie had seen of the rebel commo/ intelligence setup impressed him. Leaguers had gotten sophisticated about computers since the days when Soviet chess champ Kasparov practically had to smuggle PCs in to kids, though Eddie suspected some of Timur's tech elves had gotten training in the U.S. or Japan. Maybe he even had some American whiz-kid volunteers—though if the sampling of wanna-be warriors was an indicator, they'd all be goofballs *except* the spies. However it came about, the rebels had a damned sophisticated touch for exploiting the world-girdling and infinitely controversial Net.

Eddie's commands turned a little software robot loose, out among the satellites. The Net was amoral. More to the point, unless you did something major ballsy or major dumb, like trying to crack the Dai-Nihon insurance group's data base, what you did in it was intrinsically untraceable. That was what made the world's governments so nuts.

It was also the beauty of the Net for spying—hell, for the whole C-cubed-I panorama; command, control, communications, and intelligence.

The robot homed to the address it had been programmed to seek. Then it sent back a message, indistinguishable among the trillion or so flashing along the Net at any given instant. Eddie's screen lit "Are you ready, Eddie?"

He grinned. KGB had let him dictate his own recognition codes. They hadn't come within light-years of spotting the rock 'n' roll references. Then again, GRU had used the chunk they'd bought of the Cuckoo's Egg to build him an alter ego named for his three idols: Eddie van Halen, Willie Randolph, and Paul Newman's character from *The Hustler*.

He typed, "Ready to rock and roll." It was all mickey mouse anyway; his robot and their guard dog routines had established all the bona fides that mattered in a couple nanoseconds.

The screen flashed into today's post returns for the dump they were about to hit, complete with reference strings he could pull to bring up complete personnel and State Security records on the tiny guard detail, relief schedules, check-in times, everything. Courtesy of KGB, who fished most of it right out of the army's own net. They wanted their boy to make a good impression on his boss.

"How goes it, my friend?"

Taking his time, he tapped the hot key. The screen switched instantly to the feed from the rebel downlink. He noted in passing it bore a disturbingly close resemblance to what he was getting from KGB. It gave him a chill; armed forces' net had been penetrated big-time. He hated the ramifications. He could do nothing about them.

Then he looked up at the compact man in the League uniform coat who had spoken and laughed out loud. "Well, considering the fact that I'm trying to train a unit with twelfth-century transport to take on a twentieth-century army, and about half my boys know as much about horse-back riding as I do, which is jack, and I'm working with a mondo bizarro Mongol Horde grab bag including an ethnic Korean, humongous ethnic Gypsy twins who are in constant danger of getting lynched by their buddies for filching, and the oldest PFC in the Turkestani Defense Forces, things couldn't possibly be goddam better." *Oh, and one ethnic-Arab Azerbaijani spy from HQ. Can't forget about him.*

Ali al-'Ajawi squatted next to him. "Are you unhappy?" He sounded genuinely concerned. Eddie believed that, uh-huh. He also believed he'd collect Social Security one day.

He shrugged, grinned. "Not at all. I'm a can't-resist-a-challenge kind of guy." That really *was* true. Although this was maybe kind of a *large* challenge . . . .

"Has anything changed?" The Arab gestured at Eddie's computer.

"Not that I can see, Colonel," he said. "Maybe I'm being a mother hen about this, checking every four minutes."

"No such thing. We have these resources, such as no warrior ever has before. Why not make use of them? Like *djinn* from a bottle, eh?"

The reference hit too damned close to what Eddie had just uncorked from his computer, courtesy of KGB. He turned his grimace into a grin. "I wouldn't mind a little gin from a bottle, right now." *Jeez, was that weak, or what?*

"I wouldn't take you for a gin drinker, Lieutenant." Eddie raised an eyebrow. "Don't be surprised that I know my liquors. I'm not a practicing Muslim. Many Central Asians aren't; Turkestan is famed for its cognac, did you know?"

"No, I didn't. I'm still learning a lot about this part of the world."

He felt the Arab's eyes on him, felt the next question on its way: "Just what brings you to our desolate corner of the earth, Lieutenant?" It came casual, just passing the time, smoking and joking with a fellow troop. Sure.

You son of a bitch. What's one of Timur's major butt boys doing chaperoning a milk-run raid by a training company anyway?

"You know how it goes," he said, shrugging. "It's not just the job, it's the adventure. Not much of that left, back in the world."

He snapped the computer shut. "Can't stay on too long. Don't want the men to think I'm linking down some fuck show from Rio. They damn near lynched me when I told them they couldn't bring radios or flip players on this joyride."

Radio frequency detection did concern him—electronic emissions had a way of standing out way out here in the desert, even the very weak ones of radio receivers or satlinks. He was more worried about noise discipline; he wasn't about to have some recent poli-sci major from Tashkent U settle into position for the coming raid and decide to pass the time by cranking up 3 Mustaphas 3 or the latest Serious cut from Freedom Kills! or Duty.

Though he joked about lynching, it wasn't all that funny. He was still a long way from popular with this crew, especially among the Tadzhiks, some of whom carried lockets with photos of the late Ayatollah Khomeni on the chains with their dog tags. Fragging officers was the fastest-growing sport among all the world's armies.

Ali wasn't going to be deflected. Of course. "Still, I'm curious, my friend. You went through long and arduous training. Why not stay in the profession you worked so hard to master?"

"Challenge wasn't there," he said, a little surprised at how smoothly the lie flowed. He'd spent half his life as a spy, but lying had formed small part of it; it had been more a constant game of *I've Got a Secret*. "The developed nations keep up their balance of trade exporting military advisers to the developing ones. Brass told me *I* had to stay home as an instructor. A real crock. I was too good for my own good, you know?"

"Are you really so avid for adventure? You seem a turbulent soul. Yet I should think you'd seek the opposite of excitement."

Eddie looked at him. Ali shrugged, quietly laughed. "And I suppose you were eager to strike a blow for freedom," the Arab said wryly.

From down the rubble slope came a soft hooting, a burrowing-owl call. The sentries were bringing somebody in. Indiges loved that sort of B-movie *Beau Geste* business, and Eddie did too, for that matter. Since they were into controlling their emissions, it did make more sense than shouting, "Hey, infidel dog, sir, we got company."

Eddie stood, feeling relieved despite the pain it caused

him. President Fyodorin himself with his personal battalion of black-beret MVD guards would be a relief after this amiable inquisition. "Freedom. Sure. *De opreso liber*, and all like that." He started down the hill.

He moved gingerly. Hell; he moved like Uncle Lucky after tying one on. After two days' hard riding, he wasn't falling off his horse more than once every couple hours, which to his mind vindicated the notion of progress. But his inner thighs trembled like the branches of the poplars down by the Syr in the never-ending wind, and most of his parts hurt.

It was a cold camp he picked his painful way through, without the usual fragrant fires of *kiziak*, dried sheep shit, the fuel oil of your desert nomad. That was fine with Eddie; the stuff made his allergies act up. A *kiziak* fire didn't give off a lot of light, and they could mask the heat well enough among or under all these jumbled red rocks. But they were in Indian country now—cavalry country, if you thought about it, but Eddie was trying not to—and there was always a chance of a helicopter cruising downwind towing a particle sampler, a "people sniffer," that could detect the pungent smell of a dung fire put out in profusion.

League Air had suddenly gotten very circumspect, after the rebels finally got pissed off about the desultory nuisance bombing and blew the tail assembly off a Myasishchev-4 strat bomber with an old *Armiya-PVO* SA-5 missile over Eski-Tashkent. That Desert Wind should be forced to press a bomber design that was coming on half a century old into service went a long way toward explaining why over three weeks had passed without any decisive thrusts against the rebellion.

All the red had drained from the horizon now, leaving the sky in shades of bruise. A young Uzbek stood next to a pair of gaunt men in what seemed in the less than half-light to be patchwork robes. His Kalashnikov was pointed studiously away from them, and he kept what Eddie took for a respectful distance.

Have to have a word with the boy about that, he thought grimly. Ali laid a hand on his arm. "With your permission, Lieutenant. I will deal with them."

Eddie frowned, but he said, "Sure, go for it." The Arab seemed to know what was going on here.

Ali walked down the slope, making some hand gesture masked by his body and incipient dark. "*Ishq*," he called softly.

The two men looked at him. "*Baraka, ya Shahim*," one replied. Eddie got the odd impression he had no hair on his head, not even eyebrows.

The three of them moved away, drawing no response from the sentry who was supposedly covering the outsiders. Eddie crossed his arms. Since Ali was a major wheel—he still thought this was like having an Undersecretary of Defense along for the ride—this was by definition not a breach of security, like it or not. Eddie didn't.

"Will somebody tell me what the fuck is going on here?" he nattered.

An Uzbek named Maqsut squatted nearby, a solid man in his early thirties who wore a labor battalion walking-out tunic and didn't inevitably spit and mutter "*kaafir*" when Eddie walked past. He pointed his round chin at the strangers. "*Kalandariya*."

"Say what?"

"Sufi adepts. They belong to a *tariqa*, an order whose center is Bukhara. Of all the orders, theirs is the most mysterious. They wander alone through the desert, and the desert belongs to them, Red Sands or Black."

"Great." Though the League charter mandated freedom of religion, especially if you were white and Russian Orthodox—in contrast to Communist days, when atheism was encouraged, *unless* you were white and Russian Orthodox—Sufi *tariqa* were outlawed. The League was terrified of them, believing they constituted an underground cell structure irredeemably hostile to Russian domination. Eddie had seen secret studies where GRU went so far as to blame the *tariqa* for the defeat in Afghanistan, along with the Americans, the Iranians, the Chinese, and of course the last refuge of losers from Ludendorff to Westmoreland, the Stab in the Back by wicked civilians.

So what are they *hanging around for?* He noticed some of the Tadzhiks were muttering and making evil-eye protection signs. Maybe the Sufis weren't so bad after all, if the Shi'ites didn't like them.

Ali nodded, turned, and began walking back toward Eddie. The *Kalandariya* went the other way. They were absorbed almost at once into the gathering dark, without a peep from the supposed sentry.

"I see your fuse is smoldering," Ali said as he approached. "Forgive me for seeming to trespass on your command. We have our own resources, eyes, and ears that you are not . . . how might one say? Tuned in to."

He slapped Eddie on the arm. "Our *Kalandariya* and our computers say the same thing about our objective. It is a good omen."

Chapter
EIGHTEEN

"This is the forward dump," Eddie said to his three section leaders, who stood or squatted in a cluster around the boulder on which he had his computer spread open. The cover/screen showed an enhanced overhead photo of the dump, which he could transform to a standard contour map with a keystroke. Where the rebels had gotten the aerial he had no clue, but KGB confirmed its accuracy. "Who wants to tell me something about it, just from this?"

"It is badly sited," old Aliyev the *manaschi* said, in the

precise Russian he used when he wasn't singing. In spite of Aliyev's age—he had fought as an underage volunteer in the Great Patriotic War—Eddie had made him head of Delta section. These people respected age, and anyway he could outlast any man in the *jagun*—the hundred-man training company—in the saddle. He was also willing to give Eddie a chance.

"It is dominated by these hills here, to the north and northwest. Riflemen can sweep it at will, or observe for mortar fire."

Eddie glanced aside, to where Colonel Ali sat apart, trying literally not to look over Eddie's shoulder. *Damn, I shouldn't do that. I don't have to check with him.*

"Spot-on," he said. "You'll also notice the hills are in easy range of rockets and launched grenades, both of which we have. And which we're not going to use, at least directly."

"Why not?" demanded Shoreh, Charlie section's leader. He was a waspish, bespectacled perpetual student type from Dushanbe. He'd gotten the job because he was the spokesmen for the Tadzhiks who made up Charlie anyway. He seemed to be one of the bigger Khomeini fans. He definitely made no secrets of hating Eddie's sigmoid colon. "Isn't our goal to kill enemies of the revolution?"

Eddie could tell he'd wanted to say *enemies of the True God* so bad he could taste it. But that would not have gone over, and not just with their infidel-in-chief. To Eddie's surprise, he'd discovered that not much more than half his men were professed Muslims, and only a third or quarter observed the five daily prayers.

He smiled. It was time to cut lad Shoreh off at the knees. But he lost points if *he* did it.

"Any reactions to that?"

"Our objective is mainly to get supplies, isn't it?" asked Bravo's leader, pushing his own round eyeglasses up his nose—this was a nearsighted bunch, and no mistake. He was a gigantic Uzbek kid, an engineering student from

Samarkand, cover-boy handsome in a copper-skinned, Plains Indian kind of way. He spoke English with a flawless American accent from spending his adolescence watching MTV on sat. "There's supposed to be ammunition stored here. We don't get it if we blow it up."

"There we go, Shy Bunny." Shaybaaniy was the actual name, but the kid lit up. He seemed to get a huge charge out of Eddie's spin on it. "Glad to see *someone's* thinking. Maybe I should remind everybody that Timur has said he wants to keep the bloodshed to a minimum. When Desert Wind blows in, we fight, but we're not out here to slaughter bank clerks from Aral'sk whose only offense is to've been called up for reserve duty."

He keyed in instructions. The compound expanded to fill the screen.

"Okay, what we got is basically bunkered storage for ammo and whatnot, plus a few cement buildings above ground for the guard detail. This is the barracks, right in here next to the bunkers—what kind of shape they'd be in if anything actually blew I don't even want to know, but that's the League for you. According to our information, the detail itself's ten men, two of whom are down with the running shits."

"So naturally we must have a *plan* to deal with them," Shoreh said, as nastily as he could.

Eddie looked at him. "You got a problem with that, section leader?"

"We are seventy," Shoreh said, looking around at the others and visibly pumping himself up into orator mode. "They are eight. Why not simply sweep down and over-whelm them?"

"Don't you people remember how you got conquered in the first place? These may be fat fortyish guys who'd rather be home in front of the tube slamming vodka and watching the St. Pete Defenders kick ass in the pennant race. But they have *machine guns*. You go sweeping down on them, you get quickly dead."

"You are afraid? Better a dead lion than a live jackal."

"Give me a break. If you're dead you aren't a lion *or* a jackal. All you are is trash, swelling up in the sun. Food for fucking flies. If you'd ever *seen* a stiff, Shoreh, maybe you wouldn't be in such a hurry to be one."

He scratched his ear. "I tell you what. If we're gonna be hung on heroic metaphors, Jagun 23 of the Turkestani Defense Force is gonna be a live *leopard*. Leopards are cunning bastards. They lie invisibly in wait until they're sure of their prey. Lions just lie in the sun licking their genitals and let the babes do all the work—or is that what you're driving at?"

The others laughed. Shoreh turned red and gave him one of those *wish your skin was drying on a rock* looks. Eddie knew it was risky to ply his tongue's well-stropped edge in the hypersensitive East, but he could only use the tools he had, and that was one of the sharpest. Ever since he was a child he'd realized the only style that suited him was if-this-doesn't-work-it's-gonna-kill-me. His troopies would play him some slack because he was *amerikalik*, and therefore brash, and also because Timur said to obey him. But basically it was a race to see if he could win them over before they decided to just slit his throat.

"So now that we know why we have to have a plan, let's all find out what it is, shall we?" he said.

"Of course it is part of the plan that our brave leader stays well hidden among rocks," Shoreh said, "since it is so important to Timur to preserve the lives of all *ferenghi*."

You just don't give up, do you? Eddie gave him a big smile.

"Wrong again," he said.

"We did it!" the old man sang, dancing in circles brandishing a freshly liberated RPG-16 over his head with stick arms. "We really showed the *basmachi*!"

"Grandfather," Shy Bunny said, emerging from the bunker

with a crate of 5.45 ammunition on his shoulder, "we *are* the *basmachi*."

"Oh." Yefreytor Bakhtiyaar—Uncle Lucky—blinked rheumatic eyes in puzzlement. He wasn't old, he was *old*. He claimed to be a hundred and three, and Eddie suspected he was shaving some so as not to seem superannuated. He looked as if he'd weigh seventy soaking wet—pounds, not kilos—and sported the most impressive assortment of wrinkles Eddie had seen since he quit doing his own laundry.

"You mean we're not the Red Sticks?" he asked plaintively.

"That was the twenties, Grandfather," Shy Bunny said. "Also the other side."

Grinding up the grade from the river valley half a klick away, the convoy's lead truck flashed its headlights in a preset pattern, to get Shoreh's boys, out among the rocks, to ease off the triggers of their own RPG launchers. The approaching column had already flashed a satlink message to Eddie, confirming they were in fact the rest of his own Alfa section with the heavy transport to haul away the loot.

Eddie stood at the gate, nodding with satisfaction. Only half an hour late. By Third World guerrilla standards, that was way ahead of schedule. If they highballed it down the Syr Dar'ya highway they could be almost back at their staging base in Turkestan town by sunup, just in case Frontal Av got more vengeful than prudent.

It had gone off more or less as planned. Eddie had simply walked out of the desert and up to the wire, megaphone in hand, and called for surrender in his best your-worst-nightmare American-accented Russian. No one had so much as challenged him; as he'd been gambling, they were all asleep or preoccupied. If they hadn't been, he was additionally gambling they'd miss with their opening fusillade—panic-firing into the dark, full-auto at the air in general. He gambled a lot. He remembered the Duke of Montrose's toast, even if that old fuck Arbatov thought he was a typical American vacuum brain.

To ice the operation, as soon as he was sure he had the

tiny garrison's attention, he waved a hand. A spotter up on one of those controversial hills saw the motion through a starlight scope—a Ukrainian pirate of an American design, with entrails from Japan—and passed the word to the helpful Colonel Ali, manning an AGS-17 automatic grenade launcher. Ali dropped a perfect three-round burst of thirty-millimeter high-explosive through the old, outsized satellite up/downlink dish that was the dump's lifeline to the *Dar al-Harb*, the "World of Hurt." And that was another battle in the books.

Along with Texas Team's hit in Georgia, this was two strikes on isolated posts that had gone flawlessly for Eddie in the past several weeks. It was enough to make him superstitious; the first axiom of real war is that nothing *ever* goes according to plan. But hey, neither place had exactly been manned by Delta Force. Another axiom is that success-ful commanders tend to be lucky in their opponents.

"Good," Shy Bunny said, pausing beside him. "They brought the bus and the livestock trailers. We don't have to ride back." Eddie grinned at him. The would-be engineer was a no more enthusiastic horseman than Eddie was, though he didn't fall off near as much.

He walked forward as the lead semi pulled up. "Glad you boys could make it. We were beginning to wonder whether Al Capone might beat you—"

He stopped, dropped his foot off the step up to the cab. The Uzbek driver's eyes were withdrawn way back in his head in the purest look of hate he'd ever seen.

The passenger door banged and Tashmat Kagorovich, Eddie's designated second in command within Alfa, walked around the tractor's coffin snout. The driver spat carefully in the gravel next to Eddie's right boot.

"What the fuck?" Eddie asked.

Kagarovich was a *kumli*, a sand dweller from somewhere in the Qizil Qum. He was pure Mongol mongrel, Kypchak and Turkmen and Tatar and whatnot wound up in one wiry bandy-legged package. He had stiff red hair, one eye, and a face that was scuffed, creased, and expressionless as an old boot.

He stared at Eddie. "You didn't hear?"

"We didn't hear anything. We've been on a *raid*, Kagarovich, not back in Turkestan town with our feet propped up watching *Fucking for Cruzeiros* on satellite and eating microwave popcorn."

From a back pocket Kagorovich took a black Sony Satman the size of a deck of cards and held it up to Eddie. The whole face became picture: black-tab League tank officers leaning over a table loaded down with guns, rocket grenades, and polymere bags of white powder.

"—inspecting a cache of weapons and drugs they say was unearthed by Desert Wind ground forces following their successful attack on the southern Kazakhstan village of Ak Tepe almost forty-eight hours ago," squeaked from the miniscule speaker. "Elsewhere, violent demonstrations protesting the attack continue within ethnically Asian regions of the League as well as rebel Turkestan. Free Turkestan leader Timur is rumored to be flying at this hour to the Tadzhikstan capital of Dushanbe in an attempt to stem rioting which has led to reports of savage attacks and atrocities on ethnic Europeans—"

The driver spat again. This time he dropped a shiny yellow ball on the toe of Eddie's boot.

"*Kaafir*," he said.

Chapter
NINETEEN

"We die now," said Eric the driver, quite matter-of-factly, considering. He was hunched down behind the wheel of the horrible lime-green Moskvich, as if that would protect him from the firepower of the vast evil-looking *Gorbach* squatted in the road not thirty meters ahead, its Russian blue-saltire-on-white insignia wavering in the rising south Kazakhstan heat.

"What you did expect?" Tewfik said. "To just simply do this mazurka across no-man's-land from rebel territory?"

"You have a charming way of lapsing into Third World speech patterns in times of stress, darling," Jacqui Gendron said. "Now shut up."

An officer emerged from the helicopter, bending low to avoid the sweeping rotor even though it was mounted high up. Four troopies in lumpy battle armor trotted after, Advanced Kalashnikovs at port arms.

"Red trim for army," she murmured. "not Border Guards green. Good. This is *just* what I expected."

She opened the door. The officer's young face and resolve seemed to dent as she marched to meet him midpoint. The soles of her desert boots wanted to stick to the semi-molten asphalt.

"What is the meaning of this?" she demanded in English.

He opened his mouth, shut it, then pulled invisibly pale brows down into a frownlike state. "You cross in—inter—forbidden land," he said in English.

Inside she grinned. She'd pulled him off balance into a foreign language. That gave her a lock on initiative. She needed no more. "Is this not the area of operations for Desert Wind—the Central Asian Front?"

His lips moved as he sorted that out. "Yes."

"Then it is of course not forbidden to me! I have here—" she slapped his broad chest with a plastic laminated packet of credentials, "*papers*. See? I am accredited to cover the staff of General Colonel Anatoliy Karponin. I have his clearance to travel anywhere within his command."

He was blinking at the stiff, scuffed sheaf. She stayed in his face like a little yap-dog, giving him time to focus on nothing but Al Capone's distinctive signature scrawl: "Do you see? Do you?"

"Yes, ah, madame—"

"Ms.! It's ms., you male chauvinist. Why do you still insist on delaying me? The General Colonel has in the past been careful to maintain only the best relations with the world press!"

It was the exclamation marks that did it. The young officer jabbed the packet back at her as if it was impregnated with *white* retrovirus. "You may go. Please, be careful, you are outside area in which we can guarantee your safety from the rebels."

She turned and marched back to the car. "Have nice day," the Russian called after her.

She shut the door with a triumphant slam. "There's that out of the way. I told you we'd have no trouble with these fools, Tewfik."

"What if they find out your papers are outdated?" he asked sulkily, slumped against the side of the cramped box of heat that was their transport. "Karponin wasn't even a General Colonel when he signed them."

"And why, O my clever cameraman, do you think I gave him no peace to scrutinize my papers? Teach your grandmother to suck eggs, will you?"

She slapped her hand on the back of Eric's seat, making him jump. "Now. Let's go visit that village your mother's cousin told you about, and see if their visitor is still on hand."

The plane seemed to plummet away beneath him. Francis Marron's stomach seemed to swoop in sympathy. He bit his lip, rose, and made his way back along the clattering aisle of the venerable high-wing two-engine DeHavilland Twin Otter Air Tashkent had bought off the milk run between Los Alamos and Albuquerque. He tried not to notice the high Pamirs that formed a bowl around Dushanbe. The snow-glazed peaks put him unpleasantly in mind of the weapons of the mob in *Lost Horizons*, and they hadn't even gotten to the riots yet.

Timur sat at the back of the tiny cabin, turban-swathed head bowed. *Maybe it's a good sign that he's letting me make my sales pitch as frequently as I want.* Marron smiled mirthlessly. *Or maybe he just wants me where he can keep an eye on me.*

His stomach writhed a bit. Maybe it was the turbulence, and the razor proximity of the mountains. Or maybe it was the way the Acevedo affair still haunted him, the unfairness of it . . . .

Young gunslingers in powder-blue *tyubeteyka* occupied seats either side of the aisle, two places in front of their leader. They tracked Marron with hot trigger-happy eyes as he picked his way past. The worn-carpeted deck bucked and yawed beneath his feet the way he imagined a skateboard would—he had never actually been on a skateboard, as he had never done anything a surgeon general disapproved.

Timur closed the book he was reading as Marron sat in the seat across from him. "Mr. Marron."

The hard boys kept staring holes in the American until Timur made a slight hand gesture. Then they turned and faced sullenly forward.

"Why do you put up with them?" Marron asked quietly.

Any expression Timur wore was hidden by his facecloth. Marron was glad the rebel chieftain hadn't asked him to play cards.

"Are you familiar with the history of Khmer Rouge, Mr. Marron?" The American nodded. "Any movement attracts such youths, filled with the conviction and happy cruelty of the young. If I permit them to serve as my bodyguards, it gives them a fairly benign channel for their energies—energies which otherwise might be expressed the way they are being expressed now in the streets of Dushanbe. Also, it keeps them where I can keep an eye on them."

Marron nodded. Timur was not entirely without leadership skills—far from it. Marron had to give him that.

"I thought I'd take the opportunity to urge you again to reconsider, *janaap*." *Janaap* was Uzbek for "sir;" it was as much of an honorific as you could use with Timur without him getting curt. "Please, accept what we have to offer." He was not talking about investment capital.

"I will happily accept advice from you, Mr. Marron, though I cannot promise to follow it, of course."

Marron moistened his lips. "The United States stands poised to provide assistance far more substantial than *advice*."

"Indeed. You would supply 'advisers,' and matériel, but not for payment. Not in gold. This, truly, is what makes me hesitate to accept your kind offer of aid, Mr. Marron. *Price*. We are a mercantile folk. If terms of repayment are not made clear, we fear; who knows what the other party will demand before our obligation is fulfilled? Who knows if it even can be?

"Consider why the Sufis do not refuse payment for their teachings. A man who takes money might be greedy or he might not, so the story goes. But one who takes nothing is suspected of wishing to steal your soul."

Marron glanced aside, out the smeared window on his side. He could see a spill of suburb down the side of Dushanbe's mixing bowl valley below. You had to expect that of Third World leaders; they might at any moment dart from the path of rational discussion down some superstitious blind alley. Talk of *price* made Marron uncomfortable enough. To drag mystics in . . .

He turned. Timur's eyes bored into him like obsidian augers.

"If we accept anything from America, Mr. Marron, it will be paid for under terms agreed upon in advance. But we will stand or fall on our own. Understand this. We are prepared to pay any price, *any price whatsoever,* to force the League to acknowledge our independence."

He settled back and closed his eyes.

"And then, Mr. Marron, it shall not matter what the rest of the world does."

* * *

"The Defense Forces have fired tear gas grenades."

Drawing squiggly trails of smoke, the grenades fell back among the crowd. That was a tactical mistake. It angered the mob, and also provided physical impetus to move, breaking up the concrete inertia that held the mob short of the cordon.

The crowd surged forward. Some people held handkerchiefs over their mouths, soaked with water from plastic jerricans brought along for just this purpose. It was still shy of a concerted rush at the militia lines. It was a back and forth thing, a hesitation dance, one group thrusting up almost to club's reach of the cordon, stopping short, and falling back with cries and grimaces as another knot of rioters lunged as far as angry bravado would take them. It had the seesaw syncopated rhythm of a street fight in a film by Kurosawa, who understood these matters better than any other filmmaker: no one is ever actually eager to get his head cracked open. It's why armies drill.

Jacqui let the peristaltic crowd action propel her forward. She wore a mask made by the *Groupement;* with a subvoke mike taped to her larynx, the quality of the sound bite was not at risk. Besides, what she was saying now was going into memory, not out live. She had a reputation for going live only when big news was breaking.

She had a feeling she was going to be hitting the Net quite soon.

The crowd parted to flow around a Moskvich on its back, burning. Although it was lime green, it was not *the* Moskvich, sadly; the car they'd rented in Tashkent was lying dead in a road washout somewhere in northern Chimkent Oblast. By great good fortune it had carried them as far as the rebel-held portion of Kazakhstan before miring in soft sand and expiring. Gendron credited her personal fate with seeing to it that the subcompact breathed its last within five kilometers of a cooperative farm that possessed an airfield and a light plane that could speed her, Eric, Tewfik, and their precious cargo the rest of the way to their destination. She put great faith in her personal destiny. She was an Aries, after all, and Aries were lucky.

She didn't bother to glance back at her cameraman, knowing he was burning some good footage into memory; he was superb at what he did, even if he was a bitch. As she passed the flaming car, she craned to make sure there was no one *in* it. Burning people made good telejournalism. TéléFrance wouldn't show it, of course, but they could sell feeds to less-inhibited markets in the developing world and the Pacific Rim.

A hand gripped her shoulder. She snapped an elbow up to break the hold. With an Arabic curse Tewfik leaped back, steadied the cam on his shoulder, and pointed. "Jacqui, *look*. Ow, that hurt."

The militia line had parted. A man stepped through. He wore a dark Western suit with no tie. His face was obscured by a fold of his white turban.

"*Timur.*" Gendron was actually unsure whether she or the crowd around her breathed the name. "*Can it be? He's moving forward, showing no fear at all of the crowd—Paris, can we go live now, this is crucial—*"

She scanned for the Sons of the Sky-Blue Wolf. The boys in the blue skullcaps always clung to their man like remoras to a shark. Surely they wouldn't let him walk into this maddened mob alone . . . .

But he was alone. Several militiamen, faces working as concern for their leader struggled with self-preservation, started after him. He stopped them with an upraised hand, not glancing back, and walked into the heart of the mob.

They fell away from him like mercury from a fingertip. He raised his hands.

"People of Free Turkestan," he said, his voice booming from PVDF balloon speakers that had floated up from somewhere behind the cordon, "peace."

Hard brown hands brandished a placard, a blown-up photo from satellite news: a row of sad, bedraggled bodies lying before a bullet-pocked wall, being ignored by a League soldier in battle dress with a cigarette in his mouth and his bullpup Kalashnikov beneath one arm.

"There can be no peace with those who did this to our people!" A gangly bespectacled boy with an uneven beard straggling around his chin thrust from the crowd, long coattails flapping around his calves. Jacqui had seen him a few blocks back, up on top of a van crying death to foreigners through a Radio Shack megaphone. He had a tropism for the videocams, that one.

"I agree," Timur said mildly. He spoke the local brand of Farsi. Jacqui was glad Iran had been a major news ticket for twenty years for World Beat reporters such as herself; she understood the language. And while there was still no real-time translation software that didn't sound like Down's kids on helium, TéléFrance had Farsi-speaking human translators standing by, like operators for an outlaw telemarketing service in Mexico.

Timur gestured around him at the glass and steel World Urb boxes that thrust up from among the willows and plane trees lining the grid of *aryk* canals to define downtown Dushanbe. A lot of pallid high-mountain sky showed overhead; even foreigners hesitated to build higher than three stories, for fear of earthquakes. "But do you think to find Anatoliy Karponin here? Do you think perhaps President Fyodorin and his council are staying at the Dushanbe?"

"It is the foreigners we seek!" another student hissed. He was shorter than his rival rabble-rouser, stockier, with thinning hair and a Western-style coat hanging open over his paunch. Not telegenic; he'd never make the replays, unless he showed some real fiendish class. "The Westerners who seek to destroy Islam with decadence and guns."

"The Nikolays!" the mob screamed on cue. "Give us the Nikolays!"

"Go home," Timur said. "The only people here are Turkestanis and their guests. Or have you, in your fervor to strike down modernism, forgotten the ancient laws of hospitality?''

"They are foreigners!" the bald boy screeched. The first speaker from the crowd glared at him, jealous of the telejournalists' spots illuminating the bald boy like divine grace. "Nikolays, Armenians, Jews the lot of them! They stink in the nostrils of Allah!"

Timur faced him. "Who am I?"

"You are Timur," the first spokesman said quickly, reasserting himself.

"And what am I?"

The youth frowned, and before he could think better of it, "You are one of us" spilled from his lips.

"I am." He touched the fold of cloth that hid all his face but the bright-dark eyes. "But what am I? Am I Tadzhik? Uzbek? Am I Kazakh or Kirghiz or Kypchak? A Turkmen, perhaps? Or could I be myself a Nikolay with a broad strain of *Kalmyka* in him, that shows in the eyes?"

I can't believe he's doing this, Jacqui thought. *He's practically begging them to renounce him. To tear him limb from limb.*

"I wear the facecloth so that people will not trouble themselves with such questions. I am a Turkestani, and that is all that matters. And understand, he who lifts a hand against any Turkestani—Sart or Nikolay, Muslim, Christian, or Jew—raises his hand to strike at me."

"But what of Ak Tepe?" the second spokesman demanded.

"What, indeed? The League and its military have committed a great crime, and tell lies to the world to cover it. Does turning your hand against your brother bring the killers justice? If we act like savages, we play only into the murderers' bloodstained hands."

He beckoned. "Come here. Face me."

The bald rabble-rouser hung back. "Why should I trust you?"

Timur laughed. Jacqui felt ice water sluice down her spine. *Is he mad, or is he a genius?*

"You're afraid." He turned dismissively away. "Who is not afraid?"

"I'm not afraid."

Timur swung about to face the tall bearded youth, the first speaker, who stalked onto what he knew was the center stage of History, trying not to smirk at the rival who had popped his nerve and blown it.

"What is your name?" Timur asked.

"Mozaffar."

The shrouded head nodded. "'The Winner.' It is a good name. So hear me, young Winner. I hereby decree a special band of fighters: the *ghazi*, the champions. Those of you who join shall be granted amnesty, and shall bear the honor of the fiercest fighting for God and the *millet*. Those who refuse are the enemies of Turkestan no less surely than the Butcher of Ak Tepe.

"Which shall it be, O Winner? Be the first to join, and I shall make you a *noyan*, in command of a *minghan* of one thousand."

The boy fell to his knees on the glittering broken glass that covered the intersection like snow. "In the name of Allah, I am your man, O Timur."

"Then arise, and let me embrace you as a brother."

Chapter
TWENTY

"Okay," she murmured for her throat mike, "roll the satellite feed *now*."

She broke into something faster than a trot but not quick enough to tweak the trigger fingers of the young men in blue skullcaps clouding around Timur like space junk around a shuttle as he walked slowly back to his hotel. With broken-field skill born of long experience, she dodged through the lean and hot-eyed escort and fell into pace at Timur's side.

He glanced at her with his Chinese eyes. "That was magnificent, the way you dispersed that mob," she said. "The most courageous act I have ever seen." *Or the craziest*, she thought. She had seen enough of craziness and courage to understand how fine the differential was.

"Thank you. But it was merely what had to be done."

"I'm Jacqui Gendron, TéléFrance Global News. I'd like to do an interview with you—"

He flicked fingers in dismissal. "You must make arrangements through my press secretary," he said. "I warn you, I have little time to publicize myself."

She danced in front of him. "I ask this as a favor, Timur. I know that in Turkestan one does not approach a great man without bringing gifts. I bring you *this*."

She held up a hand. The Wolves growled and started to bring up their AKs. Timur held them off with an upraised hand.

She was holding a Sony Satman palm TV. The playing-card-sized screen showed the face of an auburn-haired woman in close-up. Fatigue and strain furrowed her fine European features.

"—medical officer for Ak Tepe, who witnessed the League assault," Gendron's voice was saying in English. "Can you tell us in your own words what happened, Dr. Rossopovskiy?"

"Ak Tepe was attacked without warning, without provocation," the doctor said. She stared straight into the camera. "Anatoliy Karponin is no hero. He is a murderer. The world must know."

"But Central Asian Frontal Command showed video of caches of arms and drugs it said was found in Ak Tepe,

Doctor," the on-screen head said. "How do you account for that?"

Dr. Rossopovskiy looked at the interviewer with eyes like black lasers. "The Frontal Command can show films of anything they want," she said, her Russian-accented English crisply precise, like breaking glass. "They can show zebras and marching bands too. None of these was to be found in Ak Tepe. The people of the village were loyal to republic and League, to the extent they thought about it at all. And except for an old shotgun and two rifles to control the pests, they were entirely unarmed. What the General Colonel Karponin showed was a fraud."

The duty officer in the Media Compliance Monitoring Facility pursed his lips in a silent-flute whistle.

"Bullshit," Justin Serafin said, dribbling crumbs from his sandwich down the front of his suit. The watch officer had run a risk disturbing him during the ten minutes he allowed himself for lunch, but the undersecretary was in town to monitor the newsbreak on Central Asia, after all. "She's an actress. Has to be. *Has* to."

Studying a readout on the big board, a young tech shook his head. "No, sir. The Psychiatric Stress Evaluation's clear as a bell. Her voice stress indicates she's pissed off to the red line, but sincere."

Brushing his mouth, Serafin gave the tech a sharp look. These technical personnel were getting awfully familiar. You had to watch these nerds like a hawk, lest their mastery of technological arcana go to their heads.

The duty officer produced a defusing chuckle. "Shit, sir, we do hands-across-the-water with the Big K all the time. They know the standard scams as well as we do. This time they just got caught."

The undersecretary turned his hot look on the shift boss. The older man met it without a twitch. *I got my twenty in, bun boy,* the shift boss thought. *Desaparecido this.* In the real corridors of power, informed word had it that the only thing more to be feared than the Federal Police was the FedPol *union*.

Serafin's fine mobile mouth writhed. "I suppose."

"Do we let it go out, sir? The networks will be drooling in their collars over this scoop."

The undersecretary thought. Policy was to use the Central Asian mess to make the League sweat, to remind them that while the geopolitical alley fight was a lot more crowded than a decade before, America was still top dog. Still . . .

"Clear it," he said sourly. "I just hate showing anything that makes a government look bad. *Any* government."

For an Oriental potentate, Jacqui Gendron thought, *this Timur hasn't much sense of style*.

The personal quarters of the ruler of rebel Central Asia comprised a suite on an upper floor of the Hotel Dushanbe. Even with the inroads economic reform had made, for an individual to possess that much living space was an extravagance in its own right. But, like a solitary dinner by candlelight with a Western reporter who had provided the rebellion with its greatest propaganda coup to date, it was a minor extravagance, the sort that could be written off as virtual necessity.

"When you announced the creation of your special *ghazi* squads today," she said, sipping the dry white wine she had not been particularly surprised to have been served, "was that a spur-of-the-moment thing, or the result of a decision you had been weighing and evaluating for quite some time?"

Timur paused in the act of holding up his checked facecloth with one hand to insert a forkful of food in his mouth. He drank no wine himself. "Is this off the record?"

He laughed softly and lowered his fork to his plate. The meal was a spicy rice *palov* with lamb and American-style tossed salad. Despite the fact that the hotel was majority-owned and largely managed by the French, the meal had a touch of tackiness, like everything in the League that wasn't

Tsarist in opulence. She kept half expecting to see a bottle of catsup off to the side, by the salt and pepper.

"Though the interview proper has not yet begun," he said, "I suspect nothing said in your presence is entirely off the record."

She smiled at him. She wore an open-necked blouse and her khaki globetrotter pants, and her orange-russet hair was drawn into a ponytail. She was a strikingly handsome woman, and knew it. Wearing her hair pulled back from her face gave her fine predator's features a severe, professional cast, while the little-girl ponytail and the candlelight softened her. It gave her room to maneuver, which she always liked and was good at obtaining.

"That's subject to negotiation," she said.

He passed that off with a laugh, took his bite, chewed and swallowed it. "It was an action I deemed appropriate," he said, "however long it took me to arrive at it."

She let a corner of her mouth turn down in amusement. *Not a bad parry*, she thought.

"You named the units after ancient champions of Islam noted for their suicidal valor—the word *ghazi* is still sometimes translated as 'fanatic' in the West. They're obviously meant to attract militant Shi'ites and fundamentalists. Does this represent a retreat from your original determination that Free Turkestan should not be a specifically Islamic state?"

"Not at all," he said. His eyes fixed hers above the cloth; they neither widened nor sidestepped at the question. "This is a revolution of all Turkestani peoples, including the Muslim radicals. My *ghazi* units are designed to attract those who have trouble containing their anger or their fervor, to give them a channel that will help our revolution rather than tear it apart."

"You yourself have taken the name of a famous conqueror," she said, "one notable for the extent and ruthlessness of his conquests. Does this choice reflect your long-range intentions?"

"Not at all. For better or worse, Timur-i-leng, the Iron

Limper, is the best-known Turk in our history. I serve as a
rallying point, as a catalyst, and chose therefore to pick the
greatest name of Central Asia. In spite of the connotations,
rather than because of them.''

"You don't want to conquer Russia?"

"*Khuda asrasin*—God forbid. We want no one else's life
or freedom or property. Ours have proven expensive enough.
The butchery at Ak Tepe shows us—and the world—what
we can expect to pay to keep them.''

She made a mouth, pouting almost. It wasn't the answer
she had hoped he would give. But perhaps he was being
evasive, to avoid alerting his enemies to his true intentions.
Diogenes searched for an honest man; Jacqui Gendron
searched always for a strong one.

"So would you describe yourself, if not as a conqueror,
then as the violent Gandhi of your people?"

Black eyes danced above checked cloth. "I would not
perhaps describe myself that way. I certainly have no objec-
tion to your doing so.''

She finished eating, cleaned her mouth with her napkin
and the punctiliousness of a grooming cat, leaned back, and
hooked an arm over the back of her chair.

"Today's world is interdependent, an ecosystem," she
said. "You can't stand entirely alone. You need friends.''

His eyebrows disappeared into the upper portion of his
headcloth. "So the seduction begins.''

Her first impulse was to laugh in his shrouded face. She
stamped it down hard. It was risky to laugh at even the most
liberal-minded Asian despot.

Besides, she admitted to herself, it was not at all impossible. He was hardly prepossessing physically: a stocky man,
shorter than she, somewhat soft around the middle, and God
knew what the facecloth hid. But physical appearance wasn't
the key to physical attraction for her.

She felt herself to be highly intuitive and highly psychic,
and revered first impressions. Her first impression of Timur

was of a man possessed of World Historical presence. A man touched by destiny. That excited her.

But still: Timur had shown himself indeed to lack his namesake's ruthlessness, and would a truly strong man shrink from strong measures? Nor had she ever loved losers—and she had to admit that in the upcoming contest between Timur and Anatoliy Karponin, the smart money rode squarely on her most recent lover.

Timur was watching her, calmly, steadily. She realized that while he was interested in her as a woman, his comment had not been about that at all. She almost blushed, for the first time in memory.

"I have a social conscience," she said. "You have needs. The workers of my country can fill those needs, for arms, munitions, electronics—"

"Your 'country.' Not your United Europe."

She shrugged. Even American commentators and columnists were beginning to perceive the cracks the stucco of EuroCommunity hid. That morning two Swedish advisers had been killed in a brush with French advisers in the Great Namib, with the result that the French national arms industry's stock had gone up in the Bourse, and the Swedish had gone down.

Timur laid down his fork and slid his chair back a few centimeters. "I shall keep your kind offer in mind. Shall we begin the interview?"

Ak Mechet: the "White Fortress." Its fall over a century before had signaled a symbolic and actual turning point in the Russian conquest of Turkestan. The adoption of the name Kzyl Orda, "Red Capital," had symbolized Turkestan's hopes for the freedom revolution would bring—hopes soon shot in the back of the neck during the purges of native Communists, or starved to the tune of ten million or so by Stalin. The White Fortress had taken its old name back at about the same time St. Petersburg and Volgograd were reclaiming theirs, in what proved a final, and futile, gesture before the League drowned the hopes of independence that had stirred to brief life at the dawn of the nineties.

Moving deliberately, as STAVKA, obedient to the council, demanded, General Colonel Karponin's Desert Wind advanced along the Syr Dar'ya River. It entered Ak Mechet without a shot being fired.

"'Procrastination is like death,'" Anatoliy Karponin told the giant face on the screen on his office wall, "if I may take the liberty of quoting the immortal Suvorov. When am I going to be permitted to move?"

For a general colonel to quote to a full marshal an aphorism that even a *praporshchik*, "warrant officer," was expected to have by heart was an almost unthinkable effrontery even in today's army. That the marshal was chief of the League General Staff sent it almost into the realm of the fantastic, along with faster-than-light travel and artificial consciousness.

But Karponin's effrontery had nothing to do with the redness of Marshal Burdeinyi's face, or the sweat scattered across it like crystal pebbles; he always looked like that, and Al Capone always talked to him like that.

"Come now, Tolya," Burdeinyi said, trying for bluffness and mainly sounding exasperated, "be reasonable. You are advancing into a virtual information vacuum. Who can know what lies before you, hey? We must also keep the political realities before our eyes—and speaking of eyes, the eyes of the world are upon us there in Central Asia, never forget. And besides, this isn't the Great Patriotic War; these black-asses can't seriously *threaten* us. Go gently."

"To answer your objections more or less in order, Marshal," Karponin said tartly, "I cannot be held responsible for the failures of our civilian associates to gather adequate information—as I cannot for their failure to nip this rebellion in the bud. The *political reality* is that the world has already turned its back on the rebellion; the Westerners may censure us for forcefulness, but in a matter of days, weeks at the most, some sensation will distract them, and all will be forgotten. And are we weak, that we should care what the world says?''

The marshal said nothing. He sweated some more. Karponin of course looked perfectly cool and dry, though the air-conditioning in the ancient barracks outside Ak Mechet he had tapped as his headquarters had as a matter of course crapped out.

How huge the pores of his nose are, Karponin thought. *One could put one's finger into them.* By the pattern of veins visible on Burdeinyi's bulbous nose, it was clear he was not obeying army regulations on the moderate consumption of alcohol as strictly as befit the chief of STAVKA. Another datum Karponin would make use of, when the time arose . . . .

''What is called for here is a short, sharp shock,'' Karponin said in his best lecture-hall tones. He was a full Doctor of Military Science. On this particular stifling late summer morning, there were only five hundred twenty-eight others in the whole League who could make that claim. Marshal Burdeinyi was not one of them. ''Permitting this treason to go unpunished strengthens the rebels; the longer they defy us, the deeper sedition will send its roots. But if we *pluck* it out''— he made a snatching gesture right into the video pickup; Burdeinyi jumped —''we can make an abrupt end to all this nonsense. The longer the process is prolonged, the harder will be the uprooting, and the more chance the West will have to cavil. All this argues for Suvorov, and speed.''

Burdeinyi sighed and visibly fought down an urge to mop his forehead. ''But the rebels haven't exactly made you pay for every step in blood, have they, Anatoliy Grigorevich?'' He shook his heavy, balding head. ''You will see. You are young and impetuous, and you will see. The nationalities tried to break away before, and all failed, in spite of the traitors and weaklings who ruled the Motherland. In the face of our calm determination, this—this seedling of rebellion will quickly wither and die." He smiled, pleased at having finally figured a way to heterodyne with Karponin's metaphor. Karponin respected him better when his false teeth were honest Russian gold, not French ceramic.

"Patience, Comrade General Colonel," the now jovial face said. "Patience and perseverance. This is what STAVKA requires of you."

The screen went blank. Karponin balled his hands into fists and slammed the knuckles down on the warped pine top of the desk.

Flies buzzed around his head, huge and black and gross. The windows stood open. Not even Anatoliy Karponin dared shut them on this heat. It was tin-smith heat, bent on hammering you out into sheets. The once-great Syr Dar'ya had been strangled down to a mere unnavigable trickle by the rape of the Tien Shan watershed in the name of Tsar Cotton, but the valley air was still humid enough to lend lead to the blows of that heat.

There were no screens on the windows. There were no stocks of window screening in Ak Mechet, even if you commanded a Front. Screen was on the government's ration list, which was to say, not to be had. *If I'm here for any time, I'll send men to tear some off some fat merchant's villa*, he thought. *These Asiatics are all capitalist exploiters at heart. They know how to look out for themselves.*

A brisk tap on the door. "Come in, Captain," Karponin called.

His aide entered with a firm stride. A bright young man from a good military family, Captain Rybalko was a veteran of the undeclared war with the Chinese animals—a tanker, or course. He was not afraid to speak his mind.

Al Capone was not a man who encouraged subordinates to differ with him. He liked them to do their jobs and keep their mouths shut. But he prided himself on his objectivity, and he always made it a point to keep one independent thinker at his elbow. It helped maintain perspective.

Rybalko's recruiting-poster face creased when he saw his

commander's expression. "General Colonel, what is the matter?"

Karponin waved a hand at the boy. "The old women of STAVKA. They've got *zasadskiy sklad uma,* the ambush mentality—our post-Afghanistan Syndrome, as the Americans suffered their post-Vietnam indecisiveness. They fear to act."

He shook his head. "I don't know what's wrong with Timur. I slapped him in the face at Ak Tepe. He must slap back, or he's going to lose all face. And face is everything in the East."

"Perhaps he doesn't know that, General," Rybalko said. "Turn on the television."

Karponin picked up the hand control, switched the wall unit from videophone to TV.

Jacqui Gendron's sharp handsome face was looking out at him, her russet hair blowing in the breeze down Fergana Valley from the blue Tien Shans behind her. Karponin's lips vanished in an angry line. *That whore. How could she dare expect me to—*

"Timur," she was saying, "who is becoming known to the world as the violent Gandhi of his people, has a startling message for the people of Ak Mechet: do not fight Al Capone."

The screen switched to the rebel's shrouded face. "Do not take up arms against the invader," he was saying. "Resist without force; disobey any orders he may give, obstruct when you can. But do not give him the opportunity to massacre you as he did the children of Ak Tepe."

His eyes blazed from green facecloth folds. "I am not the Iron Limper, though I bear his name. But I quote him now, to Anatoliy Karponin and to his masters: 'You may be able to get the bone down your throat. But if it reaches your stomach it will tear your navel.'"

Karponin tipped his head back. The laugh came from deep within, propelled by the hard muscles of his belly. Rybalko looked at him as if he'd gone crazy.

"I'm going to ram this Front up your broad black ass, Timur Khan," Karponin said. "The League can't hold me back forever, even if you're too cowardly to provide me provocation. They will release me to act. And then we'll see what tears through whose navel."

Chapter
TWENTY-ONE

Ambush country, Fast Eddie thought, feeling the footfalls of his khaki-colored mare with the black Mohawk mane jar through his tailbone. The scrub-dotted land looked countertop flat between red mesas. It was a lie. There was dead ground in profusion, between slow dun swells that you never noticed until they rose beneath your feet, in sandy-bottom wadis, cut sharp-sided by the fierce infrequent rains and deep enough to hide a horse and rider.

Of course, that was why the long-suffering League taxpayer got to pay for all those *airplanes*. Not much overhead cover in the desert. That in turn was why every third man of the two sections of Jagun 23 on exercises forty klicks southwest of Turkestan carried a Third World knockoff of the old American Stinger shoulder-fired antiaircraft missile. Eddie wondered where they got all the damned things, and wondered if Al Capone was taking them into consideration.

Probably not. To Karponin, air assets were something you burned up to clear the way for the glorious black-tabbed tankers.

They had spent the past three days drilling. The men, all mounted, scattered like grouse to a hawk, to re-form at a map reference ten klicks away. Eddie was painfully certain he would once again be the last to trickle in, along with

Maqsut, who stuck faithfully by his side. It was the horse's fault. Her name was Sertikan, which meant "Full of Thorns." It fit.

Despite her best efforts, he was spending less time as an airborne stranger now. He couldn't say he was getting the hang of *riding*, but he was better at staying aboard.

A pair of riders popped into view to the left, disconcertingly near. The newcomers were dressed in dusty ragged robes and round skullcaps of goat-hair felt that had probably once been brightly dyed but were now the color of grease stains. They reminded Eddie of the Sand People from *Star Wars*. They were Sand People from the Qizil Qum, *kumli* he had just received as guides and replacements.

They had probably been smoking and joking somewhere, knowing they could loaf to the rendezvous and still beat their *ferenghi* boss. One of them had an ancient drum-magazine Shpagin machine pistol, its shiny finish muffled in rags like its owner, slung around his neck. Maqsut greeted them and was acknowledged in guttural desert dialect. No *kumli* Eddie had met except the astonishing one-eyed red-headed Kagarovich admitted speaking Russian.

He'd gotten six new Sand People after Shoreh and most of Charlie had opted out of the unit to enlist in Timur's dipshit new *ghazi*, along with a couple of Shi'ite Kirghiz. He also received a dozen better-socialized—Hanafi—Tadzhiks. That left him understrength, with a bloc of troopies who wouldn't speak any language he understood.

He figured he'd come out smelling like a rose. He was still maybe not Mr. Popularity, but at least nobody left in the unit was eying his Adam's apple and murmuring to his buddies that jihad begins at home.

Scuttlebutt said the Shi'ites and hairier radical-revivalist Muslims—what the Western media still called fundamentalists, even though they were anything but—were volunteering for the *ghazi* in shoals. In his E-mail reports to Arbatov, Eddie wondered whether Timur had backed off from religious tolerance, or if he figured he could keep the nuts in line if they were all clumped together—wishful thinking in Eddie's book. The chief director told him not to waste effort on matters over his head. The fat bastard.

The early afternoon sun came through his aviator shades like military lasers bent on burning out his eyes. The riders topped a rise and the land fell away. At the base of the slope the rest of the unit waited, most of them dismounted so they could flake out in the shade of an arroyo that ran through a grove of what looked like dead trees.

"Why?" Eddie asked. His throat felt rusty with dust, heat, and disuse. Maqsut raised his eyebrows, which gave him a comical look. "I mean, I know why the trees are *dead*, but what are they doing here at all?"

"They aren't dead. They're saxual. The dead appearance conserves moisture. When it rains, they sprout leaves."

"How often is that? Once a century? They're not really dead, they're just as good as dead, is that it?"

"It rains here. Sometimes. Less than in our parents' time. The desert grows, thanks to the Nikolays using up all the water to grow their cotton."

Fast Eddie chewed the inside of his left cheek. League agricultural policy wasn't his problem, which was fine with him. He had problems enough. Such as Al Capone's cheapjack Desert Storm ripoff, gathering not three hundred klicks from the *jagun*'s base in Turkestan town.

Starting down the slope, Eddie noticed a man sitting in the dubious shade of a meter-high clump of camel hair grass just down from the crestline with a Brazilian Stinger across his knees. He nodded, grinned encouragement. Half of him meant it. Half didn't. *Where do I stand when it all hits the fan?*

He noticed Maqsut looking at him funny, realized he'd let a flash of his uncertainty show. *Playing spy wasn't supposed to be this hard,* he thought. *I've done it half my life.*

"Jesus, Jesus, come and squeeze us," he said in English, a couplet picked up from the tough Irish Catholic schoolboys he'd alternately run and rumbled with as a kid in the Bronx. And then in Russian, "It's hot out here."

One of the *kumli*, who had fallen in a few meters behind, laughed out loud. His companion said something in his native dialect.

"What's that all about?" Eddie asked.

Maqsut smiled shyly. "They say, wait until you feel the bite of *Qizil Qum*. Compared to that, this is the Perfumed Garden."

"Senior Lieutenant."

Eddie glanced up to see Shamsiyev, the kid Kirghiz, standing just outside the feeble glow of the fire he'd let his men build against the night's surprising chill. He nodded for the youth to hunker down beside him. "What's on your mind?" His voice caught briefly in his throat. *Kiziak.*

The youth looked quickly around. "It's about my master, old Aliyev—"

"What about him?"

"He—I—I don't want to do it anymore."

"Do what?"

"I don't want to be his apprentice anymore. I don't want to spend my days and nights droning the *Manas* song. Do you know how long it is? *Do you?* It's a quarter of a million *lines*. The *Encyclopedia Brittanica* is not a quarter of a million lines long!"

His voice had risen to a penetrating bat squeak. "Hey, now, turn it down," Eddie said. "Al Capone will hear you if you keep that shit up."

He pulled at his chin, heard a rasp of stubble. "Quarter million lines, huh?"

"*Yes.*" Eddie glared. "Yes," the boy repeated in a whisper.

"That's really longer than the *Encyclopedia*, huh?"

"Surely it must be."

"Surely it must."

It was a real Kodak Moment, one of those things they

didn't prepare you for at Bragg. You couldn't just shake your head and say, *Sounds like a personal problem, talk to the chaplain.* Not to an adolescent indige with LA Gear basketball shoes and a bullpup AK slung across his bony back.

"Look," he begun, not really sure where he was going. "I can sympathize. I mean, a kid your age, you want to be hanging out, scoping some babes—" *Fast Eddie Randolph, Youth Counselor.* "You want to have a regular life."

The boy's eyes lit. "That means I can quit?"

"No. Give me a minute, here. Just think. This has got to be your basic dying art. How many people are running around the Pamirs with a quarter-million lines of poetry in their heads?"

Shamsiyev stared down at the hard-packed dirt between his toes. "My master is one of the last."

"Be a real shame to let a tradition like that die out, wouldn't it? Sometimes we do things we don't like to do, because they're the right things to do." *Now I sound like a public service announcement on late night TV. Why did I ever want this job, anyway?*

"But why can't somebody else do it?" the youth blurted.

"Because you're the one who said he would," Eddie said, looking at him steadily.

Shamsiyev hung his head. Across the fire one of the city Sarts raised his skullcapped head.

"Bu haqiqatan qiziq," he said. "This is really odd."

Eddie picked up his own Kalashnikov. He was sensing something wrong too. Just an edge in the air, like a knife drawn softly over skin.

"That sound. Like a giant horsefly—"

"Airplane!" Eddie yelled. He kicked over the fire. "All right, everybody, you know the drill. Spread out and get ready to move *fast.*"

His internal alarm system had already cycled down from red alert to yellow. The sound was still no more than skirting the subliminal fringe, but he could tell it was the drone of a propeller plane, not the whistling roar of a fast mover.

The League had no prop-driven attack planes. Most of the world's nations had reintroduced propeller strike aircraft, far superior to jets in the counterinsurgency role. Neither League nor republics cared to admit they *needed* COIN craft, preferring to rely on the tank-busting Shtormovik—the Su-25 Frogfoot—which while slow for a jet was too fast to menace irregular troops strewn across broken country; and on helicopters, which Afghanistan had shown were vulnerable to rebels armed with an earlier generation of backpack SAMs. Supposedly the shiny new Kamov verti had a modular COIN tray that could be slid in, but it was still barely operational. Al Capone, if he had any at all, would surely not have enough to risk one three hundred klicks into rebel territory.

No. The sound, rising slowly to full audibility in the southwest, didn't have the sharpness of high-speed graphite-polymer blades in the Kamov's ducted fans. Nor did it have the low harmonic beat of multiple props in chorus. It was a single engine, with maybe a bit of asthmatic catch, and as Eddie listened, crouched on the felt-soft sand of a wadi bottom with his rifle in his hands, he felt the muscles of his face slacken in surprised recognition.

"Allah be praised," a voice said from the darkness. "What's a crop-duster doing out here in the middle of the night?"

"Crop-duster? *Khuda ozing meni asragin,* you Kazakh country cousin!" exclaimed a trooper from Bukhara, remembering his DOSAAF paramilitary training. "That's a paratroop plane! We're under attack!"

Eddie laughed out loud. "At ease," he called. "Pass the word, people. Keep your fingers on the trigger, but keep your linen dry. I don't think VDV's coming to call."

Al Capone wouldn't do that to Spetsnaz, *even if he does hate us as badly as* mujahidin, Eddie thought. There was no question his two citizen-soldiers and he were all hearing the same thing: the most commonly produced airplane of the post-World War II world, the Antonov An-2, called by NATO the Colt.

The last military biplane in history.

It was like a Certs commercial from his early-eighties adolescence: *Colt is a crop-duster, Colt is a paratroop dropship, two, two, two Colts in one.* It wasn't an *operational* drop ship, though, please God; it was a trainer, old, slow, fat, and arthritic.

Eddie remembered his first VDV training drop at Ryazan'. He was used to jumping from the massive C-130 Hercules, its four Allison engines throbbing with high-tech power. When he found out they expected him to climb in an antique box kite with fabric wings, he'd almost had an asthma attack. The fact that the Colt reeked of chemicals didn't help. Sure enough, it had turned some recent tricks as a toxic avenger.

It had never been so easy to jump out of an airplane, before or since.

Here came Maqsut, duckwalking to keep below the lip of the shallow arroyo. "What is it, *Havaa Rang*?"

Eddie grimaced at the nickname. "I'm not sure, but I am willing to bet my life it's not a quick *desant* raid."

The sound was almost overhead. Eddie stared up, straining to catch a flash of blunt wings occulting diamond-drill desert stars.

"It is so low and slow," the Uzbek marveled. "Surely we could bring it down with rifle fire."

"Harder than you think, Maqsut. Let him go. He's not going to bother us, and we don't need to tell him we're down here."

The sound began to dwindle as the Antonov made its majestic way to the northeast. "Son of a bitch!" Eddie exclaimed. "I know what that sucker's doing. He's towing a particle-sampler array."

He could feel Maqsut's raised-eyebrow expression without having to see it. "A people-sniffer. He's trying to smell us nasty rebels. And that fucking *kiziak*'s given him a noseful.''

He stood up and raised his voice. "Saddle the ponies, people. It's time to hone those old night-marching skills.''

"Do you think he'll call an attack on us?''

"Not on your life. Karponin hasn't been dropping air attacks; the council's yanking his chain, afraid of bad press or losing expensive air crew.'' Expensive air *frames*, anyway; human components had always been expendable in the heroic Soviet Armed Forces. The League wasn't much different.

"Besides, that's not Al Capone's style. He doesn't want us scattered all over hell's half acre. He wants us all in a bunch so his tanks can roll us out into a nice red Bukhara carpet.''

"Then why do we run?'' Maqsut's tone was questioning, not challenging. Like most of Eddie's desert warrior wannabe's, he was painfully eager to learn.

Eddie rose deliberately, feeling twinges from his bruised tailbone and raw-rubbed inner thighs. "Because if you want to play in the big leagues, you play to what the other guy *can* do, not what you think he's *going to* do.''

Two hours later, ten klicks to the southwest, the two sections of Jagun 23 were roughly backtracking the biplane when a *kumli* outrider from Charlie called out that he'd seen a streak of light low in the northern sky.

Eddie called a halt but didn't order the column to disperse or dismount. He felt Sertikan gathering herself below him to try bucking him off, slapped her hard on the side of the neck to show he was still paying attention.

He had about decided that the Sand Person was seeing UFOs when the horizon pulsed with a yellow flash. It settled quickly to a false-dawn hint of glow, truncated by a line of sawtooth hills.

"Somebody got tired of being sniffed,'' Eddie said. "Time to de-ass the four-legged BMPs, everybody. We'll take two hours down time and then go see if we can find the wreckage."

Beneath the same clear sky, on the desert west of the ancient city of Samarkand, half a dozen men huddled around a boy who sat on the sand with his beardless face bathed in the glow of a plasma screen.

"Truly, God is great," said a bearded Turkmen who looked like a grizzled chow dog in a turban. "This weanling communes with the angels of *Khuda* on high, and we leap to do his bidding. And this very machine is itself old enough to be his grandfather. Indeed, your Timur is a wonderful man, to entrust so much to the young."

"He's your Timur too," snapped a youth not much older than the boy who sat cross-legged with the notebook computer unfolded on his lap. Until two weeks ago he had been a student of *mirasist* literature at the great university in Samarkand. Now he was an artillerist, serving a BM-13 launcher with its tubes angled skyward like a giant's closely held fingers. "Unless you don't consider yourself a Turkestani."

"*Salaam, muslimlar jaan,*" said the old Uzbek who drove the launcher truck. He had driven tractors for a cooperative farm along the Karakum Canal, until the land got too poisoned to use. "Peace, dear Muslims."

The chow dog wouldn't let it go. "The boy takes divination from the letters dancing on his screen and tells us where to fire our rockets. It smacks of black magic! How can we trust one too young to've even topped his first ewe?"

"I bet ewes are what you top too, back home in Turkemenia," said another youngster, a Samarkand Tadzhik sitting with his back against the empty ammo crate on which the satlink antenna rested. Samarkand Tadzhiks were notable smart-asses. "You know what Zohair says: 'An old fool is worse than a young one; for the young may always grow wise.'" The lettering on the crate was Roman, and read REPUBLIK INDONESIA.

"Smart-assed Samarkand Tadzhik," the chow dog muttered in his own dialect of Turkic.

The youngest boy had never looked up from his keyboard. The light on his face turned red.

"Fire," he said.

The fallow cotton field north of Samarkand was littered with the hulks of trucks too clapped-out even to serve as transport in the Turkestani Defense Forces. In the midst of them a BMP armored personnel carrier, knocked out during the fighting in the city, bulked like a rhino among water buffalo.

Because the Soviets made a lot of military matériel over the years and never threw any of it away, and because war toys were still the only exports the League could reliably sell, the world was full of Soviet weapons, from new to ancient. By the middle of the eighties the manufacture of ammunition, replacement parts, and after-market upgrades to Soviet equipment was a thriving industry worldwide. The nations of the ostensible European community pulled in almost as much hard cash from replenishing Third World stocks of formerly Soviet hardware as they did selling their own armaments.

The growing Muslim superpower Indonesia was a lot closer to Central Asia than EuroCom was, and more immediately interested in the fate of the rebel state. Also, its wares were cheaper.

The BM-13's launch tubes may have been welded before Stalin murdered his last million, but the rockets they fired at coordinates fed by satlink to half a dozen launchers dispersed at random over two hundred square kilometers were cutting-edge. The warheads were not especially smart by contemporary standards. That was why the rebels—whose income from cotton and *Liga* economy cars only stretched so far—could afford them. They were smart enough to sense the greater mass of the BMP magnetically, and make minute adjustments to their steering vanes.

Blue-white lightning flickered as shaped charges clawed open the BMP's thin top armor.

"Direct hit," reported Ali al-'Ajawi, watching through binoculars from the top of a hill.

Yilderim the Tadzhik let out a whoop of triumph and danced around in a circle with his hands clasped over his head. "Allah be praised," breathed Sher Khan, the giant Pushtun with the hennaed beard. He thought the whole thing smacked of demonomancy too.

Timur let a slow breath billow his facecloth. "Allah and the youth of Turkestan, who trained themselves to use computers despite the Nikolays' discouragement. You've done me proud, Yilderim."

Ali lowered his glasses. "We can sheave artillery. That doesn't mean much. We taught the Palestinians to do that in '82, park their launchers in a vacant lot, fire at a map reference, and drive away before the Israeli Skyhawks could find them."

Yilderim stopped dancing and started to pout, his eyes swimming behind his thick glasses. "This is a bit more sophisticated, Alijaan," Timur said gently.

"True. But it's one thing to fire to coordinates fed to you via a satellite link, and quite another to use the remote-sensing data for targeting yourself."

"We can't test that without tipping our hand," Yilderim said sulkily.

Timur laid a hand on the techie's shoulder. "Peace. We've succeeded in what we set out to do here. The time has come for the Butcher Karponin to make his move."

He turned away from the others, then looked out at the black line of poplar and willow that traced the course of the Zeravshan River, several klicks beyond where the glow of the stricken armored carrier was dying back to darkness.

"And the time has come for us to goad him into making it."

Chapter
TWENTY-TWO

Finding the downed aircraft was not much challenge. A pillar of black smoke led them, just like in the Bible. It was two hours after dawn, with the heat already pressing down like a sheet of lead and the smell of burning aviation fuel and fabric dope like burrs up in their sinuses, when the two sections of Jagun 23 reached a ridgetop and looked down on the wreck.

It was a Colt, all right. A few furtive flames still gnawed at the broken carcass like rats. Beside the furrow it had plowed augering in, a metal pole had been stuck upright in the sand. It was the sort you might carry along to hold up one end of a volleyball net on the beach.

"Uh-oh," Eddie said. From the pole flapped a green banner. Eddie's team wasn't first on the scene.

The green banner meant *ghazi*. They were down on the flat near the wreckage in a circle of laughing, bearded faces surrounding a man in torn khaki coveralls. He staggered blindly from captor to captor, from blow to blow. Eddie saw the heliograph wink of desert sun on blade, and the man fell, a red arc hosing from his neck.

"Well, shit," Eddie said. "Bravo, disperse into firing line along the ridge and dismount. Cover our asses. Delta, follow me." Without waiting to see if he was obeyed, he spurred Sertikan down the steep slope.

The man who had gone down stayed. The *ghazi* seemed to lose interest in him, clustering instead around two more survivors in flight suits. They forced them to their knees with the flash suppressors of the AKs, then backed off into a wide circle.

A pair of aspiring heroes in green *tyubeteyka* rushed forward to splash colorless liquid on the kneeling pair. One stood up, screaming and struggling with his hands behind his back. A *ghazi* smashed him in the face with the buttstock/ receiver of his bullpup assault rifle and he fell back down.

Eddie was among the *ghazi* then, shouting, "Back off, you sons of camels!" in Persian. They scattered away from Sertikan's hooves in surprise. He swung down from the mare's back, let her reins drop in the sand, and hoped like hell she didn't bite him in the ass when he turned his back. It would spoil hell out of his entrance.

A Tadzhik with a Moldavan extended-service NCO's tunic open over a black-striped tanker T-shirt confronted him with a sneer. "So the Blue Sky Riders have come to grab a share of our glory."

Eddie's jaw muscles contracted. The apparent top *ghazi* was not much taller than he was, with a soft rounded face and wire-rim glasses. Eddie had bumped into him before— his original unit had been part of the same *minghan* or regiment as Jagun 23 before he transferred to the *ghazi*. His name was Abdulsattah, and he was hard. Mean, anyway.

Blue-Sky Riders was the *minghan*'s nickname for Jagun 23. Given the traditional Turk and Mongol veneration of the Blue Sky, Eddie had taken the soubriquet as an extreme compliment until a chagrined Shaibaaniy pulled him aside to explain that it was a sardonic reference to the place where the unit's commander spent more time than actually on the back of his mount.

Eddie keenly felt the lack of Shy Bunny. The outsize Uzbek was back home in Bukhara on compassionate leave. His mother had been killed in a car accident. Though he'd done his time in cadre, it still struck Fast Eddie as strange, sometimes, how life—and death—went on in the midst of war.

"If there's any glory, here Abdulsattah, you're welcome to it," he said, sidling nearer to the captives. "What's that smell?"

Abdulsattah laughed. "Petrol. We were just preparing our sport with the *kaafir* dogs when you arrived." His old second-in-command Samirov, a pock-faced giant from Termez, was still with him, Eddie noted. Samirov's huge face leered at him over Abdulsattah's shoulder like the full moon setting.

Eddie broke the circle. The prisoner still on his knees stared at him with eyes blue and wild and empty as the Turkestan sky. Gasoline shone on his cheeks like tears.

"This is a bad thing," Eddie said, aware that the hostility pressing in from all sides was directed at him as much as at the Russian captives. "Mistreatment of prisoners is forbidden."

Abdulsattah sneered. "You *kaafirlar* stick together, eh? Your heart cries out for their plight."

"Timur himself has ordered—"

"Timur is not here. Only us, and these *kaafirlar*. Maybe you should join them, *amerikalik*?"

He smiled and struck a match. His teeth were perfect.

Eddie acted without thought, without intention. Abruptly the three fat white sighting dots were forming a line before Abdulsattah's face, the two on either side in sharp focus, the central one blurred. Just as they should be.

The Glock had no external hammer and no safety; it came up ready to roll. For some reason the piece had been returned to Eddie during his confinement for "debriefing"—he wasn't really a prisoner, after all. He had practiced drawing and dry-firing it with the stolid zeal of a Zen swordmaster. It was something to do.

The holes of Abdulsattah's face opened wide, eyes and mouth and nostrils, and its color fell away. In those eyes Eddie saw a flash of surprise, of terror, as they stared into the barrel of the Glock, four-tenths of an inch wide, an infinity deep. But nothing of doubt. Self-delusion had predeceased Abdulsattah by fractional seconds.

The safety slug exploded on impact with the flat bone of Abdulsattah's cheek. The three hundred tiny shot within had enough cohesion and kinetic energy to punch through the zygomatic process half a centimeter below the right eye and ring loose hell in the brain behind.

The right side of Abdulsattah's face collapsed. His head snapped back, blood squirting from the corners of his eyes. Eddie took little for granted, but somehow he knew there was no call for a follow-up round, the second benediction of the classic anti-terrorist double-tap.

The match fell into the sand along with Abdulsattah's flopping body. Flickered. Died.

Eddie pivoted with ballet precision. His body snapped into the Weaver stance, left arm extended, right hand cupping pistol hand and pistol, pulling tension to lock body and arms in a rigid triangle. The three dots floated before the front of Samirov's tunic.

"Call off your wolves, Samirov," he told Abdulsattah's second-in-command. Inside he felt turbulence like boiling water, but without heat. He had fired at human targets before and was confident some of his targets died. But there had always been *distance*. He had never killed anybody like this, close enough to feel their fluids drying on his face in the angry sun.

"Do it now, Samirov. Have 'em drop their weapons. They might shoot me to pieces, but no power on this earth will prevent me pumping one in your belly. You know what a Glaser is, asshole? You'll be hours dying, and it'll hurt like one mother fucker. Takes a lot longer than burning, brother."

The *ghazi* second-in-command was staring at him. Samirov's jaw had dropped. A rope of saliva fell out over his hanging underlip, unreeled toward the ground. A mewing escaped him, then, turned into a strange gobbling, choking sound. He doubled, eyes impaled on the Glock's black muzzle, and then he sat down hard and began pumping at the sand with both legs, looking for all the world as if he were working out on a leg machine at Nautilus, sculling himself backward, away from Eddie, away from his pistol. The fat warm smell of fresh shit filled Eddie's nostrils.

Well, Brother Samirov's departed controlled flight, Eddie thought. *Swell.* Behind him he heard the click-*slam* of a Kalashnikov bolt being thrown.

The last time he'd dived right in amid things in the vague expectation of being backed up . . . if it hadn't been for the handy little Glock, the four dudes from Naval Infantry *Spetzsnaz* would probably still be dancing on his face in that fucking bar in Georgia. The Glock wasn't going to be enough this time. If the Blue Sky Riders decided it was time for all good Central Asians to show solidarity, he would in short order be spritzing from so many holes he'd look like one of those hoses the goyim used to water their nice suburban lawns. . . .

"Drop your weapons," he heard someone say behind him. Maqsut.

A *ghazi* stared past Eddie in disbelief. "But are we not all Turkestani?"

"*Gapirmang!*" another Blue Sky Rider snapped. "Shut up. Only those who follow the will of Timur may call themselves that. Now do as *Leytenant* Eddie *khaan* says, or we'll trickle your blood in the sand."

League Undersecretary of State Pavel Valentinovich Vorov'yev stood at the dacha's great south-facing windows, gazing out at the Ural pine forests near Kuybyshev and contemplating decadence.

Behind him council members punished the buffet and clattered to each other about the intractable Red Sands crisis. He swirled wine in the cut glass goblet, gazed moodily down into it. A California sauvignon, supposedly laid down before the American ban on domestic wine production. To serve it at a council meeting, even an informal one, was something of a slap at the Americans, with whom the League took pains to maintain a wary *rapprochement* since the Americans' sullen realization that their aid had financed not rehabilitation but rearmament.

He sipped the wine. It was very good. There was fine

vodka at the buffet. But when one is surrounded by decadence and cannot materially affect it, one would be a fool not to partake. That was decadent thinking, he knew.

The medals on the chest of his Western-style suit, dark blue, severe, and immaculately tailored to his marathon-runner's frame, were another form of decadence. Mere ostentation. Empty display.

The damage the fool Gorbachev had done ran too deep. There was too much to undo. The League was still saddled with press freedoms and traces of the market economy, which could be squeezed but not entirely done away with. Worst of all was this pretense of *autonomy*.

It had gone off in their faces. Now the black-asses were in open rebellion, and the achievements of the glorious armed forces rang as tinnily and emptily as the service medals on a youthful undersecretary's chest. Vorov'yev had served his country with distinction fighting the savages in Afghanistan, had earned the rank *podpolkovnik,* lieutenant colonel. And what of that? All of them bore military rank, the thick-bodied balding men grazing at the buffet behind him, and they seemed to have as little substance as their reflections that flitted ghostly in the glass before him.

"So pensive, Pasha."

Vorov'yev turned. Marshal Burdeinyi, chief of STAVKA, looked every millimeter the elder military hero, with his astonishing white eyebrows and shiny dome of skull, innocent of hair as a dolphin's, his oil-drum chest lit up with medals like the exploding scoreboard at the Moscow Sports Palace. Yet he had never heard a shot fired in anger.

"I find myself momentarily overcome with luxury, Marshal."

The marshal produced a laugh like pebbles in a tumbler. The hand he laid on Vorov'yev's shoulder was soft as a brick. "You sound like a damned *perestroikachik.* The grave responsibility we bear demands compensation. Surely you don't begrudge us our simple dachas, do you, Pavel Valentinovich?"

Vorov'yev held up his goblet. "Like you, I enjoy the wine, Marshal." Burdeinyi laughed again and patted him on the shoulder.

The lodge had been built after the League's formation, as one of the incoming regime's rewards to itself. It was sunk into the side of a mountain, all gleaming glass and hardwood, passive and active solar for the sake of being *kulturnyy* in the world of the nineties. Not thirty kilometers away the country's biggest emergency command post, the bolt hole for the president, his council, and STAVKA in of the oh-so-remote case of war with the League's friendly rivals of the West—or the less-remote case of war with those smooth-faced barbarians the Chinese—lay buried beneath a massive slab of living rock at Zhiguli.

The rulers of the *Liga* had done themselves proud in more than just comfort. An entire SAM battalion surrounded the estate, and a regiment of picked OMON troops patrolled the perimeter, though their jackbooted feet were not permitted to sully the immaculately manicured grounds short of actual emergency. Less than ten kilometers back in the hills lay a League VDV-*Spetsnaz* training camp for mountain and forest warfare. The dacha lacked Zhiguli's cement and stone, but was comfortably safe from assault.

"It's beautiful, is it not?" the marshal said, looking out across the deck and the rose garden right below the window at the broad green lawn.

"Very beautiful."

"The president was wise to convene us here. I find the mountain air quite stimulating, Pasha. And the gardens—do you know that roses grown here have won prizes all over the world?"

"Is that so?"

The marshall glowed with pride at being so *kulturnyy*. "Indeed it is. Our roses are the best in all the world."

The best roses come from Fergana. The best in the League; some say in the world.

The best gardeners likewise come from Fergana.

The dacha's master gardener was old. He had served the masters of the state for almost half a century, since shortly after Stalin's death. When the lodge was built, it had gone without saying that he and his staff—the youngest of whom was a grandfather—should be installed here. The rulers of Russia deserved the best, it was traditional, and the master gardener and his staff were the best.

The old man parked his wheelbarrow laden with tools covered by a burlap sack and looked up. A story above him the lodge's southern windows shimmered like a glacier wall. In the thin hot midday sun he could see a tall young man and a stout older man standing behind them. Their eyes looked at him without seeing.

Half a dozen of his assistants trudged after him, two bent low beneath the weight of a ladder. They weren't charged with tending the roses alone, but all the estate's greenery. Sometimes the trees needed pruning. Today there was much pruning to be done.

He remembered the blue high Pamirs looming like guardian giants above the valley where he was born. He had not seen those mountains in fifty years.

He would not see them again.

His assistants gathered around him. They were all Kirghiz too. He knelt beside his barrow, threw back the rough burlap.

Inside were stacked Yugoslav MGV-176 machine pistols. They were manufactured by the Gorenje company, which at one time made household appliances. They were stubby and short and very handy, with folding stocks and M88 noise/flash suppressors built onto the barrels. Clear plastic drums holding one hundred seventy-six rounds of .22 Long Rifle each were mounted on top, after the fashion of the old Lewis machine gun.

The stooped old men were used to handling gardeners' tools, not weapons. The MGV-176 had been designed with men like them in mind.

* * *

Drifting back to the buffet to fortify himself for the afternoon council session with another glass of wine, Pavel Vorov'yev heard a sound like a bird tapping at the window. Frowning, he turned back.

The huge sheet of glass starred along a line from lower right to upper left. The window fell in, jagged sheets of glass and a flurry of powdered-glass snow.

Marshal Burdeinyi spun around. His blue eyes stared at Vorov'yev through a mask of blood and terminal surprise. The front of his tunic was stitched in brilliant crimson.

Chapter
TWENTY-THREE

General Colonel Anatoliy Karponin took a sip from his plastic cup of vodka and set it to hold down the bottom edge of the map he had unrolled on the table in his personal trailer. He liked maps—real maps, not computer displays. He resolutely refused to turn his personal sanctum into a bizarre technocratic wonderland of flashing, beeping displays.

Someone knocked. "Advance," he called, and turned in his chair to see a sentry in battle dress, his face a bizarre mask of green and black combat paint, hold the door open for Captain Rybalko.

The young officer's republican guard still held most of its crispness, showing little effect from the muggy Syr Dar'ya night. Karponin nodded millimetric approval. Soldiers responded well to officers who were willing to share danger with them, but they only respected those who continued to look like officers.

"What's happened, Captain?" the general asked. Rybalko

was one of the few privileged to disturb him here when he was snatching a few minutes' rest. One reason he extended such privilege to an officer so junior was his confidence it would not be abused.

The captain hesitated. Karponin felt surprise; hesitation was as small a part of Rybalko's nature as his own.

"General Colonel, there are no new developments to report. But there is a situation which continues to develop . . . ." His voice tailed off. He cleared his throat.

"General Colonel, please rebuke me if I overstep. But as we advance along the Syr, the rebels are massing in the Qizil Qum desert, to the south and west of us. These satellite photos—" He drew a manila envelope from beneath his arm.

"I've seen the satellite photos," Karponin said quietly.

"The rebels have no tanks or planes, and what artillery they have is scattered about. Their positions tend to be dispersed. While our satellites can show us the activities of even an individual enemy soldier in real time, the Red Sands are too vast for us to learn much by canvassing them square meter by square meter."

"I understand the limitations of our wonderful technological toys, Captain. Our coverage is also interrupted by sandstorms this time of year."

"Yes, sir. But the rebels do have trucks. And they are streaming into the desert on our flank."

"Which I am exposing." A whisper. Rybalko snapped to attention.

Karponin leaned back in his leather-covered chair. "Captain, you are correct. But understand: we're not fighting the German Irredentists here. We are fighting an undisciplined, badly organized, ill-equipped rabble with little chance to beat us in an open fight. They don't have the mobility to attack us by surprise, even with all the trucks in Central Asia.

"The enemy that concerns me more is our own government. The men in the field face the same vacillation, the same ridiculous concern for world opinion, that betrayed us in Afghanistan. That permitted the *nationalities* to humble the Union, and force this charade of a League upon us."

Rybalko was practically vibrating with tension now, uncertain whether his general was about to level him with a mighty blast or start babbling treason. *A little fear will do the boy good. Complacent, he's useless to me.*

"I can take Tashkent within the week, as I have sworn to do. But Tashkent's just a city. Timur won't throw his army away defending it; he knows I can take it from him."

He joined hands before his face, forefingers extended. His hands were large and surprisingly soft for a man of his reputation. "A protracted war is a rebel victory. Our esteemed leadership will lose what resolve the assassinations instilled in it. They will *make terms,* and the League will become a joke. I need the rebels to concentrate against me, so that I may use my speed, mass, and concentration to destroy them. They'll never do that unless they think they have a chance to win.

"And so"—He spread his hands—"I expose my flank."

Timur walked alone between the desert and the stars, head down. "Timur-*jaan,*" Francis Marron called, walking toward him from the encampment purposefully, but not fast. The Sons of the Sky-Blue Wolf were never far.

Timur stopped, raised his head. Marron caught a glint of starlight in the black eyes. He shivered. He couldn't see Timur well, but somehow he had never seen anyone look more desolate.

"You should be more careful," Marron said, coming up to Timur. "An assassin could get right up next to you, and *bang.*"

"I'm not unprotected." An easy gesture toward his escorts. Timur met Marron's gaze, and whatever the American had seen there was gone. Perhaps it was just a trick of the light.

Marron shook his head. "Sorry, sir, but that just won't

cut it. A resolute man could easily get as close as I've gotten, if he didn't care about coming back."

"I certainly respect your opinions in these matters, Mr. Marron; I know you have a good deal of experience in the field."

Marron turned his head aside, just in case it was light enough for Timur to see the way his mouth twisted.

Timur walked on. "In any event, that which I have set in motion will not stop simply because I am removed. An assassin would spend his life in vain."

That's what you always think, you Third World charismatic types, Marron thought. *And how wrong you always are.* He almost spoke the thought aloud; Timur's crazy tolerance-fixation encouraged those around him to speak their minds. But Marron was too cautious, too worldwise. Even the best-intentioned fool had a temper, and with his teenaged Wolves prowling nearby, Timur's most transient whim could be deadly.

"I feel duty-bound to tell you, sir, you're putting yourself in a highly risky position."

"Do you say this as a friend of Turkestan, or as a representative of your government?"

"I—I'd have to say both. I'm here to observe your revolution at first hand, but in so doing I have developed the highest respect for you, sir." To his surprise, it was true. Timur was a fool. But he was a man on horseback, a visionary. Marron had been a child during Kennedy's Camelot. His parents had believed and always taught him that JFK was a pure leader, and he had grown up searching for a man of the kind his parents had described. Timur was perhaps the closest he had come.

A magnificent fool, he decided. He found it mattered to him, the outcome of this final shot at dissuading him from folly.

"Timur, the world is an interdependent place. Nobody goes it alone. I apologize for lecturing you about it, but it's true." He surprised himself again by apologizing. In the course of Marron's professional life America's proconsuls had not often apologized for patronizing their clients.

"I am hardly alone, my friend. We are tens of millions strong."

"I mean *countries*. No native resistance movement has ever succeeded without external help. You have none."

"I've heard that theory. I find it debatable, myself—but I decline to debate it with you, Mr. Marron. I've too much on my mind."

"I understand fully, sir. I'm grateful to you for giving me this time, you know I am. But, even at this late hour, it's not too late to accept American assistance—"

Marron was trotting after Timur like a dog, torn between anger and frustrated tears. "You can have me shot for saying so, but without our help you don't stand a chance!"

Timur halted, faced him. "Mr. Marron, I have oftentimes feared I would become the sort of man who would order another killed for speaking what he felt to be the truth; you are so concerned in your country with substances you think are dangerous, but never will you admit the truth, which is that power is the deadliest drug of all. If power makes me into such a being, I pray that an assassin may strike me down.

"But I think we can win with what we have. Even now our forces gather in the Red Sands Desert, to strike at the flank the butcher Karponin has left open in his arrogance. He had made a mistake in this single-minded drive for Tashkent, and it gives us an opportunity to smash his army, better armed and better trained though they are."

Marron opened his mouth, but there was really nothing to say. Timur wasn't finished anyway.

"I appreciate your offer, Mr. Marron. But there are strings attached to American aid. I fear that if I touch what you offer, those strings will adhere to the backs of my hands.

"I thank you for your concern for our fate. Good night." He turned away with finality and marched back toward the blacked-out tents. Marron stood looking after him, fists balled and mouth open, breathing deeply.

If that's the way you want to play it, he thought, *then the blood is on your hands.* His knees trembled with outrage. Timur wasn't just a fool, he was a murderer, who was going to sacrifice his own life and the lives of thousands if not tens of thousands of his followers to his crazy pride. Addicted to his outmoded, dangerous notions of freedom and autonomy, he was going to put a match to everything he claimed to be fighting for.

It made it that much easier to do what was necessary.

Sondra Mohn caught the telephone before the second ring. She was fully awake and alert by the time she pressed it to her ear.

"Yes."

"We're getting a satlink communication from Turkestan. Our CIA boy with the rebels."

"Marron."

"That's the one."

Some of the younger men at State were becoming informal to the edge of impertinence. She made a mental note to squash this one at the first convenient moment.

"We've got him on-line now, if you want to talk to him."

"No." The man did not mean literally *talk,* he meant that she could get on her terminal and connect to State, from which she could be patched on in order that she and Marron could type at each other. But to career women of Mohn's generation the secretarial pool was much like La Brea Tar Pits to a saber-toothed tiger: once it caught you, it never let you go. In a computer-dominated age Sondra Mohn refused to so much as touch a keyboard, lest her fingers stick to the keys.

There was voice-recognition software, now, so you didn't have to type to talk to computers, and Mohn made use of computers in their place. But she had nothing to say to Mr. Marron. She presumed he knew his business, because NSA and CIA alike were aware of the consequences of palming an incompetent off on her come appropriations time—especially with Enforcement Affairs insisting that the old intelligence agencies were redundant, inefficient, and unnecessary.

Also, she had no wish to prolong the contact. It was fairly safe; Timur was really enough of a radical idiot not to restrict access to the Net, and a low-power satellite link was inherently hard to detect and trace. There were "smart" software routines that could be turned loose in the Net to keep watch for spies, but even in the unlikely event Third World rebels had access to such tools, they were so painfully ingenuous she honestly doubted they'd think of using them. On the other hand, if something did go wrong, she did not want the blame for keeping the spook on-line for too long. Her philosophy of power was to avoid incurring gratuitous ill will. Her methodology of power incurred a great deal of it *necessarily*.

"I have a printer in my bedroom," she told the telephone. "Feed it through."

"You've got it." The duty man at State rang off, leaving Mohn determined to put him in his place good and hard.

She forgot her resolve when Marron's report whispered out of her laserprinter. After no more than a glance, she had the telephone clamped between the old-fashioned hairnet she wore at night and her heavy flannel nightgown, pressing a preprogrammed button—single buttons posed no threat.

"*Allo*," a muzzy voice said at the other end.

"Ambassador Kapushtin? Mohn. Listen, Ivan, I have a little information that might be useful to you . . . ."

Chapter
TWENTY-FOUR

The three BMP-2s of the advance guard's combat recon patrol resolved out of the desert between two low sawback ridges in a shimmer of heat. Fast Eddie tried to whistle, but his lips were too dry. He sucked them, trying to bring moisture to relieve his dry mouth. His gum had all melted in the Red Sands heat. He had left even his precious Glock behind so he could carry an extra liter of water, but today he didn't have a drop to waste.

"Jagun 23, this is Six," he said for the benefit of the hands-free mike on the headset he wore over his Yankees cap. "Three Bravo Mike Papas, twenty-five hundred meters north, headed our way. We're going to cross them: Bravo, engage eastern target, Charlie, middle target, Delta the one on the west end. Alfa will reserve for a follow-up; we want these bad boys rattled good. Wait for my command, and remember, *Khudaga tanklar bering*."

"Your pronunciation improves, Eddie-*janaap*," came the dry voice of Shy Bunny, back from his compassionate leave and seemingly in high spirits—maybe too high, as if he were planning to take his grief out on the enemy. Eddie still read his reliability as high, for an indige anyway. "*Allaaga shukur*—that means, 'thank God.'"

"Yeah, Roger that. Wait for my command." He avoided the use of the word *fire*. You never said *fire* to indigenous forces unless that's what you wanted them to do. He was pleased with the way 23 had pulled together, but he could never let himself forget what they were.

If only it were a little clearer what I'm *supposed to be.*

He hit the squelch and said "Steady" to Asraar, the missileer for Alfa, his own section. The young electrician's apprentice from Samarkand sat next to him behind a camel-prickle bush, peering through the computerized sight of a tripod-mounted TOW-missile.

Because this was the only time they were going to be able to prepare, the launcher was emplaced in a fair approximation of a by-the-manual TOW fighting position, a hole dug two feet deep in the tough khaki-colored *syerozem* soil, shaded by a canopy made from a desert-pattern camouflage

tent from a sporting goods store in Bukhara, held up by four
tubular aluminum tent poles from the same source. To foil
overhead reconnaissance—including satellites, in case the
League was picking over the entire Qizil Qum square meter
by square meter, which he guessed would take a couple
years minimum—clumps of tough feather grass had been
piled on top. Even if remote infrared sensing had enough
resolution to pick up a variation that small, he guessed the
feather grass, each clump of which held a big fist of dry soil
in its roots, looked no more dead up there than it did on the
ground. If they left the stuff up there, it would probably
thrive; it was perverse and mean as everything that lived in
this desert, including humans.

Asraar's fingers tapped lightly on the sighting unit's
plastic housing. "I am steady," he said. "What about you,
qimmatlik amerikalik?"

Eddie wiped sweat from his eyes, glanced sideways at
Asraar, looked away fast. After all his time in the Muslim
East he was still a little dubious about the fact that a man
could call another "dear" without trying to be fresh. Of
course, in the Muslim East, he likely was trying to be fresh,
but it wasn't the necessary case.

"I'm cool," he said. "Only thing that spooks me is this
shit." He tapped the earphone of the lightweight headset.
"Squad-level satlink communications, and the damned thing
weighs less than the old AN/PRC-70s we used in basic."
Headset, electronics, milliwatt power supply, and the half-
meter-long half-moon-shaped phased-microarray smart antenna resting beside the TOW pit altogether weighed fifteen
kilos. And Sertikan, hidden with Asraar's mount in a little
gravelly draw behind them, got to hump it most of the
time.

"We don't have this stuff outside Special Forces, and
neither do the, ah, neither does the League," Eddie said in
a leading tone. *Time for a little intelligence-gathering, here.*
Anyway he really wanted to know how these ragged-ass
rebels got gear like that.

Asraar laughed. "They could buy it from the Japanese, just as we did. These are consumer electronics, and very reasonably priced. I cannot speak for you Americans, but I think the Nikolays do not trust their soldiers with communications tools this powerful."

Hmm. He wondered if the Americans felt the same way.

One thing was damned sure: Timur's little elves hadn't trolled in all this neat poop in only eight weeks. Jagun 23's four TOW-2 launchers were outmoded, though still effective, as were the simpler but shorter-ranged and less-powerful MILAN launchers Alfa and Charlie sections carried. Because they had been superseded by smarter weapons systems, they were fairly cheap these days, and the various marks of Soviet/League RPG anti-tank rockets the unit carried for close-in work had been falling off trucks and walking out of dumps for years. And as far as Eddie knew, any hobbyist could pick up the parts to make a satlink walkie-talkie at Radio Shack, more or less as Asraar said. But his missile men had photocopied manuals for their weapons in hand long before he arrived, and knew how to use their pieces.

Something had been seriously wrong in Central Asia for months in advance of the uprising, if not years. In Soviet times, Asian troops seldom got weapons training of any sort, and *never* in Western weapons. Timur had been training and prepping the hard core of his army for a hell of a long time, right under the nose of the KGB.

The Chekists fuck up again, he thought with savage satisfaction. It was going to be fun calling attention to that fact in his next sitrep to Arbatov.

If he ever got to make it.

From Bukhara in the south, in the green Zeravshan valley above the confluence with the Amu, to Ak Mechet on the Syr is about five hundred and seventy-five kilometers by air. What lies between is the Red Sands.

From Samarkand to Bukhara the Zeravshan runs mostly

west in a north-bent arc. The valley's northern boundary is a writhe of ridges and mountains that runs on west across Qizil Qum almost to the Amu and the desolate Zaunguzk Plateau before zagging back to the northeast like a cobra rearing to strike. About midway between Bukhara and the White Fortress, the cobra's hood is a bowl of hard-crusted sand a hundred kilometers across, dotted with weird alkaline deposits and patchy clay pans called *takyr*.

Fast Eddie had Jagun 23 strung out over nearly a kilometer, in pairs, mostly to keep his troopies from getting lonely. When soldiers—indiges in particular, but everybody—started feeling abandoned or feeling that they were the last living thing on earth was when they bugged out, especially when the shitstorm of an artillery barrage began to thunder in their ears and squash the air right out of their chests.

It was an enormous front for a company of just shy a hundred men to cover. But they weren't talking holding off an infantry assault here; if they were still on hand when the Motor Rifle boys de-assed their BMPs, it was definitively *game over*.

Away to the west a column of smoke rose into a sky whose blue stung the eye. They had been watching tiny sun-glinting arrowheads darting about in that direction for the past hour, as League attack planes worked somebody over. Eddie hoped Frontal Aviation stayed infatuated with that set of victims. He had his Strelas and his ersatz Stingers, but Jagun 23's best defense was that the Red Sands were huge and it was small and spread out.

He raised his binoculars again. The BMPs were coming hard and fast and arrogant, as befit Al Capone's fair-haired sons of bitches. The only thing keeping the pedal from the metal was fear of throwing a tread on the uncertain ground or nosing into a hidden wadi; they were going to smash through these black-ass rebels by the sheer size of their cocks alone. It was as if man-portable anti-armor weapons had never been heard of.

"Stupid fucks," Eddie said. It was idiots like Karponin who had cost them the war in Afghanistan, at least as much as Gorbachev and his reformers.

It didn't mean it was going to be easy to kill his comrades. His countrymen.

Fast Eddie—Aleksandr Pavlovich Gorsunov—had always come the bad boy, smart-mouthed, rebellious, prone to dart off in his own direction. But at crunch time he had always done what he was told, whether it was abandoning his mother and his country as a small boy, or joining the American Army as a bigger boy, or joining *Spetsnaz* when he was as big as he was likely to get.

That fat bald fuck Arbatov had told him to go to Turkestan and become a rebel, and the fat bald truth was that he hadn't needed Lt. Shadrin's hamfisted threats against his father to make him go. Fast Eddie/Little Alex did what he was told because that was what he did. That was what he was.

Arbatov had ordered him to do his absolute best in Timur's service until he was told otherwise. That was what Eddie planned to do, no matter how it made him feel. He didn't *let* himself feel, not now, nothing except the methedrine brew of fear/exhilaration/anticipation that preceded the first shock of battle.

Besides, this would be an *extremely poor* time to do anything but his best. This was what he was trained for, and if he held anything back, he would wind up expeditiously dead . . . if he were lucky. If he got captured, it was going to be a die-roll as to whether he went down as an American spy, a League traitor, or a KGB spy, depending on how alert his buddies in GRU were. However the call went, they would fry him in his own grease, and Mr. Chief Director Arbatov would not lift one blunt-instrument finger to save him.

Two klicks' range. *Fuck it.*

"Bravo, Charlie, Delta TOW crews, fire now."

Three TOWs whooshed away in clouds of white smoke and tan dust. Eddie felt his scrotum contract. His professional pride was in this now, even if self-preservation hadn't quite kicked in. He ached for his boys to ring up all three, even if they were just indiges, and on the wrong side.

White light splashed the lead BMP's western flank. That was the nice thing about crossing fire with your anti-tank missiles. Like most Soviet-designed AFVs, the "armored infantry machine" was hard to hit, sharp-nosed and low to the ground. Crossfiring attacked their side armor, thinner, flatter, and more vulnerable than the frontal glacis.

He panned his glasses left. A gush of flame flipped the turret off the westernmost vehicle like a poker chip. The third vehicle was slewing off to one side, spilling black smoke.

"Yeah!" Eddie exulted, pumping the air with his fist. "Three for *three*."

"*Khop*," Asraar said, *great*. He sounded subdued. *He* wanted to shoot a rocket too.

"Bravo, Charlie, Delta TOW crews, cease tracking, out of action. Boogie *now*." The backblast of a TOW could fry a man if he stood too close, and threw all kinds of crap into the air. An alert enemy could spot it and try to make the missileer duck by throwing a lot of lead in his direction, or even dodge the operator-guided projectiles—possible if your timing was perfect. That hadn't happened; no doubt these crews had not remotely anticipated a sudden smashing attack like this. But any survivors—and Eddie had been up against it enough to know there are *always* survivors, no matter what it looks like—knew exactly where the rockets that had damaged their vehicles had come from.

"Machine gunners, commence firing. Be ready for my signal to pull out, and run like hell when I give it." The Blue Sky Riders had an assortment of light MGs, mostly Kalashnikovs in conventional and bullpup designs that looked like AK assault rifles on steroids, but also several antique Degtyarevs with wooden stocks and funky drum magazines. Even firing from rests, they had the chance of a televangelist entering into the kingdom of heaven of hitting anything at this range. That wasn't the point; Eddie just wanted them to ring some nice loud hits off hull metal, kick up some dust, convince the Leaguers that the desert was crawling with rebels like crabs on a Krasnoyarsk whore, all intent on lifting white skins to bind their Korans with. Green troops whose invulnerable armored fighting machine has just been blasted into flaming junk don't take much convincing.

Eddie punched up the stopwatch of his fancy Seiko digital watch, which was one of the few functions he'd figured out, and divided attention between it and the battle. The norm for the bulk of the advance guard, following in column maybe ten klicks back, to come up to support its stricken patrol was twenty minutes. Like the Soviet economy of old, the League Army ran on norms. Since these were Karponin's troops, and Al Capone was a maximum hardass where drill was concerned, they would probably come in about on schedule. If they tried too hard to beat the norms, they were going to have some vehicles go down from shedding tracks in this rough country, which was fine with Eddie. Jagun 23's mission was to slow down the Leaguers and piss them off, inflicting as much damage as possible on their transport.

Squaddies were bailing out of the lead and eastern BMPs. Nobody had gotten out of the west-end vehicle, and the way flame was gushing out the top, he didn't figure anybody would.

He tasted bile at the back of his mouth. *Well, at least I didn't pull the trigger on them.* He was much too sophisticated to buy that, of course. But he was also too smart to waste much worry on it now.

The lead carrier didn't seem to be on fire at all, in fact. Neither did it seem to be going anywhere. That and the place it had been hit made it likely the track had been cut. Which made it a paperweight until somebody with the proper equipment came out and bent a new one on, a completely arduous task even when it wasn't fifty C and you weren't being shot at by wicked rebel terrorists under the guidance—of course!—of soul-bought American mercenaries. As good as a kill, by his mission profile.

The BMP was still a *dangerous* paperweight. As he watched, the muzzle flare of one of the quick-firing 23mm cannon that the tracks had been retrofitted with in emulation of the American Bradley began to wink from the turret. From the turret angle and the dust puffs he saw when he looked left, it was shooting in the direction of the Alfa section launcher.

"Alfa, this is Six. Anybody hit?"

"No, Eddie," Shy Bunny said. "They're not yet close."

"Don't let 'em get closer. Go ahead and pull out, and don't stick your heads up."

"But—"

"*Now,* dammit!"

Asraar was peering at him out of his shallow firing pit with huge beseeching eyes. "I can knock him out, please," he said. "He isn't even moving."

"Forget it. Once we're out of range, he's out of the fight. We don't have missiles to waste on cripples."

He glanced at his stopwatch. Almost five minutes had passed. Screw it. The lead vehicle in any League unit was the one with the radio link back to HQ, and this one had probably spent the last five minutes screaming for an air strike.

In contrast to Western doctrine it was iron-shod League policy to *deny* air and artillery support to units in trouble. Inheritors of the Soviet military tradition refused to reinforce failure, preferring to use their big guns to secure or expand victory, in support of elements on the advance. On the other hand, in this target-poor environment the recon leader might just get his airplanes anyway. League strike jocks had to be frustrated and hungering to dump on *somebody.*

"That's it," he said. "Jagun 23, it's time to go."

Chapter
TWENTY-FIVE

As the rebels rode south, strung out over terrain dotted with gray-green shrubs called wormwood, just like in the Bible—though Eddie, who'd watched a lot of Western movies on late-night TV, knew they were nothing but sagebrush—the ground began to jitter beneath the feet of their horses, who jittered back. Thunderclaps rolled like tsunami across the desert as self-propelled howitzers and 122mm rockets worked over the ridges they'd just left.

Ridges running parallel to the League axis of advance striated the arid land. That was convenient; it slowed the lead elements' advance, and made it take longer for the main force to catch up when the lead got hit. It channeled the League fighting vehicles into the breaks between ridges, and provided natural vantage points for the rebels to ambush them from.

It also offered convenient aiming points for the League's fine artillery. Desert Wind commanders may have been following a battle plan more suited to taking on Americans than rebels who weren't much more than guerrillas, but they did know how to read ground, and they knew perfectly well where they were going to be ambushed from. At the first flash of a rocket motor, they were going to rake the high ground big-time.

With not much time to learn the terrain, Eddie was thrown back on improvisation. That was how he preferred to play it anyway. Intricate plans and elaborate strategies weren't his game, and besides he had no faith in them: the reality of battle was more complex than you could ever plan for.

He already had his first fallback line picked out and conveyed to his section leaders. It was on the *third* ridge system back from their original positions. That gave the League force two potential red zones that had to be sterilized with artillery and approached with care, and also gave the rear echelon types time to get mightily pissed off at the regiment for slowing its triumphant advance.

Under normal circumstances horses can't outrun APCs. But this country slowed horses far less than BMPs, and the League was burning a lot of time pouring troops out of their track-laying cans to bust an ambush that was long gone.

In an hour Jagun 23 reached its rendezvous. As it began digging in, the earth shook. The second ridgeline took its pounding without complaint.

An hour and a half later, Jagun 23 heard the clatter and whine of tracked vehicles approaching. The men began to exchange nervous glances and watch Eddie very closely. "If the rockets come—"

Eddie shrugged. At that moment he didn't actually care. The way he had it worked out, if a BM-21 rocket came in and smeared him all over the rocks, it would extricate him very neatly from a situation he could see no other way out of.

He was quite aware that reasoning was nuts. But it worked, which was enough for now.

No rockets landed. Instead League tracks appeared around the flank of the ridge to the north. The regimental commander wasn't screwing around with reconnaissance patrols anymore; this was the lead company in wedge formation, with three T-80 main battle tanks in line-abreast out front.

"Astakhfirullaa," someone breathed. *By God.*

"Jagun 23, T-80s and BMPs, 2000 meters north. TOWs and MILANs will engage by depth on my command. Leave the tanks to God. Fire."

This time eight launchers fired, the four TOWs and four MILANs. Eddie watched until he saw explosions, then called "Cease tracking" and ordered his rocket teams back over the hill and away. Nobody argued. There was something about those tanks, low-slung and massive, that made you go cold all the way through.

The first impact he saw was a flier that gouged a big harmless hole in the earth. Ideally both kinds of missiles guided themselves to the target, provided the operator kept it in the eye of his computer sight. But no weapon system is infallible.

He noted six vehicles smoking; there had been another miss, or one BMP had been double-teamed. "Machine guns, fire fifty and get the hell out. RPGs fire and flee too." He'd ordered the men with RPG launchers to load OG-7 high-explosive rounds into them. They wouldn't defeat a BMP's armor; but then, they couldn't actually reach the vehicles from here. The idea was to create noisy explosions to convince the Leaguers they'd run into a major strongpoint.

Eddie could see soldiers diving out of undamaged BMPs as well as the ones his men had hit. Everybody's doctrine— not to mention reflex—was to get the troops out of their APCs at the first sign of a weapon that could destroy them. They couldn't really fight effectively from inside one, the Infantry Fighting Vehicle concept notwithstanding, but they could all go up in the same greasy pyre.

RPG rounds began to explode, well short of the League troops—they were designed to self-destruct after less than a kilometer's flight, to prevent their warheads' falling into enemy hands or creating a safety problem when battle was over. Soviet and League farmers had been blowing their legs off stumbling over stray ordnance from the Great Patriotic War—and malcontents had been scrounging leftover explosives and weapons—for half a century.

It didn't matter. Eddie's troops weren't looking to cause casualties. The reality, alkaline-harsh as the Central Asian soil, was that in a stand-up fight they couldn't lay much hurt on a full League regiment before they were wiped out. Their job was to slow them down, shake them up. And damage their transport.

Return fire was starting to whip the ridge's foreslope.

Eddie called a pull-out, both by his fancy satlink set—which miraculously hadn't gone down yet—and arm signals. The rest of the Jagun scampered back over the crest to where squadmates held their horses.

Pulling back from combat is a tricky, treacherous game. The difference between deliberate withdrawal and full-scale rout is a tiny attitude switch. In a way, it's easier for irregulars than it is for regular forces, because if they're trained right they don't have any expectation of holding the line and absorbing what the enemy dishes out. Eddie took pride in the fact he'd brought these boys up right; they knew they could scatter to the four colors of the old Mongol compass and regroup again, and they weren't ashamed to do so.

As they rode away, the military crest of the ridge, on the far side of the summit, erupted in a wall of smoke and horrible noise. The mobile artillery had evidently held position after its last bombardment, waiting to see if the regiment needed it again before it pulled out of range. Eddie grinned at Maqsut, who gave him a thumbs-up. The League column was now going to play inchworm, tanks and APCs advancing to the forward edge of artillery support, then waiting for the tracked howitzers and missile trucks to catch up. That was slow. It made it less likely the League would catch them. It also meant that Division, imbued with Al Capone's straight-ahead philosophy—and with his staff undoubtedly ringing them up every ten minutes to wonder why the hell their lead elements weren't pulling up at the Sonic Drive-in just north of Bukhara yet—was going to be chewing nonstop on the regimental commander's butt.

When they had the mass of the next ridge south between them and the shelling and they could hear again, one of Eddie's riders hollered "*Astakhfirullaa!*" and brandished his Kalashnikov over his head. "These Nikolays aren't any trouble at all. We should stand and fight—they're just no good."

"You talk like a fool," old Uncle Lucky said in his quavery voice. "The *basmachi* are tough; we've got the best of them now, but they won't give up."

"Uncle Lucky," Eddie said gently, "as the man said, *we're* the *basmachi.*"

The ancient shook his head firmly. He was wearing something that looked like a horribly decrepit hunting cap, and the greasy tattered earflaps flopped like wings.

"When I was a Red Stick and fought the *basmachi,* they were bandits," he said. "They fought against the revolution, which was going to bring peace and justice and freedom to all Turkestanis, Sarts and hillmen alike. We beat them, and then we found out that the revolution wasn't about those things at all. It was about trading one set of European masters for another—and a worse lot, at that. The Bolsheviks tried to kill us off, one and all; of my old Red Stick band, only I survived, by the will of God."

He took out a handkerchief, blew his nose, and wiped his eyes, which struck Eddie as awfully unsanitary. "They killed my children. My sons and daughters—all. *Allaaga shukur* that I found a new young wife later, before the war against the fascists, or my line would have ended.

"The Nikolays stole and tortured and killed; *they* were the bandits. So now I fight them, and they are *basmachi.*"

"They're all asleep by now too, if they were listening to you, grandfather," jeered Dinmukhammed, a lantern-jawed Uzbek carpenter.

"You might be a wiser young man than your prattle suggests," the centenarian said. "For though I dearly loved my beautiful Qoqigul, the women of Samarkand all longed for me; and their breasts are as succulent as the melons they grow, and *esiz,* alas, I was not always strong. So I might *be* your grandfather—"

Something pulled Eddie's eyes up from mistrustfully watching Sertikan's hooves pick their way down the rock-littered slope. A shadow flashed across them.

He heard a rush of jet engines, and the hillside bloomed in a thousand wildflowers of yellow flame. Sertikan reared, screaming. Eddie clung to her mane and miraculously didn't go flying off in the feather grass.

A Frogfoot was streaking away, not five hundred feet above the gray valley floor. As Sertikan's forefeet dropped to the ground, a SAM-7 Strela sprinted after the plane. The little shoulder-fired rocket guided to the engine tucked up near its starboard flank and exploded.

Nothing happened. The Su-25 didn't even have the grace to waver in flight. It banked away to the north and crossed the ridgeline out of sight, leaving not even a smoke trail behind to mark the hit.

"Fucking Russian piece of shit!" Eddie raged, trying to bring his mare back under control. "A Stinger would've had the bastard." The Strela warhead was just too damned light.

The vicious crackle of the cluster bomblets going off was replaying itself as the sound waves bounced back at them off the ridges. Eddie heard the screaming of men and horses. The nearby riders stared at him with round eyes. The bomblet pattern had missed his immediate area, slashing across part of his section and the Singer's.

"Spread out!" Eddie shouted, waving his arm and almost losing Sertikan again. "Just scatter. If the wounded can't ride, just leave them."

He put his head down and dug his heels into the mare's yellow flank. Belatedly catching the drift that this wasn't a good time to assert her autonomy and empowerment, she took off obediently to the southwest.

He passed a couple of men lying inert in patches of maroon-stained earth. He didn't stop to try to first-aid them. Beyond, a horse lay kicking on its side, legs tangled in its own guts. He said "Jesus" and reined up just long enough to unsling his Kalashnikov and quiet the animal with a burst.

A couple of hundred meters farther on he broke through some *alhagi* scrub and down the fortunately collapsed bank of a shallow wadi. Giant Rahman was sitting with his twin brother's head cradled in his lap, bawling.

Rahim looked as if some kid had opened him up to see what made a Gypsy work. As Eddie reined in, the crimson arc pulsing from the base of the man's throat sputtered and died.

"Leave him!" Eddie shouted. "You can ride behind me."

"*Yoq*, no, I can't," Rahman sobbed. He stood up, hefting his brother's huge limp body in his arms as if it were a child's. It reminded Eddie of a painting he'd seen in Moscow by a contemporary Russian artist, of the painter standing by the roadside in his skivvies, holding in his arms the body of his chow dog who'd just been killed by a hit-and-run driver.

"Come on!" Eddie yelled. Rahman started a slogging run through the soft sand, and Eddie realized that one of the twins' horses was standing calmly over by the bank with the reins looped over its neck, sublimely unaffected by blood smell and commotion. Deciding there was no accounting for horses, or indiges either, Eddie gave Sertikan full throttle and took off.

The country opened out here into apparent flats that were actually scored by tortuous twining wadis. Ten klicks farther on, it reared up into bluffs and foothills and then some rocky junior-grade mountains before falling away into the vast red bowl of sand at the desert's heart.

It was great country for fleeing. Riding the wadi bottoms lessened the chance of being spotted from the ground or even air. Eddie took stock via his comm unit, whose smart antenna was lashed behind his saddle. His section commanders were uninjured, and only six men seemed to be missing. That was enough of a loss to demoralize irregulars, but morale still seemed high. The boys had a sense of having hurt the Nikolays worse than the Nikolays had hit them, and of being able to keep it up.

They didn't see the Su-25 again, and eventually the hair settled at the back of Eddie's neck. He hadn't really expected the strike plane to make a second pass, and intellectually he wasn't that worried if it did. Though slow for a jet, the heavily armored Shtormovik was still a fast mover. It was suited for its primary role, hunting out the conspicuous and relatively stationary targets made by APCs and tanks and shredding them with bombs and rockets and machine cannon firing depleted-uranium slugs. But its pilot could only see troops on the ground by accident, and with the Jagun strewn across klicks of desert, even the sprawling kill zone of a cluster-bomb dispenser would only catch a few of them if he did.

It was helicopters that worried Eddie. They *could* catch and kill dispersed infantry. They could also spot effectively for the motor rifle division's powerful, long-range artillery, or drop VDV *desant* squads south of the rebels to play anvil to the advancing regiment's hammer. His lightweight surface-to-air missiles could knock hell out of choppers, even the well-armored Hind "flying tanks." But helos could take them to pieces if League commanders were willing to suck up some losses—and they would be, the way the terrain and harassing ambushes had slowed them up, and the way Anatoliy Karponin was undoubtedly shrieking at them to advance, advance, always advance.

Eddie looked up at the sky. The midafternoon sun spilled below the brim of his cap and splashed his face like acid despite the thermonuclear blast-proof sunscreen he'd smeared over every exposed surface of his body before dawn that morning.

No choppers. Far to the south what looked like a vapor trail drifted across the sky—except it was angled sharply down, into the planet, which didn't look good for Frontal Av.

Eddie was afraid. He wasn't that afraid of death—that fear didn't prey on him. He was afraid of the powerlessness. At the crucial junctures of his life he had been without power—when the bigger, older kids teased him for being a Jew, when his mother went away, when he was sent to America, when he was sent to Central Asia. He hated that feeling worse than anything.

The motor rifle regiment grinding behind didn't make him

feel powerless. It could squash him and his little force, no question, but on the evidence it couldn't *catch* them. This wasn't Europe's rolling hills, or the dead-flat Southern Desert of Arabia. The speed the League relied on was cut to bone.

But he had felt powerless when the Shtormovik struck, when he'd ridden past the inert bodies of the soldiers, when he'd seen Rahim die in his brother's arms. They were rebels, they were supposed to be his enemy. But they were *his men*.

The day had gone their way, so far. That would change. In war, it always did.

After all, why should war be different from real life?

They popped a new trick on the League. While three sections took up ambush positions well to the south, Eddie handed off command of Alfa to Maqsut and stayed back with Charlie Section, now under one-eyed Tashmat Kagorovich, who'd taken over when Shoreh went to the *ghazi*.

Charlie was overall the greenest section, but from its cadre of *kumli* desert dwellers the newbies had learned fairly quickly How Not to be Seen, as the old Monty Python routine had it. They went to earth with RPGs and a MILAN launcher prepped and let the lead company roll over them and past.

From ahead, the TOW launchers—including one detached from Charlie—engaged the tanks; it was time for God to collect on one or two, keep the black-tab bastards inside from getting too smug. While that was going on, Eddie and Charlie popped up out of their wadis and engaged the rear BMPs of the wedge formation with RPGs from two hundred and fifty meters.

It was beautiful: complete confusion. One of the T-80s went up like Mount St. Helens. Before the squaddies had even begun to tumble out of their carriers, the BMPs were slammed from behind, and when the troops did get their asses in the grass, they found themselves under concentrated small-arms fire from well within effective range.

The body of the regiment was trailing the lead company by about five kilometers. Following doctrine—charge!—it lunged ahead to support its embattled unit.

Eddie let the firefight cruise for five minutes. He himself let off a couple of magazines from his Advanced AK—after all, no one could really tell that he was aiming his bursts over the heads of the League soldiers, and everybody was having such a wonderful time busting caps that he could have been playing solitaire, for all anyone noticed.

When he called for the section to pull out and exfiltrate around either end of the League company, he had most of the riflemen and BMP gunners firing north, to their own rear. With any luck they would still be doing that when the rest of the regiment pulled into range, and Regiment, thinking itself under fire by bad ragheads, would fire up its own comrades. Mix-ups like that are lethally common in warfare even without outside help.

Russian blood was being spilled. Eddie felt only exaltation, a sensation he knew would pass as quickly as his earlier despondency. He had taken on a bigger enemy and won. That was the biggest head rush he knew.

It had not been without cost. A *kumli* and two Tadzhiks were dead, two other Tadzhiks injured but able to ride unassisted, and the MILAN launcher smashed by a burst of 30mm grenades from an AGS-17 automatic launcher. On the plus side, one T-80 was toast, and the exultant rebels were claiming ten or a dozen BMPs knocked out. Eddie wasn't sure about that, but from the glimpses he got as they worked from wadi to wadi, there was a lot of wrecked machinery out there. And the surviving T-80s were suppressed— it's tough to get tank drivers to advance in the teeth of dug-in AT rockets; that's what infantry is for, to go dig the missile troops out.

Also, even if the regiment didn't fall for a firefight with its own lead company, at the minimum it was going to stop and spill its infantry into fighting line two klicks from the ambush zone, and everything would come to a halt while they advanced on foot to clear the ambush. Another success—and when the roiling gray curtain of a barrage popped up ahead, the other section leaders happily reported that they were already clear.

Eddie and Charlie had almost caught up with the others where the bluffs reared up, when they heard the distinctive drumming of helicopter rotors.

Chapter
TWENTY-SIX

It was a lean shark of a Mi-28 Havoc, coming transverse out of the northeast, skimming the hilltops ridged like dinosaur spines. Like its American opposite number the AH-64 Apache, it reminded Eddie of a frozen dachshund, except its nose didn't droop like the Apache's.

The craft almost stopped as the 30mm cannon under its straight nose fired. The burst hit somewhere beyond Eddie. "Dismount and take cover," he yelled, rolling off Sertikan. He remembered to pull on her reins; under the guidance of old Nizam the Cameleteer, in charge of four-legged transport, the Jagun's horses had been taught to lie down on command. To his surprise, the dun mare obeyed. Maybe she was smarter than he'd thought she was.

The Havoc was sliding forward, drooling dark gray smoke from its gun. When it was almost over Eddie's head, two Stingers slammed it from opposite sides. It vanished in a ball of yellow fire.

"Shit!" Eddie yelped. It would be just his luck to get soaked with burning helicopter juice. But the chopper had been moving faster than it appeared; momentum carried the wreckage safely past him before it struck a hillside and went rolling to the bottom in an expensive avalanche of fire and wrecked technology and men Eddie hoped were safely dead.

There were more choppers now, Havocs and *Gorbach*—Hinds, both troop carrier and strike varieties. VDV was coming to the party.

"Sections report!" Eddie hollered into his communicator as he hugged the ground beneath a camel-prickle thornbush. Shy Bunny and the Singer came back immediately. There was no response from Kagorovich.

My luck to lose my main desert hand right off the bat, Eddie thought. The *kumli*'s communicator might just be down. But that would be too easy.

He buried his face in the dirt as a shadow swept low overhead, mashing him with downdraft and stinging his face with a whirlwind of dust and thorn-bush shrapnel. He spat out acrid dust.

"Forget the strike ships unless they're tearing you up," he commanded. "Same principle as on the ground: hit the transport choppers. Use AT rockets if they ground or hover too long. Acknowledge."

He expected argument—indiges liked to hear themselves talk, and these Central Asians had a particular fondness for dispute. But his two section leaders who remained in touch acknowledged immediately.

He raised his head to see a SAM guide to a Hind's starboard exhaust. The explosion popped the main rotor neatly off and sent it spinning away like a Frisbee. The helicopter dropped like a brick and blew up.

Maybe I've done a few things right with these boy, after all, he thought.

He glanced back over his shoulder. Asraar was on his belly thirty meters down the shallow slope, his two horses—his own mount and the animal that carried the heavy TOW launcher—lying near him rolling their eyes.

For indiges whose military experience consisted of labor

battalions and DOSAAF, these Turkestanis were pretty hard-core. Asraar grinned hugely and held one thumb in the air.

Then he came apart before Eddie's eyes, in gouts of white light and blood and dust and intolerable noise. Eddie buried his face, trying to blink dirt out of his eyes, as the earth shook and freshets of soil splashed off his back.

The noise of explosions all around was so intense that when it stopped, it took several heartbeats for the fact to register. Eddie raised his head. Asraar was ruined, rags of meat hanging off chunks of white bone. So was his packhorse and the TOW launcher it carried.

Eddie bit his lip. He could guess what happened: a salvo from the 57mm rocket pod beneath a helicopter's stub wing had caught them. He was fortunate the one remaining TOW-2 missile hadn't been set off by the blasts. Of Asraar's mount there was no sign. Eddie caught sight of Sertikan, though, racing away with tail held high, terrified by the explosions.

Rockets were stringing their white smoke trails every way across the sky now. Jagun 23 was letting fly with every backpack SAM it had. *Good. No point saving them, unless you want to be buried with one.*

Another helicopter dove away out of sight behind a hill, flying pennons of dark smoke. At least four thick black columns were rising from the pyres of downed aircraft. The survivors were sheering off now, curving back to the north. *Running.*

Through the ringing the rockets had left in his ears, Eddie heard cheering. His surviving men stood up out of the scrub to wave triumphant fists after the choppers. He thought he could see at least half of them. They had been well dispersed, which was the next best defense to not being seen at all.

Still, another attack like the last would finish them.

He sensed a buzzing sound, fumbled his headphones, which had gotten dislodged to hang around his neck, back into place. "*Eddie*-jaan," Shy Bunny's voice said, "*south—*"

He spun. An Mi-24 transport was just rising up from behind a rise above them. That meant—

"Shit. *Desant* squad in our rear! Bravo, try to break west around the flank. Delta, go east."

Taking off, even lightened by disgorging its infantry squad with weapons and gear, the big *Gorbach* was logy. An RPG anti-tank round hit it on the windscreen. Eddie saw the interior light with the brilliant flash of the shaped-charge warhead. The Hind dropped straight down. It didn't explode.

He ran hunched over up the hill. He could see several others from Alfa—Rahman, Uncle Lucky still or again mounted on his horse, Dinmukhammed, Moon the ethnic Korean. They acknowledged his hand signals and passed them on. Someone out of sight tugged old Uncle Lucky off his mount, and the remnant of Alfa ran in a crescent line up the hill.

Dinmukhammed was first. He popped up onto the crest with a yell and began firing his old-style AKS-74 from the hip. The snarl of a Kalashnikov light machine gun answered.

Dinmukhammed toppled backward and rolled back down, coming to rest against the mound of sand that drifted around the base of a feathery camel's-hair bush almost at Eddie's feet. The carpenter's half-lidded eyes stared unflinchingly into the sun.

"—*chopped us to pieces!*" The voice from the Hind's speaker crackled as much from terror as atmospherics. "*Must be a thousand of them, and they've got everything— heavy machine guns, SAMs, triple-A—*"

Nikolay Stepanovich Kuliyev, still a junior lieutenant by grace of a superior combat record but back in Hinds by grace of insubordination before the Ak Tepe strike, grinned beneath his red handlebar mustache.

"Get the coordinates for that call, Ivan Mikhaylovich?" he asked the instrument man in the seat next to him.

Ivan turned to him. From the tilt of his head, Kolya guessed his face was as blank as the visor in front of it.

They had covered the landing of a VDV *desant* battalion in the pass through the bald red sandstone buttes that the advancing League column would use to pour into the great sandy bowl beyond. In spite of the fact that it was a natural ambush point, the rebels held it only lightly; Kolya guessed they were expecting their missile-armed skirmishers to delay the Desert Wind armor even longer than they had. Now the ship was free to hunt.

"Tell Tiger lead we're taking this call," he told his young commo man.

"But I—" the boy sputtered. "I mean—"

"You thought I lost my nerve, and that's why I came back to join you?" Kolya laughed that big-chested laugh of his. Keeping the stick with his left hand, he drew his huge Ruger .44 Magnum from its shoulder holster.

"I don't kill unarmed civilians," he said, "but I'd rather shoot rebels than export-grade Stoli. Go on, boy; tell Tiger we're on the way." He snapped the cylinder shut and banked the chopper right.

As he gently boosted the cyclic to accelerate the ship, he was half gratified and half chagrined to learn that Viktor, in the dropped gunner's bubble in front, had learned to do a passable imitation of his own rebel yell.

Shaking his head, Eddie policed up Asraar's rifle, his sack of spare magazines, and the RPG-16 slung across his back. He fastened the sack to the harness of the light ruck he wore to carry his own spare magazines and the satlink antenna, slung the rifle and the launcher across his own back. It was unwieldy, but *leave nothin' for Charlie* were the words he'd been raised by.

He moved up the hill, hearing the crack of fire from the more cautious members of his section—who had taken up covered positions to engage the League airborne troops instead of standing up like a *ghazi* idiot—and the stop-and-go popping of return fire.

He dropped just short of the lip of the hill, bellycrawled

to the top, peered around a rock. The hill flattened, then sloped down for maybe seventy meters before beginning to rise to the next higher level. The VDV squad had done a good job of becoming one with the planet, as was to be expected—these were *almost* his peers, after all, though still quite a ways shy of *Spetsnaz* or Green Beret mil spec. From the muzzle blast plumes kicked up as they returned fire, they seemed to have dispersed in good order.

The indiges of Jagun 23 had proved to be hardy, quick-learning, and adaptable. They had readily picked up their field-expedient dragoon drill. They failed to wilt under the merciless eye of the desert sun, even though the city Sarts for the most part had pulled far less time with their butts in the actual sand than Eddie himself. They had endured incoming artillery and air bombardment without coming completely unhinged, and had already sucked up losses Eddie estimated at better than a quarter of their number. Whatever Timur was selling, they were buying by the bale, and they bought Eddie as a combat leader.

What they mostly were not was good shots. And while Eddie had drilled them in simple fire and maneuver, most of their training had been geared toward the kind of shoot-and-scoot hassling they'd been dealing Al Capone's armor all day. The VDV facing them were mainly conscripts, of course, but they were better trained and drilled than standard-issue grunts. In a stand-up fight they could mop the foothills with Alfa, and probably the whole Jagun.

But as a little Jewboy in the Bronx, Fast Eddie had learned that fighting fair was a luxury he couldn't afford. He ducked back and crawled to the nearest man to his right, who to his relief turned out to be Maqsut, undamaged and calm as usual.

"We're gonna bust caps at these boys but not expose ourselves. Got that? We make noise, keep their minds on us, and let Bravo and Delta get around behind them."

Maqsut smiled and nodded. *"Yakhshi."*

"Like I told you before: don't bother aiming. Just use the

good old Nam Spray.'' To demonstrate, he rolled onto his back, held up his AK both-handed, and blazed off a long blind burst in the approximate direction of the enemy.

"Pass it on,'' he said, and started crawling the other direction.

It didn't exactly take *encouragement* to get his indiges to fire blind. Most of them were launching bullets as rapidly as the three-shot regulators on their advanced AKs would let them. Maybe one in three were shooting literally blind, eyes tight shut—which actually wasn't a terrible proportion, even for regular line troops.

When he was scuttling along his line, passing the word and checking on his boys, he was also not having to fire his piece at Russian soldiers. He wasn't going to, if he could help it. He would remember who and what he was, no matter how hard it was.

By the time he finished, Shy Bunny and Aliyev called in to say they'd worked their horsemen behind the VDV squad, flowing around hills east and west of the one across which Alfa and the Leaguers faced each other. Alfa was burning through its ammunition at a fearful clip, and must have convinced the airborne squaddies that whatever men the rebels had were staring right down the muzzles of their Kalashnikovs.

"Do it to it,'' he commanded.

Dust flew in miniature geysers along the crest of the hill and among the shrubs where the Leaguers were hidden. Eddie saw frantic movement as troopers scrambled out of suddenly compromised positions. It was every soldier's nightmare from the first war on: being taken from behind. *Surrounded*.

This was a serious departure from the book: a foe caught between hammer and anvil was not supposed to turn paper to the anvil's stone. The squad leader—probably a *praporshchik*, a warrant officer or extended-service noncom—had a tough call. Doctor of Military Science Anatoliy Karponin's pet doctrine of balls-out attack was the universal antidote for ambush or encirclement. The question was, which way would the *paras* break?

Clouds of white smoke abruptly boiling off the ground in front of Alfa's position provided the answer. One of Eddie's squaddies screamed "Gas!" and took off down the hill.

"No, wait! Hold your line, dammit, it's only smoke."

Eddie fired into the grenade smoke, aiming high, looking to herd the charging soldiers away from him. He saw figures moving in the smoke, and something khaki-colored bounced on the similarly colored earth right in front of him.

He ducked. He had instantly recognized what his boys called a *ragada*, an RGD hand grenade—he'd thrown them himself, often enough. It went off with a spiky bang, showering him with clods of dirt.

And someone tucked-and-rolled over the hilltop, right beside him.

They stared at each other. The Leaguer was a boy, beardless, his helmet gone, his hair yellow and surprisingly long. The blue and white stripes of a VDV T-shirt showed at the neck of his bulky flak jacket.

His blue eyes took in Eddie's own fair skin, light eyes, and Yankees cap. He swung up his assault rifle.

Eddie was faster. The boy's vestfront exploded in tatters. The 5.45mm rounds didn't penetrate, but multiple impacts knocked him on his butt.

He had a chance, then. Had a chance but didn't take it. He was VDV, and he thought he was a hero.

"American swine!" he screamed in Russian, raising his rifle again.

His head exploded before Eddie was conscious of having made a decision.

"You stupid son of a bitch," Eddie screamed in English, "*I'm Russian!*" He let the whole magazine go in a yammering burst, furious at the youth for forcing him to act.

A hand caught his arm. He spun, lips skinning back from teeth in an animal snarl, ready to use his hands or the big knife strapped to his belt.

It was Maqsut, looking concerned. "*Yakhshi*, Eddie-*janaap*," the Uzbek said. "Well done. But you can stop now because, as God wills, he's dead."

Eddie pulled free, dropped the orange plastic banana magazine, and slammed a fresh one home. Around him he heard only scattered firing. "What about the others?"

"They broke through. Some we killed. The others—" He pointed north across the Red Sands. "They prefer the desert to our company."

"Good for them. Let's get the hell out of here before more choppers come."

From rolling foothills the land gave way to a line of sandstone buttes like the sterns of docked supertankers. Once Jagun 23 was threading its way among them, Eddie felt safer. No way the tanks could follow them here, between these strangely smooth walls that looked as if they had been shaped by giant potter's hands.

Helicopters were another matter. They had burned every last surface-to-air missile they had in the last fight. But Al Capone was advancing on a front almost a hundred klicks across, according to reports Eddie had pulled in from the Net. Surely he had more pressing things to do with his air than flout his own beloved doctrine by reinforcing failure.

At the head of the column Eddie was back on Sertikan, who had been trolled in by a desert man from Charlie. He was happy not to have to hump it, but the blessing was decidedly mixed. His right thigh throbbed from the nip the mare had given him to show how happy she was about seeing him.

As he feared, Tashmat Kagorovich was dead, decapitated by a rocket. Jagun 23 had taken stiff losses—thirty-two missing and presumed dead, eleven more injured. But his men had hurt the League, especially in the fight with the helicopters and the lone *desant* squad. They had come out of battle exhilarated, the blood singing in their ears, as it must have sung in the ears of their nomad ancestors when they sacked some great and ancient city.

Of course, the downside of a combat-adrenaline head rush is the worst come-down known to science. The Jagun was beginning to return to earth. The chatter was dying, heads were slumping, horses were showing a tendency to wander off the narrow path that wound between the sheer buttes.

As for Eddie . . . he was doing a good job not thinking. The sun had fallen out of sight to the west, and though the late afternoon was little brighter than dusk, here the rocks were blaring the heat they'd been absorbing all day back at them. It was hot, and still, and the irregular clopping of the horses' hooves rebounded off the walls like volleys of stones, and the smell of hot sandstone enveloped you, made it easy to lose yourself in fugue and fuzz and fatigue. . . .

He felt it, beating on his back and the sides of his face off the rock walls close to either side: a rhythmic pulsing of the air.

"Shit," he said, as a man behind him screamed, *"Halikuptaar!"*

Chapter
TWENTY-SEVEN

The mottled dragonfly shape of an Mi-24D *Gorbach* swung into view a hundred meters ahead and fell into the gorge like a raptor. The roar of twin Isotov engines and the rotor throb filled the narrow passage and threatened to burst Eddie's head.

As the monstrous shape swept overhead, Eddie saw flame dance beneath its snout. He yelled and threw himself off Sertikan. Eight riders and mounts disappeared in sprays of blood and flesh as 23mm high-explosive shells raked them. Jagun 23 tried to scatter, to seek cover as it had been so endlessly drilled. The sandstone walls held most of it trapped, at the mercy of the great, flying, hunting thing.

Eddie was off Sertikan, kneeling, pulling Asraar's RPG-16 around his shoulder. They had one chance. Others still had RPGs, but only he had the knowledge.

Without a lot of luck, it wouldn't be enough.

"You can't hit a flying helicopter with that!" exclaimed Maqsut, clinging to the unyielding wall behind Eddie.

"I don't have to," Eddie said. "Not dead-on, anyway."

The column was strung out for half a kilometer. The Hunchback's momentum carried it beyond the column's tail before it climbed and banked to come back for a second run. It slid down smoothly between the sandstone walls. Eddie knelt, aimed, and almost at once fired.

"Missile launch!" Viktor sang.

"Yob tvoyu mat'!" Kolya said. It didn't look like a SAM launch, not enough smoke. So it would probably not track him—but the same smooth walls that trapped his quarry held him too.

He put the big ship's nose down. Too low and he'd splinter his rotor tips against the rock faces to either side, but if he could get under the missile . . .

And then memory kicked in, and he knew what had been done to him. His bellow of outrage was subsumed in the piercing crack of the rocket-propelled grenade exploding almost over his head.

RPG rounds are designed to self-destruct at the limit of their flight range, which for Eddie's was eight hundred meters. The Pushtuns of Afghanistan, for millennia the perfect spiritual masters of improvisation at war, had figured out a way to use the Nikolays' own safety feature against them.

The Mi-24—*Gorbach*, Hunchback, Hind, whatever—was a huge target. In flight, it was still virtually impossible to hit with an unguided AT rocket. But Eddie *could* get the small but potent warhead within its destructive radius of the chopper when it blew, if his timing was dead-on.

It was.

The blast sheared two of the Hind's five rotor blades off clean. Only the skill of one of the League's top rotary-wing pilots could keep it from dashing itself to flaming wreckage against the gorge walls or floor.

Not even Kolya the Cowboy could make the landing soft.

Kolya groaned and stirred. He'd banged his forehead against the instrument panel when the ship angled in. He hadn't blacked out—if a blow to the head did that to you, it generally broke something—but for a while his attention had sort of freewheeled.

He felt tugging on his right arm. "Lieutenant Kuliyev! Lieutenant? Kolya, for the love of God, come on!"

He looked around. It was Ivan, leaning over him, trying to pull him out of his seat. "Viktor—?" he asked.

The visor had popped off his instrument man's flight helmet, and the boy was unable to repress a sidewise flicker of his eyes. Kolya looked out the starred windscreen and groaned. The aircraft's nose had struck an outcrop, and its ten-metric-ton weight had collapsed the gunner's compartment.

"Shit," Kolya said. "Oh, no."

He tried to get up. Pain lanced through his back, and that weird loopy unbalanced feeling he knew so well, as if the upper part of his spine had slid off the lower.

"Vanya, my back," he said. "Get out of here. Save yourself. I can't move."

"Come on, Kolya. We've got to get out of here. The ship could blow—"

He screamed, wheeled around, clumsy in his flight suit. Blood from a gash across his back sprayed Kolya's face. Craning in his seat despite the agony in his back, Kolya saw a long-bladed knife slash at Ivan's face and futile upflung hands.

The boy fell across his seat. Behind him a man stood in the passenger space with muted light from the sprung side door falling across him. His face was young, younger maybe than Ivan's, but with Asians it was hard to tell. His black eyes were wide, uncomprehending, as if he were as much a victim as the boy he had just hacked to death.

Nikolay Kuliyev never believed in making excuses for his enemies. He took out his American revolver and blew apart the Asian boy's head.

"Stop! Goddam it, *don't go in there*!" Eddie did a Pony Express flying dismount off Sertikan as she was braking, that in other circumstances he would have been purely proud of. When they saw the attack chopper go down, what was left of the Jagun had gone howling forward at full gallop. Shamsiyev, the disaffected apprentice *manas* singer, had reached it first.

Eddie's command had been too late to stop the Kirghiz boy, but it brought the other squaddies up shy of the door. Eddie shouldered through them. Their bearded faces snarled. He was losing them; the sudden savage attack when they thought they were safe was turning them feral and ugly.

From inside the helicopter, shots, booming loud. Eddie pushed the two men nearest him into the others and dove through the door.

Even after the late-day gloom it seemed pitch-dark inside the craft. He hit the deck in a paratroop tuck, somersaulted to the far wall.

The smell of gunsmoke and spilled bowels filled his head. His eyes adjusted enough for him to see the pilot was still in the seat right ahead of him, waving a by-God humongous Dirty Harry six-shooter in the air. He was trying to swing it back to bear on the new intruder, but for some reason couldn't.

Eddie lunged forward between the seats, grabbed the gun hand's wrist. It seemed as big around as his thigh; this was one big mother, for a chopper jock.

"Will you knock it *off*?" he grunted, wrestling the gun hand with both of his. "A quick surrender is your one and only chance of getting out of this with all your parts attached."

The big red-mustached man had gotten a look at him now. "An American!" he bellowed, despite the fact Eddie had addressed him in Russian which he frankly thought was better than the pilot's. "A goddam American! This is just what we need, you sticking your long Yank noses in our business!"

Eddie gave a *kiai* grunt and whipped the back of the man's hand against the panel. Numbed, the fingers released the pistol. It dropped with a clunk on the rubberized metal deck.

Eddie let the wrist go and slumped back against what he immediately realized was a lifeless body already slumped across the instrument operator's seat. *Fuck it.* He opened his mouth to speak, but all that came out was an infinitely weary sigh.

The chopper driver hit his safety harness release, started to get out of his seat, then settled back with a groan. "If my back wasn't fucked up, I'd tear you in two, you meddling little fuck."

"Hey, buddy, anytime. Any fucking time. You and me're going round and round—*after* you get out of traction. Right now, you're gonna help me get your fat ass out of here."

With grumbling bad grace the red-mustached giant put his oak-trunk arm over Eddie's shoulder and let him help him to his feet. The two worked their way around the instrument operator's seat and turned around.

Turghun Aliyev stood in the doorway. His Kalashnikov was leveled from the hip.

Once again Eddie was acutely conscious that his ass was waving in the breeze. *Why does this always happen to me?*

"This man's a prisoner, Aliyev," he said warningly.

The aged head nodded slowly. "Our duty to Timur demands we guard his life as our own."

"That's the way to talk."

The old man looked at the body of his apprentice, sprawled practically at his feet. A tear welled from each eye, and made snail tracks through the red dust that caked his wrinkled cheeks.

"But this man has taken much from me. He must repay that debt."

Eddie shook his head. "Whoa, wait a minute, here. Remember what you said just a minute ago, about *duty* and *prisoners*—"

"You misunderstand me, *Leytenant*. I warrant his life and safety with my own. No harm shall come to him, except from his own kind."

"Fine. I'm real glad to hear you say that. Now help me get him the hell out of here before the gas tank goes."

The casualties Kolya's attack had inflicted broke the back of Jagun 23 as a fighting force. The survivors were so subdued they didn't even gripe when Eddie made them fashion a crude stretcher out of a tent and tent poles and lash the captured pilot to it. He didn't kid himself; he had been blooded beside his men, but without the presence of Aliyev at his side, dusty yet immeasurably dignified in his brimmed skullcap and Western-style suit, he would have been twisting in the wind for true.

They reached the top of the buttes, where they could take cover under sandstone overhangs overlooking the central bowl of the Qizil Qum, and dug in.

They spent a sleepless night tending wounds, maintaining weapons, and watching the light show as Al Capone kicked the crap out of the *ghazi*.

Chapter
TWENTY-EIGHT

"The mood is subdued here at the headquarters of the Turkestani Defense Force as the second day of the Battle of

the Red Sands winds to a close," the young woman said into the glare of TV floods. *"Troops of the defeated rebel army have been streaming south past Timur's tent city since midafternoon. Already observers from nations around the world have begun an exodus from the camp, as the magnitude of the catastrophe has grown clearer with every hour."*

"Jacqui," Tewfik whined in her ear. "Jacqui, why aren't you filing? For heaven's sake, everyone in the *world* is scooping you on this!"

She brushed at her ear as if trying to drive away a gnat. Certainly it looked as if the story was breaking. Likewise the rebellion.

The *ghazi* had awaited the League armored columns in positions dug into the sand of the great cobra-head bowl in the midst of Red Sands. They fought with fanatical courage, and they inflicted savage losses on Anatoliy Karponin's troops, launching anti-tank missiles at thin rear armor from concealed firing pits, throwing themselves bodily against main battle tanks with shaped-charge mines strapped to their chests.

But they did not fight a battle of dispersal and constant movement, as the irregular Jagun before them had done. They stood and slugged it out. That gave Karponin the opportunity to use his artillery and his strike aircraft and his darting *desant* units, as well as his beloved tanks. Inevitably, the superior weight of League metal and League manpower told.

"TDF command has at last confirmed what our colleagues with Desert Wind have been telling us: Timur's elite ghazi formations are broken, bypassed, in flight, or destroyed. The bulk of the Turkestani Defense Forces, massed behind the ghazi line, are fleeing south toward the Amu. Meanwhile League Frontal Aviation is claiming over a thousand trucks of various sizes destroyed, despite ferocious opposition from SAMs. . . ."

Jacqui turned and began to walk away between the tents, away from the satisfied drone of her rival telejournalist. Tewfik trotted by her shoulder.

"If you're not going to get the story you came here for," he said, "can't we at least get *out* of here?"

"Twefik, there's something wrong."

"Of course there's something wrong. The Russian Army is on the way!"

"No. That's not it. Something's wrong here. What's happening now . . . I don't how, but I feel it, I know it: it's not the *story*."

"Not since Desert Storm, whose name this whirlwind assault echoes, has the world seen a multinational force of such size—nor, apparently, a victory so one-sided. . . ."

"You're crazy," Tewfik said.

She stopped, faced him, smiled. "Of *course* I am. I've always been crazy. That's why I'm the best, and not the bitch back there with the plastic tits."

Timur and his *orloks*—an ancient Mongol term, literally "raging torrents," which meant field marshals—were gathered around a table with their heads bent over an old-fashioned paper map when Francis Marron burst into the room. His collar was open, his hair disarrayed.

He pointed a finger at Timur. *"You."*

Timur raised his shrouded head. "Mr. Marron," he said mildly, "you're distraught."

"Your army's been destroyed," Marron said. "The ones who aren't dead are only alive until the league can hunt them down. The dream is over, Timur. The revolution is dead, and you killed it."

Blue-skullcapped guards seized the American's arm. Timur waved them off.

"If that is the case, I accept full responsibility."

"That won't wash, Timur. We're talking about people's lives here. You held them in your hands. You had a chance to preserve them, safeguard them. But you threw them all away. Because of pride, and some crazy anachronistic idea of *freedom*!" He spat the last word out like shit.

Sher Khan, the huge Afghan, growled deep in his throat. The small, slim raghead, Ali, smiled grimly.

"Freedom is something we think worth dying for, Mr. Marron," he said. "In this backward corner of the world."

Marron shook his head. "You're nuts. You're all nuts. Karponin will bulldoze your precious ancient cities and send your people to rot in camps. And the rest of the world won't make a peep.

"You could have had help. You could have had a *sponsor*. If not us, somebody. But no. You had to go your own way. And your own way led right to hell!"

Timur stood upright, unflinching. "Are you finished, Mr. Marron?"

Marron hung his head. "Yeah. Yeah, I'm finished."

"Then I beg that you excuse us. We have much work to do."

Marron allowed the Sons of the Sky-Blue Wolf to lead him away. "Mr. Marron," Timur called.

It seemed to take all Marron's willpower to roll his head around on slack muscles.

"Thank you for your concern," Timur said.

A few minutes later Timur excused himself for a walk in the nighttime air. He stood on the northern edge of the encampment, gazing north across the sand.

He heard steps behind him. "Timur."

"Ms. Gendron. I'm surprised to find you still here."

Her laugh was brittle. "If you are, you don't know me. I'm a bitter-end kind of woman."

"So you believe you are going to witness the bitter end of the Red Sands rebellion."

"No," she said quietly. "I don't know why, but I don't."

They stood for a while in silence. Wisps of Middle Eastern rock drifted by on a slow heavy breeze.

"Ms. Gendron," Timur finally said, "I owe you a substantial debt for the coverage you gave our revolution at a crucial moment."

She thrust her head forward. Her eyes were bright and feral. "Does that mean there's something going on? Can I have an interview?"

"I won't tell you. What I will do is promise you that, if you remain patient a very little time longer, you will have all the story you could desire. And it will be yours exclusively."

"Does that mean you win," she asked, "or does that mean you lose?"

When he turned his head to her, his eyes were bright with what she was startled to recognize as mirth. "Either way," he said, "it's a great story, don't you think?"

Rotor wash raised spiky wavelets on the surface of the small brackish pool as the *Gorbach* settled out of the starry sky. Tall and confident, General Colonel Anatoliy Karponin stepped onto the hard-packed soil before the engine whine died.

The colonel of the Ukrainian Republic regiment bivouacked by the pool came to meet him. "General, this is a most delightful surprise."

Karponin laughed. Two separate League Army videocam teams scrambled from the chopper, almost jostling each other into the pond in their zeal to ensure that the great man's every word, his every gesture, was recorded in his hour of triumph.

"You don't think I'd miss something like this, do you *Polkovnik* Novikov?" he asked. "Where is it?"

The colonel nodded over his shoulder at a tree that stood by itself about fifty meters above the pond. Karponin strode toward it.

The center of the bowl in the midst of Red Sands is an arid place. But the higher ground surrounding it does provide a watershed of sorts. At the lowest point, a few pools accumulate, giving sustenance to clumps of habitation too tiny and depressing to be called *koopkhoz*, like the one, now deserted, through which the officers walked with their entourages trailing behind.

"One of our chemical-warfare platoons found it, when

they were checking to make sure that the rebels had not poisoned the pond," the colonel said.

"I see," Karponin said, halting to inspect the tree from a few meters away. It was the kind known in the West as Russian olive or oleaster, with drooping willowy branches whose leaves, darker above than below, were gray with a silver sheen like fine field-mouse fur in the light of the crescent moon.

"These trees are native to the Amu and Syr basins," Colonel Novikov said. "This one may be an accidental tourist." He reached out to pluck one of the tiny pale-green fruits from among leaves and needlelike thorns. "These are a popular food for birds; one might have dropped a seed here in its feces. Or it may have been planted deliberately, as a windbreak or just to relieve all this desolation—"

"I know all that," Karponin interrupted. "I am a Russian, not an American; I have not forsaken nature. Now, where is this controversial plaque?"

Novikov nodded. An aide stepped forward and shyly proffered an oblong tablet about twenty-five centimeters by twenty, wrapped in plastic.

One of Karponin's half-dozen bodyguards thrust forward, a short, broad man with a face far less picturesquely scarred than his master's. He wore tanker insignia, and around his thick neck wore an Israeli-style sling from which hung an Advanced Kalashnikov with a short submachine-gun-style barrel dropped in.

"Is it safe?" he demanded.

Novikov laughed, somewhat nervously. "More than safe. We've even run it through a mobile medical X-ray unit. It's just a bronze plaque, with a most remarkable inscription. "

"General, this whole area is completely secure. The soil around the tree is packed solid; there've been no mines buried here. As for snipers"—he stepped back and encompassed the low surrounding hills with a wave—"the perimeter is secured by an entire VDV battalion. Your man's concern is entirely unwarranted, General Colonel."

He gestured at the plastic package. "Aren't you going to open it?"

Karponin eyed it as if it were a fresh goat turd. "This won't do. Put it back on the tree where you found it, so I can discover it."

The colonel frowned. He obviously didn't understand. That was part of the reason he was a colonel while Karponin—several years younger, by appearance—was about to accept his marshal's baton from a grateful League. Karponin had always been an admirer of Douglas MacArthur, and he had taken especially to heart the example of the great American commander in wading ashore through the Philippine surf again and again until he had the footage he wanted in the can.

At a nod from the still-bemused Novikov the young aide unwrapped the plaque and gave it to a soldier, who stepped up and hung it from a nail driven into the tree trunk.

Karponin looked to his video crews. "We're ready, General."

The spots came on, sandblasting the scene with white light. Karponin nodded and marched forward with forthright stride. Head lifted and turned to a precise angle to express his best three-quarters profile to the camera, he read the inscription.

It was in Russian, with Arabic script below. It read:

ANATOLIY KARPONIN DIES BENEATH THIS TREE.

So the nigger has read his Sun Tzu. He didn't say it aloud. In today's climate there were some sentiments it was improvident to express, even in the presence of the loyal League Army press and archivists corps. And maybe this lovely scene would help bring about a climatic change.

In the original, which Karponin knew by heart, a rival of Sun Tzu's disciple Sun Pin had been lured to a great tree on which was inscribed, P'ANG CHÜAN DIES BENEATH THIS TREE. As P'ang Chüan read it, ten thousand crossbowmen concealed in a defile shot him to pieces.

In his paranoid delusional way, Timur had obviously thought to re-create that legendary event. But it had all gone wrong for him, as his whole nigger-foolish revolution had. There were no ten thousand rebel crossbowmen in these hills, only a cordon of Karponin's toughest troops.

It was a moment of the most exquisite irony, the most perfect symbolism. Even Karponin's genius for self-promotion could not have contrived a more perfect climax to Operation Desert Wind.

He set back his head and began to laugh.

The living core of the Russian olive had been hollowed out from above by patient hands. As Al Capone's laughter reverberated across the oasis, his image was perceived by a fiber-optic video pickup threaded from the heart of the tree to the surface of the shiny bark. Ni-cad batteries fed a tiny current to the satlink antenna concealed within a thick branch.

Al Capone was still laughing when a return signal pulsed downward from the great unseen satellite-based Net overhead.

The ten kilograms of League Armed Forces—issue plastic explosives that had been sealed in the tree's bole by the gardeners of Fergana exploded. The wood of the trunk splintered into shrapnel, riding the shockwave.

Before they could raise him up and bear him to his waiting helicopter, Anatoliy Karponin died beneath the tree.

Chapter
TWENTY-NINE

Out in that hot night, the tribes begin to move. Kypchak and kumli; Uzbek, Tadzhik, Turkmen, Tatar; Kazakh, Karakalpak, Kirghiz; the Great Horde, the Middle Horde,

*the Little Horde, the Golden Horde: the sons and daughters
of the Sky-Blue Wolf. They move.*

The survivors of Jagun 23 had worked their haggard way
to the northeast rim of the great cobra's-hood bowl, hoping
to slip away southeast and lose themselves in the most
desolate part of the Red Sands. One of the *kumli* knew a
route through the middle of it that he claimed Chingis Khan
himself had used when he pulled his epic end-run on
Ali-ed-Din II Muhammad of Khwarizm. Fast Eddie believed
that route must lie farther west, nearer the Aral. The really
significant thing about the desert man's road was that it
didn't run through the middle of Desert Wind.

At midnight they were still on the move when they heard
engine sounds. Eddie deployed three sections into ambush
with their remaining AT launchers. Telling Aliyev to keep a
particular eye on the captive, he took Alfa and a *kumli* from
Charlie forward to investigate.

It was a truck of magnificent age, grinding up a track that
was scarcely more than imaginary. Its bed was surmounted
by a high tarp cover. A whip antenna had been fastened to
the hood, and a tiny flag that looked suspiciously like the
multicolored banner of Free Turkestan fluttered from it.

"What the fuck, over?" Eddie started to rise.

Maqsut laid a hand on his arm. "Let me," he said. "If
they are ours, the sight of a foreigner might set them off."

"Good idea." Eddie got ready to rock and roll on his
AK, just in case.

Maqsut walked slowly down the hill, waving his hands
over his head. The truck stopped. Several men climbed out
of the back and covered him with Kalashnikovs. He exchanged a few words with them and then with the driver,
then signaled Eddie to come down.

Eddie did. "What's this? You boys must have balls bigger
than your brains to be headed north after the last two days."

Once he said it, he realized it hadn't exactly been diplomatic. The newcomers looked at each other and laughed as if he were the funniest stand-up turn on sat.

Eddie looked at Maqsut. The Uzbek shrugged.

"We're the Free Turkestan artillery," a chicken-neck kid in a Tashkent *tyubeteyka* announced. "We're going on the offensive."

Even heroes need sleep, thought *Polkovnik* Efremov, commanding the Russian lead regiment leading the League thrust into the Red Sands. *Screw Al Capone if he doesn't like it*.

Around him his men were digging gratefully in for a few hours' rest. They had fought a stiff battle today against the so-called *ghazi*. Men and machines were in no condition to proceed.

He carefully scanned their surroundings with night-vision binoculars. He was not really happy with their disposition; this was dune country, the first they had come into—rather to his surprise, for he had imagined the Red Sands Desert to be full of the famous crescent dunes of Central Asia, the *barkhan*. It wasn't practical to encamp a "daring thrust" armored regiment on sand dunes, so he had been compelled to pick a spot more or less surrounded by high ground.

He doubted the bandits were going to move against him. Today's fighting had produced a decisive League victory; and the rebels his men had sent running before them showed no sign of slowing down shy of the Iranian border. But he took nothing for granted, as a matter of principle, and so he would plant patrols and observation posts on the surrounding dunes.

He lowered his glasses. He had done what he could; his men had done what they could. Division was calling for him to press on, quoting bales of armed forces aphorisms about warding off inaction and warding off passivity. He'd told them they could shoot him if they wanted, but his immediate concern was warding off the collapse of his command.

Entering the door of his personal trailer, he heard an outcry behind. He stopped and looked back.

The southern sky was alive with climbing streaks of light.

Standing in the headquarters tent, watching the monitors from which Ali al-'Ajawi coordinated the hamstringing of Al Capone's army, Jacqui Gendron got the story Timur had promised her.

The Indonesian smart rounds Timur had bought for the BM-13s Khaalis provided him had boosters that increased their range dramatically. From all sides of the vast depression rockets reached out for the concentrations the satellites overhead showed their human operators. So refined was the sats' real-time surveillance capability that rebel rocketeers could pick their targets according to priorities that had been drilled into them in advance.

Least important were the tanks: *khudaga tanklar bering*. Seeker-heads would sense their mass and guide rockets into them if they were in an impact zone, but they were incidental to the secondary targets, the APCs that bore the troops.

Highest priority was *resupply*. No modern army lives off the land, and in this desperate land every gram the army consumed had to be replaced by freight hauled overland: fuel, lubricants, ammunition, replacement parts, treads for the tanks and APCs—and of course, food and water. As they were used up—and war consumes stocks at a terrifying rate—the army would become first immobile, and then impotent, and finally dead.

In the north, more of Khaalis's BM-13s had been left behind on either side of Karponin's axis of advance, dug in, concealed under tarps, with clumps of hardy bunchgrass on top to fool aerial and satellite eyes. They began flaying the convoys rushing to feed the voracious army with miniature cluster-bomb dispenser rounds. The bomblets would do no harm to tanks, and little to BMPs, but tore hell out of soft targets like lorries and tanker trucks. The hidden Stalin Organs also launched Brazilian-made rounds that sowed mines along the supply line, both anti-armor and anti-personnel.

Enemy artillery was excellent, and its counterbattery capability had been steadily improving as the League creaked and lurched its way into the computer age. But the League gunners had a problem. They could sometimes backtrack the incoming rockets to their source. But by the time they fired a comeback mission, the launch trucks would have simply driven away, to find a new location in which to reload, fire, and move again. The rebel artillerists had only to stay in range, and their laptop computers and cheap satlink antennas would tell them where to shoot.

With his skirmishers and his *ghazi*, Timur had drawn the advancing army into an apparently victorious charge into the heart of wasteland. Then he cut off its head, and cut its lifeline. It was a trick not unfamiliar to that destroyer and progenitor of Central Asia, Chingis Khan.

As dawn begin to seep up out of the eastern sand, carefully orchestrated mobs spilled onto runways throughout League-held Kazakhstan and the Turkmen Republic. They would be cleared away, eventually, by tear gas and machine gun fire. But they would prevent air support or resupply of the beleaguered army for crucial hours of daylight.

Reports were still flooding Timur's command center when the sun arrived, but the outcome was already clear. Rebel rockets had caused few casualties. But they had done what they were meant to do.

Desert Wind had blown itself out.

Timur returned to his own tent. What could be done, he had done. He had no taste for the celebration that had broken out in the command center. He needed rest to face the future squarely.

In Tashkent he lived like a prince. In the field he lived more like an anchorite, with a small wardrobe, a low portable desk with a satlinked notebook computer on it, and a cheap modern Bukharan rug to sit and sleep on.

He was hanging up his jacket when he heard the tent flap

rustle. He turned, wondering if one of the League infiltrators he knew his camp must harbor had come to repay the favor he had done Anatoliy Karponin.

It was Jacqui Gendron. With her hair hanging unbound around her shoulders, taking fire from the light of the kerosene lantern hung from the center post, her features seemed softer, younger.

"You've won," she said.

He watched as she unbuttoned her blouse, let it slip over her shoulders. Her breasts were small and pointed. The nipples stood erect in the dawn chill. She kicked her boots off, skinned her khaki slacks down her slim shanks, and came to him, naked.

Colonel Efremov stood inside the door of his trailer, fully dressed with service sidearm in hand, feeling foolish. If the firing outside, that had burst out and then faded away as quickly as a spring rain squall on the Caspian, signaled a rebel attack, then a mere pistol wasn't going to do him much good. But he could not stand the thought of waiting for death empty-handed.

A knock on the door. "Colonel Efremov, it's safe to come out now. They're all dead."

He emerged into milky dawn light spilling over the dune tops. Bodies sprawled on the ground, the nearest not ten meters from his trailer.

He walked to it. It wore a robe that seemed made all of patches. A hood had fallen back to reveal the thrusting Persian features of a totally hairless man. No eyebrows, no beard, no hair on the scalp.

Efremov shuddered. *Fanatics*. The army had been briefed on the Sufi cults, the *tariqa* of Central Asia. The dead man belonged to the most mysterious and most fanatical, the Kalandars.

An Advanced AK with a submachine-gun-style barrel lay by the dead man's outflung hand.

"They were coming for you, Colonel," the head of his

security unit said. "God knows how the devil-worshiping bastards made it this far before we cut 'em down." He crossed himself, Orthodox-style, and spat.

An explosion shattered the eerie post-coital silence that followed a firefight. Efremov whirled to see a dirty brown ball of smoke rolling into the sky on the west side of camp. He heard more blasts, shouting.

He ran, his security boss racing after, trying to catch up to his superior and keep him out of danger but hampered by his battle dress.

A pair of ragged figures were racing for the dunes. Efremov arrived in time to see them knocked down by a horizontal storm of gunfire.

They had done their damage. Efremov watched as water bled into the sand from a thousand holes in the fat flanks of a big tank truck. The saboteurs had used claymore mines.

"A feint," he said, lips curling back from his teeth. "The attack on my trailer was a feint. They were after our *water*."

The security officer clutched his arm. "Colonel—up there."

A man on horseback had appeared on top of a dune, alone in the eye of the rising sun. He wore a triangular Mongol hat. A long straightened-sperm RPG-16 lay across his saddlebow. In the binoculars someone pressed into his hands the colonel saw that his broad flat face was largely obscured by mirror shades.

The man held up something: a canteen. Deliberately, as if a thousand edgy soldiers did not have him zeroed in their Kalashnikov sights, he unscrewed the cap. He put the canteen to his lips, tipped his head back and drank, wiped his mouth, and carefully replaced the lid.

Then he cocked his arm and threw the canteen.

It landed halfway down the dune's flank and rolled almost to the hastily strung perimeter wire. Every eye in camp followed it.

The Battle of the Red Sands was over.

PART III

The Land Of Flowers

Leave the Turks in peace, so long as they leave you in peace.

—*hadith* [saying of Muhammad]

Chapter
THIRTY

Hands clasped behind his back, League Undersecretary of State Pavel Valentinovich Vorov'yev stood gazing out the dacha window into pinewoods that stood black in the shin-deep snows northeast of Moscow. As it always did when he stood in such a position, the long white glass-fragment scar stretched taut across his right cheekbone itched.

His visitor was a fit light-skinned black man in his early fifties, with a square honest face and a dignity-adding frosting of gray in his hair and mustache. He was photogenic enough to be a TV news anchor and had been, before American press restrictions forced CNN overseas. Like so many modern Americans, Talbot White had gotten along by going along.

"Mr. Undersecretary," the American emissary said, "I don't know how to say it any more strongly: *we are not helping Timur*. I admit it was considered, maybe even tried. But he wasn't having any of it."

"I don't disbelieve you, Talbot," Vorov'yev said, turning with a smile the same temperature as the hoarfrost clinging to the windowpane.

He spoke so quietly that the American goggled slightly behind his square wire-frame glasses and said, "What?"

"I believe you—speaking unofficially. But it doesn't matter."

"What are you talking about?"

"The League is in turmoil since that idiot Al Capone led his Operation Desert Wind to such a cinematic defeat."

Despite the tension pressing in on his skin like Jupiter's atmospheric pressure, White had to suppress a smile. He had seen much of Operation Desert *Storm* from firsthand, in his reportorial capacity. Having invited the comparison, Karponin deserved the posthumous ridicule heaped on him; his PR ploy made his defeat seem that much more comprehensive.

On the other hand, White thought, *if Desert Wind produced the same lack of political consequences Desert Storm did, we wouldn't be* having *this conversation*.

"The republics are upset by their losses—hypocritical swine that they are; the bulk of casualties were Great Russians, in the League and Russian Republic armies. The Balts, who have been scanting their commitments since the day Operation *Sukhovey* commenced, are threatening to pull out of the League Armed Forces altogether. The other republics blame the Balts for not doing their parts. Georgia and Armenia, meanwhile, are in a state of terror that the Mongol Yoke will descend upon them at any moment. Popular militias are forming on a scale not seen since the virtual civil wars of the early nineties, and the governments of those republics are handing out arms to them. And on our borders, our traditional enemies sit fingering their knives and smiling. Do not deny that this is true, Mr. White."

White shook his head—not *No, it isn't true*, but *No, I won't deny it*. Last week he had been in Germany, pleading off the record for the *Bundeswehr* to call off large-scale maneuvers scheduled along the Polish frontier; Central Europe and the Balkans were having hysterics, and the Germans had already announced they would defy a European Council vote condemning the exercise. He felt something near admiration for the way a German general officer could tell him *Fuck off and die, nigger* with no more than a flick of ice-blue eyes.

"The Central Asian rebellion threatens to destroy the

League. At the center we understand the danger inherent in that, as the fools in the republics do not."

Things fall apart; the center cannot hold, White mentally quoted to himself. But he said, "I understand your concern, as both an official of the League and a citizen of the Russian Republic. But even shorn of the republics, Russia is a superpower."

"The wolves are gathering, Mr. White, and not all of them wear sky-blue hats. You cannot understand the implications this crisis holds for us, and I am not permitted to enlighten you. I would not if I could; they are our concern, not yours. What you need to know—and your President Callendar, and his ever-so-clever National Security Adviser, is that we will not go down alone."

He dropped his voice back to the quivering edge of audibility. "And we still have the means to ensure that we do not."

Like the missiles of Tyuratam, just a stone's throw away from rebel Uzbekistan. "Are you threatening us?" White said, more in disbelief than outrage.

"I am stating fact. Whether or not you had a hand in setting loose this monster in Central Asia is irrelevant. It must be stopped up before it pulls the League apart.

"Or the world will be left with no superpowers at all. Good day."

The blood had long since been scrubbed from the cement beneath the old men's black-slippered feet. They cast no shadows; the north China sun was an unemphatic disk behind a scrim of white gauzy cloud, giving little light and less heat. As the two men in their quilted blue coats walked, they kept their round, close-cropped heads down, and their breath smoked as they spoke.

"The situation in Russian Turkestan is most unstable," said the younger, a weanling of sixty-five. "Perhaps we should emplace a full diplomatic envoy."

The elder was eighty-one, but his steps were firm as they

walked past a pair of guardsmen with rifles at parade rest
and cap straps beneath their chins. The Party's security
ministry had a large contingent in place this morning, as
every morning, holding back the crowds that thronged the
dawn streets of Beijing, so that the rulers of the last
Communist nation on earth might enjoy their stroll in Gate
of Heavenly Peace Square in imperial isolation.

"We have dispatched a representative," he said in his
quiet, almost plodding way. He was a man who weighed
and tasted and learned the shape of each word before he let
it out of his mouth. When he was a boy in school, his
classmates rode him endlessly, thinking he was slow. They
had learned better. "One who is quite expert in the history
and culture of the region."

"But do we not need someone expert in politics and
economics and military affairs? The eyes of the world are on
Central Asia."

"Our intelligence services have people in place, of course,"
the elder said with a touch of admonitory firmness. "Our
representative is the one we deemed appropriate."

"A professor," the younger said, "and a woman, at that.
These are Muslims. How seriously will they take her?"

"Timur professes himself a believer in equality of the
sexes. He will take her seriously, or lose some of his gloss
as a hero of modernization. As to why we chose her, instead
of a trained diplomatist—though the League seems para-
lyzed by its defeat last year, the continued existence of Free
Turkestan is controversial at best. Our veto alone prevented
the U.N. Security Council from condemning the rebellion,
after all, and no legitimate government on earth has yet
recognized the secession."

A shadow of a smile passed over his face, like a cloud
over the sun. "And how could they, since the governments
of Uzbekistan, Tadzhikstan, and Kirghizstan are *already*
recognized, and have been for years? Governments-in-exile
though they now are, they remain the legitimate authorities.
We could scarcely send a professional diplomat to treat with

rebels. Dr. Shih is an intelligent young woman, eminently qualified to do that which we need her to do."

The younger man glanced at the elder from beneath thick eyebrows. The elder's face was serene, untouched by worry or years, as smooth as a baby's.

"There is one more matter I should bring up," the younger man said, his voice dropping further. "Our intelligence services have turned up evidence that the woman has ties to dissidents, and may have taken part in the illegal outburst here in Tienanmen."

The older man permitted himself a full smile. *So the young dog tests whether the older has left his throat unprotected.* Well, the boy was here to learn.

"Perhaps you are not completely familiar with Sun Tzu," he said.

The young man missed a step. Mao, whose divine ten-story countenance beamed down upon them from the wall beside them, had cribbed from Sun Tzu almost as extensively as he did from Confucius. Since the passing of the man, if not his cult, the politically ambitious were well advised to familiarize themselves with the original article.

"I have not studied him as profoundly as you, of course. I humbly beg enlightenment."

The smooth moon face nodded. "Recall the thirteenth chapter."

" 'On Making Use of the Cracks in the Door,' concerning the employment of secret agents." the younger man said quickly.

"Just so. The seventh paragraph tells us that 'what is called "foreknowledge" cannot be elicited from spirits, nor from gods, not by analogy with past events, nor from calculations. It must be obtained from men who know the enemy situation.' "

"Yes."

"Now, recount to me the five types of agents which constitute what Sun Tzu called the 'Divine Skein.' "

"Native, inside, doubled, expendable, and living," the younger man recited.

"Precisely. At the moment, our professor is in the category of living agents, 'those who return with information.' " He smiled a great benevolent smile.

"Do you see, then, how convenient it is that, should circumstances dictate, she can be shifted from the fifth category to the fourth without loss to the state?"

Little Tarim saw them walking across the former cotton fields toward the village at sunset: six men bent under the weight of heavy packs, wearing odd bulky clothing patterned in earth tones, strung out in a vee, kicking over hard khaki clods and trampling weeds. To his terror and exhilaration they carried guns, long and black, held across the front of their hips.

Tarim was eight. His village, on the brink of the Muyun Qum, the Camel's Neck Desert of Kazakhstan's rebel Dzhambul Oblast', comprised eleven families, Uzbek with a strong admixture of Kirghiz. It had seen no fighting: Desert Wind had blown far away in the west. But the settlement, small as it was, had sent three young men as volunteers to Timur's army. Tarim had listened intently to the stories of the two who returned to help organize the population for defense.

It seemed to him the strangers were not threatening. If they meant to attack, would they not be sneaking, making use of what little cover was offered by furrowed, fallow fields awaiting recultivation in food crops less demanding of soil and water than the League's accursed cotton? Would there not be more of them? Six men weren't much of an assault force.

But he could take nothing for granted. Akim and Dmitriy never tired of emphasizing that. Tarim hid in the weeds on the bank of a dry *aryk*, behind the pale green spray of a tamarisk shrub.

They were going to pass within fifty meters of him, two

walking the narrow dirt road, the others fanned out in pairs in the fields to either side. He flattened himself into the winter-dry stubble, wondering what he should do. Could he run to warn the village without being seen?

The farther away of the two men on Tarim's side of the road suddenly stopped and looked straight at him. Tarim's heart jumped into his throat. He was the biggest man the boy had ever seen—except that there was a second man the same incredible size right on the other side of the road.

The enormous man waved. "Come ahead on out, little buddy," he called in the worst Russian accent Tarim had ever heard. "I see you."

Tarim froze. On the road stood a tall man. His face was the color of pale skin tanned well by the sun, and even at this he was clearly as handsome as any actor Tarim had seen on the television set the widow Chichek had bought with the money she got from the government after some drunk accidentally backed a tractor built on the chassis of a PT-76 light tank over her husband in the Ukrainian Republic. He was clearly a hero. He waved to Tarim.

"Don't worry," he called. "We won't hurt you. We're Americans."

Americans! At last! With a happy smile Tarim jumped up and ran to greet them.

"Despite the apparent withdrawal of the Baltic states from the war effort, and in the face of increasingly severe street demonstrations in Moscow by Russian Republic citizens who fear that the rebels may press their advantage by launching a jihad, the League military buildup continues slowly in government-held areas of the republics of Kazakhstan and Turkmenia, which surround rebel Central Asia. As yet, League forces show no signs of readiness to force a showdown with the insurgents, led by mystery man Timur. President Fyodorin continues to rule out the use of chemical or nuclear weapons against 'League citizens on League soil.' Unofficial armed forces sources insist, however, that

counterguerrilla operations by elite 'caravan hunter' teams continue to inflict serious damage on the rebels.''

The man on the bed grunted.

"Though Timur last week refused the latest demand by Iran's ruling Islamic Revolutionary Council that he turn his rebellion into the holy war that Muscovite protesters so fear, cross-border fighting between Iran and the League is reported daily both by satellites and observers on the ground. Substantial numbers of League troops likewise remain tied down on the borders with the People's Republic of China and Central Europe. In a possible move to relieve the tension along the western frontier, League Foreign Minister Zhuravlev met yesterday with German Foreign Minister Hofstädter. Though the talks were private, rumors hinted that the talks concerned possible League support for German claims to East Prussia, Silesia, and the city of Gdansk, formerly Danzig, now part of Poland. The rumors prompted widespread demonstrations throughout a Central Europe already alarmed by increasing German militarism."

The scene on the hospital-room wall switched from BMP-2s rolling across the chemical-yellowed mud of the Aral Sea fringe to a crowd waving signs—at least half of which were in English—and then to a dark-mustached man in a turtleneck, who said, "We remember too well the last time the Germans and the Russians got in bed together. The child born was World War II."

He was replaced by an anchorwoman with a beautiful but nonthreatening milk-chocolate face. The face said, "European Council Chairperson van Damme today issued a statement condemning both Germany and Poland for their anticommunitarian stance in refusing to sit down at the negotiating table."

"Coming up this hour on the Satellite News Network, Australian peacekeeping forces in Papua New Guinea fire on strikers at the Panguna Copper Mine seeking independence for the island of Bougainville, and a member of Jakarta University's controversial 'Gang of Four' physicists

announces that recent discoveries by the team may indicate that the speed-of-light barrier may not be unbreakable after all. But first, Americans today bade farewell to a fallen hero. . . ."

Switch to a flag-draped coffin being lowered into the earth. "Though as secretary for Enforcement Affairs he was one of the most influential men in Washington, Larry Doyle never lost the common touch. During his NFL playing days he was known as America's best-loved nose tackle—"

An honor guard in full midnight-blue FedPol battle dress, swept bicycle racer's helmets with heavily polarized Lexan visors, and bulky Kevlar body armor with steel and ceramic inserts, raised bullpup submachine guns and blasted a salute at the low overcast. Vader's Raiders, everybody called them.

"—and even as secretary he was beloved of millions of children in America's crime-ravaged streets for his continuing portrayal of McGruff, the Crime Dog. Now he has been struck down by an assassin's hand while playing that famous role. . . ."

"Holy Mother of Kazan," the man on the bed said in disgust. He needed a drink. He would not ask for one. Even where he was now they had AA, but he had five years and hadn't needed meetings all that often for a long time. Credit his wife: *darling, how are you now?* He was free to call her, that was the irony. He had been authoritatively advised not to—for her sake, not for his. He missed her and their daughter a whole lot more than the booze. He reached for the remote control to switch channels.

The door to his room opened. His mouth tightened under his extravagant red mustache. *Not time for PT again.* He was determined not to let his reinjured back make him a cripple, but there was no way he could fool himself into thinking he enjoyed the therapy.

A small man in a cast-off Western suit coat that managed to be at once neat and shabby entered. His mustache and eyebrows were silver. He wore a white skullcap with a rolled-up black bottom.

The man on the bed moaned. This was worse than physical therapy.

The old man drew up a straight-backed wooden chair next to the bed and sat down with vast and compact dignity. "Good evening, Lieutenant Kuliyev. I hope you rested well after our afternoon session."

"This is a war crime, Aliyev," Nikolay Stepanovich Kuliyev said. "Amnesty International is gonna hear about this."

"You did your duty most bravely, Lieutenant Kuliyev. But in doing so you caused a substantial loss to my country, my people, and me personally. International law requires that we feed you and shelter you and tend your wounds. Do we not do these things?"

"You do," Kolya the Cowboy acknowledged in a mutter.

"But Timur's law requires restitution. We both know it could be worse."

He sat for a moment as if meditating, then raised his face to the window. His old eyes looked out unfocused as the Russian Colonial heart of Tashkent came alive with lights.

"As always, you will learn the lesson by heart first in Russian, then in Kirghiz. This evening's verses concern how Manas's wonderful horse rescued him from the Tanguts."

Kolya clutched his sheets and made an inchoate noise.

"Come, now, Lieutenant. You are making excellent progress. You have only two hundred forty-five thousand seven hundred lines left to learn. Shall we begin?"

Tex extended a huge hand toward the village, two hundred meters away. All the square adobe structures were burning brightly, except the headman's three-room structure in the middle. Tex thumbed a button on the little transmitter, and the headman's house erupted like a volcano.

Rocket-propelled grenades began to cook off and whiz away into the night, drawing tails of light behind them. The men of the half-detachment of Texas Team started walking away across the plowed dry earth, except for Tex and his twin brother Buddy, who stood there with the flickering light of flames and explosions playing on their Moon Pie faces.

Georgie clutched Buddy's sleeve. "Come *on,* you idiots. Or do you want an OG-7 to land right on top of your fat heads?"

Letting his M60E3—at eight kilos a "lightweight" 7.62mm machine gun—dangle from its sling around his water buffalo neck, Buddy wrapped a hand in the front of Georgie's blouse and without looking plucked him off the ground. "Who you callin' *fat,* Buttercup?"

"Tell him, Buddy," Tex said.

Twenty meters away Pete stopped and looked back. "Quit screwing around. It's time to move out."

Buddy dropped the Georgian. "We just wanna watch the fireworks. You never let us have any fun."

Georgie was brushing at himself as if he feared Buddy had given him cooties. "You're just pissed 'cause you didn't get to rape anybody."

"Least I got me a dick to rape 'em with." Buddy smirked.

Georgie made a growling sound and twitched a hand toward his Arkansas toothpick.

"*Move,*" Pete said quietly.

A fresh series of explosions rumbled like out-of-season thunder. Tex shook his head and laughed. "Another rebel atrocity," he said, stooping to shoulder his pack. "Ain't it just a shame?"

Chapter
THIRTY-ONE

The boys of Fast Eddie's old Jagun 23 were exalted, smoking and joking as they urged the company's mounts out of the semitrailers. Fast Eddie stood to the side with his hands in the pockets of his bombardier's jacket, trying not to breathe in too much of the stink of diesel, dust, and camel shit. He was happy to let his troops do the work. He and Sertikan, having picked up a few nicks in their hides together in the Red Sands, had come to a sort of modus vivendi based a whole lot more on respect than affection. That didn't mean Eddie had much use for the general run of horses, though, and as far as he was concerned camels were *still* the ultimate evil. Next to the Mets.

Shriveled old Nizam the Camelteer wandered past, leading the big bull Bactrian he called Burannyi-Karanar. "Do you know why the camel smiles, Eddie-*bahadur*?"

"Because only bloody camels know the secret one-hundredth name of *Allaa*," Eddie replied in a long-suffering tone. "You know what, Nizam? I've heard that line so damned much I promised myself I was gonna kill the next person who told it to me."

Banter died and heads turned. Nizam went pale beneath the hoary stubble of his cheeks. His turban started to come loose and slump into his face.

Eddie smiled. "Fortunately, it was a Nikolay caravan hunter."

The troopies roared. Nizam turned colors and made catfish motions with his mouth and pushed his turban up his forehead and finally laughed too. He was a genuine nerd, and the speculation among the farm boys as to why he named his favorite camel Debbie Gibson was frankly rude. But he'd just gotten back from his first actual combat mission on the snow-clad desert north of the Syr Dar'ya, where he'd held up fine in the firefight with caravan hunters.

Eddie slapped the old man on the shoulder to let him know he was okay. He wondered if he would ever actually feel anything again.

The tent city north of Chimkent looked as if the circus had come to town—or at least how Eddie always figured it would from TV and books; Barnum & Bailey brought no tents to Madison Square Garden. Timur had several permanent floating tent cities that he shuttled among. It kept him from getting a static "fortress" mindset and kept the League at least semi in the dark as to his whereabouts at any given time, in case it wanted to risk a bomber to rebel SAMs or try its cruise missiles, which still weren't up to the standards of the early-nineties Tomahawk of the *real* Desert Storm. They might even consider using nerve gas, trusting that they were too big and mean for the thermonuclear U.N. retaliation the use of such weapons was supposed to incur.

Mostly Eddie figured living in tents gave a real old-fashioned Sky-Blue Wolf steppe-nomad nostaligia head rush to the indiges. Even if the felt yurts of the Golden Horde had largely been supplanted by the synthetic domes of K-mart.

The tent city was a vibrant place, full of bustle and music and laughter. Eddie let it bounce off him like grains of windblown sand.

He wandered along in his Yankees cap and mirror shades and real leather bombardier's jacket that would buy him rations of shit from the animal-rights people back in the USA, scuffing the toes of his Asics athletic shoes in the yellow dust, just to be wandering. He was important now: a hero whose unit had inflicted unexpected casualties on League troops while unwittingly helping goad them headlong into Timur's fire-sack trap. He was *noyan,* a baron or marshal—which wasn't exactly as grand as it sounded, covering a range from Big Colonel to Little General, but meant he now commanded a thousand-strong regiment. A guerrilla star who had just come off from smoking his third caravan hunter team, when no other unit had ever beaten more than one.

A mannequin modeling the latest nouvelle millennium military drag, by the way he felt. Man-shaped plastic, built around an armature of nothing.

He was a teetotaler who had spent three days drunk after returning from the shattering defeat that turned out to be a victory of shocking completeness. His binge hadn't dimmed his luster with Jagun 23. They figured his getting lit was an arcane Western jock ritual. The ethnic Turks among them, especially the city Sarts, understood the appeal of a good snootful themselves.

When he came out of it League soldiers were still wandering out of the Red Sands to surrender.

He was a traitor to the Motherland. Or a hero, silently serving. He didn't know which. For months Arbatov had answered his repeated and frantic requests for information, for clarification—for some kind, any kind, of *response*—with echoing sepulcher silence. He was isolated. He was alone.

What had he done? He didn't know. He preferred to stay numb, to put his mind on hold through relentless work, drilling and studying and practicing and working out, and when that ran dry by the exercise of sheer will, rather than have the question tolling in his skull like the bells that made old Edgar Allan so nuts. He went through the motions, whether it was grab-assing with the squaddies to keep morale up or staring full into the bearded face of a League commando and not seeing his wide eyes die as he whipped a bullpup RPK light machine gun out from under its mylar wraps and firing it between the hairy humps of a Bactrian camel, point-blank into the man's chest.

At least he hadn't *known* any of the caravan hunter faces he had looked into that winter. The three teams he had zatzed were all BON, special-ops units organic to the paratroops, whom VDV jealously maintained in competition with *Spetsnaz*, GRU-controlled and not so discreetly overseen by the KGB. Many of them had cycled through the same para schools at Ryazan' and elsewhere as he had, but VDV was large, not an exclusive club like Special Designation.

He had not made many friends in training anyway. His

classmates regarded him as an outsider, a rival, a threat. He had responded by outperforming all comers at any task set before him in a cold fury, and laying serious hurt on anyone who crossed over the line from verbal abuse to physical.

Still, if he was to look into a familiar face as his finger closed on the trigger, he wasn't sure what he'd do . . . No. That was a lie. The problem was, he knew too well what he would do, with his life stretched out like a chicken on a Singapore counter, waiting for the cleaver. He'd shoot a friend as dead as any stranger.

He did a stutter step and a little sideways dance, to avoid tripping over the guy rope of a hemicylindrical blue tent. *You're thinking again,* he told himself. *Nasty habit. Everybody always told you* not *thinking was what would get you in trouble. Whole lot they knew.* Maybe he should try getting drunk again.

He turned a corner to see a bearded man in a black pullover sweater slip up behind a man with a slung AK and slash his throat with a quick swipe of a knife.

"Mr. Timur," the woman in the sage-colored skirt suit was saying, "the Nature Conservancy, International has sent me here to issue the strongest possible protest against your program of privatizing former League and republic lands. Precious little is left of the various riparian and Tien Shan watershed environments as it is. To expose them to commercial exploitation—"

Though there was still snow on the ground a few kilometers away, the day was quite warm. A small fan swiveled its head left and right with idiot fixity of purpose, stirring air turned taupe by afternoon sunlight filtering through the roof and walls of the multichambered tent. Seated Western-style on a folding chair behind a camp table, Timur waited politely until it became apparent the woman's word flow had sputtered out in indignation. Though she carried a British passport, she was American. The Nature Conservancy was another operation that had been driven out of North America.

"Ms. Longchamps," he said in his fine English, "it was my understanding that the purpose of your organization was to buy up lands for the purpose of preserving or restoring natural environments. Implicit in that policy, I should think, is the understanding that governments make poor stewards of such resources, as they do of all things. Has your own government administered the lands it seized from your organization well?"

Longchamps's face flushed. She was an extremely attractive woman with dark blond hair and pale eyes. Angry color ornamented her. "No. They've made them into test ranges and labor camps."

"And did the Soviets care for the land well? Has the League?"

"For God's sake, no. I've seen what they did to the Aral and the Syr."

"Why are you so concerned that I am removing the land from such a careless proprietor?"

"Because giving it over to capitalist exploitation is just as bad, and because you're so caught up in encouraging individual enterprise and this whole laissez-faire thing."

"You have traveled widely. Surely you must know that the worst environmental excesses of the capitalists pale before what socialism did to the former East Germany? Or my own land, for that matter."

She sat down, exasperated. "The earth is more than a resource to be used up. In the name of capitalism or communism. "

"I could not agree with you more. Understand, when we fought for our land, it was for our *land*, the parched and poisoned soil of Turkestan. We were sickened by what the Nikolays did to our earth for their cotton. Sick of having babies born deformed and adults dying young from exposure to pesticides and fertilizers no Western country would permit. The beauty of nature is a value too."

"Human values aren't the real reason—" Longchamps began.

Timur held up his hand. "Please. I have no desire to debate you. Instead I wish to make a proposition."

She settled back suspiciously. "What's that?"

Timur nodded his shrouded head toward the third person in the room, a dark man in a dark suit who sat quietly to one side, sweating.

"This is Senhor João Soares of Rio. Sys."

She raised her narrow Anglo-Saxon nose. "A Brazilian."

"My company has always opposed the destruction of the rain forest," Soares said in that same flat defensive tone that non-White Tribe South African businessmen used to have to cultivate.

"His company," Timur said, "wishes to buy the Chatkal Forest Management Zone south of Tashkent and give it to your organization."

"Naturally, we would wish that you consider yourselves to be administering it in trust for the people of Turkestan," Soares said.

"But . . . why?"

"Public relations," Soares said. "My company manufactures consumer electronics. We would like a share of the emerging Turkestan market. Given the lead possessed by the Americans and Japanese, and even the Europeans, we want to do something to make an impact. Government mismanagement has made conserving the environment a popular issue here."

"A publicity ploy."

Soares took out a handkerchief and swiped at his forehead. "It would benefit you, it would benefit us, it would benefit the Chatkal. It would please the Turkestanis. My company has a long-standing commitment to improving the environment."

Longchamps moistened her lips. She visibly longed to say something scathing, but somehow it wasn't coming.

Just as she found her voice, three shots cracked behind the tent.

Eddie was running, his Glock 23 out of the concealment holster inside the back of his cammie pants where the tail of his bombardier's jacket covered it. The scene turned into one of those slow-motion tunnel-vision dream things, where your whole being is focused on one thing and you run and run and can't seem to get any closer to it. At vision's end was the stricken sentry, the blood just rushing out of him like people from a burning theater, and his murderer, clinging to him like a lover.

The knifeman was paying no attention to anything but holding on to his victim. No matter what the movies show, a human with his throat slit doesn't just silently fold his cards and float off into the white light. You splash and thrash and, given the opportunity, can emit a whole lot of noise, even if it's only a panicky gurgling whistle.

Eddie had an adrenaline-stretched instant to be amused that only a few heartbeats before he'd been ragging himself for thinking too much, and here he was reverting to the Indiana Jones School of Action Without Thought. It also gave him time to recognize and really hate what he was going to do next.

One thing he'd never picked up on the streets of New York—along with AIDS or a serious drug habit—had been the white New Yorker's hatred/fear of firearms. Maybe he came from too low a stratum of society. He'd always liked the things, and had a feel for them, handguns particularly. He was still better with a pistol than any other form of firearm known, and God knew he'd checked out on them all.

He respected firearms. One thing a good firearm is not is a club. Yet when he got within reach of the knifeman—just beginning to lower his now limp but twitching victim to the ground—he gave him a hard crack with the Glock's square receiver, right behind the ear.

When he was a kid, Eddie saw a movie where somebody

tried the time- or at least fiction-honored expedient of removing a sentry by clocking him on the head with the butt of a gun. And the sentry, quite realistically, grabbed his head with both hands and screamed, *'Aiiieee!''*

But Eddie had no intention of knocking anybody out. His gut had realized that one man skulking about camp slitting people's throats in broad daylight was liable to have little friends, armed—as the knifeman himself was—with nasty little AKR Krinkov submachine guns slung across their backs. Eddie wanted to be quiet, but he also wanted to mash the fucker's skull in.

Also contrary to the movies, a Glock is not all plastic. Knife boy fell across his victim. A quick check left, toward the front of the tent. Big tent, no one else in sight. Important tent, too, if it was worth putting armed guards over . . . or cutting their throats to get inside.

Eddie had no time to follow up that speculation or even see if he had put the knife wielder down to stay because his peripheral vision caught a second man backing into view around the other rear corner of the tent, locked in a butt-to-crotch two-step with another slashed sentry. Eddie sprinted toward him.

He saw Eddie in his own vision's fringe, released his victim, who was beyond the point of making trouble. He squared off facing Eddie in a crouch, holding his knife low and point up, making come-to-me gestures with his free hand. He was not in a deep enough crouch. Eddie did a quick tae kwon do skip step and raised the guy's Reeboks a couple inches off the hard-packed dirt with a front thrust kick to the balls.

That *is* a good way to keep someone from making noise. All the breath came out of the killer in a single voiceless rush, like a particularly bad consonant in some unprounceable Third World tongue. He did make a tiny dry rat-squeak, unsuccessfully trying to inhale on his way to his knees and on down to the ground in a fetus ball.

So far, so good . . . but along this side of the tent, the

third member of the team with his Krinkov in his hands, a serious assassin about his business, was walking right toward Eddie.

He opened his bearded mouth—they all three had beards, so far, not that that was remarkable in this part of the world. Since he was going to make noise anyway, Eddie shot him three times in the chest.

The battle computer in his head was clicking away. Two sentries, two attackers to take them out—plus a third man. Probably the trigger man. This was the killing team.

That meant a second unit out in front of the tent, to pull discreet security, to make sure the quarry didn't escape, and to give backup in case something went wrong. Something like an intruder stumbling across the break-in attempt and firing shots. . . .

He dropped to the ground at the rear of the tent. Fortunately this was not one of those seamless-whole affairs where the roof and walls and floor are all one piece. He ripped loose several metal stakes holding down the bottom and slithered underneath.

The chamber of the partitioned tent was half-lit and stuffy. It was also unoccupied. He noticed rolled-up bedding to the side—a futon, for Christ's sake?—an open notebook computer with a smart satlink rig beside it, some books. Whoever lived here certainly spared every expense when it came to lush living. Holding the Glock in both hands, he rose, crossed swiftly to the hanging-flap interior door, took a breath, pirouetted through.

Three people sat at a table. A man in a turban had his back to Eddie, close enough to touch. A second man in a business suit poised half out of a chair to one side, uncertain which way to bolt.

Across the table from Eddie and the turbaned man sat a great-looking Western woman in a lady executive suit. She was looking at Eddie and opening her mouth to scream.

He pushed his Glock at her into Weaver stance and fired twice. She fell on her side, shrieking as if she had a compressed-air bottle in her aerobics-flattened stomach, unaware that she hadn't been hit. The man who had loomed up in the doorway behind her made no noise. Eddie's two rounds had taken him full in the face. He dropped his AKR and fell.

Over the ringing in his ears Eddie heard a muffled exclamation from the tent's third section, beyond the door. He dodged past the table, vaulted the screaming woman's chair, and went through in a low dive.

Another terrorist was in the antechamber, sure enough, along with yet another foreign woman, Far East Asian from the Gestalt flash Eddie took in of her before concentrating wholly on the tall, bearded man with the muzzle of a Krinkov jammed up under her right ear.

Slowly Eddie stood up, keeping his arms extended and his pistol trained on gunman and hostage. He was glad he kept in shape. Holding down on the terrorist while rising wasn't as easy as it sounded.

"Death to Westernizers and infidels!" the man shouted in Persian. "Death to enemies of the True God! Death to cowardly dogs who spurn the banner of jihad!"

He spoke not the Turkic-flavored Tadzhik dialect but pure middle-class Tehrāni. Behind the hostage's ear Eddie could see a gold locket hanging from the gunman's neck by a chain. He was willing to bet it contained a picture of a dead Asian religious and political leader, and not Mahatma Gandhi either. He bet all the gunman's little friends had them too. *An Iranian? What the fuck, over?*

"Give it up," Eddie replied in the same language. "You don't have a chance."

"I'll kill her," he man said in a less declamatory voice. "I'm willing to die, American."

Eddie had been trained in counterterrorist tactics by U.S. Special Forces, SAS instructors on loan, and *Spetsnaz.* "Okay," he said.

The woman put one hand over the other and drove her elbow hard into the pit of the gunman's stomach. He gasped and doubled, easing his death grip on her. She dropped flat on the Bukhara rug floor.

Eddie had ten rounds left. He gave the Iranian two in the chest and blasted three more into him on the way down, just to discourage him from using his submachine gun. Then he raised the Glock to cover the front door in case the man had buddies outside.

"Get the gun away from him," Eddie said in English. Then he said it again in Russian and—you never know—Persian too. One of them took, because she picked herself up, took a step forward, and gingerly kicked the Krinkov to the side of the tent, out of the dying man's reach.

Still covering the entrance, he gave her quick sidelong scrutiny. She looked Chinese, with a pointed-oval face, heavy black hair in bangs, jeans, and a dark blouse. She was holding herself together quite well for somebody who had just been taken hostage and seen a man killed. She only showed it in the width of her black eyes and the spots of color flaming high on her cheekbones. She was even more striking than the round-eye woman in the other room.

"It's okay," he muttered, as much to himself as her. "You don't have to thank me for saving you. It's all part of my job description."

"*Saving* me?" she demanded, in English with an accent like fine porcelain. "Save *me*? I saved myself, thank you very much."

A man with a leveled Kalashnikov burst in the door. He pointed the assault rifle at Eddie. Eddie took up slack on the trigger.

The woman dodged between them and shouted "Wait!" in Uzbek.

Eddie eased off the trigger. The five assassins he had seen all wore standard *Pasdaran* drag, beards, black pullovers, dark pants. The getup wasn't all that unusual in the Turkestani Defense Forces, but that much uniformity was. Take the man—boy—staring at him over the sight-shroud of his old

AKS. He had on MVD cammie pants, a Satanta T—and a sky-blue skullcap.

Come to think of it, the two sentries Eddie had seen go down outside had blue *tyubeteyka* on too. Tumblers began to click into place in his head.

At the same time the Son of the Sky-Blue Wolf was visibly deciding that since this intruder pointing a gun at him was blond, it stood to reason he was Russian and so he should just forget about the woman and shoot him. Someone came into the room behind Eddie and said, "Enough. This man saved my life."

Eddie saw a look of dumb devotion smear itself over the youngster's face. The Kalashnikov quit staring him in the eye.

Deliberately he lowered his own weapon. When he straightened and turned he was not at all surprised to see that the turban worn by the man who had sat at the table covered all of his face except his eyes.

They were black eyes, intense, with slight epicanthic folds. Eddie met them and felt a shock go through him like an iron bar.

"Timur," he said.

The eyes turned to crescent slits. After a beat Eddie realized the man was smiling. "Ah, I remember you! The turbulent American from the schoolyard, who was so ready to defy the odds to take up the cause of the oppressed. You've done it again today, though I daresay this time the beneficiary of your daring was not perhaps so blameless."

Eddie's head began to spin. He tasted vomit. He'd almost died. He had killed three men, maybe four. Now, for the second time, he had the chance to kill Timur.

But Arbatov's orders . . . fuck Arbatov. Eddie went slowly to his knees, laid his sidearm down at Timur's feet, and bent forward to touch his forehead to the blood-soaked carpet.

Chapter
THIRTY-TWO

Wet from her shower, Jacqueline Gendron emerged into Timur's sleeping chamber from the portable unit in the corner. The high points of her naked body glistened in the low lamplight, as though the point of her shoulder and her ribs and smooth flare of hip were molded from polished bronze. It was a fine body, long-waisted, long-legged, firm. Her pubic hair was a discreet dark vertical band tucked beneath her slight belly; it required little maintenance to be suitable for the latest Eurothong bikini fashions.

She sat beside the man on the futon she had insisted they buy and vigorously toweled her hair. "I was so worried when I heard," she said. "Almost totally frantic. I caught the first plane available out of Tashkent." Unspoken but loud was her resentment that he had not arranged for transport to be available to her at all times—as a journalist of importance, as the great man's mistress.

He studied her minutely. The night chill of high-desert spring had raised goose bumps on her arms. He was a middle-aged man, of no extraordinary appearance, with precisely no pretense of being a seducer; he was a man who scrupulously avoided the trappings of the Eastern potentate as much as he could without losing all credibility. He was hardly the sort to purchase sex. Since his wife had . . . gone . . . he had resigned himself to doing without. He never expected to see a woman so beautiful so close again.

"It was terrible," he said, slowly.

"What?" Breathless. "The fear of death?"

He shook his head impatiently. "Not that. I've never seen a man die. Not actually . . . before me."

He turned his gaze to the lamp, began to unwind his headcloth. "It made me think again of the deaths I've caused. So many, the men, the women. It seems so easy, when great issues lie at stake, to make the great plans and give the great orders. But to see what they translate into . . ."

"One doesn't make an omelette without breaking eggs," she said with a head flip.

His hands froze. "I'm sorry you missed the incident. It was very vivid. You would call it 'good telejournalism.'" He felt tension pass through her like a rope jerking taut. *Why do I provoke her?* he asked himself. *Is it to do away with the suspense of awaiting her attack?*

She smiled. A coldness passed through him. She was mercurial, unpredictable, and what that implied was terrifying. He had passed almost six months in her company, and yet he hardly knew her at all. *How can I presume to decide for others, when I know so little about what is in their minds, how they will behave?*

He set his headcloth aside. Gently she touched his face. It was an average face, a Sart face, with a bit of Mongol flatness in the bones of the cheeks and a bit of Persian roundness in the flesh. Only the eyes were different, obsidian mirrors set within slight epicanthic folds. *Like the eyes of a Buddha,* she liked to say.

"Do you think that's all I care about?" she purred. Her touch thrilled and burned like brandy. "The story?"

"I know that you are a professional, and good at what you do," he said stiffly. She had him all adrift again, like an old-time traveler on the great Silk Road, who'd let the night's goblin voices lure him into the trackless Takla Makan to die with his camel.

She ran fingers down his chest. Timur the mighty, villain to much of the world and Great Liberator to the rest, was dressed only in a Western-style undershirt and baggy Russian undershorts. His body was soft but carried little excess.

Where the hem of the shirt rode up, he showed the purplish striations of vanished flab. He hadn't exactly wasted down to an ascetic, but something had diminished him.

"I care about you," she said.

She kissed him on the cheek, stood up, turned half away from him, and stretched. "What did they want?" she asked.

He shrugged, hung his fingers before him in a knot between his knees. "Jihad," he said. "They wanted me to call down the *djinn* of holy war."

"Why not?" she asked. "You can sweep out of your desert like a conqueror of old, a Temujin, a Tamerlane. The old world is decadent; it needs a cleansing, the way a pine forest needs fire."

She dropped to her knees before him. Her hazel eyes glowed in the lamplight. "*Do it*. The sword is there, it awaits your fingers."

"I'm not Tamerlane, damn it!" he shouted. She refused to flinch, only settled back on her bare haunches with a private smile. He covered his face with his hands.

"I'm fighting for freedom, not domination. Can't people understand—that I am not the Timur of the old times?"

"You chose the name, dear. As for *freedom*"—She pushed back, stood—"that's the dead wood in worst need of clearing out, so a strong new forest can grow."

"I don't believe it. Only freedom makes life worth living."

He looked up at her, expecting the worst. They had had this discussion before. Jacqui used approval and disapproval like touches of a quirt. His own wife had used soft, mute resignation sometimes; yet mostly they had talked. They were modern that way, as they were in marrying for love. All the same, the sad blank expressions laid over silence had happened more and more frequently, before the end, before...

Jacqui rose and walked away like a bored lioness. He set himself single-mindedly to watching the play of her scrupulously maintained buttocks. He had never before appreciated what escape there could be in the carnal, in pretty flesh. Another trap he might set himself, another thing to beware.

She sat down in front of a travel mirror she had unfolded on a trunk, next to the Ripstop shoulder bag she had not yet unpacked. She began to work her fingers through her hair, which she had permitted to grow to almost shoulder length, untangling snags.

"I understand you appointed a new chief of security. The man who saved you, the rogue American. He sounds like quite a colorful little bastard. What a chance to tweak their dicks in Washington and Moscow, no?"

He shook his head. "No. No publicity. He was quite insistent."

"Insistent? *Insistent*?" She turned to stare at him, face congealed in contempt and something like shock. "You let a mere adventurer, an *American*, tell you what you may do?"

"I chose to honor his wishes." He raised his head. "As I chose to make him an *orlok*, a field marshal. What I give him is what I think he deserves, and the choice is *mine*."

"What?" she demanded. "Are you going imperious on me?"

He held her eye and didn't flinch.

She laughed, rose, and came to him. "It's about time," she said. "You are a great man, my love. But you still must learn to act like one."

And she was a warm, moist, pressing presence, and her nipple was hot and insistent on his bare arm, and he was happy, for a time, to put thought in abeyance.

The face of the Secretary-designate appeared on the screen. "Dr. Mohn." The sleek head nodded. "Good to hear from you. But I'm afraid I don't have much time to chat."

You precocious little snot, Sondra Mohn thought. *Do those bags under your eyes come from the long hours or the coke? I hear you're not being backward about savoring the rewards of having greatness thrust upon you.*

"I'm so sorry about Operation Clean Sweep," she said sweetly. "It started out so promising."

Justin Serafin's mouth twitched. "We've had a few setbacks, is all."

And hitting the iceberg was a minor inconvenience on the Titanic'*s maiden voyage.* Gun battles, riots, the nation's already overloaded detention system swamped, plus massive obstruction from local, state, and even federal officials—not to mention *employees*—outraged to discover that they weren't immune to Clean Sweep's broom.

"It's so tragic what happened to poor Larry," she said. "Have you made any headway tracing the murder weapon? We all know how easy it's become to lay one's hand on major firepower since private ownership of firearms was banned, but a Barrett Light .50 is serious ordnance even by the standards of the streets."

Serafin watched her a moment, full lips contracting to a line. "The weapon used in the assassination is not common knowledge, Dr. Mohn."

"Yes, the media are quite obedient about telling the public only what you want them to know, aren't they, Justin? Give an old lady some credit; when you've been around politics as long as I have, you acquire sources in the most *unexpected* places. You'd be quite surprised what I know."

"If you have pertinent information on the case, it's your duty as a citizen to step forward and share it with us. To hold back would be anti-communitarian." He smiled thinly. "Not even our highest officials can hold themselves above the law."

"I'm sure I know nothing Enforcement Affairs is unaware of at the *highest levels*," she said, poison-sweet. "Certainly nothing I'd be afraid to testify to in open court, were I called upon to do so. And should some mishap befall me, I've made arrangements with certain of the foreign media to make public the details—just so you could make sure they tally with your own information."

Serafin sighed. He slumped farther down in his chair, adjusted himself. "Are we finished with the threat behavior now? I really am busy."

Mohn permitted herself a flicker of smile. "I need someone you've got."

"One of my agents?"

"No."

"Then who?" He was starting to sound testy again.

"Francis Marron."

It was his turn to smile. "We just went to a lot of trouble to put him behind bars."

"It should take less to get him out again. For you."

"What do you want him for? He's washed up."

"A situation has arisen. He is uniquely qualified to deal with it." She paused. "*Uniquely* qualified."

"The Russia thing?"

"The Russia thing."

"Quietly, of course."

"Of course."

"And whatever happens, we can tack a little something onto the CIA's image deficit? Just another nail in the coffin, before it goes in the ground?"

"Justin, dear, it was never my intention that you go away with nothing for your pains."

"We run the operation? Top to bottom?"

"I'm interested in results, not details."

"A pleasure doing business with you, Doctor."

"And you, Mr. Secretary."

Sitting out under the stars beside his own modest tent in the midst of his bivouacked *minghan*, Fast Eddie Randolph hit the SAVE AND CLOSE FILE key of his notebook computer. The screen display returned to menu, as innocuous as a laundry list. He punched in a brief memorized sequence.

He could smell the green shoots stirring in the hard-spirited soil, awakened by the melting kiss of the last snow off the Tien Shans, reaching upward in anticipation of the brief rains to come. Around him the encampment slept, silent except for the muted percussion of the wind on tents. He liked to keep his men busy enough that they had little energy for getting into trouble on their downtime.

His own Jagun 23 was mostly gone to the camp-follower

tent city subsidiary to Timur's floating HQ, bleeding off the
tensions of their last hunt. Seeking in women and recreational
chemistry the same release that he had been hunting on his
random, driven walk among the tents that afternoon.

Hope they have better luck than I did.

He sighed, leaned back, and raised his head as if to watch
the little software robot he'd released spring upward from
the polymer-shell half-moon of the satlink antenna, to begin
its trace-foiling careen through the great illicit Net, out there
between him and the stars. He always linked-in out in the
open, with nothing overhead to interfere with transmission.
Superstition, he supposed.

For six months he had been sending those robot messengers,
dutifully and regularly. For six months the reply had been
silence. The silver cord had been cut, and he was all adrift.

But he had done his duty, now. Accomplished all that
could be asked of him by his Motherland—and more than
her self-appointed guardians had ever anticipated, he suspected
to the point of certainty. Against all odds, he had catapulted
himself into the rebel king's innermost circle. He was poised
to strike. This was triumph, the greatest of his young life.

So why the fuck does it feel like betrayal?

Chapter
THIRTY-THREE

"Hey. Hey, there!"

Dr. Shih Tai-Yu kept walking, arms folded over the notebook computer she held against her chest, a few stray strands
of blue-black hair blown in her face by the crisp breeze.

She heard running footsteps, tensed, felt a thrill of rolling-
eye panic. *I won't let them see me afraid!* shrilled in her

brain, while her rational mind tried to reassure her the nearest
Chinese security forces were across the Tien Shans, pictureque
and very forbidding, to the west.

The thought hit: *The assassins!* A hand seized her biceps.

She turned into the hold, snapping up her forearm to
break the grip.

The man let go of her, jumped back with hands held up
and out, as if surrendering. "Whoa, lady," he said in
English. "Sorry. Didn't mean to set you off."

She glared at him. He wore athletic shoes, baggy camouflage pants, a leather jacket, and a blue baseball cap with the
letters NY worked together in what looked to her like a bad
parody of a Chinese character. He was short for an American,
not much taller than she.

"I just wanted to see how you were doing," he said.

Still flustered and angry at him for it, she nodded curtly
and started walking. Head up, not tipped demurely toward
the ground like a proper Asian woman.

He trotted after. "You know, when somebody saves your
life, some kind of acknowledgment is, you know, customary. Doesn't have to be anything formal. A simple *thank you*
usually does it, though your more concrete rewards like
money, sex, or writing your rescuer into your will are all
acceptable."

She turned to face him, cheeks sunburn-hot. "You rescue
me? I rescue myself, thank you!"

She walked. He skipped along sideways beside her. "You
have, like, the cutest accent in the world, you know?"

"Pig!"

Fast Eddie stopped, looked after her. " 'Pig,' " he repeated, half under his breath.

He sprinted, planted himself in front of her. Her eyes
blasted him like chain guns, and in the sudden tensing of
her posture he read the intention to plant either a knee or the
tip of one of those cute little kung fu slippers in his nuts.

His thighs flinched toward each other and he danced back a step. "Wait! I'm sorry! I'm sorry, I'm sorry, I'm sorry."

She glared at him a moment, then let a little pressure bleed out her nostrils. "All right. You are sorry. I already know that."

He made a shot-through-the heart gesture, hands over chest. She started walking.

"Look," he said, pacing her again, "I'm sorry if I came off like a male chauvinist jerk. I'm not really a chauvinist. I'm just a jerk."

She sighed.

"I'm still letting off emotional overpressure from that, in the big guy's tent," he said. "It kind of makes me forget my manners."

She looked at him, for the first time as if he might be human and not an ape escaped from some nearby zoo. "You feel . . . pressure . . . from killing those men? Even after several days? It seemed to come so easily."

"It does and it doesn't. When you do it—kill somebody— it's like the most natural thing in the world. In a situation like that it's all you can do, and there's no talk, no posturing, no thinking, really." He shivered. From her expression he knew she thought he was showing her an act. He wished he was. "It's afterward that it all comes down on you."

They walked side by side through the city of tents. The day was hot. Hard to believe Eddie and his men had been fighting in ankle-deep snow the week before.

"You're right about saving yourself, babe. That was a good move you put on the Iranian. Good timing too."

"I had no wish to be a hostage, and I certainly did not wish to die."

"You knew what he was saying? Your English is great. You understand Persian too?"

"The language of a gun in your ear is universal, I believe."

He laughed. "You saved my life too. Thanks for not

letting that homeboy in the blue beanie pull the trigger on me.''

She smiled. ''I experienced quite an intense struggle with my conscience.''

''So who won? Wait—don't answer that.''

She nodded solemnly.

''You're a pretty cool customer, babe. The round-eye woman from the big man's office had to be carried onto the plane for Karachi strapped to a stretcher.''

''Perhaps Westerners are less mature than we Chinese are.''

''Um. Yeah. By the way, I'm Eddie. Fast Eddie Randolph.''

''I am pleased to meet you. I am Dr. Shih Tai-Yu.''

''Doctor.'' He pushed out his lips. ''So what brings you to Uncle Timur's Permanent Floating Carnival and Sideshow? The nightlife? The great tanning beaches? You got the whole Red Sands between here and the Aral; room to catch a lot of rays.''

''I am professor of Altaic languages and culture at Beijing University.''

''So you specialize in Turkic dialects, like Uzbek and Kirghiz and Kazakh? Hey, why are you looking me like that? You figure I'm just another couch-potato American, don't know anything about anything but *Happy Days* reruns and who won the Super Bowl?'' He hoped she wouldn't ask him who *did* win the Super Bowl. In old movies they were always tripping up spy bad guys by asking them American sports trivia like that. Eddie didn't know who won the Super Bowl even when he lived in New York. He hated football.

She dropped her eyes, a minor victory he enjoyed. ''Actually, my specialty is more the Mongol group of tongues. And I admit, I did not expect you to know what 'Altaic' meant. I offer sincere apology.''

''I sure don't get those very often. It's okay. People are always underestimating us Americans. It's not hard to do.'' He cocked his head, half closed one eye. ''Is that what I meant to say? It didn't seem to come out right.''

Shih giggled. Eddie raised his eyebrows at her. "Whoa. The jade Buddha cracks. The professor has a sense of humor. That kind of thing could be very dangerous, you know."

Instantly she sobered. "I am sorry. I will be more careful."

"Hey, wait a minute. Did your leg come off in my hand? I was *kidding*."

"It is just that, when people say that it is dangerous to talk a certain way, where I come from it is wise to listen to them." She looked at him curiously. "You also, I would think."

Whoops. The cover slipped a little there. Are things that bad back in the States? He shrugged. "I never listen to what people say. It's part of my charm."

"I do not believe that. I think you listen to everything people say. Perhaps you take it too much to heart."

"So you're a counselor now. A lady of many talents. Say, can I walk you somewhere?"

"You already have." She stopped, bowed slightly. "Thank you very much, Mr. Randolph. It was most instructive." She turned away and vanished.

Into Timur's big office-and-living-quarters tent. He stood blinking after her like a high school junior left stranded on the stoop without a first-date kiss.

"Dr. Shih," Timur said in Uzbek, rising from his cross-legged carpet squat as a sullen Sky-Blue Wolf escorted the woman into his receiving chamber. Flowers flashed on all sides like frozen explosions. "A pleasure to see you. Please, sit down. Will you take tea?"

The prevailing local conception of tea ran to bland Japanese imports and a Xinjiang blend that tasted to the refined Beijing palate like boiled ditchweed. Perhaps as a gesture at old-nomad solidarity, the half-Mongol Shih perversely liked the stuff. Or had done a good job convincing herself she did. She sat on a maroon and black Bukhara rug and nodded.

An earthenware teapot sat on a tray at Timur's side. He poured Shih a *piyaala* full and brought it to her.

"Thank you, sir." She sipped. "For a powerful man, you seem oddly uncomfortable with the perquisites of power. I hope it gives no offense to say so."

Halfway back down, Timur checked himself momentarily, looking intently at her from the folds of his headcloth. "No offense given, Doctor; I am not easy to offend. Tell me more, if you will."

She gestured around the tent. "Your surroundings are not luxurious. You have these beautiful flowers, tulips and orchids and the little purple ones that look like lilacs—"

"Turkestan lilies," Timur said. "Some of these are spring wildflowers, others hothouse grown."

"Am I correct that they are freely given by the people, sir?"

Timur nodded. "Truckloads arrive daily at all my encampments. I keep some, give the rest to whomever wishes to share the beauty."

"Why are there no roses? Turkestan is famous for them."

To her surprise she saw him shudder. "No roses. I . . . cannot abide them."

"Your flowers are gifts, and you pour your guests tea by hand. Yet you are one of the most powerful men in the world."

"That's hardly true," he murmured.

"Forgive me, sir, but it is. You have torn your land from the living flesh of the world's last great empire. Your people worship you. You are a focus, an inspiration, to the aspirations of people all over the world who feel themselves oppressed by foregin conquerors, especially in the non-aligned nations. Is that not power?"

The eyes closed briefly. "The U.N. has condemned me as a reactionary."

"Sir, that only increases your cachet among those who wish they could secede. You saw the satellite coverage from

New Guinea. The Bougainvillean strikers waved your portraits at the Panguna mine.''

"As the Australians shot them down." The pain in his voice sounded authentic. "Is that one of the perquisites of power you find me uncomfortable with, the ability to cause pain and death?"

Shih's silence showed that she had understood the question to be rhetorical. After a moment, he said, "My own people riot against me in Bukhara and Termez."

"They are in the minority. Your followers would crush them in a moment, if you gave the word."

He nodded, agreeing without evincing pleasure. His black eyes bored into hers.

"You are correct. But I will not give the word." He laughed, a sound quiet and bitter as the wind across the alkali pans that surrounded the dying Aral. "It is because of my insistence on toleration that they riot against me. They wish me to crush the enemies of God."

"You really believe in freedom and toleration? When the rest of the world rejects them as reaction or sentiment or folly?"

"I do."

"You seem too good to be true, sir."

He stared at her. Her face was beautiful, oval, with high slanting cheekbones. Her eyes were large and bright. In neither face nor eyes did he read dissembling or concealed sarcasm. Perhaps he was becoming too accustomed to their presence. Or maybe she was a skilled actress.

He held out the bottom of his facecloth to sip his tea. Lowering his cup, he looked at her. "Just what are you doing here, Doctor?"

She smiled shyly. "I'm a spy."

She had told him that, quite bluntly, when to her surprise she was instantly ushered into his presence on arrival at the tent city. She had received endless hours of briefings from her government, but they were of a decidedly Delphic nature, either contradictory or flat incomprehensible. The only thing successfully made clear was that she was supposed to observe what went on in Timur's camp and report back to Beijing.

Why they sent her instead of a trained agent or diplomat she had no clue. One thing she was sure of was that she had no chance of maintaining her cover when her superiors themselves would not or could not make clear exactly what it was supposed to be. She guessed the old men of the Politburo had no real idea of how to read or respond to the Red Sands rising, and that her mission was a manifestation of that ambivalence.

Perhaps it was the sense of borrowed time, of playing on after the recess whistle had blown, that she like so many black-hand dissidents had lived with through the years since Tienanmen Spring, that made her risk everything on a single cast. Or maybe she was just tired. Timur's response had been to laugh hugely. Since then he had treated her as a valued friend, ignoring the occasional dark look or verbal jab from his tall orange-haired companion—currently back in Tashkent, thank heaven.

"I know why you were sent here, Doctor," Timur said. "I want to know what you are really *doing* here. What is your personal agenda?"

She sipped brackish tea and decided to gamble on truth again. "I want to see how long it takes before the power you hold corrupts you."

The harsh *afganets* wind blew out of the southwest. The setting sun skimmed orange light along the ground and turned the desert beyond the outskirts of the tent city and the faces of Eddie's men to flame.

Holding his newly received assault rifle vertical beside him, muzzle up and buttstock snugged inside his left elbow, Eddie paced off ground from the armored department-store mannequin. The survivors and replacements of Jagun 23 trailed along, smoking and joking like spring break at Daytona Beach.

At first glance the weapon looked like a standard bullpup rifle, black, with the magazine fitted behind the pistol grip. Up close it was plain weird. Instead of a long receiver to take a reciprocating bolt, it had a short, fat cylindrical housing, mounted along the long axis. A well for the box magazine let into the underside.

The rifle was a radical new design by an American émigré firm based in Mexico. It took the concept of caseless ammunition—the coming trend in military procurement, except in the United States and the League, who seemed wedded to their brass—several steps beyond the usual kludgy derivatives of the original, oversold Heckler & Koch G11.

Conventional "cased" ammunition has cases made of extruded metal, which add cost, weight, and environmental burden, and impose the mechanical problem of getting rid of the damned things once they're fired. The MRS "rotary" fired bullets glued to small tiangular-section blocks of propellant. Inside the housing rotated a cylinder with three evenly spaced longitudinal channels cut into it—like chambers of a revolver's cylinder, but open, and triangular in section. Turning, each chamber stripped a caseless round off the magazine and carried it up to align with the barrel, where an electric charge fired it. A fraction of the rapidly expanding propellant gas was vented to spin the cylinder and keep the weapon firing. It was compact, high-tech, and mechanically simple.

Eddie was aware of the snags implicit in a unit's using too many different types of ammunition. It complicated resupply, and if in the heat of action you grabbed the wrong box, you could be well and truly fucked. On the other hand, the regular League forces issued three calibers of small-arms ammo: the big old 7.62 × 54mm rimmed round used by machine guns and sniper's rifles; the shorter 7.62 Lite used by the classic AK-47; and 5.45mm, used in latter-day AKs and light MGs.

Eddie wanted his men armed to the max. On-line scuttlebutt said the rotary beat the ass off conventional assault rifles. Besides, he loved fancy war toys. Always had.

At twenty-five paces he stopped, turned. His squad leaders shooed their men out of his line of fire while old Uncle Lucky handed over a loaded magazine. Even with a little battery for the electrical initiator inside—there was another pair inside the rifle itself, just to make sure—the fifty-round box was barely over eight inches long. The triangular rounds used space more economically than ones that were actually round. The ammo units were so short the magazine looked as if it were meant for a handgun.

He clicked the box into the well, made sure it was seated, worked the charging lever at the front of the cylinder housing to rotate a round into firing position. He adjusted his earphones over his Yankees cap, seated his extremely cool yellow shooting shades more comfortably on his nose, and leveled the weapon. At this range he disdained to take a shoulder weld and use the integral optical sight; he just tucked the thing under his arm in the midpoint position and ripped a quick burst at the dummy.

The mannequin was wearing a timeless creation in Kevlar and steel/ceramic inserts, the Hard Corps IV vest by Second Chance. It was still the world standard for personal protection, though the new polygraph—polymerized graphite—ballistic cloth armor might give it a run. The inventor used to put on a vest and let pepole plunk him in the chest with an old .30-06 from about ten feet, a convincing demonstration of his armor's effectiveness, if not his sanity.

Eddie's burst hit the dummy. Stuffing and bits of plastic flew *everywhere*.

The rotary fired ammunition designated 7/4mm—seven slash four. That meant the bullets were 7mm wide; the lesser overall bulk and weight of caseless offered an alternative to the worldwide trend toward ever slimmer projectiles. They had silver-gray polymer nose caps which, on impact, pushed back into the hollowed nose of the jacketed lead slug, causing it to expand. The vest ate those without difficulty.

The nasty little sharpened 4mm tool-steel penetrator rods inside the lead sabots just kept going.

Eddie's finger came off the trigger. In sudden ringing silence the crowd held its breath as the upper half of the mannequin kind of caved in on its lower torso. Then everybody erupted in applause and hooting laughter.

Eddie looked at the rifle, made a vaudeville *not bad* face, tucked the weapon under his arm, and strolled forward to check out the damage.

'*Allaa agbar,*'' Maqsut breathed at Eddie's side. ''That thing's a real *shaytaan.*'' Which meant, it kicked *ass*.

That 7/4 caseless ammo cost the *world*. But it sure ripped the shit out of the dummy, armor and all.

''Well, damn,'' Eddie said. ''Timur's Own Personal Life Guards and Marching Band could seriously *use* this shit.''

Leaving the men to take turns shooting the marvelous new weapon, and Maqsut and Shy Bunny to make sure they didn't shoot each other with it, Eddie went off to the side and cracked his notebook comp. He was not a man who deferred gratification well, perhaps because he'd done too much of it already, during two years in solitary—and before. He wanted to see how soon he could lay hands on some more of the things.

A flashing message on the screen when it lit told him he had priority electronic mail waiting. Reflexively he punched it up.

His heart almost seized when he saw the first page. It wasn't what the text said; it was some innocuous crap from an old bulletin-board pen pal . . . apparently. What electrified him was what it *meant*. Code words identified it as a front for a communication from his puppet masters, League KGB, from whom he hadn't heard since before the Red Sands battle.

He glanced around hurriedly to see if anyone was in position to read over his shoulder—what that phony front page was for. He hit the hot key to bring up the real message.

It read, *"Terminate Timur immediately."*

Chapter
THIRTY-FOUR

"Ooh, baby! Let me feel it! Let me feel all your big hard cock!"

The two teenaged Sky-Blue Wolves may or may not have understood English. There was something about that deep-throat moaning that was universal. They looked at each other, faces comical in the starlight, and then rabbited almost out from under their blue *tyubeteyka* to investigate the source of the sounds, somewhere beyond the nearest tents.

Fast Eddie Randolph watched them go. *Dickheads,* he thought dispassionately. Their devotion was unquestionable, but he'd never had any faith in the judgment of Timur's adolescent paramilitary groupies. As part of Timur's pre-revolutionary core, they had sacred-cow status; even as field marshal in charge of guarding Timur's body Eddie had not been able to dislodge them.

Until he recorded some soundtrack off a hard-core satcast out of Belo Horizonte and dropped off a cheap GoldStar flip player behind some tents to run it back for them. *That* got them going. He slipped into Timur's tent.

The darkness inside was almost physical. The still, thick air smelled of flowers and synthetic cloth and tobacco and the sweat of petitioners. Light shone faint around the edges of the flap that covered the doorway to Timur's audience room.

Eddie drew a knife. It was even bigger than a Rambo-style big knife, with a heavy, tapering, single-edged blade. A Khyber knife, common as camel dung in that part of the world. Untraceable. *Quiet*.

He moved forward soundlessly. Tendrils of darkness seemed to brush his face. The audience room was unlit and untenanted. The light he had seen was bleed-through from Timur's sleeping chamber.

Eddie ghosted to the next opening, held his ear near the fabric flap. Dialed high, his hearing detected the calm but not quite rhythmic breathing of an adult male, awake and engaged in no strenuous activity, and the small unconscious noises everyone makes unless they're trying not to. Eddie could smell him now, the slight masculine scent, a whiff of soap and talcum powder. There was perfume too, definitely feminine, but definitely background. Timur's companion, the lanky TV-reporter bimbo who always eyed Eddie like a piece of spoiled meat, was in Tashkent playing Woodward and Bernstein.

Eddie already knew Timur was alone. As head bodyguard he monitored everyone who went in and out of the great man's presence. He was a very conscientious bodyguard.

He was a very conscientious spy too; a very conscientious killer. He had killed his own comrades at the behest of the Chekists. He had gotten next to the rebel leader—literally so, now. And after echoing months of silence, the summons had come.

He could do it now, quiet and quick, be well on his way to some border by the time the alarm was raised. Or not. He had laid no careful plans for escape. The act was all, and after . . .

He lowered his knife hand, so that the blade was concealed by his hip. Then he stepped through.

Timur knelt like a man at prayer, reading a book. He raised his shrouded face at the soft rustle of the door flap. Eddie read his smile at the corners of his eyes.

"Ah, Eddie-*bahadur*," he said. "At last you've come."

* * *

The flat space on the roof between the blue dome and the parapet of the *madrasa*—built by some risen steppe dweller bent on demonstrating that the effete poets and scholars of great Bukhara had nothing on a man whose idea of "one for the road" was to open up a vein in his mare's leg and drink his fill—felt as if it had been heated with a blowtorch. Trying to ignore the burning sensation in the soles of his sneakers and the seat of his pants, Fast Eddie panned the rifle scope's magnifying and particular eye along the broad thronged avenue.

Another coming trend in military hardware was modularity. The demo rotary had a long, heavy sniper barrel you could drop in, and a fancy electronic scope to snap on in place of the plain-vanilla assault-rifle optics. Eddie was a good rifle shot but no sniper. On the other hand, the handful among Jagun 23 who were expert marksmen, scattered across the flat hot roofs before the hill of the fortified Ark, all had appropriate if less high-tech weapons. This was his toy, and he intended to hang on to it.

"They're moving now," said Shy Bunny's voice in his ear. Eddie acknowledged absently as the people in the street flowed through his circumscribed vision like debris bobbing on a stream, faces slightly blurred by motion.

The cross hairs painted on the glass before his eye by a microlaser array centered on a medium-sized man surrounded by a mob. Eddie stopped tracking the weapon. As if feeling the pressure of Eddie's vision, the man lifted his head. His features were obscured by a fold of his green turban. The cross hairs turned from yellow to red as the scope's microprocessor decided it had a mortal lock on him.

"Timur," Eddie said under his breath. All alone in that sea of hate. It made Eddie's sphincter knot. There wasn't a sky-blue skullcap to be seen; Christ knew how he'd manage to ditch his pet Wolves. The problem was, the crazier the things Timur tried, the better they worked. Or this would still just be the plain old Uzbek Republic. And Eddie wouldn't be a traitor.

For the benefit of the mike taped to his Adam's apple Eddie said, "All right, this is Six to all units, everybody listen up. Timur's started for the mosque. Everything in hand there, Singer?"

"Well enough," the old Kirghiz answered back. The Russian EPW he had press-ganged as his apprentice *manas* singer was up and around on crutches and doing PT on an outpatient basis, so Aliyev had got him transferred out to Timur's tent city where he could keep up his lessons. The big bushy-lipped son of a bitch still loudly had no use for Eddie, but Eddie was relieved all the same. Though Aliyev didn't have Shy Bunny's charisma or Maqsut's calculating strategist's brain, he might have been the most valuable of Eddie's lieutenants, for the steadiness he brought Delta section and the legitimacy his unwavering support lent Eddie. Eddie wanted to give the old guy all the leeway he could, but he'd been spending an *awful* lot of time in Tashkent with his pet bear.

"The crowd here is sullen, but calm," Aliyev reported. The Kalyan mosque, with its minaret that dominated the Bukhara skyline, was one of Central Asia's most revered. Eddie had his biggest contingent there, but he couldn't command it in person. This was not a good day for infidel dogs, even ones who happened to be *orloks*, to be getting fey with the holy jim-jams.

"Stay awake," Eddie said, then grimaced. That was the kind of pep-talk bullshit he always hated to get from his own COs. There were a hundred thousand people in the narrow streets, and most of them were minded for some serious ass-kicking. His boys weren't going to be playing with themselves. "Six out."

He moved the scope. A face on a poster leaped at him, many times the size of life but no more attractive. A face he'd seen but briefly, though he would remember it a long time. The face of the terrorist in the doorway to Timur's audience room, before Eddie put two bullets through it. Your usual raghead martyr's poster. *Swell*.

Shi'a had been gaining ground in Bukhara the last few years, partly in reaction against the dominance of its ancient and solidly Sunni rival Samarkand in the Central Asian *mirasist* independence movement, in part because it for some reason had been attracting refugees from the Shi'ite intramural strife that had helped make Iran such a fun place to live in the nineties. It had also drawn far more numerous refugees from the sliver of Turkmenia still held by League loyalists who, squeezed between Iran, Afghanistan, and Free Turkestan and far gone in paranoia, had been making a run at the land atrocity record, as if to demonstrate the League had better claim to the name *Timur* than the current pretender. Bukhara simmered with anger toward the infidels of the World of Hurt. Though the revolution had begun in Uzbekistan—and Timur was widely presumed to be an Uzbek himself—it was still not much of a surprise that the first open defiance of the revolutionary chieftain should come from the city's volatile street mobs.

Eddie swept the scope back the other way, across Timur making his slow stately way through a mob that pulsated with fury at him but could somehow not lay hands upon him. Off to the right, orange hair and khaki, Timur's squeeze and her fruitbar Maghrabi videoman catching it all. Eddie was mildly surprised the bitch wasn't right there matching him stride for stride and being digitalized for the ages too. She had a major rep for getting herself in stories, and getting the stories into her. Maybe she couldn't take the heat. Journalists liked to brag how bold they were, but when the shit really hit the fan they hunkered down and screamed privilege of the press.

Something tugged at his preconscious, and he twitched his vision field back to Timur. *"Jesus Christ,"* he breathed. At Timur's side, a slim figure in blue jeans, the sheen of midnight hair in the sun: not his imagination, then. *The babe Dr. Shih. He's letting her tag along for* this? He shook his head, wondering which of all of them was craziest.

"Six to Jagun 23. Remember, if anybody makes a play

for Timur, lay waste to everybody within seven meters of him who isn't that little doctor. I'll take the heat for it.''

"It is bad luck to spare the Chinese, Raging Torrent," came back laughing from one of his *kumli* desert rats. *"Raging Torrent"* was the literal translation of *orlok*. It was a better nickname than Blue Sky.

"Put a sock in it, Yoldash."

All around him the crowd screeched and waved its placards. Its fury fell on him like a hail of stones. He kept his head high, his step sure. He was an accomplished faker by now.

Shih Tai-Yu trotted alongside like some brave sleek dog. "Is this what you bargained for, when you sought power?" she shouted.

"I never sought power." He did not raise his voice, but her face told him she heard. Had his voice always possessed such power of penetration?

"Isn't that what tyrants always say?"

The word stung him like a slap. *Tyrant.* He felt his eyes water. "Is that what you think of me?"

"Yes. No. I don't know." She hugged her arms under her breasts and shook her head. "I don't think you are yet. I don't know what you'll become. I can't think clearly. This crowd frightens me."

"It frightens me too." It frightened him for what it might become: a storm of fire to inundate Turkestan, the Muslim lands of the League, the *Dar-ul-Islam* beyond, perhaps. It seemed to him the world was well doused with aromatic fervor and hatred, the most volatile of fuels—not just religious, and not just among Muslims. It would take so little to set off a jihad firestorm that could consume the world.

The prospect that the crowd that surrounded him—two hundred thousand lungs screaming denunciations at him for not raising jihad's green flag—might turn on him and tear him to pieces did not frighten him at all.

"I never wanted power for myself," he told her. "I only wanted the ability to . . . change things. To make them better."

"Doesn't everybody begin that way?" She held her hands over her ears as if that could stanch the anger of the crowd. "No one—no one wants to do evil. *Doesn't it always start with good intentions?*"

He sat his jaw behind his facecloth and told himself she couldn't hear him anymore anyway. It saved having to confront the void of words within him.

He mounted the steps of the great glazed-brick mosque, turned, and spread his hands. He hoped his words were still oil, his people water.

"So you let them riot, and wave pictures of terrorists, and call for your downfall. Did you loose your troops on them? Did you disperse them with a whiff of grape?" Jacqui Gendron sat down heavily on the bed in the spacious suite at Bukhara's Amu-Darya Hotel. "No. You have no understanding of the uses of power."

Timur stood in the center of the bedroom, all at sea, his headcloth coming loose. The Amu was built under foreign supervision, and the paint hadn't started to peel yet. In fact, the room was luxurious, done in shades of butter and lemon as if it had been decorated by a movie set designer.

At length he sat down beside her. "I don't want power. I just want freedom for my people."

"*Faugh.*" She stood, massaged her lumbar spine, stretched backward, facing away from him the while. "The world is teetering on the brink of disorder. It cries for a strong man to pull it back. You could be that man."

"I don't *want* to be that man, Jacqueline. I don't want to save the world; I wouldn't know where to begin. It seems my hands are more than full with Turkestan."

"If you'd shot some troublemakers today, your hands wouldn't be so full. Why not let that American pit bull do it? He has the crazy edge to him. *He'd* be happy to do it, and your precious hands would be clean."

Reflexively he raised his hands, looked at them as if checking for bloodstains. He turned the motion into near-supplication. "I calmed them. I spoke to them, shamed them, for themselves and Turkestan. The mob broke up. Isn't that power enough for you?"

She held up her hands, palm upward, fingers clawed. "A great man must not be afraid to bloody his hands."

"Then I have no wish to be great."

"That choice is yours to make," she said crisply, and went out of the room.

Chapter
THIRTY-FIVE

With the engine of Japan's economy, overstressed by government interference and the trade war with America, sputtering on the verge of throwing a rod, the Indonesians were crowding the Japs hard and wanted the world to know it. The businessman from Bandung was small and smooth, with a walnut-colored baby's face, mirror shades, and a sharkskin suit. He also had two enormous Jordanian rent-a-goons with necks wider than their heads. Renting out Hessians— conscript mercenaries—was a favored revenue enhancer for half the world; Jordan played the game on a more modest scale. Hiring its elite Arab Legionnaires as bodyguards was this season's status symbol. They were called *Husseinis*, because everybody in Jordan is named Hussein.

Deplaning from the 767 in Tashkent, Mr. Hussein took the lead, the businessman from Bandung went second, and Mr. Hussein brought up the rear. As they entered the terminal, the lead Mr. Hussein found the way blocked by a thin, disheveled Westerner in a rumpled tan jacket, who stood blinking at the snow-capped mountains through the green-tinted floor-to-ceiling windows, as if trying to figure out just exactly which mountains they were. Mr. Hussein reached out a satchel-sized hand and took him by the upper arm.

Francis Marron jumped. For a moment he was back in Carson City: the grip on his arm, massive and implacable, the sense of looming male bulk behind him. Pain shot deep in his bowels, tears started in his eyes. *They lied to me again.*

He sees his friend's head, shaking, emitting tut-tut sounds like a scratching chicken. "Too bad what happened in there, old buddy old pal," said Dick Torrance, the original Swinging Richard. "But you know how it goes these days— Tough Love incarceration for all you white-collar criminal types. But hey, just remember to be grateful they're letting all the real hard-core mothers, the mother-stabbers and father-rapers, letting 'em out early to make room for the dope dealers and data pushers and the other hurt-promoters, huh?"

But no. The grip was impersonal as an assumbly-line robot's, the breath warming his cheek studiously minted—the man still had his clothes on. Not prison, then. His heart opened its wings like a startled bird in a rib cage, even as the first Mr. Hussein carefully steered him out of the way and let him go.

Marron blinked around. The people flowing past him were speaking Russian and what seemed two other tongues, familiar but never understood. *Yes, Tashkent.* He was back in Central Asia.

The knowledge hit him like the slam of a cell door. He knew where he was, and why. His good friend, old buddy old pal, had let him out of prison. But only on condition. He had a *little job* for him.

He was still caught in the nightmare. It had just changed venue.

* * *

" 'All right, you son of a bitch. Freeze.' '' Shih looked at him. She sat. He paced. "Did I hear incorrectly, or did you actually say that?"

The wind walked in the shade of the poplar trees down by the wide slow Amu. Eddie nodded glumly. "I did."

Timur had calmed the jihad-maddened masses in Bukhara, which as far as Fast Eddie was concerned came closer to magic than politics, and then had gone to a tent city outside Samarkand to hold court for a while. Francis Marron had followed him there. Eddie was not a happy camper when he learned that. He acted without thought—as usual, more Zen than smart.

She pursed her lips. She looked astonishingly cute when she did that. He hated it when she looked cute after he'd unzipped and stepped on his dick in front of her. Which seemed to be every time they strayed into each other.

"Perhaps you have seen too many American police movies, to burst in upon Timur and Mr. Marron and myself with all those guns," she said in hypothesizing tones. "Or perhaps you suffered momentary—what to call it?—testosterone poisoning."

He made a noise. "Look, the guy has a . . . a rep. There was a dude in Central America a few years back, Acevedo the name was. Leader of a movement down there that favored telling the Americans to keep their hands off the region—no geopolitical games, no drafting the countries into the war on drugs or tobacco or whatever. The U.S. took exception to that, and Señor Acevedo got suddenly dead. Marron's name was . . . *connected*."

She cocked her head to one side. "But the League accuses you Americans of supporting the rebels. Why would your government send an assassin after Timur?"

"I—" He balled his hands to fists, opened them again. No answer fell out on last fall's fallen leaves. "I don't know. It's just—I don't know how good your life expectancy gets to be, if you go putting too much faith in governments. Any government. The League says the Americans are backing Timur, the Americans vote to censure him in the Security Council. Who can say what they really mean—or if they'll mean it tomorrow?''

She sat for a moment with her face turned toward the water and her eyes turned toward the past. That's how it looked to Eddie, at least. Evening was settling on the Amu Dar'ya Valley like a gray blanket, bringing an insidious river peace. Big-winged birds flapped through the dusk ungainly as pterodactyls, seeking night's shelter amid the *tugay,* the riverside forest. Bugs rose in clouds; swallows slashed them through like scimitars. A hummingbird came and faced them, hovering eight feet above the sliding water. Eddie wondered what the hell it was doing there; he didn't think the little bastards drank water, just sucked nectar or whatever.

"You speak very objectively about your country," she said, brushing back a strand of hair black as a magpie's wing. "I would have expected an American soldier of fortune to put up more patriotic display."

He looked at the trees on the far bank so she wouldn't see his eyes. "Let's just say I'm Timur's man now, whatever I was before."

He trusted himself to look at her then. "You probably think I'm a total jerk-off—uh, jerk."

She laughed. "I think you are very refreshing. Gauche, perhaps, but you are unafraid to be *you.* That seems very American. Is it?"

Not no more, if what I see on the evening satellite is any indication. "Don't be judging America in terms of me," he said easily. "You're bound to do someone an injustice."

"You are also very facile. Very skilled at evasion."

"Hey, babe, they don't call me Fast Eddie for nothing. Come on, I'll walk you back; it's getting dark."

When Jacqui Gendron returned from Tashkent late to find the American back and talking with Timur over tea, she was pissed. But not for long. Another mood predominated, and didn't put up with competition.

When the American saw her, he jerked as if an ant had bitten him. He rose, looking disorganized and scared, and excused himself. Despite Timur's invitation to stay, he stumbled out into the velvet-painting Samarkand night.

And that was fine with Jacqui.

"In world news tonight," said the seamless television face, *"two eras come to an end. In a press conference this evening in the nation's capital, the American Federal Police Agency claimed responsibility for the death of noted infopusher Fred Derwillis, gunned down leaving a brothel in Bogotá, Colombia. Derwillis, a pioneer of the hypertext concept in computing, was the creator of the outlaw* Encyclopaedia Universalis *information network, who had fought off numerous American extradition attempts.*

'Apparently the assassination was timed to coincide with the final dissolution of America's controversial Central Intelligence Agency, whose functions are being absorbed by the FPA's parent Department of Enforcement Affairs."

Enforcement Secretary Serafin appeared then, his hair slicked, his cheeks smooth, his eyes puffy. Francis Marron felt his scrotum contract.

"Today we finally recognize that the Cold War is long dead and buried," Serafin said. *"The war we're fighting now is against the hurt-promoters who prey on the minds and bodies of our children. The message we sent today was clear: this war knows no borders, and we're in it for the win."*

His face was replaced by the face of Dick Torrance, the original Swinging Richard, with a shock of black hair in his eyes and his mouth in a mean fox grin.

"Francis," the head said, and shook, as Marron's fingers scrabbled at the carpet which served as inadequate intermediary between his butt and hard-packed soil. "Francis, you're dragging your feet. This just won't do, at all, at all."

Marron covered his face with his hands. When he looked

again at his satlinked notebook computer, the screen was blank.

Timur sat on the futon and unwound the cloth from his head. The act had a ritual quality to it. It enabled him to breathe more easily in more than the physical sense; with the headcloth he put aside a burden, a life, a lie. Without the mask he was no longer Timur. *If only I didn't have to put it on again tomorrow.*

He looked up into the eye of a palm-sized camcorder. Its scrutiny stung his face like a splash of acid.

He jumped up, waving splayed hands like palms fronds between the camera and his face. "Jacqui, what are you *doing*?"

She danced back, evading him easily and laughing with silver malice. "Come on, Timur. I am a photojournalist, I live for the visuals. Can't I have *something* to remember you by?"

He looked in her eyes. His hands dropped to his sides. He nodded. "Very well. Take your pictures."

She was wearing a loose robe in pastel swirl, that left her long shanks bare. He came to her, purposefully, heavily, opened the robe. She was nude beneath. He dropped to his knees. Laughing, she aimed the camera down, following him, holding the focus as he buried his face in her.

In his own tent, not far from Timur's, Fast Eddie tried to gear down and go to sleep and *not* think about Dr. Shih Tai-Yu. He cracked his notebook comp for a quick look around the world in general. He was getting to be a real Nethead.

There was just one message in his personal mailbox. He thought about blanking it, then thought, *What the fuck, over.* He punched it up.

It read: *"Alyosha, it is imperative that we meet at once."*
It was signed *"Arbatov."*

Chapter
THIRTY-SIX

The wind scattered sand in fistfuls like a gambler throwing dice. It would have ruffled the hair of Arkady Arbatov, chief of the Fifth Chief Directorate of the KGB, if he'd had any. Ruffled his eyebrows, though.

Fast Eddie stood with hands in the pockets of his baggy khaki pants, looking at Arbatov across the floor of the natural amphitheater in the heart of the Red Sands. That same wind had shaped these yellow sandstone walls.

"You said we had to meet," he said. "We're meeting."

Arbatov removed a handkerchief from an inside pocket of his ill-fitting tieless suit, mopped at his gleaming forehead. "You did not pick an appropriate meeting place."

Eddie fished an apple from his pocket and began to eat. "I like it. I like the desert. The dry heat clears my sinuses."

Arbatov's eyebrows lowered like thunderheads. "You should show more respect," Arbatov said. "You are surrounded."

"I am?" Eddie's right hand was still jammed in a pants pocket. He wiggled the thumb.

The sandstone bowl filled with thunder, loud as a sun-tipped ICBM lighting off from the silos of Tyuratam, not many kilometers northwest of here. It was a noise that threatened to crush the skull. That strong man Arbatov, that giant, staggered as it reverberated. He barely paid attention to the geyser of dust that squirted up practically between his legs and rose higher than the dome of his head.

"That was the sound of a 14.5-millimeter Steyr-Mannlicher Anti-Matériel Rifle, fired by a one-hundred-and-three-year-old *yefreytor*. Shoots pretty good for an old guy, huh? You let me have the home field advantage, Arkasha. Panic move; not bright. Now, are you convinced, or would you like me to start having the heads of your *Komitet* goon squad rolled down to us, one by one? You have a very sexy little MiG/Mitsubishi *Uragan,* just big enough for you and about thirty of your favorite leg-breakers, parked on an old road five klicks from here. You can start talking like a human being. Or you can start walking back to your plane." He took a bite of apple. *"Alone."*

Arbatov straightened arthritically and put his hands in his own coat pockets. *Probably has a hideout piece in there,* thought Eddie, munching. It didn't give him much concern. The day he couldn't beat a sixty-year-old Chekist to the draw was one day longer than he had any business living.

"Very well," Arbatov said, with ursine dignity, "we have made the appropriate noises. As I shouted, so you echoed. Now we must talk."

Crunch. "So talk."

"You must kill Timur."

"Horsecrap."

"It has become vitally important. It was always your mission—"

"It was *never* my mission. Just how fucking stupid do you think I am? You wanted me to *help* Timur, and you wanted me in place to feed you information so *you* could help him. You wanted him to fry Al Capone, not that that's any hair off my balls. Why? Was Karponin getting too big? Did you figure he was going to lead the armed forces in a *Putsch* against your precious League, maybe just put you State Security buttholes out of business for good?"

Across the drifted sand that floored the yellow stone bowl, Arbatov locked eyes with Eddie. He must not have liked what he saw. He dropped his gaze to stare at the toes of his cardboard shoes. No Giorgio Armanis for him; he was an anachronism, and Eddie guessed he knew it.

The huge man sighed. Even over twenty meters of wind

Eddie heard the gust. "We wanted Timur to win. Karponin's death was incidental; he did not worry us. He was a fool."

"You got that right. But what the fuck, over? You boys are supposed to help keep the League together."

"We are Russians first of all—the leadership of the committee, as well as I—and you."

"What's that got to do with the price of poontang in Peshawar?"

"You are not really a Westerner, though your time in America has affected your habits of thought and speech, and hardly for the better. You know we supported Mikhayl Gorbachev to the end. How could we not, when he was the hand-picked successor of the great Andropov, who brought the Committee for State Security for the first time to a position of dominance in the affairs of *Rodina Mat'*? But it was more than simply loyalty to the political line of Yuriy Vladimirovich Andropov. We—most of us—truly believed reform was necessary. Truly a comic irony, is it not, that the dreaded KGB should favor reform over repression?"

"My sides are splitting."

"It was not from cosmopolitanism that we believed in reform. We knew, better than any, how horribly the engine was strained. We knew it would break down unless something was done. We had to sacrifice some power, or lose all."

"That's ancient history. Where's your point?"

"So American you have become. So impatient, so uncaring for history—"

"That's a load of crap, but *that's* beside the point. What the hell does any of this have to do with Timur?"

"We recognized the League for a good thing. Let us speak openly as Great Russians: it was a means by which Russia could maintain herself as a virtual empire, without having to pay the concomitant costs. This is not without precedent; in classical times there was—"

"The Delian League," Eddie finished. "The old Athenian scam. It was supposed to protect the Aegean Greek cities from the Persians. All the city-states paid their dues to Athens, which spent the loot any damn way it pleased—mostly on monuments and the Athenian fleet. When anybody tried to back out of this snug little arrangement—'' He shrugged. "Well, what else you gonna use your fleet for?''

He laughed. "You know, deep down I always wondered if that's what the Kremlin was up to. Gorbachev, Yel'tsin—they planned it all along.''

Arbatov hung his head. "I underestimated you Americans. I see that now.''

"Don't reason beyond the evidence, old man. You underestimated *me*.''

Arbatov grimaced. He dabbed at the sweat dripping from his eyebrows. "The League was a success. Everyone admits that. The European Community honestly believes we structured ourselves in emulation of *them,* more fools they. But we did not make the rage and resentment go away. We only made them vanish from view, like painting over rust. Even before the Red Sands revolt broke out in Tashkent, it was apparent to us that the League could not hold.''

"Maybe I'm slow, but how does that add up to giving a helping hand to the rebels?''

"You know the armed forces would never consent to letting the League peacefully dissolve. But if it does not dissolve, it will explode.''

"So you set the dynamite. You were gonna destroy the League in order to *save* it? Say, you bozos really didn't learn anything from Vietnam either, did you?''

"We saw it more as venting steam to save the boiler. The Muslim republics were the most unmanageable. Their religious and nationalist aspirations were too intractable, and their population increasing too rapidly—in a few years, there would be more Muslims in the League than Europeans of any sort. Holding on to Central Asia was the most obviously self-defeating course—although, ultimately, we were prepared to let all the republics go, if we must.''

"But why? What's left?''

"Russia. The Motherland. *Our* nation."

"But what about Great Russia's 'messianic rights,' and all that other happy horseshit those Rad-Trad fruitcakes are always going on about? I mean, you're still talking about blowing off your big, bad empire."

"I have one word to answer that: Siberia."

"Why do I have this impression that the more you say, the less you tell me?"

"You are very impertinent for a senior lieutenant."

"Yeah, but I'm about spot-on for a field marshal, even a Third World one. Since you bring it up, you're taking a pretty lofty tone for somebody with an unknown quantity of firepower aimed at the middle button of his burlap blazer."

"You would not dare harm me."

Eddie let the wind, singing along the fluted white and yellow walls, provide his answer.

Arbatov wiped his face some more. "Very well; I know where the crayfish hibernate. You wonder why we are now willing to let the League be stripped down to the bare Russian Republic, and I gave you the answer. Siberia. The greatest repository of raw materials remaining on the surface of the earth. With those resources, properly exploited, Russia herself, the Motherland, could be as great a superpower as the League or Union ever were. Greater. Without them—" He spread his hamhock hands. "We are a Third World country. Black-asses in whiteface."

"I remember, back when devolution was going down, there was some noise about Siberia splitting off. Came to big nothing, though."

"Not then. And of course, the Siberian populace is predominantly Great Russian. There is affinity between her and Russia west of the Urals."

"There was a lot of affinity between England and her American colonies too."

"You have hit the eye and not the brow. You speak in terms of explosions; let us change metaphors. We—the *Komitet*—felt that the League was grown gangrenous. Better to cut off the leg before the mortification got too near the heart.''

"Only you decided to let the leg amputate itself," Eddie said, "with covert guidance from all you master surgeons at KGB Central."

"Precisely."

Eddie snorted. "So why the sudden change in plans? The operation's a success, Doc. Where's the problem?''

"Now we are caught between hammer and anvil. Karponin's death gave the moderates a winter's grace. They accomplished nothing; the non-Russian republics are in turmoil, on the verge of outright rebellion."

"So what? That's what you wanted. Kiss 'em good-bye, and get on with your life."

"*We* would like nothing better. Unfortunately, hard-liners have seized the upper hand in the armed forces—both of the League and of the Russian Republic. They aren't willing to let the League break apart."

"Tough."

"It could be tougher than you imagine, Senior Lieutenant Gorsunov. On you and me and everyone in the world. A faction within the regime has already sent a message to the Americans: if the League falls apart, the League will launch its missiles at Germany and China and America. These madmen would rather burn the world than see it run by their rivals."

"Bullshit. And the name is Randolph, Edwin A. Gorsunov is dead."

Arbatov rolled hands into fists as big as Eddie's head. "I swear to you. Before God, it is the truth. You must kill Timur. Or billions will die."

"Fuck that noise. *Fuck* it. You think your problems will dry up and blow away, just because one man dies? Wake up and smell the coffee, Chief Director. The League's had it, it's dead as the Union, and if the crazy bastards in the Kremlin don't realize it, then there's not one damn thing you or I can do."

"The symbolic impact—"

"Would make him a martyr. You're just seeing a little brushfire. Waste Timur, and it's a firestorm."

"There will be many firestorms, if the reactionaries start World War III."

"Then there's *nothing we can do about it*. Face it, Arkasha: if we're living in a world where crazies can get their fingers on the button, then it's all only a matter of time before they push it, isn't it? If we all go together when we go, I'd just as soon get it the fuck over with."

"Please—"

"At least we'll die free. I don't know that I *want* to live in the world that's coming around, the world as it'll be if this rebellion goes down. A New World Order where we're all the property of the secret police and the social scientists and the military and the bureaucrats, where who we fuck and what we smoke and when we take a crap is all regulated by five different agencies, all of whom contradict each other. That's no way to live. But I'm not making that choice for anybody else. If the fucks in Moscow blow up the world, *they're* making the choice."

For a moment Arbatov just stood there and blew like a racehorse coming off a furlong. "If you have no loyalty to the Motherland—"

Eddie went white. *"Don't hit me with that crap!"* he screamed. "Who sent me out here to help the rebels? *Who ordered me to kill the Motherland's fucking sons?"*

Up there among the rocks, out of sight, fingers took up trigger slack at the *orlok*'s obvious fury. Arbatov sensed it, took it like a blow, but he was a brave old bastard. He held his head up and drove on.

"The American Federal Police are feeling triumphant from their victory over the CIA, and savage over the collapse of their precious Clean Sweep. That is a volatile combination. Your father—"

"I don't have a father. There was a Party hack the Party gave me who called himself that. He was like everything else the Party issued: a lump of shit."

"So you turn your back on your oath, and your people, and even on your own flesh and blood?"

"I turn my face toward the light, Jack. We will be free."

"You seek to crush water in a mortar."

"I'm not your errand boy anymore. This marionette snipped his own damn strings. I won't kill Timur. I won't do anything for you. Make *that* a notch in your nose, you aphoristic son of a bitch."

Arbatov exhaled through flared nostrils. "You should not think that I did not know that by coming here, I would put myself in your power," he said.

"You want the last word?" Eddie laughed. "You asked for it, you got it. *Liga*." He threw down the apple core, gave Arbatov his back, and walked away.

"You think you've cleared away all your illusions, stripped away all masks," Arbatov yelled after him. "What of the mask Timur hides behind?"

Slowly Eddie turned back to him. "Say a word against Timur and I'll have my men shoot you to pieces. Slowly."

Arbatov swallowed. He thought about it. Then he said, "As you wish. But seek the truth for yourself, if you think you can face it."

Eddie held up a warning hand. "Seek the Land of Flowers," Arbatov said. "You'll find the answer there to a question you don't have the guts to ask."

"Never talk to me again," Eddie said. He climbed up over the lip of the sandstone bowl, and the endless desert swallowed him up.

The *Uragan* reentered League airspace over the yellow poison flats on the Aral's eastern edge. As it did, a slim Sukhoi-27 interceptor, painted a delicate robin's-egg blue, rolled in eleven klicks behind it.

The MiG/Mitsu was a radical design, with two pusher-prop engines in the rear, a delta wing, a bone-in-the-nose canard. Its engines gave off little heat, its polymerized graphite fuselage produced a poor radar return. It was hard to see, and hard to track.

The interceptor pilot knew where to look. He saw it, a tiny dart of white, rapidly growing larger as the SU-27 overtook it. And what he saw, the television eye of the AA-13 missile under his right wing saw also.

A buzzer in his ear announced that the Japanese microchip in the missile's nose had memorized and fixated upon the *Uragan*'s shape. It was a point-and-shoot missile, and now it would follow the aircraft relentlessly.

A bulky-gloved thumb depressed a button. The Sukhoi rocked gently as the missile hissed away. The pilot watched the white plume stretch out before him, as a second chime told him that the missile was guiding true.

He pulled the Sukhoi's needle nose up level; he was several hundred meters higher than the *Uragan*, and had entered a gentle dive during target acquisition. He kept the plane on course until he saw a flash of yellow light.

He was over the *Uragan*, then. It looked as though a great white shark had bitten off the rear of the craft: the twin engines had vanished, and much of the wing. The airplane was beginning to fall like a leaf.

The pilot smiled and chinned his radio. "The target is destroyed," he said, and banked his aircraft right, toward his home airfield on the fringe of the great Baykonur Space Complex.

Chapter
THIRTY-SEVEN

At a little after noon, Marina Kuliyeva left the small private clinic near the Skifovskiy Surgical Institute on

Moscow's Sadovaya, where she worked as a drug and alcohol counselor, to walk the six blocks to the apartment she shared with her parents, her daughters, and her husband—if God and Timur ever let him come home again. Today was ostensibly a school day, but all classes had been canceled; something to do with the civil disturbances. She welcomed the chance for a lunch at home with her children. It helped distract her from the nagging, unanswerable question: *When is Daddy coming home?*

As she went down the cement steps, pitted by ice and the salt scattered to combat it, two men in long overcoats approached, one from either side. She stopped, watching them with open wariness. She was a tall, willowy, darkly beautiful woman, who kept herself in rigorous shape. Shape to run, to fight if necessary.

"Marina Mikhaylovna Kuliyeva?" asked the younger of the two. His breath smoked; winter in Moscow had more staying power this year than in the Tien Shans.

She nodded cautiously. "That's me."

"You must come with us. You are under arrest."

She recoiled. Ferret quick, the man seized her wrist. As her eyes filled with angry, surprised tears, she looked past her captor and his partner. For the first time she realized she faced a firing squad of video cameras.

"What's going on here?" she demanded. "Take me to my daughters!"

"Have no fear," the older man said. "We will."

Beside the unmetaled road a small stone marker read LIGKHOZ 23. Inside the wire, a large wooden sign read, WELCOME TO GULISTAN. It had a bunch of roses painted on it, red, faded brownish like bloodstains by weather and sun. *Gulistan* literally meant "land of roses" or "rose garden." By extension it meant "the Land of Flowers." Synecdoche they called that, unless it was metonymy.

The tape strip across the gate said KARANTIN. *Quarantine.* It had those little trefoils of interlocked circles like short-handed Olympic symbols on it, that stood for *biohazard*.

The tape was faded translucent and cross-linked brittle by the sun. Eddie stepped over it and walked on toward the building. Whatever hazard had been here was unlikely still to be viable. He thought he knew what it was.

The farm had that indefinable air of abandonment. Nothing really overt; this wasn't the inner city, where the walls of derelict dwellings were paint-sticked with graffiti by punks and displaced Central Asian toughs, and the windows shot out by *para* gangs of angry VDV vets out looking for some hapless lone *militsioner* to tie to a lamppost and garrote, and the hallways stank of the piss of the homeless who had begun to throng Soviet cities after Amnesty International made the government quit putting them in concentration camps. All was intact, except for maybe a couple of panes of glass blown out by the wind.

But the stucco had flaked a little bit too much off the main building's adobe walls, and the henhouse had fallen down, and the tractor parked beside a toolshed had turned into a tractor-shaped lump of rust. People had cared for this place, kept it up better than most cooperative farmers did. Then they stopped.

Eddie rounded a corner, almost tripped over a red tricycle lying on its side. He stood on tiptoe to peer through a window, feeling absurdly like a Peeping Tom. Inside was a dormitory-style room. The bed still needed to be made. A good Sony TV with a videoflip player sitting on top of it rested on a wooden crate. It was as if all the occupants had been called away at once and had somehow neglected to return.

They had been carried out, if Eddie's guess was right. By health workers in bulky protective suits, working hastily and afraid to touch anything they didn't absolutely have to. Whether to set matters right or loot.

Eddie's lips twisted. It was ironic that they'd been so afraid. Had they been at risk, they would have already been dead.

He walked on. The buildings gave out and he stood looking out on a vast rose garden, row upon once-meticulous row, the bushes now overgrown and winter-barren. *The best roses in all the Fergana Valley came from there*, the Kirghiz waiter with the retro-Chinese pigtail had told him. *That's why they called it* Gulistan.

Then he shivered and made a complicated hand gesture. To avert evil, like.

Eddie stooped, picked up a rock, threw it as far as he could. Carrion crows rose squawking in indignation from among the bushes, and flew away southwest on the wind like damned souls.

"So who wants to watch the Nashville Satellite Network?" the big man demanded. He took a hit of coffee, wiped his red handlebar mustache with the back of a freckled hand, and slammed his mug down on the mess hall tabletop. "Don't everybody speak up at once."

The off-duty boys from Bravo and Delta sections of Jagun 23 laughed in a desultory way. Though they were under explicit instructions from Eddie-*khan* and Senior Lieutenant Aliyev not to forget the Russian was a prisoner, they thought he was a pretty good guy to hang out with. He was never going to be accepted completely; he had caused the deaths of comrades, after all, though nobody's blood relation— which was fortunate, because if he had, not even the threat of execution would have kept him alive. But he knew how to live, and he knew how to laugh, and when he laughed, others did too. That translated to a wary popularity.

"I would rather set my tongue on fire and beat it out with a camel-prickle bush," a young Sart from Kattakurgan announced proudly, "than listen to that crap." Everyone tittered, Eastern style. Kolya Kuliyev guffawed. It was a Cowboy kind of thing to say.

Musical tastes in the unit ran to rap and Moroccan-roll, notwithstanding both were big-time passé in the West. The only thing they hated worse than C&W was Serious. Kolya was with them, and absent *orlok* Eddie too, as far as hating Serious went. They were all confirmed Airheads—as Serious fans called anyone out of tune with their duty-bound, socially conscious, anti-individualistic post-rock sound. It was a play on A/C, which could stand for either "anti-communitarian" or "air-conditioning."

A Kirghiz kid with a powder burn from a VDV Kalashnikov still plainly stamped on one chipmunk cheek picked up the remote control for the mess hall TV. He began to cycle through the channels in the endless and traditionally futile quest for something worth watching. Even an all-male military unit, a third of whom were adolescents or just past, could only watch Brazilian porn feeds so much of the time.

"*Yob tvoyu mat'!*" Kolya exclaimed. His hand clamped on the Kirghiz kid's biceps. The kid rolled his eyes, hurting and apprehensive, and the squaddies eyed one another. Was Nikolay the Nikolay about to make a break for it?

Kolya enveloped the boy's hand with his own, pressed his thumb down on the youngster's, hovering over the backup button. The screen flickered, and there was an evening-news feed from Moscow State TV, showing two men and a tall, dark woman on a city street.

"—ovna Kuliyeva, wife of Junior Lieutenant Nikolai Stepanovich Kuliyev, who has been a prisoner of the Central Asian bandits since the battle of the Qizil Qum last summer. She and her daughter Anya were among several hundred family members of suspected defectors arrested today in a League-wide sweep—"

The Kirghiz cried out as Kolya crushed his hand and the controller in one convulsive squeeze. It took ten of them to subdue the big Russian, bad back and all.

"Frank," the face on the screen said, "just what the fuck do you think you're *doing* here? This isn't playtime. You got a job to do."

Francis Marron sat there, feeling as if a small hand were holding his tongue. *If I answer and he's not real, that makes me crazy. If he's real and I don't answer, that'll make him mad.*

"Frank, there is a very specific thing you have to do. When you've done that you send us a specific signal, and then we come and clean up the mess and make sure you get away okay. It's all worked out."

Yeah, he thought. *It's all worked out. It was all worked out before.*

His very own buddy had laid it out for him. He sees it now, like a nightmare video.

"*Look, pal. You can go down easy, or you can go down hard, but one way or another you're going down.*"

"*But I didn't do anything,*" *he says weakly.*

Torrance laughing. "*You are looking at this from a very outmoded perspective, my man.*" *He reaches forward to slap Marron's cheek.* "*Hello! Hello! Are we awake yet? We are the* government, *we determine reality. The government says you did it, so you did it. All right? The question is, whether you're going to admit it or not.*"

"*I'll fight you,*" *Marron says.*

"*With what? The securities charges add up to a RICO rap. That means no lawyer will touch you. If he does, we land on him and take him for everything he's got, because hey, who can say if one of the dollars he used to pay for his boat or his condo or his kid's braces might have been the fruit of one of your illegal enterprises. And if some bleeding heart fool agrees to represent you for nothing . . . well, that's going to cast serious doubt on his* competence, *isn't it? Not to mention his morality—stepping forward to defend an antisocial fuck like you.*"

He shows his eyeteeth. They are very sharp. "*The U.S. attorney handling this case did a year as an intern with the Attorney General's office in Managua under the Sandinistas. They know how to handle obnoxious defense attorneys down there. We learned a lot more than just how to* desaparecido *people down in Central America, good buddy.*"

Marron shakes his head with exaggerated swings, as if this is all a nightmare he can somehow dislodge from his brain. "*I won't do it, God damn you, I won't!*"

"*Sure you will, good buddy, sure you will. You'll stand*

up there in court, and you'll stand up there in Congress, and you'll say exactly what we tell you to. We're going to sink fucking Central Intelligence, and you're going to be a good little torpedo. And in exchange for that, you do a little light time in some federal country club and walk away."

"No no no no—"

"Yes, yes, yes, yes. Or—let me see. You lose everything— got that? And everybody who invested with you—everybody who trusted you—they lose everything too, poof! Because, who knows if they may have gotten hold of some of your tainted money too? And, let's see. Your daughter. You obviously have not been instilling her with proper communitarian values. We might have to take her away from you. There's a serious shortage of foster families, so we'd have to put her in a camp. Not a National Service camp—not that I'd want my daughter in one of those, nothing unpatriotic or anything, you understand—but a girl's shock incarceration camp. It's supposed to do wonders for attitude adjustment. Of course, if you're squeamish about your daughter getting fucked with a broomstick . . ."

It was after midnight when Eddie, exercising an *orlok*'s privilege, let himself into Timur's tent. He pushed through the waiting room and the reception chamber and into the inner sanctum, not caring what Timur was doing or whom he was doing it to.

But Timur was miraculously alone. No Shih, no orange-haired journalist bimbo, not even his latest shadow Marron. Just the man himself, reading a book by the light of a kerosene lamp. He looked up.

Eddie faltered. The fugue state that had carried him back from the high Fergana Valley dissipated, leaving him adrift and wondering what the hell he thought he was doing.

"Ah, Timur-*janaap*," he mumbled, "sorry to bother you. Maybe I should come back tomorrow."

"Not at all, Senior Lieutenant Gorsunov. Why don't you sit down and join me in some tea?"

Chapter
THIRTY-EIGHT

He had broken down, of course. Given them everything they wanted. And they stuck him in the hell of Fort Carson and left him to rot.

Now they had taken him out again.

"Frank?" Dick Torrance said. "Talk to me, Frank. We have a *situation* here, the pressure is getting very intense at this level, if you know what I mean. We be rolling for *mucho* high stakes here, buddy. I can't afford to have you go blank on me—"

"Mr. Marron?"

He broke the connection with a fumbling guilty snap, spun to face the entrance to his tent. As he did, he realized that this wasn't a dream, wasn't hallucination. He had really been speaking with Torrance. *This time*.

"May I come in?"

She was standing with one hand up at the top of the doorway, putting on her best Bacall slink. It was wasted. He bobbed his head as if it were attached to the body of a stuffed dog in the back window of a taxi.

"Please do."

The warm air that accompanied her in was scented in jasmine with undefinable accents. The perfume she had chosen came from a Third World country that wasn't signatory to the accords that allegedly kept cosmetics free of unsafe or environmentally impious substances. Breathless rumors—carefully disseminated and nurtured by corporate agents—whispered that the scent contained actual human pheromones, designed to drive any viable male into a sexual frenzy, and derived from human corpses. It was hooey, but then, no human pheromone had ever been isolated. As fraud, it was no more brazen than nuclear winter.

It was intensely illegal anyway. That was what gave it its real aphrodisiac edge, mostly in the user's perception. It was not really that expensive. So much was illegal these days, and what was legal so encumbered with taxes and regulations that much of what actual business got transacted was perforce on the black—on the left, as the Russians said back in their bad old days. Here, as in so many other ironic ways, the ostensibly free world had passed the League going in the opposite direction.

She entered and sat down across the tent from him. The yellow light from his turned-down kerosene lamp softened her features, turned her eyes large and luminous and topaz-colored. She wore khaki pants deceptively similar to her usual telejournalist kit, but cut closer and lacking the pockets. She wore a lightweight mauve blouse that just happened to be unbuttoned to her navel.

"Mr. Marron," she said, "I've been watching you."

Yes, he thought, *with distaste.* He flicked his eyes hurriedly to her face, then, to see if he'd unintentionally spoken the words aloud, or if she'd heard them anyway. Sometimes it seemed to him that everyone around him was hearing everything he thought.

He made himself nod. His capacity for thought and volition had gone away somewhere. Until they came back, he could just play the role. He could do that with anybody; he'd been raised to it since birth.

She leaned forward, allowing her blouse to fall open a little farther. If he craned his head slightly, he could see her nipples. He did not.

"I think you are the one man I can talk to," she said breathlessly. "There's an energy in you. A power. I can *feel* it."

Yes, he thought. *I'm crazy. That's not power you feel, that's schizophrenia.*

"A great opportunity exists here in Turkestan," she told him. "This is a World-Historical moment."

Jacqui was playing to herself; but then, she was always her best audience. "Timur has proven himself unworthy to seize this great moment, to play the role of the strong man, the Napoleon, the Alexander—the Tamerlane. For a long time I wondered why. Now I know."

She reached out to touch her fingertips to his wrist, where the end of his cuff exposed skin. "I have been researching Timur's background in Tashkent. I have learned something, a terrible secret." She executed a quick the-walls-have-ears glance around the tent.

"Timur is a fake. An impostor. More than that—" Her voice fell to the bottom of her throat, *"he's an agent of the KGB."*

Marron watched her, apparently alert and receptive, wondering exactly what he was supposed to make of what she was telling him. If he was supposed to care.

Interpreting his silence as the stunned variety, she put herself beside him, so quickly she might have teleported there. *That's funny,* he thought. *I never used to think in fanciful terms like that.*

She laid her palm on his chest. His Brooks Brothers shirt was open against the heat beating up from the ground. His chest hair was chestnut-colored, and slightly grizzled.

"You are touched by Destiny," she said. "I feel it in here."

He glanced at the open screen of his notebook computer. It was still blank; Torrance wasn't watching him. He smiled. This woman was so sure of herself, so sure she knew everything about him. And yet she knew nothing at all.

"Yes," she said, running her fingers inside his shirt. "You feel it too, don't you? You are American. Americans are always confident; they are touched by destiny, and they know it. We Europeans, we are decadent, we hate to admit it. But the future belongs to you."

"To me," he echoed. If he hadn't been so numb, he would have laughed aloud at the absurdity of it.

"To you." She took one of his hands in hers, held it up as if she could tell him something new about it.

"These are strong hands. Capable hands. Hands that can seize the moment. Seize your destiny."

This was too much. "Seize it how?"

"Kill Timur."

"What?" He frowned in incomprehension. He started to pull his hand away.

She held fast to it. *"Kill him,"* she whispered, and licked the lobe of his ear. Her blouse had come all the way open and fallen halfway down her shoulders. Her small breasts pressed his arm and chest.

"Kill him. He's obstructing History. It is the destiny of America and Russia to rule the world together. He is standing in the way. You have the chance to remove him. *Kill him.*"

"Kill him? Kill Timur?" He started to laugh.

"That's it," Dick Torrance said from the turned-off computer screen. "Kill the puke. She's got it."

This woman was trying to seduce him into doing the thing he had been let out of prison and sent back to Central Asia to do. The thing his old friend had been badgering him from the screen to do since he had arrived.

She thought she could fuck him into doing that. After all the times he'd been fucked already. It was too funny. Big fat tears started rolling from his eyes.

When he started to laugh, she knew she had him. That was what her script said, and as a good advocacy journalist she always made sure she had her stories well written before she went out and got them.

She slid off her khaki trousers. She wore nothing beneath them. She writhed against him, smooth and lively as an eel, while her fingers adroitly opened his fly.

He wasn't hard. That was no problem. The powerful men, the movers and the shakers—the only kind she cared for—were mostly older men, preoccupied men, and not uncommonly saddled with a dependency on one or another form of synthetic self-esteem that interfered with their responses. For business and pleasure both, she had learned a good many tricks.

He gazed past her shoulder at the open screen. He saw news footage playing there now. Footage of him being led from the Senate building in leg irons.

He had just finished testifying before a secret Senate subcommittee how the CIA had orchestrated the Red Sands uprising. Swinging Richard was swinging along beside him, grinning all over his long fox face.

"That was great, buddy boy. Just great." He slapped Marron on the arm. "Too bad you're headed for a long stay at Carson City."

"Carson City? That's maximum security! You—you told me I'd do easy time."

"Hey." Torrance held his hands up by his shoulders. "I lied. By the way, your wife's going for a divorce. This legal thing is just a pretext, something that'll look good when she files. The real truth is she was just fed up with you."

Marroon stared at him, lips hanging loose. Disasters were coming too fast to process. "Elinor? Divorce—?"

"It was bound to happen anyway. You two just didn't communicate. Did you know your wife loves it in the ass? No, of course not. You see, old buddy, you were just too big a weenie ever to find that out—"

The body memory of the impact of his fist on the side of Torrance's face made him hard, though he still felt no excitement.

Jacqui moaned. She pushed him back, and straddled him, and sank herself upon him.

Chapter
THIRTY-NINE

"When did you make me?"

Eddie sat down and accepted a *piyaala* from Timur. The tea was hot enough to burn his lips. He never felt it. What he felt was the quavery release/relief he imagined serial killers felt when the cops snapped the cuffs on.

"The first time I saw you, there in the schoolyard." Timur began to unwind his blue-checked headcloth. Eddie watched, too surfeited with emotion to be surprised. When he was done, Timur tossed the cloth aside with a relieved grunt, as if the cloth were lead.

The face that looked at Eddie was . . . just a face. Middle-aged, mildly handsome. Remarkable only in how unremarkable it was.

Then why the mask bit? a voice asked at the back of Eddie's skull. It was as if someone else were in there with him; the only question that might have had real relevance to Eddie was what would become of him, and he didn't care. He was drained of curiosity. Whatever came, he accepted in advance.

"I wish you wouldn't stare at me so fixedly," Timur said. "It makes me quite uncomfortable. There is nothing supernatural about my spotting you so quickly; you had *plant* written all over you. I know the signs; I was KGB myself for twenty-five years. First for the Soviets, then for the League."

Eddie breathed shallowly, as if the sound of his breathing might drown important words. "You mean you—Timur was a double agent all along?"

"I mean nothing of the sort." Timur giggled, and then the laugh erupted from his belly in full-blown Western fashion. "My boy, not only am I not Tamerlane, I'm not even Timur."

"What?" Eddie said.

Timur picked up his cup, drained it, and set it down again. "The man known to the underground as Timur was an authentic resistance leader for many years, a very brave and clever man who never had the resources to be more than a gnat buzzing in the Nikolays' ear. Eventually he got unlucky, and was arrested in Samarkand, his stronghold.

"There were already riots going on at that time. KGB transferred him to its regional headquarters in Tashkent to prevent his rescue by street mobs. They wanted to try to buy him off, or, barring that, discredit him with a show trial: lots of media, lots of manufactured evidence that he was a drug kingpin or something equally unpopular. The League can be quite as heavy-handed as ever the Soviets were, but they knew better than to make him an out-and-out martyr."

He braced his hands on the carpet and raised his rump off the cushion to give his tailbone a momentary respite. "I spoke to him in jail. I wanted to help him. I could offer him the things he lacked: organization, equipment, direct intelligence of his enemies' actions. I had quite a thriving network built up by that time myself, and it was all at his disposal. But he refused. He called me *agent provocateur*. He was really very vehement."

"What happened then?"

"He died. Suicide. One of his many secrets was that he was diabetic, which he withheld until it was too late for our doctors to save him." Timur smiled. "So I combined his network with mine, and I became him. After that, things went as you saw them on the evening news."

Eddie sat for a while and stared into the yellow glare of the lamp. Finally he asked, "Why?"

Timur leaned back with his hands on his thighs. "A long time ago there was a Sart, mostly Tadzhik, whose name was Ivan Yakovovich Mukhtaari. His father dreamed of nothing so much in the world as to have his son become fully assimilated, to shed the stigma of being a black-ass. But the father died while the boy was still in his teens, of cancer.

"In college the boy was a good student, able at both the humanities and mathematical subjects. He could have been many things: a scientist, an economist, a lawyer. What he became was an analyst for the Committee for State Security. How better to secure a place in the *nomenklatura* and fulfill his father's dream?"

He shook his head and sighed. "Our Ivan Yakovovich worked hard for his new masters. The *Komitet* was just beginning to notice computers then. It picked our young man to be among the first to learn to work with them, in spite of his ethnic background. He was sure his father's spirit saw him and was proud, though as a good Communist he was properly ashamed of such beliefs.

"The young man met a young half-Kirghiz woman from Fergana, from a farm where they grew the world's finest roses. Shaaira, she was named, "poetess," and she was, she was—along with many other things. She made the young man happy, happier than he ever thought he could be.

"As a poet she was a student of the language and cultural traditions of the Central Asian *millet,* and sometimes in private she spoke critically of the Soviet state. A serious crime, but these were the seventies, you see, when the Red Star was in its ascendancy. The Union was destined to lead the world into a glorious Communist dawn, and how could the views of a brilliant but unworldly woman impede the historical process? So the young man neglected his duty to report her.

"Despite their occasional differences, they were happy, those two. Not even the fact that they could not seem to have children came between them. Soviet doctors gave them conflicting information as to why. In the end it didn't matter, because after eight years of marriage Shaaira conceived and bore a daughter, and two years later she bore a second."

"No sons?" Eddie asked.

"No. Two daughters only. Most Turkestanis would have

been disappointed, I grant, but this young man—no longer quite so young—was so well assimilated that he didn't mind the lack of sons. For all her love of tradition, Shaaira was in her own way quite modern. So all of them were happy.

"Then when the girls were six and eight—some thirty-one months and seven days ago—Shaaira took them for a month's stay at the farm where she had been born, and where her own parents still lived."

Eddie tried to moisten dry lips. *"Gulistan."*

Timur nodded. "League Farm 23. You know it?"

"I've been there."

"You are very clever to have learned so much. You must know what happened then."

"Given what I saw, and the time frame, I'd say *white.*"

Timur lowered his head. A tear dripped on the back of his hand. "Is it any wonder that I cannot abide roses?"

Eddie opened his mouth, was for once too wise to let any sound out. His curiosity had come back strong, was building up within him like pressure in his bladder. But he sat several agonizing minutes in silence, waiting for Timur's self-control to return.

"A hundred million people died of *white* in four weeks around the world," Eddie said. "It's terrible that it took your family—God, I'm sorry, and I wish I could think of something to say that wasn't lame. But—*why*? How did that cause you to do...what you did?"

"To betray my country, you mean? To betray my father?" Timur rubbed his eyes with the fingers of one hand, the gesture used to close a dead man's eyes. *"White* came late to the Fergana Valley. It is isolated, and little traffic goes in and out, even today. The American contravirus that stopped *white* was already available, had already arrived in Tashkent. But as was so often the case with *white*, within twenty-four hours of its first appearance no one at the farm remained alive. The official explanation was that the health authorities only learned of the outbreak after it was too late. I grieved, but I accepted. I died with my family, but I believed.

"Then, three weeks later, I was reading a digest of communications to and from our provisional military government—martial law had been declared. I chanced upon a reference to *Ligkhoz* 23 in a report from the commander of the Turkestan Military District himself. He had known of the outbreak in plenty of time, it seemed. But the Land of Flowers was thought by military intelligence to nurture sedition as well as roses. The military governor had simply availed himself of the opportunity to get some unruly black-asses out of his hair. He was really quite forthright.

"From the moment I saw that, I was the enemy of everything I had stood for before. I make no excuses—not for that. As for where my anger has led me..." He shook his head and spoke no more.

Eddie sat and tried to assimilate it all. It was as if his whole world was spinning inside his skull on maglev bearings.

"So that's why you were able to do all that with just a bunch of raggedy-ass indige followers," he said. "You had it all, didn't you? Every goddam thing KGB had, you had in the palm of your hand."

"Of course." Timur held up a finger. "Do not deprecate the 'raggedy indiges,' please; they did the fighting and the dying, not I. But yes. I was a hacker—cracker, more correctly—of the most insidious sort. I held the keys to the whole KGB computer system in my hand. I helped *create* that system. Passwords, structure, everything. That's what I had to offer Timur. If KGB operatives were closing in on underground members, I could steer them away. I could discredit informers. I framed most of the competent officers in General Vorontsov's command in Tashkent. I could do many things."

"Now, hold on a minute. All during the war, you knew... exactly what Al Capone was up to. And the tactical information you fed us, the targeting info you gave your rocket launchers—"

"We used League tactical sensing satellites. What the KGB knew, *I* knew. What they had, I had." He smiled. "How do you think I knew your real name, Aleksandr Pavlovich?"

Eddie shuddered. "Don't call me that again. Please."

Timur made an easy gesture. "As you will."

"Something else . . . how come you didn't stop them busting the, uh . . . the original Timur?"

"I let that happen. It is so amazing how it goes. How arrogant you become. You experience a moment of epiphany, of blinding clarity. And then you feel as if you have all truth packed within your head. I had such a revelation when I saw the report on the Land of Flowers.

"But it's just another illusion. I acted as if I had godlike knowledge when I permitted KGB-Samarkand to arrest the real Timur—and it turned into a bungle. He spurned me and died. That was not at all according to plan." He closed his eyes. "If only I had learned that lesson . . ."

Eddie sighed. This was all very interesting, but it was time to bite the reality sandwich.

"So what happens now?" he asked. "Are you going to kill me?"

"It would reflect very badly on my judgment to make a man *orlok* one week, and execute him the next," Timur said. "Especially since I knew all along that he was a KGB plant."

Eddie sat there and felt deflated, somehow. As if not getting killed was anticlimactic. Life's a bitch, and then you don't die.

He felt Timur's gaze and looked up into it. "Will you kill me?" Timur asked.

"No. I had the chance once before and didn't take it. I guess you know that already."

"But why *won't* you kill me?" Timur asked plaintively.

"Because you're the only real thing I know."

Timur made an explosive, exasperated sound. "That's not *true*. I'm a liar. I've lied to you. I've lied to everybody. I'm not Timur; I am Ivan Mukhtaari."

"You're Timur," Eddie said flatly. "What you were before means nothing."

Timur dropped his face into his hands. "What kind of KGB assassin *are* you?"

"A piss-poor one, I guess. An unwilling one. I just resigned anyway."

"Then what are you?"

Eddie shrugged. "Head of your bodyguards. One of your *orloks*, if you still want me to be. If you don't, then I guess I'm just a grunt in the ranks. However it goes, I'm your man. Now and forever."

"With enemies like these," Timur said with a moan, "who needs friends? Eddie-*bahadur*, I love and honor you, but you drive me crazy. Go."

Eddie stood. "One thing, before I go. What am I to you? Please. I . . . have to know where I stand."

Timur sighed. "You are my chief bodyguard. If you won't honor my request to kill me, who better to keep me alive? Now please, go away."

Chapter
FORTY

She came awake with a start. *Someone's outside the tent!* She sat up, blankets falling away, her hands reaching out in the darkness.

For what? She had no weapons. She didn't know how to use them if she did. For all her bravado with the amusing American Eddie, she had been all but petrified with fear that day in Timur's tent. She least of all understood how she had been able to bring herself to drive an elbow into the gunman's stomach. It had been some neural fluke, she knew; she could never duplicate the act.

If the terrorists have found me, I hope they kill me quickly. Unconsciously in the darkness she raised her head, simultaneously showing defiance and her throat.

"Tai-Yu? Dr. Shih? It's me. Eddie."

"Eddie?" As always, she split the *d*'s scrupulously: *Ed-die,* as if it were two words. He always claimed to find that charming, but she was sure he was only making fun of her.

"Yeah, babe. It's me. Can I come in?"

She looked down at herself. She was wearing an Indiana University sweatshirt given to her while she was guest lecturer at the school's Uralic and Altaic Studies Program. She was covered, but it was still highly improper for an unmarried female comrade to permit a man into her sleeping quarters. Not that anybody back in the People's Republic thought there was *anything* proper about Shih Tai-Yu. Still, the grip of socialization was strong, even though she recognized it for the sham it was.

But Eddie had always been a gentleman, in his own uncouth way. And there was something in his voice—

"Come in."

He stumbled inside in such a rush that she drew back with a small mouse shriek, fearing her trust had been misplaced. Instead he collapsed in a heap at the foot of her mound of blankets.

"I need to talk to you," he said, hanging his head between his knees like a man about to pass out. "I need to talk to *somebody.*"

She sat up. Her hand reached out to touch his shoulder in the dark, then stopped, as if of its own volition. She ached to touch him, to soothe him, but she could not.

"What happened, Ed-die?"

He blew out a long breath. "I talked to Timur. It's . . . strange." He shook his head. "He isn't what he seems to be."

He looked at her, and the ghost of a grin shaped his lips. "Then again, babe, neither am I."

"What do you mean?"

"Do you really want to know?"

She nodded.

He told her. From the time his father came in to wake him and tell him that his mother was going away, to right now.

Everything but Timur asking him to kill him. It didn't seem right to talk about that. It was just an aberration anyhow; Timur didn't really feel that way. It had been a test of some sort—

It seemed to him that he talked forever, that his story was too big for one night to hold.

But when he finished, it was still dark and his cheek was laid in the hollow of her neck. Her hand stroked his head, in a tentative way, the way you'd stroke someone else's pet.

"So now you probably hate me," he said, his voice muffled by her shoulder.

"No. I am not sure what I feel. You don't know who you are; for all your life, others have systematically taken away everything that might help you know." She shook her head. "I feel sorry for you."

He reared up. "Don't! Don't dare feel sorry for me, goddam it!"

She refused to flinch. She looked into his eyes as best she could in the dark.

He took hold of her again, hugged her hard. "Well, okay. Maybe you can feel sorry for me. Just a little bit."

She laughed. "Ed-die, you are just like little boy. A bad boy."

He peered up at her from beneath his eyebrows, making her laugh all over again. "You're not afraid of me?"

"Why ever should I be?"

"I'm a KGB spy. An assassin, sent to kill Timur."

"But you quit, didn't you?"

"You bet your sweet little— ah, yes."

"You tell me Timur started out being a KGB agent, before he was Timur. I don't fear him. I think he is a very good man."

Eddie nodded fervently. "He's the best man I've ever known. The best in the world, probably."

She grabbed him, held him at arm's length. "You should not think that. It is not good for you. It is not good for him."

He shook his head, smiling ruefully. "I guess maybe

there are some things only men understand. The way we're brought up—''

''Don't you start that! We are not that different. It is only an excuse.''

The art of difference-between-the-sexes debate was one of the few cultivated to a higher degree in the West than in China. But Shih Tai-Yu had been in enough of them to know she didn't have the energy to get embroiled in one now. In her limited experience there was little enough debate and almost no communication to them, just attitudinizing and self-justification. To block that conversational path, she drew him close again.

He kissed her neck. There beside her throat at the base, above the little bowl within the clavicle.

Reflexively she grabbed the hair at the nape of his neck to pull him away. She realized the tingle running through her body was not at all unpleasant.

More gently than she had first intended, she drew his head up. When he faced her, she put her hands on his cheeks. They were stubbled with half a day's growth of beard, not silky like an Asian man's, but spiky and harsh.

Still, his face was not unattractive, if you like the drawn and pointed Western features. She liked his. He was quite handsome, in an exotic way. It was part of her flawed nature, that she failed to share the belief of the community in which she had been raised, that *different* equated to *ugly*. Maybe it was her Mongol genes that made her so anti-communitarian. Maybe it was her father.

She kissed him. He looked as if he were about to start talking again. That was really why.

He pressed her to him, kissing her so hard he seemed to be trying to pressure-weld their faces together. She couldn't breathe, and started to squirm, wondering if this perhaps was a bad idea.

His hands were pulling up her Indiana sweatshirt. Her breasts were round and high, and full without being big. Her nipples were dark.

He bent to circle one, lightly, teasingly with his lips, flicked it with the tip of his tongue. She cradled his strange blond shaggy Western head and wondered what on earth she was doing.

Acting like a schoolgirl who's escaped her chaperone for the very first time, an internal voice told her. *After a mere thirty-four years.*

Her previous lovers—the unlamented De, for example— she had only accepted after long acquaintance. Their liaisons had been fumbling, perfunctory, stunted by the puritanical weight of the People's Republic's disapproval. The lovers themselves seemed unreal to her now, transparent almost, like paper dragon kites faded by the sun. They were drones and mayflies, she knew, as she always had known, the usual camp-followers of academe; true solid Chinese men would have nothing to do with a scandalous half-Mongol bitch like her, who didn't know her place and didn't want to. Her former lovers were both drabber and less fully adult than this wild Americanized Russian she was opening herself to.

She smiled, then bit her lip with sudden pleasure. *If I've waited so long to let myself go, at least I've gained enough wisdom to make the most of it.*

After two hours, during which Marron's mind had been elsewhere while his cock just sort of stood there and took it, Jacqui finally raised herself off him and collapsed, sweaty and happy and replete. She hadn't had such a workout in years.

Confirmed socialist though she was, she was not without some concept of value-for-value. Also, the challenge of making him come had begun to pique her; she was agile, skillful, and incredibly fit, and neither her most passionate exertions nor her most professional had made perceptible impression on him. She laid her hand on his chest for three long, shuddering breaths, then slithered down to envelop the head of his cock with her mouth.

He shuddered. A slight moan spilled from his lips, along

with a trickle of drool. Jacqui smiled around his cock. She was finally getting through to him.

She clamped her lips firmly over his glans, worrying the top of the shaft just below the notch on its underside where it joined with the head, the most sensitive spot, with the tip of her tongue. Her fingers jacked lightly up and down his rigid penis.

Within two minutes he cried out, clutched her shoulders, bucked, and came. She took in all his yield, and wondered how long it had been for him.

Then she snuggled up beside him and fell promptly asleep with her shoulder in his armpit, satisfied that she had conquered her conqueror.

He raised his forearm and let the fingertips of his right hand dangle on her upper back like the leaves of a Russian olive trailing in the Syr Dar'ya. He continued to stare at the tent ceiling, lost in darkness, with the same lack of expression as he had for the last few hours.

Dick Torrance tried to speak to him from the screen. He managed not to listen.

Chapter
FORTY-ONE

The wind had risen with the false dawn. It whipped Timur's headcloth as he strode through the gloom toward the vehicle park. Eddie trotted behind, clutching his Yankees cap to his head. Though Timur was a couple centimeters taller than Eddie, his legs were no longer, but it always seemed Eddie had trouble keeping pace with him.

"You sure you don't want to just fly back to Tashkent?" Eddie yelled. "It's a pretty long haul by road." The highway wound well up the Syr Valley, before swooping back over the tag end of the Chatkal spur of the Tien Shans to Tashkent.

"We will take the road that follows the rail line through the desert," Timur said.

"That's more direct, but the road's a shitload worse."

"It will be well. I need to feel the desert wind in my face."

"You picked the right day for it."

Timur had chosen to rise early, to slip away before the usual crowd of favor-seekers and hangers-on were abroad. That seemed to include Jacqui, who was nowhere visible, which was fine with Eddie. Eddie had left Shih snoring gently in his blankets after a Sky-Blue Wolf rousted him out; she could catch up later.

On the other unfortunate hand, up ahead Francis Marron stood waiting beside a beefy *Liga* Karakoram four-wheeler with the top off and the windscreen down. He was staring out west, where the mesa country, mauve and gray-green and dingy yellow with incipient dawn, flattened toward the Qizil Qum, as if he saw something marvelous among the shadows.

Timur stopped just short of Marron's earshot. "I want you to take your Jagun up north. There's a caravan hunter team operating beyond Turkestan town."

Eddie looked to Marron, back at Timur. He pressed his lips to a thin line. Naturally insubordinate as he was, he wasn't quite up to saying *bullshit* to Timur this morning.

Timur laid a hand on his shoulder. "Don't worry for me. Nothing will happen between here and Tashkent."

"I don't like it. He's a killer."

"He is harmless. He is . . . disturbed. He was badly treated back in America, after he left here. He is trying to find himself again."

"You're liable to find him with his hands around your throat. He was ready enough to wax Acevedo down in Costa Rica, and he wasn't even nuts then."

"Eddie, I know that you are my chief bodyguard. But if

something befalls me as a consequence of my own action, the fault is entirely mine, and not yours. Now, go.''

Eddie started to turn, found he couldn't let it go. "But your life—you belong to Turkestan.''

"That's an illusion. Should I start thinking that, you would be amazed how soon it would turn itself around in my mind so that Turkestan belonged to *me*. Great outrages are only committed by men who know beyond question that what they are doing is *right*. Hitler, Stalin, Pol Pot—each believed he was just what this bad old world needed." Timur turned toward the truck. "Your friend Dr. Shih helped me articulate this. I had realized it for quite a long time, but I feared to admit it to myself." ·

My friend? What does he know about that? Eddie started after.

"Our lives belong only to us, Eddie-*jaan*.''

Eddie stopped, dropped his chin to his chest. "My life belongs to you," he said, little-boy sullen.

Timur spun with a flourish of his headcloth tail. His eyes flashed like obsidian knives. "Are you still looking for a father?"·

Eddie sidled away, not meeting his eyes. Timur stepped close to him, invading his space.

"You are still trying to please your father," he said in a low, tense tone. "Aren't you? Look at me.''

Eddie nodded. His angry words to Arbatov, denying his father, had been no more than the outburst of a hurt and angry adolescent. A child telling a parent, *I hate you*.

"Your father divorced your mother because a man could not hope to rise in the Party while married to a Jew. Is that someone to admire? To please?''

Eddie thrust out his lower lip rebelliously. Timur dropped his voice till it almost vanished in the current of the wind.

"How do you think the Americans caught you in Germany, Alyosha? They turned your father; his price for immunity from prosecution was to turn over one of GRU's most successful moles: *you*. Of course, it was all engineered by the KGB, who promptly redoubled him. Pavel Il'ich Gorsunov would not betray his *Party*."

"You're lying," Eddie said. But he knew it was the denial that was a lie, even as he spoke it.

Timur's eyes didn't flicker. "Turkestan needs no father, Eddie. Neither do you. Grow up. Take the rest of your life and make of it what *you* choose. Not what others choose for you."

Eddie stood there so filled with things to say that his chest was constricted, as if by an asthma attack. Then he threw his arms around Timur, hugged him so hard the older man's back made crackling sounds.

"I'll never see you again," he said. His eyes were streaming.

He turned and went away from Timur then. With all the strength he had, he made himself walk, not run.

"I love the sunset," Timur said. "Of all times of the day, it is my favorite. The light turns everything strange and wonderful, and the peace of evening settles in."

Timur, driving the Karakoram himself, had parked on the crest of a ridge southwest of Tashkent. The western sky was an eerily luminous pale blue, that bore the same relationship to the normal sky blue as a corpse's complexion does to that of a living man. Lower down it darkened into striations of yellow, then orange, then finally red.

"Yes," Marron said. "It's very beautiful." He had been staring as though hypnotized at a blunt little darkling beetle with a slate-and-white-striped carapace, scurrying along the flank of a miniature hill of dust that had accrued around the base of a clump of camel's-hair. When Timur spoke, he raised his eyes to the west.

He had always loved nature, but in a very conventional, Sierra Club poster way, taking in grand vistas like a wide-angle lens. After prison he found himself more oriented to the particular. Like the crawling bug, spilling microcosmic landslides away from its six milling feet, or the way the wind stirred the fringe of Timur's headcloth below his right eye. To try to absorb the world of light and air a quantum at a time was impractical, he knew. But he also knew he would not have time to take it all, no matter how big the bites. So he preferred quality over quantity, and was content.

"It soothes me," Timur said. he looked at Marron. "And you, my friend? What of your troubled spirit? Does anything ease it?"

Marron put his hands up to grip the padded dash. A muscle stood out in his cheek, a tooth-grinder's diamond.

"The face on the television keeps telling me to kill you," he said.

"Is that what you were sent here to do?"

"Yes."

"Do you want to kill me?"

Tears ran down Marron's face. "No. You're the only thing I have left. The only good thing in my world."

"Do you want to help me, Francis?"

Marron nodded convulsively.

"Prison was very hard for you, wasn't it?"

". . . yes . . ."

"When you were there, you wanted nothing so much as to get out."

Nod.

Timur nodded slowly. "I feel sometimes as if I am in prison. I am in the midst of a wilderness of howling, where every path I see leads to death and devastation for millions of innocents. My pride and anger brought me here, and I don't know how to escape."

He looked at Marron. The American was crying, sobs shaking his stiffly braced body like temblors. He made no noise.

"I know my confinement is as nothing compared to yours," Timur said softly. "But I am not as strong as you; I cannot bear it much longer."

He turned in his seat and stared at Marron until the American's bloodshot eyes met his. "I want to be free of my prison, Francis. But I cannot leave on my own."

"I—" Marron sniffed. "Am I your friend, Timur?"

Timur laid a hand on his arm. "You are my true friend, Francis. Whatever happens. Shall we drive on?"

Jacqui Gendron swept into camp a little after 2000, with a tired and bitchy Tewfik and a couple of surly Sky-Blue Wolves for retinue. Outside Tashkent, Timur was using a gigantic tent that had once served outdoor festivals—it was of course owned by Khaalis's *yurt*—with a much smaller residential tent at the rear. As she marched to the entrance of the living quarters, a piece of shadow detached itself and approached.

The young Wolves growled and unslung their weapons. After spending a travel day with Jacqui, they hoped they could kill something. But the figure that materialized out of the black belonged to yet another of the bizarre foreigners with whom it amused their master to surround himself.

She looked him over with a practiced, professional eye; reading desperate men was one of her major stocks in trade. In the darkness her slight smile was invisible.

"You're looking for a story?" he asked. His voice was cracked like an old painting.

"Always," she said coolly.

"Tomorrow," he said, "you'll have one." He turned away and the night absorbed him.

Timur was sitting cross-legged at work with his notebook computer when she came in upon him. She rushed over to him, knelt beside him, and flung her arms around him.

"Oh, darling, you should not have slipped away like that! I have been *so concerned*."

She raised up the lower hem of his facecloth and kissed him on the lips.

Kneeling like a samurai to seppuku, Francis Marron opens the cover of his notebook computer. He turns it on, activates the satellite link. By default it shows an English-language newsfeed from South America.

The world is full of rioting. He feels violence and anger wash over his face like waves of heat. The fury of it makes him blink.

When he opens his eyes, his old friend is there.

"We know a secret, Francis, you and I. Don't we? We know you're going to choke. You don't have the stones to do Timur. You couldn't do Acevedo either. That's why the original Swinging Richard had to zatz the little spic—but he was still willing to let his old buddy, old pal take all the credit."

He smiles. His eyeteeth are prominent and pointed. *"That's the most important thing in life, isn't it, dude? Knowing who your real friends are?"*

A shudder wracked Marron. When it was gone, a newsreader's face, unfashionably haggard, was saying, "—repeating the top story of the hour: at a Moscow press conference acting Secretary of State Vorov'yev has just announced that President Fyodorin has been taken into custody by elements of the League and Russian Republican Armed Forces . . ."

It was nothing to him. He stretched his fingers with a ripple of popping joints, and began to type a message.

Chapter
FORTY-TWO

Half an hour before dawn Eddie snapped upright out of a fitful sleep and said, "Bullshit."

"Your pardon, Eddie-*khan*?" asked Yoldash from beside a dried-sheepshit fire.

Eddie stood up and started buckling on his web belt. "He said I'm my own man," he said to no one in particular. "Well, okay. *Okay.* I'm gonna start doing things my own way."

Yoldash sat with his head tipped to the side, a respectful

look on his young, imperfectly bearded face. Eddie was completely mad, of course, but that did not diminish his standing as a hero. Just like old Aliyev's songs: real heroes were always pretty wacky.

Eddie tugged the mag out off the butt of his Glock, scoped it quickly. Standard party mix: .40-caliber safety slugs and silver-tips. He rammed it back home.

"Tell the Singer he's in charge till I get back. I'm going into Tashkent. Personal business."

Through a morning whose heat was a razor's kiss, the vertis came in low, hugging the serrations of the red and khaki land, their polymerized graphite bellies brushing camel-hair on the hogsbacks. They came in fast, their black polymer propellers, hooked like cat's claws, pulling them through the air at three hundred fifty miles an hour. The pilots were good, fighting ground turbulence at a speed at which terrain features were past almost as soon as they were perceived, and an altitude at which the slightest miscalculation would drive you halfway through a ridge.

There were four of them, covert-missions penetrator models jointly designed by the French, the Argentineans, and the Iraqis. They were quiet, cool, and next to invisible on radar. The pilots were British, American, and Israeli. Lest the brittle League budget should be strained in these high-risk times, the United States was picking up the tab for all of it.

And all they asked was one single ride-along. Hell, it was more return than they *usually* got for military aid.

The great festival tent bubble with people and happy noises. Wearing a white headcloth and his customary Western suit sans tie, Timur sat on a rug on a low platform before the multitude, hearing petitions, dispensing arbitration. A few blue skullcaps hung around the edges, playing with their weapons slings and glowering.

He seems to be in an excellent frame of mind this

morning, thought Dr. Shih Tai-Yu, sitting discreetly to one side as befit a foreign observer. His sayings were more by nature of advice than judgment; he arbitrated rather than decreed. The amazing thing was that no one seemed dissatisfied. He was either wonderfully wise or a wonderful charlatan. Considering what Eddie had told her, Shih thought he was probably both.

Eddie . . . It had hurt her to awaken to find herself alone yesterday morning. *You should have expected nothing else,* she told herself sternly. He was an American soldier of fortune—not to mention a League spy. How could she be anything but a random conquest to him? She had never held the interest of a man for long anyway.

Jacqui Gendron was also on hand, in a holding pattern off to one side of the dais, murmuring comments for her throat mike and badgering her cameraman, Tewfik, who was reducing the proceedings to data. She looked unusually sharp and vital this morning, as if she'd been drawn with more attention to detail than normal.

Shih wondered why Jacqui was expending such concentration on routine palace doings. The outer world was falling in pieces, and while Turkestan was a central cause or at least catalyst, at the moment most folk had more pressing concerns than how Timur handled bean-patch property disputes.

Into the audience tent came Francis Marron. He stood for a moment with the morning sun haloing around him, resplendent in a white linen suit and standing taller than Shih had seen him before. He surveyed the scene, seemed to sigh, and made his way forward through the throng. Insistent as they were on crowding as close to Timur as possible, the petitioners flowed away from him.

Seeing him, Timur brightened. He rose, held out his arms as if welcoming a brother.

Marron raised his right hand. It held a small black pistol. He fired three times, deliberately, while every other being in the tent turned to ice. Whether all or any shots hit, Shih could not actually see, but Timur dropped to his knees, arms still outspread.

He raised his head as Marron stepped up to the platform. Holding his right arm stiff before him, the American shot Timur through the forehead.

Gunfire crashed as the Sons of the Sky-Blue Wolf, coming out of their shock fugue, unlimbered weapons and flared off at Marron. The American stood upright, almost at attention, swaying slightly as red splotches blossomed on his white suit like all the roses of Gulistan.

For a moment bright flashes filled the tent as the Wolves kept their trigger fingers clenched. Without consciously moving, Shih found herself lying on her belly, yelling, "Stop! Stop! Cease firing!" in Uzbek and Russian.

The spasm of firing stopped. Shih felt the air throb with moans and screams as the crowd surged forward toward its fallen hero.

Crouched by the side of the platform, Jacqui felt her heart, balloon-sized in her chest and thumping like a gas-powered village water pump. She wanted to pump her fist like an American sports fan. The instant she laid eyes on Marron she had given the word, and by prearrangement gone live via satellite. Every viewer of TéléFrance and its subscribers had seen everything.

It was the diadem of her career.

Add to the stunning live coverage of the assassination of the world's most controversial leader the one-hour special report she would broadcast at one tomorrow morning—prime time in EuroCom—called *Timur: the Man Behind the Mask*, revealing for the first time both his face and the thunderbolt of his past. . . .

She noticed Tewfik flat on his belly beside her. She suppressed her mike with her thumb. "Tewfik! Tewfik, you coward, stand up! We're missing the action."

He didn't respond. The fool's nerve had finally broken. Not in a compassionate frame of mind, Jacqui seized the short black hair on top of Tewfik's head and pulled it up to look him in the eye.

And eye was what he had—the right, which had been pressed to the viewfinder of his videocam. A Blue Wolf bullet had gone in the other one. *Thank God he got most of it*, she thought.

The Tashkent camp had the aura of desertion, like a boomtown gone bust. Eddie slowed the little *Liga* scout car way down, looking warily around him as he nosed among the tents that sprouted from the desert like Cubist flowers after a spring rain. The usual prohibitions against motor vehicles was in effect, but fuck that noise: there were no traffic cops around here.

There should've been *somebody*. Eddie made a note to chew the ass off the Turkmen he'd left in charge of security while he and 23 were off playing Boy Scout on the Syr Dar'ya.

It was not entirely strange that there should be fewer people than usual around. After Timur made one of his flying moves to the new HQ, it generally took a few days for the whole menagerie of hangers-on to catch up. But nobody?

Eddie knew with painful clarity that he was being stupid. The smart play would be to poke around until he turned up someone, anyone from the Turkestani Defense Forces, then move in by the numbers. He was acting like your standard Hollywood cop, charging into a possible confrontation without calling for backup.

Fuck that noise too. Timur might be in danger. He put the hammer down, sprayed sand and pebbles across the tent fronts.

Timur's camp-meeting tent stood at the eastern edge of a plaza. Its side belled and collapsed forlornly like the sails of a drifting ship, and its flaps snapped in the wind. There was nobody in sight, not even the ubiquitous Sky-Blue Wolf sentries under Eddie's nominal command.

He brought the car to a swerving stop before the big tent,

jumped out, and dashed for the entrance, so hyped that he went down when his feet hit the ground and had to scramble to get upright.

The smell that greeted him at the door knocked a measure of sanity back into him. Stale and sweet, *oh* yeah. He stopped, took a deep breath—through his mouth—glanced at the car several meters away. He had been so out of control that he'd left his nifty-drifty MRS assault rifle propped against the passenger seat. No time for it now: either seconds counted, or nothing counted.

He drew his Glock, went in fast, into a crouch and side-scuttling right, arms braced into a firing triangle, ready to engage any target.

There was none. There was nothing but bodies lying in that graceless unheeding way of the dead beneath a buzzing smog of flies.

The inner walls looked as if someone had thrown buckets of red paint on them.

In a dim, distant part of his consciousness Eddie was very glad he was in combat mode—pure Zen, no thought, no intention. He waded through carnage toward the platform, sidling around bodies, stepping over them only when he had to, peripheral vision steering his Asics clear of blood-soaked swatches that could turn to slick mud beneath them.

A body lay facedown on the dais. A pool of blood surrounded its head like a halo, dark red turning black. Eddie's soul dropped to his shoe soles. It was small to be Timur, but death makes you small, just as death makes you heavy.

Right in front of the platform Francis Marron lay on his back with his arms outspread. He had been dressed all in white like a televangelist gone before the flock to explain just what he'd been doing in that motel room with the boy scout, the goat, and the *faux*-fat butter. Marron's outfit was mostly scarlet now; he'd been shot all to shit. His face, though, remained untouched. The half-closed eyes held a bemused, dreamy look, the lips a smile's ghost.

Eddie jumped lithely onto the podium, held the Glock up in his left hand while his right reached for the prone man's neck. The gummy Jell-O feel of skin and flesh beneath told him he didn't need to spend a lot of time probing for a pulse.

He took the body of the cast-off-suit-coat shoulder and rolled it over.

Ali al-'Ajawi, erstwhile major of artillery in the League Armed Forces, stared past Eddie's knee with jellyfish eyes. The blood that had poured from his slashed neck was congealing, hardening his coat and shirt into a rusty red cuirass.

Eddie's lips curled back from his teeth. He put his fingertips to the dead man's cheek, pushed gently. The head moved freely. Ali had been nearly decapitated.

As best Eddie could see for the blood, the cut looked clean. It was possible to cut a man's throat that comprehensively at a stroke, but rare. Eddie guessed he'd been garroted with a fine wire loop.

His hyperextended senses caught a footstep. He dove over the body, rolled, came around in prone firing position with his Glock out in front.

"Lieutenant Randolph, I presume," an unmistakably American voice said in English. "I've heard a lot about you."

Expert combat shooter that he was, Eddie was focused on the fat white dot of his front sight. As his eyes shifted focus, the attenuated figure that had come into the tent behind him resolved into a tall, loose man with a shock of black hair hanging almost in his eyes, wearing a white duster over a pale yellow shirt and mauve slacks. Pastel hell was back in style for those who couldn't handle Serious launch-tech jumpsuit white.

Deliberately Eddie rose to a Weaver stance. At no point during the process would his first shot have missed the center of the intruder's sternum by as much as a centimeter.

"Hey, I'm impressed," the stranger said. His lips smiled. His pale eyes did not. He held his hands up to the sides, palms out. "But hey, you don't need that for me. I'm not packing. I'm Torrance, Richard...."

Eddie sized up the intruder, the way he moved, the way he held himself. Eddie knew two things: the man *wasn't* Special Designation, not anybody's; and he thought he was hot shit.

There was one more thing he knew. Eddie had been through interrogation and interrogation-survival classes run by both sides, been leaned on by the dreaded KGB, and with Texas Team had worked cadre in several of the Third World's perennial atrocity pits: Iran, Syria, Iraq. He knew the eyes of a man for whom inflicting hurt was always pleasure first, then business.

"What's a FedPol snotsucker doing here?" Eddie demanded.

Anger whipped across Torrance's face. Then it was gone, leaving only a sharp-toothed smile.

"Just doing my job, Eddie, old pal. Which right now means saying, you're under arrest."

Eddie had never shot an unarmed man, but if he was going to start, this looked like an ideal candidate. His left forefinger began to pull.

"Well done, Agent Torrance," a voice said from behind Eddie. It spoke American-accented English and rang like a great gold bell. If the figure on the Nazi recruiting poster could talk, it would sound just like that. "But please keep in mind, the prisoner is ours."

Eddie turned his head slowly, still holding down on Torrance. If the figure stepped off that Nazi poster, it would look just like that, too. Though it probably wouldn't be wearing American cammies.

"Hello, Alex," Pete Yermakov said. "You've been a busy boy, haven't you?"

Chapter
FORTY-THREE

Upside down, the ridge crest came rushing at Eddie's face at a hundred and fifty miles an hour. He screamed and jackknifed. The ridge swept by. He felt the heat wash from its sunbaked rocks, could swear fronds of camel's-hair stung his face. Or maybe that was just a random swirl of sand caught in the blast from the verti's curved black props.

I never thought I'd regret my eyes didn't swell shut from getting the crap kicked out of me.

He hung back down again, making strangling sounds: "Ah. *Arragh*." Vomit had dried on his cheek like ropes of rubber cement. At least gravity and the wind had carried the puke away from him, and his stomach was vacant now.

Over the muted snarl of the engines and the wind of his own demented passage, he heard gigantic laughter. "Did you see 'im? See how he jumped?"

"Yep. Brother Buddy, you surely are one sick individual."

He twisted to look back at the verti. Buddy Lynko filled the open hatchway, holding Eddie by his ankles. Invisible behind him, his brother was holding *him*. Eddie was secured to the craft by upwards of seven hundred pounds of Texas beef. It didn't calm his stomach.

He started thrashing violently, trying to break the hold on his ankles—or better, Tex's grip on his brother's web gear. *If we both go, I'll have a nice wad of blubber to land on. In hell, anyway.*

"Whoa!" Buddy sang. "The little fish is floppin'. He's tryin' to get away. How 'bout it, Tex? Should I oughta let him go?"

"Naw. That way's quick. Too good for a traitor like him. We're gonna take him home and skin and fillet him *proper.* Best you haul him in now, boy."

"Here! Don't photograph *this*." Inside the tilt-rotor craft Mr. Perfect was trying to hold his hand in front of the late Tewfik's videocam, as Buddy laid Eddie on the deck red-faced and gasping like a trout beneath the mask of dried blood and vomit. Buddy made sure to give his head a good crack as he did so.

Stray-round circumstance was compelling Jacqui Gendron to run the cam herself. She batted Pete's hand away. He sat back gaping at her, shocked rather than angry.

"Aw, lay off her." Swinging Richard was leaning back on one of the longitudinal paratroop-style benches with his legs crossed, looking cool. "I don't know about your people, but mine will want a full report. The video will play like a motherfucker at the debriefing."

Georgie rubbed his prominent nose and scowled. "But wait, we can't let the Americans see us—"

"Don't be stupid, man," Cat Delgado said. He was sitting on the end of the white-plastic box that held what used to be Timur. "We're blown already. But after this score—shit, GRU'll have to make us *generals.* We're set for life."

"Yeah," said Torrance. "We be cool. Give me five, my man." He and Delgado slapped hands. They understood each other perfectly.

Pete smiled thinly at Jacqui, made himself appear to relax. His blue eyes watched Torrance and Delgado closely, then slipped shut.

It had all gone splendidly. Mr. P knew his former CO well. Gorsunov was an odious little yid who thought he was smarter than everybody else. He was *not* a coward. Nor was he stupid. He was damned near as good as he thought he was.

It was just that Pete was *better.*

They had lost their dedicated fuel carrier and the second security squad's verti, overrun on the LZ outside the tent city—who knew the niggers could react so quickly? But that didn't matter. The mission was an overwhelming success; they had two traitors on board, one on ice, one trussed for roasting. All that remained was to loaf home to loyal Kazakhstan at 250 kilometers an hour to save fuel and the pilots' nerves, the hatches open to let the wind blow away the baking Central Asian heat.

Bored, Buddy took out his garrote and stared, making cat's cradles in air with the fine wire he'd slipped between the ivory handles. "Did you see the way I did that little raghead? Did you?" He made a loop, started to tighten it on Ali's remembered neck. "Tightened it up just enough so he could feel, so he'd know what was fixing to happen to him. And then—bang! I cut him. I *cut* him."

"Yeah," said the Cat, Delgado, "we know, man. We were all there. So what?"

"Yeah," Georgie said. "Put that thing back in your pants. Don't play with it here—there's a *lady* present."

Pete half opened his eyes. Across the cabin the French-woman, Gendron, was sitting next to Torrance, talking fervently. She was leaning forward conspicuously, and her blouse was unbuttoned *way* down. The American wasn't even trying to keep his eyes from straying.

Pete's lips twitched in disgust. *Decadent animals*. But he refused to let himself be drawn into anger. If they became obnoxious, a flight to Kandahar for two could be arranged. Texas Team were due to be the heroes of the hour; no one would ask too many questions if foreign nationals turned up missing from their ostensible care.

Tex turned from watching the desert slide past the open hatch and gave Eddie a kick. "Can't we get out of this here armor, Pete? It's real damn hot."

Texas Team was all bulked up in American Second Chance assault vests, steel/ceramic inserts and all. They *were* real damned hot. Kevlar doesn't breathe too well.

"Negative, Lynko. We're still in Indian country, and as long as we are, the armor stays on. And get the prisoner away from that open hatch. If he falls out of the airplane, I'm responsible. I promise I will not be the only one to suffer.''

Tex hooked two fingers into one of the quiescent Eddie's sneakers and grudgingly dragged him farther into the aircraft. Letting him go, he sat down on the bench and picked up his M60E3, began examining it. Though he looked like a compleat gross slob, he was a perfectionist where the tools of his trade were concerned. Otherwise he would never have survived in the unit under Little Alex—or Mr. P.

Simms hurried to Eddie's side and bent anxiously over him. The prisoner was still breathing, but that was the most you could say for him.

"We shouldn't be doing this," the Canadian said. "We— we're supposed to be upholding the rule of law.''

Everyone ignored him.

Eddie lay in a halfway state that combined the worst features of being out cold and being awake. He couldn't move, couldn't focus, and kept slipping beneath the surface of subconsciousness' cesspool where bad things lurked. Every so often the vivid memory of a boot in the face brought him to full consciousness with a whimper, and then he was in the World of Hurt for true, his whole body an oscilloscope of pain, the sine wave of aches that throbbed to his heartbeat spiking intermittently with agony intense as a tooth snapping. When he was awake, he could dwell on what was waiting for him in obsessive detail, and he still couldn't move, couldn't focus.

"Hey. Hey, are you in there, bunky? Wakey-wakey." A pinch and light slap on his cheek brought him back from a place where faces surrounded him, huge gibbous faces that might have been painted on hot-air balloons, illuminated from within.

He was rolled onto his back. His arms were fastened with nylon passive restraints, fingertip-to-elbow behind his back. Lying on them strained his shoulders painfully. He was in too much pain for it to make much difference. *Lucky for me, huh?*

He opened his eyes as far as they'd go. The tall American

was squatting over him, his hands on his thighs and black hair hanging in his eyes: "So. You're the amazing Fast Eddie."

He grinned and shook his head in disbelief. He was a lot less easily amazed than Francis Marron, he clearly wanted Eddie to understand.

"Who—the fuck—are you?" Eddie had lost a couple of teeth, and his mouth was gummy with congealing blood.

"Dick Torrance. The Swinging Richard to my friends. You can call me Federal Police Agent Torrance."

"FedPol pussy. Fuckin' . . . figures."

Torrance slapped him again, not lightly. "You have a smart mouth, pal. Just because you're well and truly fucked doesn't mean things can't get worse. *Lots* worse. Know what I mean?"

Eddie spat blood at him. He missed.

Torrance laughed. "Francis said you'd kill me." He put on a parody scared-kiddie voice: "Are 'oo gonna kiww poor me?"

"Yes."

Torrance stared at him. That wasn't the answer he expected.

Eddie snapped his legs up, wrapped them around Torrance's neck. Hunkered down as he was, Torrance was badly balanced, unable to brace. Before anyone could react, the former gymnast threw his wiry body in a hard right roll.

The motion whipped Torrance diagonally across his body and out the open hatch.

Dick Torrance, the original Swinging Richard, fell like a comet, but with only a scream for a tail, no glory.

"Adios, Scheherazade," said Eddie in the plane. Moving fast for a fat man, Tex had just snagged him by the back of his shirt in time to keep him from following Torrance in a suicide glide.

Tex flung him toward the rear of the aircraft. He landed hard enough to momentarily loosen him from consciousness. When he flashed back, he was surrounded by blank cow looks. *If they've never read Don Westlake, fuck 'em.*

Tex's meaty fist crashed his face like a rich kid's party. He went out again.

"Jesus *Christ*," the British copilot exclaimed, his long rubbery face going pale. The tilt-rotor aircraft carrying the BON security squad was trailing Texas Team's to portside, half a klick back. "Did you see *that*? My God, they threw that poor man out of the aircraft!"

"Yeah," the American pilot said. He was a contract man who had flown overseas work for the FedPols before. The half of his Black face his polychrome wraparound shades left visible was not impressed. "Sometimes you get two suspects, see, and you want *one* of them to talk."

The deplaned man struck a lion-colored outcrop of rocks on the flank of a ridge slanting across their flight path. He bounced upward, did a sort of cartwheel, landed in a rag-doll sprawl across a hunchbacked boulder. The Brit imagined he saw a scarlet smear across the rocks. His mouth worked, as he thought it might outmaneuver the sour vomit that was trying to escape.

The verti bucked downward. "What the fuck?" the American demanded, fighting his controls as the cockpit filled with a whistling roar.

The windscreen filled with the blunt broad nose of an identical craft *right there*, impossibly close. The American screamed. He had never in his life imagined anything like this.

Reflex took over. He slammed his aircraft's nose downward to avoid the head-on collision milliseconds away.

The verti drove into the same ridge that the falling man had struck.

Chapter
FORTY-FOUR

"Da!" Nikolay Kuliyev exulted. He wanted to pump his black-gloved fist in the air, but he needed both hands on the joysticks if he didn't want to produce another tsunami of debris and yellow flame like the one rolling across the desert below. The verti wasn't actually *designed* for maneuvers like this.

At the moment they were flying backward. Keeping the engines rotated up to the *hover* position in which the craft more or less emulated a helicopter, Kolya let remnant momentum spin them around their vertical axis.

Cheers and wolf calls erupted from the twenty Blue-Sky Riders in the cabin behind, picking themselves up from where the violent maneuver had flung them. This was *great*. They wanted to see it again.

"See?" he said when he had the ship flying the proper direction again. "I told you there's nothing to flying these."

He glanced to the side. Dr. Shih Tai-Yu was sitting extremely still. She looked as if, had she not been belted securely to the copilot's seat, she would have been up clinging to the back of it like a frightened cat.

Sher Khan the Pushtun thrust his great bearded face between them. "Well done, Nikolay," he said—*Nikolai* as in "Russian," not the pilot's given name. Waging "bad war" on the orders of Mikhayl Gorbachev—sainted in the West—Soviet soldiers had doused the Pushtun's favorite niece's eight-year-old son with gasoline and burned him before his mother's eyes. To the Tiger Lord, Russians didn't have names. Even the good ones.

He pointed to the lead aircraft, which was flying ahead and to their left, completely oblivious. This model of verti had poor rearward visibility, which was why Kolya had just scored his first career air-to-air victory in an unarmed aircraft. "There's more work to be done."

His lips set in a tight smile beneath his red handlebar, Kolya nodded. He glanced left; the burning wreckage had passed from view.

"That's one for you, Marina," he muttered, and gave the ship more throttle.

At a nod from Pete, Tex left his fist cocked and let Eddie's head thump back to the rubberized decking. As he stood up, a smile spread itself across his vast face like the moon coming out of earth's eclipse shadow. "That was a pretty good one the little fuck pulled. Can you imagine the look on that skinny son of a bitch's *face*?"

Always eager to second his even bigger brother, Buddy produced a series of straining, grunting laughs. Tex screwed up his face.

"Kee-rist, Buddy, when you laugh like that, it makes you sound like you're trying to pinch a redwood log."

That made Texas Team howl even louder with laughter. "Did—did you have your camera going for that one, Ms. Frenchy?" Buddy asked Jacqui. "Maybe we can catch his expression on the instant replay."

She was still sitting where Torrance had left her to go taunt Eddie. She was used to fast-breaking events, but this break still had her a little winded.

Instinctively she rose to move to the unit leader's side. Despite his exertions in the flatiron heat, he smelled of soap on clean male skin. She liked that. It was the kind of smell a man touched by destiny should have.

He had the hard-edged look of a man who knew how to kill and to survive. Maybe he would last longer than the last one she thought Destiny might anoint. Not Marron. Marron was a poor pathetic fool, never truly touched with greatness;

sometimes it's necessary to delude the spear carriers in the world historical drama a little bit as to their importance in the script, to get them to do their spear carrier thing and die. But Torrance...she liked his fire. She had thought he had potential.

But destiny, like evolution, is both pitiless and opportunistic. Torrance was weighed in the balance and found wanting. Destiny's advance scout Jacqui Gendron was ever ready to move on.

The American Special Forces soldiers were eyeing her now. Keeping a sidelong watch on his brother, Buddy strutted forward with an exaggerated swagger. "Hey, there, honey, we got a while left to drive. Why don't you and me slip on back to the rear and I can remind you what that good old white meat tastes like."

"Hey, dude," Delgado the Cat said with an upward flip of the head. "You planning to share that action, aren't you?"

Buddy smirked at him. "The line starts here. My brother goes second. Ain't no Lynko takes sloppy seconds to no greaser."

The Cat's face contorted. He reached for his knife.

Tex let the feed-tray cover fall on a fresh belt of linked 7.62 and swung the machine gun to bear on him. "Easy there, boy. We're all brothers in socialism. I'm already tore up with grief at beating the shit out of a former beloved comrade-in-arms. No tellin' *what* it would do to me to blow one away, even if he is a chickensquat Cuban."

"Guys," Simms said urgently. "Guys, stop this."

Jacqui pressed herself against Pete.

He didn't look at her. He was a *beau ideal* hero-warrior-jock, what every Youth League leader and American high school coach wanted his charges to be. He personified the Spartan virtues they never tired of proclaiming—in fact, he possessed Spartan virtues Coach and the YLs didn't know the Spartans had. To him a woman's purpose in life was to serve as outlet for urges that couldn't otherwise be satisfied, and to breed more soldier ants.

Jacqui hit him and bounced. She knew it. She looked fearfully around her, wondering how far this would go. These really were hard men; whatever of civilized restraint had been socialized into them had carefully been socialized back out again by the military machines of two nations, and they were zazzing on a violence high like crystal meth.

Delgado took his hand away from his knife. Tex laughed and pulled the Maremont back across his knees.

Georgie, who had had his back pressed to the fuselage next to Tex, slipped over to sit by Jacqui, hemming her between himself and Pete.

"C'mon, honey," he said. "Let me take you away from this."

Jacqui clutched Pete's arm. *"Please."*

He deigned to turn his sculpted head. His ice-blue eyes stared right through her.

The verti jerked to impact.

"What are you doing?" Dr. Shih Tai-Yu was frankly astounded that she was able to ask the question in a perfectly level tone of voice. She had never been particularly comfortable flying, and no pilot of any airliner she had ever ridden in had flown his aircraft over another and bounced his underside off the top of it.

Kolya was showing a chipmunk peek of incisor beneath his mustache as he chewed his lip in concentration. "Trying to force him down."

"Oh."

You insisted on coming along, said that hateful voice that dwells inside her head, *and everybody's. See what happens when you try to do something* effective?

Three hundred meters from the carnage in Timur's pavilion, a hand had grabbed her and drawn her between some tents. She found herself confronting Timur's Pushtun *orlok,* Sher Khan, who was as tall as the twin monstrosities back in the tent but nowhere as fat. He had men from Eddie's regiment backing him.

Marveling at her own composure, she quickly described the death of Timur and the commandos' arrival, and how she had escaped amid a horde of petitioners fleeing the interlopers' guns. The Afghan took it in, calling occasionally upon God to witness the perfidy of League and Americans alike.

Then she saw an unexpected side to the ragged rebel forces. Using satlink voice communications augmented by runners, Sher Khan quickly discovered that the aircraft which had brought the raiders were parked in the desert on a ridge just north of camp. He also got in touch with a truckload of volunteers Aliyev the Kirghiz had sent to follow Eddie back to camp in case he needed help.

Working with calm economy—aside from the pious interjections—Sher Khan took control of the scattered and confused Turkestani Defense Forces in the tent city. He sent several hundred north to catch the raiders on their landing zone and play anvil to the Jagun 23 hammer just about to arrive, and led the rest in an encircling movement converging on Timur's tent in the center of camp.

The intruders were already withdrawing as they got there. Word had just come from the north that the Nikolays had surrendered quickly when they found themselves surrounded, and that two vertis had been captured.

The two odd aircraft Shih had seen parked outside Timur's tent when she fled were just tipping their engines horizontal and banking away to the north when Sher Khan burst through into the *maydaan* or central plaza with Shih panting at his heels.

A breath stuck in her throat when she saw the open car parked before the tent. It hadn't been there when she left. Lying across the passenger seat was a funny-looking rifle, very like the one that was Eddie Randolph's current favorite toy.

Inside she found Sher Khan standing over Ali's dead body with tears dripping from his beard. "Hurry," she said. "They have taken Eddie."

"But how?" he had asked, dabbing his eyes with the tail of his *kameez*. "We have no planes."

"Yes, we do! Your men just took them."

"*Bismillah*, yes! Ah, but what honest man ever profited

from the counsels of the Chinese? We have no one to fly the
Devil's craft.''

"Oh, yes, we do.''

The nose of the enemy verti was just visible beyond their
own craft's snout. It looked terribly close.

"So how about it?'' Kolya asked, not looking away from the
windscreen. "Do we keep trying just to drive him down? It's a
pretty crazy thing to be doing. You are *real* sure you want to?''

Shih Tai-Yu watched a trickle of sweat crawl out from
under his headset and down his rugged face. She didn't
think it was from the heat. The craft was bucking in the
draft of the other's props, and he seemed to be keeping
them in formation by strength of will alone.

What is Eddie Randolph to you? her interior voice asked.
And the answer was, not much, perhaps. She found him
attractive, and she found him amusing. He was a friend.

She had said good-bye to too many friends, and not had
the chance to say good-bye to too many others. She saw
Timur lying dead in the tent, saw unarmed people fall
before the casual guns of the men who now rode the other
aircraft. She saw the tanks hit Gate of Heaven Square.

She had seen enough.

"I'm sure,'' she said, with a convulsive nod. "Force
them down.''

Kolya grinned. "I was hoping you'd say that,'' he said.
"Hang on.''

Chapter
FORTY-FIVE

Pete Yermakov stood behind the pilot's seat, staring up at
the squealing, thumping, crashing sound. "What is it?'' he

demanded. "What's going on?" For all his consummate strengths and skills, this was a situation he could do nothing to control. It had him near frantic.

"Bastard's trying to force us to land," the pilot said through clenched teeth.

"Won't he batter himself to pieces?"

"Undercarriage is strengthened to take the shock of landing. He can just bang hell out of us."

The American at the controls kept banking the plane right and left and right again. The unseen aircraft kept pace, kept bumping it from above like an amorous killer whale, driving it ever lower. The pilot chopped his throttle. The craft slowed dramatically. The nose of the other verti appeared at the top of the windscreen, then slipped back again.

"Bloody hell," the copilot muttered.

Inexorably the ground was drawing closer. "Why can't you shake him?" Pete asked shrilly.

"He's good. Also he's crazy."

A zigzag line of daylight dots appeared overhead. The copilot grunted and clutched his thigh.

Shih turned in her seat. "What are you doing?" she screamed in Uzbek.

Two of Eddie's riders were holding a third as he leaned out the hatch and cut loose with a Kalashnikov. "We're helping you force them down," one said proudly.

"If you kill the pilot and crash the aircraft, will that help your *orlok,* you sons of bearded mothers?" roared Sher Khan.

The youngsters hauled their comrade back inside. "Oh," the first boy said.

Blood welled from the copilot's leg. Realizing what had happened to him, he began to scream. Mostly out of fear and anger; the real pain hadn't hit him yet.

"Fuck this," the pilot said. "I don't get paid enough for this shit." He started to descend, scanning ahead for a flat patch he could settle down on.

Pete whipped out Eddie's Glock 23, which he had been carrying stuck into his web belt as a trophy, rammed it into the pilot's ear. "Try to land and I'll blow your head off, you coward."

"Go right a-fucking-head," the pilot snarled. "Then *you* play crash-'em cars with this psychotic."

Pete's beautiful face went white. "I could fly this if I had to," he said in a spray of spittle. But he was confident to the point of arrogance, not megalomania. He jammed the pistol back between belt and body armor.

"There's one more thing I can try," the pilot said, "but you'd better be ready to de-ass this bitch in a hurry, just in case."

Pete nodded and dove back into the cabin.

When he sensed the other verti starting to fall away beneath him, Kolya let it go. No point risking a crack-up if the other pilot was surrendering. The bad guy was a pretty decent flier, Kolya had to admit, probably a lot better than he was at flying these hybrids.

But the other verti driver had a severe disadvantage: he cared whether he lived or died.

The two craft had lost speed as well as altitude during their Apache dance. Now Kolya saw the other verti's engine pods begin to tilt upward.

"*Yob tvoyu mat'!*" he exclaimed. "No, you don't do this." He dove.

"*What are your doing?*" Shih yelled. It seemed to be her leitmotiv for the day.

"He's trying to touch down in hover—"

Her lower teeth crashed hard against the upper as the verti struck the other craft.

"—mode," Kolya continued as they bounced high in the air. "That way they can jump right back up again and run when we start to land."

The other verti plowed into a broad, shallow wadi, raising a bow wave of sand. Proficient to the last, the pilot prevented his ship from putting in a wingtip and flipping.

He even managed to follow approximately the course of the dry streambed.

"But no way they touch-and-go now," Kolya finished with evident satisfaction. The verti lost speed radically as he turned his own engines upright, trading thrust for lift.

He killed forward momentum by kicking the craft into a rudder turn, skidding around the way he had when he'd dropped the first verti, but at a lot more rational speed. "Okay, *dushman*," he yelled over his shoulder to Sher Khan, "get your men moving. A few at a time; I'll drop 'em in a semicircle. And make it *fast*—those bad boys aren't gonna be knocking off for lunch down there."

Braced in the hatchway between cockpit and cabin, Pete had ridden out crash-landing standing straight up. "Texas Team, clear the ship," he was shouting as the verti slowed to a stop with a dying scream of sand on polymers. "Simms and Georgie, you've got the prisoner. Everybody else, be ready to move out *right now.*"

He looked at the pilot, who was busy flicking switches. "Can you get her up again?"

The copilot looked at him with a strained face. "Not with that bloody lunatic up there."

"I don't know yet," the pilot said. "Right now I want to reassure myself we're not going to blow up right away. Then I first-aid my right-seater. *Then* I'll see if she'll fly."

Pete nodded. "Stay tight, then." He started away, turned back. "If you bug out on us, remember we've got satellite communications. You can't *even* run fast enough to get away."

The pilot's face went darker. "Get the fuck off my aircraft."

Georgie and Simms were just going out the hatch with Eddie slumped between them. The stork-legged Canadian had the quarter-moon shape of a satlink antenna strapped to his back. Not that Pete intended to make use of it. This was his game. He was going to play it out to the last.

The Frenchwoman touched his arm. He fought down the urge to strike her.

"What about me?" she asked.

"Stay here and finger-fuck yourself if you like," he snarled. He jumped out into the white-hot sunlight.

The wadi was about forty meters wide, winding in a vague way to the north-northwest. The team was deployed around the aircraft, communicator headsets and insect-leg mikes in place. Tex had the bipod down ȯn his Maremont and lay prone in front of the nose, covering the wadi. His brother hunkered by the tail, covering south-southwest. Upper-body bulky from the vest of 40mm grenades he wore over his body armor, the Cat lay in the sagebrush along the meter-high eastern bank.

He called for Pete's attention, pointed east. The enemy ship was lifting up from behind the end of a ridge, its engines in hover position.

"I think he just made a drop-off," Cat said. His heavy-lidded eyes were almost closed against the glare. Like his namesake, he was a thoroughly nocturnal animal. "They've dropped off three other groups, two behind that round hill to the northwest, the first almost due north, probably on the edge of the arroyo."

"Shitfire," Buddy said, "ain't that one of *ours*?"

"We never should have trusted those BON weenies to guard the LZ," Georgie said bitterly. He had the still semiconscious Eddie facedown in the sand with his boot in the middle of his back and both muzzles of his CAR-15/M-203 combo aimed at the back of his skull. "They could fuck up a wet dream."

"That's a big ten-four," Tex said.

As they watched, the craft curved around, still playing helicopter, touched down out of sight just south of southeast. *Dropping another team into the wadi*, Pete thought.

"Okay. Cat, you and Buddy strike north along the wadi. Georgie, Simms, keep charge of the prisoner, head up into the scrub on the west bank—"

"Hey, we got company," Buddy called.

Pete looked south. The verti had risen to a couple of hundred meters and was flying slowly toward them.

"It's the eye in the sky," Georgie said.

"Tex," Pete said.

Tex sat up, turned around, swung his big black machine gun up from the waist. He started hosing quick bursts at the aircraft, letting muzzle-jump spread the wealth around.

Kolya Kuliyev banked and dove away as bullets passed through the verti with thin whistling cracks. "Okay, bad idea," he said to Shih, still strapped in the copilot's seat. "This thing isn't a gunship, and it isn't armored, and we don't know what else they may have. I'm not usually the cautious type, but unless we wanna risk stranding our pals, our only option right here is to park somewhere where we can keep an eye on things, maybe lend a hand if things get scaly."

Shih just nodded. Her lips and throat were too dry to actually produce words.

Buddy let out a rebel yell. "You sure showed him, Tex! He's beatin' cheeks, big time."

Pete watched the verti fly toward a mesa a kilometer to the west. "Georgie, Simms, stay here and keep a watch. Give a yell if that thing comes back."

Tex had stood up and was letting his M60 hang from its sling as he dusted himself off. "What about me?"

Pete grinned. "You and me." He pointed with his chin at the round-topped hill two hundred meters northeast. "Straight up that hill."

A molasses grin spread across Tex's vast face. "Rock an' roll. Rock and *fuckin'* roll."

Kolya brought the verti to a feather-light touchdown on the mesa's flat top, just out of sight of the other craft. The morning sun starred the windscreen like a bullet strike. He sighed, feathered his props, and leaned forward to adjust the pillow at the small of his back.

"Now we watch. And wait."

"Yes, Captain Kuliyev," Shih said demurely. She unbuckled herself and stretched, trying to remobilize tension-knotted muscles.

Then she grabbed up Eddie's rotary rifle from the deck beneath her feet, dodged out of her seat, and was gone.

Eddie came back from his walk in the dreamtime with the packed-in sensation of lying in sand, sun cascading like scalding water on his face, and something tickling his nose.

He opened his eyes to slits, which was as far as they'd go. An immense fat green-bellied fly doing a careful recon of his nose took fright at the small, agonized motion and buzzed off.

There were dry weeds around his head and voices nearby: "Why don't you call for aircraft to help you?"

Great. The orange-haired French bitch. Timur's ex-squeeze. He thought he'd dreamed her.

He was distracted from a fuzzy fantasy of choking her by Simms's high-pitched voice, Boy Scout polite, as he remembered it: "You see, Ms., we're still deep in rebel-held territory, and the risk from surface-to-air—"

"You see any *tanks*, babe?" Georgie cut him off. "That's all fast-movers are good for. Tanks and bunkers and other shit you can see from a long way off, and that can't go hide in the bushes where you'll never see 'em again between your first pass and the time you curve back around for a bomb run. We don't *need* 'em; this is snoop-and-poop stuff." Eddie could *feel* his nasty grin. "That's where we live. We are the best."

The fuck of it was, it was true. They were the best. Eddie had made sure of that himself.

Chapter
FORTY-SIX

Aliyev the Singer obeyed orders better than his boss did. When Eddie split, he left firm instructions for the old Kirghiz to stay behind in charge, and keep the other sections with him. Aliyev did those things.

As Aliyev saw it, his duty required him to keep the other section leaders on the Syr Dar'ya with him. But Eddie had not forbidden *leave*. Therefore Aliyev decreed that each section might send five men back to the encampment outside Tashkent on furlough.

And if those men chose to follow their *orlok* and keep an eye on him . . . a commander had no right to interfere with what his men did in their free time.

Moon, the small square man with the blacksmith grip who hailed from an ethnic-Korean *koophoz* south of Tashkent, led five Blue-Sky Riders in a swift march down the wadi. Eddie had taught them well. They moved in single file, slightly staggered, so that a single high-velocity jacketed round couldn't punch them all through at once like doves on a fence. They hugged the eastern bank, to reduce their chances of being spotted and to enable them to take cover quickly if they were. They walked hunched well over, to keep their heads below the bunchgrass and bushes that lined the wadi's banks.

They were good.

It was an irregularity in the sand not far from the bank, too small to be called a mound, too insignificant to attract the attention even of alert and seasoned guerrilla fighters.

It was enough to conceal a claymore mine, buried in a

depression scooped in the sand by a single swipe of a
monster fist. At a word from Delgado in his lie-up on the
far bunk, Buddy triggered the device when Moon was
within five feet of it.

Though the Riders were well dispersed, the fan of steel
marbles tore Moon and the two men behind him to bloody
rags. The surviving pair kept their heads; they didn't freak
at the horrific blast and the sight of their comrades coming
apart before their eyes, and they didn't freeze when the Cat
took them under fire. They kept a grip on their weapons and
themselves and rolled over the top for cover.

Buddy was waiting, hidden seven meters in from the
bank behind a wormwood bush. He dropped them both with
two quick bursts.

Sometimes good isn't enough.

Eddie's keepers were arguing. Jacqui wanted to know
why they didn't stay by the aircraft where it was safe and
shady; Georgie explained none too politely that it was a
perfect bullet and missile magnet, and just swollen with
highly combustible fuel. He sounded right on the edge. The
physical danger part of action didn't really appeal to him.
Great. If she rides him, maybe he'll snap—

A hard-edged boom, followed by a quick succession of
pops. "What was that?" Simms said. He sat up like a
prairie dog sentry, craning around.

"It sounded like an explosion," Jacqui said. She was holding
the videocam on the soldiers and their captive and hoping she
had enough storage flips to take it all in. Her own satlink
antenna had bitten the big one along with Tewfik.

"I know that. I just can't see a damned thing in these
bushes."

"For fuck's sake, get your head down," Georgie said.
He himself lay sidewalk flat, keeping his CAR-203 trained
down the arroyo.

"Georgie, don't be an old woman. I've got body armor
on. I just don't want anyone creeping up—"

His head exploded.

"Astakhfirullaa," breathed a young Uzbek who wore a purple skullcap embroidered in red and black. "A head shot at six hundred meters, over open sights. A miracle!"

Sher Khan lowered his ancient Enfield. "It is nothing," he said. "When I was young and we played the ridgetop game, we would not deign to take such easy shots. It was considered no sport unless we were at twice that range."

He spoke of a game—whose reality had never been confirmed by outside observers—in which young Pushtun hillmen lay on opposite hills and tried to see how close they could shoot to one another without actually hitting. His three youthful companions stared at him in awe. They were Asian too, which meant they understood perfectly well that Sher Khan was a lying old windbag who was secretly pleased to the roots of his red-dyed beard to have nailed the Nikolay. It was still an impressive shot.

"Now we know where some of our enemies are," Sher Khan said. "We move—swiftly, but cautiously too."

Mr. P and Tex hit the hill at a run, Pete slightly in the lead, with twenty meters between them. The first group of rebels, to the left, had beaten their comrades into position. They took the two under fire from the top of the hill.

Texas Team had been together a long time. The squaddies knew each others' minds. Without word or signal passing between them, Pete dropped flat into a bush while Tex spun and hosed the hilltop with a burst from his Maremont, clamped against his hip.

Even two hundred meters away, a 7.62mm machine gun is a fearsome, intimidating weapon. Shooting with little chance of actually *hitting* anything, Tex might be able to make the rebels flinch, pull their heads down. *Achieving fire superiority* was the military-speak for it.

It was the furthest thing from his mind.

He stopped shooting and took off at an angle left around

the hip of the hill, zigzagging, leaping over bushes. He was still an immense target, completely irresistible. The four rebels blazed happily away at him.

For all his bulk Tex was a skilled broken-field runner, and he was playing to the buck fever that was endemic to indiges. The rebels busted a lot of caps at him but couldn't get the range.

Before they did, Mr. P read their positions from the clouds of detritus thrown up by their muzzle blasts. He popped a 40mm white phosphorus grenade on them.

White streamers unfolded behind the hilltop like the tentacles of a reef creature. Screams. Tex dropped to cover as Pete broke open the single-shot launcher slung under his assault rifle, ejected the spent and smoking casing, slammed in another WP, and let it go too, firing at a high angle so that it fell behind the crest.

Then they were both up and running as hard as their well-tuned legs would drive them. That was how you busted ambush: you assaulted into it, hoping to demoralize your attackers by sheer ferocity, transmute the triumph of catching you in the kill zone to bladder-clearing panic. Morale is a curious thing, either spider-silk strong or friable and fragile as butterflies' wings. Pete and Tex intended to crumble the rebels' morale into brightly colored powder.

Nothing snaps your mind back into focus like a cold blade nuzzling your throat. Eddie was just lying there trying to adjust to the odd fact that the long lanky thing flopping around in the sagebrush like a caught trout was that hopeless well-meaning Canadian goof Simms, at least from about the upper maxillary down, and trying to filter out the air-raid-siren keening of the Frenchwoman, and suddenly here was Georgie, sitting on his chest and sawing away at his larynx with that fucking Arkansas toothpick.

"That's it, you slippery little son of a bitch." Georgie sprayed Eddie's face with garlic-scented saliva. "Pete says we gotta get you back alive, but fuck it man, that's it, that's fucking *it*."

Georgie was the excitable type, and having most of Simms's brains and one of his eyeballs hanging off his uniform was not calming his mind. Otherwise he would have remembered that if you want to cut throat with a knife like his—double-edge, straight taper to a needle point—the way to do it is punch it in the side of the neck and *rip*. Fucking *does the trick*. What he was doing was better suited to slicing a sourdough loaf than homicide.

Eddie braced his heels on the mound at the base of a tuft of bunchgrass and pushed, snapping his body into a bow. Georgie said "Whoops" and bounced up into the air. His big knife came away from Eddie's throat.

Georgie was an excellent knife man, even if prone to pop his composure; he reversed the weapon and drove it down both-handed, intending to give his erstwhile CO a field-expedient lobotomy. He had landed farther up Eddie's body, straddling his sternum and restricting his upper-body mobility more than before.

Eddie threw his head right so hard he felt a pop at the back of his neck. The blade plunged into the dry soil with a librarian's disapproving *tsk*. Its edge laid Eddie's scalp open to white occiput.

"Ow, *shit!*" Inspired by the liquid pain at the back of his head, Eddie whipped up his feet, locked them under Georgie's chin, and flipped the Georgian backward off him.

There was no airplane hatch convenient, though, so a single scissors throw was not going to end this little wrestling match. He *could* have just snapped himself up onto his feet—that acrobatic training again—but if whoever splashed Simms was still holding down on that spot, his reaction was going to be to launch another bullet right away at any head that happened to present itself.

Eddie rolled his knees under him and came up to a crouch, doing a little plowing with his face and getting a mouthful of hot sand in the process. He had thumped the back of Georgie's head hard on packed earth when he threw him off, momentarily disorienting the dark-haired man. Georgie was on his knees too, probing with his Arkansas toothpick like a bug antenna.

Eddie put a shoulder down as a pivot, scythed a leg around in a sort of Cossack-dance kick. The knife went flying. Georgie lunged at him. Eddie kicked him in the face. Georgie sat down hard, shaking his head, his tail whipping from side to side, blood pouring down his mustache from his nose.

He twisted and dove for the knife. Eddie ran at him in a duckwalk like Chuck Berry on speed, kicked him in the flank. Unable to extend, the only way to get power in the kick was to run it into Georgie; Eddie fell over him, tucked a shoulder, and rolled.

The Georgian had a wiry monkey agility. His fingers closed on the dagger's elephant-ivory hilt despite the kick. He turned and flew at Eddie, the knife blade down, ready to pin Eddie to the earth.

From his back Eddie fired a front snap-kick to the point of Georgie's chin. Georgie's head whipped back with a sound like a handgun going off. He spasmed like a cat hit by a semi, fell on his back, and laid extremely still.

Eddie sat and fought for his breath watching Georgie. His shoulders felt as if somebody had doused the muscles in lighter fluid and torched them off. Georgie's chest did not seem to be moving.

He stood up, remembering to keep his head down. There were *advantages* to being a short shit, and he'd learned to recognize and use them years ago. He cast around for the knife; maybe he could saw these goddam wraps off his arms somehow. On the other hand, they were designed to be hard to cut, and the knife had finally gone missing.

" 'So what's it to be, then, O my brothers?' " he quoted in a broken-glass whisper.

Jacqui Gendron came lurching at him from stage left, strong fingers bent into claws. Fast Eddie was not the type to beat on women, but he wasn't dogmatic either. Without bothering to look at her directly, he put a sidethrust kick in her belly, more push than blow. She sat down hard.

"Fuck it," he gasped. He turned and ran instinctively west, away from the sudden storm of gunfire that had broken out from the far side of the wadi.

Pete and Tex hit the crest at almost the same instant as the group of rebels who had been dropped on the southeastern side of the hill. One of the rebels was quick and maybe lucky; he popped up and fired a burst that caught Tex right in the massive belly.

Tex staggered back three meters. Then he laughed and blew the rebel to pieces with a burst from his M60. The armorplate inserts of his vest had stopped the 5.45mm rounds from the Advanced Kalashnikov, and Tex's bulk and giant's strength had absorbed the shock of the impacts.

Both sides went to earth on opposite sides of the hill. While Tex pulsed brief bursts of fire to either side of the hilltop proper, to keep the bad guys' heads down, Pete pulled a CS grenade from his harness. Texas Team didn't carry nonlethal agents to be nice: lethal gas was too tricky and dangerous actually to be used in combat. But why bother, when tear gas generally did fine at fucking your opponents up so you could shoot them?

He started to pull the pin. And a voice in his ears wheezed, *"Lieutenant, your two men are down. The bastard Eddie has escaped!"*

Chapter
FORTY-SEVEN

"Death cards," Buddy said, straightening up. The three in the arroyo were as dead as the two he had personally waxed on the bank. Textbook claymore ambush. "What we need is some death cards." He grinned hugely; his brother would sure be proud of him, thinking of a touch like that. He lived to impress his larger twin.

"Say what?" Delgado's voice asked over his headset.

"Death cards. You know, some ace of spades or something to drop on the bodies. So people'll know who killed 'em."

"What a *coño*."

Buddy's face turned red, like a wall poster of Mars. "Hey, I know Spanish, you little *Marielista* butt boy—"

"*Six to Texas,*" a headset voice cut across him. "*The prisoner has escaped. Heading in a westerly direction, over.*"

"This is Buddy with Delgado," the outsized Texan replied. "We copy. We're on our way."

"Allah be praised! We have driven them off!"

Lying on his side, gritting his teeth in his beard against the pain of the 7.62 round that had cracked a rib in his right side before glancing off, Rahman the Gypsy nodded. "*Yakhshi.* Take them under fire, make sure they keep heading in the right direction."

The others nodded and obeyed. Rahman smiled through the pain. *Keep them headed in the right direction* was a favorite phrase of Eddie-*bahadur*'s, right up there with *fuck that noise*. He was beginning to grasp what their commander called fundamental leadership skills, he thought.

He sat up despite the agony it sent like a lance through his side. If the infidels—Nikolays or Americans, he wasn't clear on that—were routed indeed, it was time to get on with the business of rescuing Fast Eddie.

Shih was breathing hard, and her hands felt as if she'd plunged them into broken glass. She kept herself in excellent shape, as a People's Republic comrade ought—she was communitarian to that extent, anyway—but it was *taiji* fit, exercise-floor fit. Slogging across the desert was hard work, work her body wasn't tuned to. The country was far more broken than it appeared; you were constantly scrambling up and down, and the swathes of soft sand sucked your feet in and filled your sneakers with hot sand and turned your thighs to gelatin. The sparse ground cover concealed nasty little burrs, and when she fell or had to use her hands to scramble, they stuck in her.

She was still not entirely sure why she was doing this. She had been passive all her life; why was she turning into Woman of Action now, on behalf of someone she suspected of fucking and forgetting her?

Her heart felt as if it were trying to hammer its way out of her rib cage, and it wasn't all from exertion. She was heading with all the speed she could muster toward a group of the world's most accomplished killers, armed with a weapon she didn't know how to use and wasn't even sure she *could* use. But for all her terror and doubt and exhaustion, she could not bring herself to turn back to the mesa where the red Russian waited with the verti.

There was shooting ahead of her. She was unsure of the distance; it didn't *sound* close, and she saw smoke from a hilltop perhaps half a kilometer ahead. She did not pray— she didn't know how—but the little girl inside asked her father's spirit that *please* all of the enemy soldiers were up there instead of hiding in the brush and the narrow unexpected wadis. And that Eddie was still alive.

She slithered over an outcrop of pink sandstone slabs that thrust from the sand like a cypress knee. She could just see the enemy aircraft now, grounded in the wadi not two hundred meters ahead. She started forward.

Like a yeti who had wandered down out of the blue *Bam-i-Dunya* that floated like heavy clouds on the eastern horizon, he rose from a bush: one of the enormous twin white devils. Sunlight turned his glasses to twin circles of dazzle, eerie blank brightnesses. He grinned.

"Hey there, hi there, ho there, little darlin'," Buddy Lynko said. "Fancy meeting you here."

* * *

Eddie ran through the desert. Maybe *stumbled* was a better word. For a trained gymnast and seasoned Special Designation desert warrior, he was making a conspicuously piss-poor showing. Then again, the fact that he had been captured, beaten within an inch of his life, and dangled out of an aircraft, and had his arms wrapped up behind his back, and hadn't even gotten much *sleep*, might mean he wasn't at the top of his range.

He tripped over a wormwood shrub, fell. *Excuses won't keep those bastards from putting a bullet in my ear if they catch me.*

He struggled to his knees. Sweat poured down his face, the salt stinging an open cut in his forehead and forming blinding pools in his eyes. He longed to wipe it away. He tried to get at his eyes with a shoulder, couldn't. He shook his head violently, and that cleared his vision a fraction.

That reminded him that he would not last long out here without water. On the other hand, in terms of threat assessment, death from dehydration looked about as likely as death from old age right now. No matter how hot it was or how much you exerted yourself, it took *time* to die of thirst. He didn't have much of that.

West ahead of him rose a steep-sided mesa. He would steer toward that—and around it. Without hands to climb with or roll rocks down on ill-intentioned heads, the heights were no friends to him. The convoluted desert below, with its wadis and bushes, was a better environment to hide in. But if he could get the bulk of a formation between him and pursuit . . . *Hell, it can't hurt.*

He got to his feet and staggered on.

Buddy stooped to lay his CAR-15 on the ground, then held out a vast hand, palm up. "C'mere, li'l darlin'. I won't hurt you."

His smile gave him the lie. It had the wet shine of a toad's eyeball. She brought the rotary up to her hip, aimed as best she could at the middle of him. She had plenty to aim at, anyway.

He walked toward her. "You stop there," she said in English. "I will shoot you. *Stop.*"

He grinned more widely. "*Naw.* You ain't got the guts, honey. An' even if you did—I got body armor on. You put the muzzle of that puppy right up against my big old belly and give me the whole magazine, I'd scarce even feel it."

He was getting close. Despite the fact that she was armed and he was not, she felt her feet backing away, sinking in sand that seemed to suck them in like tar.

He's right. You could never shoot him. And if you did, even that would be futile. Like everything you've done. Like everything you are.

"That's it, honey," he said. "You're getting the big picture. Now it's time to get somethin' *else* big." He tittered.

Damn him, can he read my body language so well?

Her eyes jumped to his belt, which was straining to contain his giant belly. She saw the ivory handles dangling, the wire looped between them. And she knew what he intended to do to her. He would strangle her as he raped her.

He read the knowledge in her eyes and laughed. "You got that right, little darlin'. And there ain't one thing you can do about it. Now make it easy on yourself and hand me over that piece."

Fury roared up within her like a blowtorch flame. She sought words to express that flaming anger, but her circumspect Middle Kingdom upbringing provided nothing useful. Her vulgar, boisterous American/Russian lover did, though.

"*Fuck that noise!*" she screamed in English. "Fuck it!" She mashed the trigger down.

Buddy saw her finger tighten. He laughed. He had nothing to worry about unless the barrel climbed and sprayed his face, and he was already charging forward with that startling rhino speed. . . .

The 7mm expansion jackets on the rounds flattened

harmlessly against the vest. The Teflon-coated tool-steel penetrators slid with savage oily ease through Kevlar, laminated ceramic and steel, Kevlar again, and finally flesh.

Buddy shrieked. The force of the bullets smashing through his lungs and entrails squirted blood black from his mouth.

Through heartbeat thunder and the carpet-beating sound of his feet in sand, Fast Eddie heard a familiar female voice screaming a very familiar phrase. "Jesus," he gasped, "*Shih!*" He turned and ran toward the sound as gunfire and a whistling bellow tore the air.

What he might actually be able to do to help her, he had no clue. But that was Eddie.

Tex had just crossed the wadi southeast of the verti when he heard his brother's death-scream. The blood drained form his exertion-reddened face, "*Buddy,*" he murmured. He changed course to run toward the cry and the shooting.

Despite his size, he could move quietly at speed. He dodged around a clump of brush and ran straight into a turbaned man fully tall as himself.

Distracted by the commotion not a hundred meters off, Sher Khan had not heard the big man bearing down on him. At the last heartbeat he sensed approach, started to spin, but by then it was far too late. The monstrous man collided with him, his black American machine gun stunning his left arm with a funny-bone blow.

Sher Khan reached for his Khyber knife. With an instant's more forewarning, Tex Lynko was quicker. He snatched his saw-backed Randall survival knife from its hilt-down harness before his left shoulder, slashed across.

Blood from the tall man's slashed throat washed across him in a wave. A red-dyed beard twisted, and the man fell.

"*Dushman* mother*fucker,*" Tex ran on, leaving the Afghan to bleed.

Two more rebels in his path, dark skullcaps, baggy-sleeved white shirts, turning from a crouch to face him with parodic surprise on their bearded nigger faces. He fired the M60 from the hip as though it were a submachine gun. They sprayed blood and screams and fell. He ran.

Disoriented by the horrible noise still echoing in her ears and the nausea surging in her belly like the Yellow Sea in a typhoon, Shih ran south as fast as she could. She had to get away from what she had made of the giant *gweilu*, from the guilt of inflicting that much damage and suffering on another human being. At the same time, she was seized by the irrational fear that despite the punctured, sodden-mattress look of him, despite the purple tissue bulging from his mouth and nose, the huge man would rise up laughing to come for her with his garrote and cock in hand.

A spatter of desperate running steps, and the nightmare came true.

He stood before her, his face great as a harvest moon, his round glasses silvered with sun. But no, he was intact, and instead of a garrote he held a monstrous black gun.

Both stopped. He looked at the rifle in her hands. He looked at her face.

It had worked before. She had found the courage to use it before, and in spite of everything, it had worked. She pointed the rotary at the middle of his chest and pulled the trigger.

Nothing happened. She had fired the entire magazine at Buddy.

Tex smiled. He swung his Maremont to bear on the tiny girl in the blood-soaked T-shirt and jeans.

A catamount weight landed on his back. He went to his knees. The Maremont roared, firing wide of the mark. The force of the muzzle blasts buffeted Shih like fists. She threw herself to the ground and covered her ears with her hands.

Scalding blood and breath were pulsing down the back of Tex's neck. Pushto curses chuffed in his ear like animal grunts. He struggled to draw his big knife, but the M60 was in the way. The point of the long Khyber knife slammed into his assault vest with sledgehammer force.

The composite armor was enough to turn the blade, even with the Tiger Lord's brawny arm driving it. Then Sher Khan found an armpit, and his knife drank deep.

Tex roared.

He got his Randall out then, stabbed backward over his shoulder. He felt it bite. The curse-chant never broke rhythm.

Tex grunted as the Afghan's knife sank into his right buttock. It withdrew, thrust again, and this time Tex screamed full-throat as it sank into his bowels. He stabbed wildly, blindly, not noticing that he severed his own right ear.

From the sand scant meters away Shih watched as the two fought like prehistoric monsters in some Hollywood epic. The pain of wanting to help Sher Khan was like the bite of one of those huge horrible knives. But if she tried to intervene, those flailing massive limbs would break her in half.

She expected that part of her, hidden deep till now, that had pulled the trigger on Buddy to force her forward to destruction. Instead it whispered, *Stay. You can do nothing to help.*

Another facet of the jewel strength she had discovered within her, she knew then, was recognizing when you were truly helpless, and acting accordingly. But whatever she did or did not do, the scene before her—the horrible masculine orgy of blood and anger and agony and thrashing, thrusting violence—would live in her nightmares as long as she herself lived.

However long that might prove to be.

Jesus Christ, what's that noise? Eddie wondered. *It sounds like a tiger killing a water buffalo.*

He was heading what he took to be north now at a rubber-kneed trot. He thought he was getting close to where Shih's shout had come from, but his internal direction-finding equipment was all screwed up.

"Hey, amigo," a voice said from his left. "You wanta hold it right there, man."

He stopped and just stood, sweat running down his face,

angry frustrated ironic bile running down his throat. "All right, Delgado," he said, not even looking. "You got me. Why don't you just go ahead and kill me?"

"No, Aleksandr Pavlovich," another voice said from behind him. "He won't do that at all."

Eddie wheeled, sat down hard, and stared up into the blindingly perfect features of Mr. P.

"Because *I'm* going to."

Chapter
FORTY-EIGHT

Eddie had nicknamed his second-in-command after star pitcher Ron Darling of the Mets, whom teammates called Mr. Perfect for his habit of trying to put every pitch over the corner of the plate.

Eddie *hated* the Mets.

Shih, honey, he thought, *if you're anywhere around here, this is as good a time as any for a miraculous rescue.*

He stood up, swayed, and said, "Let's do it. Kill me." He squinted up at the sun. "I got nothin' better to do."

Mr. P looked at him and sighed. Then he knelt and carefully leaned his CAR-203 into the center of a clump of camel's-hair.

"What's that?" Eddie demanded. "What do you think you're doing?"

"I don't need a gun to dispose of a filthy Jew like you." He stepped forward and backhanded Eddie across the face. "I think it'll be more fun to beat you to death."

Eddie sat down hard. He felt blood running from his nose and lips. Not exactly a new experience today.

"Now this is what I call a fair fight," he said. "You never could resist a challenge, huh, Pete?"

Pete grinned and leaned forward. With all his might Eddie kicked him in the crotch. Pete grunted, then grabbed the front of Eddie's shirt and hauled him to his feet.

"Just what I always thought," Eddie said. "No balls."

Mr. P buried a fist in Eddie's stomach. Eddie bent over and hoped the air would come back eventually.

When it did, he said, "This is going to be fun. I can tell."

Pete took him by the hair, hauled him up. He punched Eddie in the face.

Eddie backpedaled, managed to keep his feet. "Wha' vuh hell's *wrong* wif you?" he demanded, numbed smashed lips deranging his speech. "You been seeing too many American movies? You never hit someone inna face wiv your *fist*."

"I know precisely how hard I can hit you without damaging myself," Pete said. Eddie noticed him waving his hand all but imperceptibly, as if trying to shake the sting. "I think of this as experimentation. Testing the human mechanism to destruction."

"Yeah?" Eddie started to topple forward. Pete closed.

Eddie planted his left foot and wheeled, bringing his right foot back and around and *out*. A spinning back kick is the most powerful blow a human body can deliver, which is helpful to know when you're as small as Fast Eddie.

Under most circumstances he wouldn't use one in a real fight: takes too long to develop, too easy to read. But Mr. Perfect was suckered *perfectly*, moving forward off balance and expecting anything in the whole world before an attack from his well-drubbed victim.

The heel of Eddie's sneaker caught Pete square in the sternum. The Second Chance vest kept the blow from squashing his rib cage into his heart, but impact sent him flying. He landed in a huge cloud of dust.

With a scream of savage joy Eddie skipped forward. He had killed Georgie with a sloppy-ass kick from flat on his back. If Mr. P raised his head trying to stand up, Eddie was going to kick his perfect blond Aryan head right fucking *off*.

Unfortunately, they didn't call him Mr. Perfect just to blow air. He knew better than to try to stand into an attack. He rolled away. Eddie chased him, aimed a kick for the kidneys—armored too, but what the hell, he could get lucky.

The millisecond Eddie fired the kick, Pete reversed back into him and cut his down leg right out from under him with a neat sweep kick.

Eddie fell across his antagonist. He butted him with his head, laid his brow open further on a Kevlar-covered insert edge. Pete started short-punching him in the spareribs.

Great, he thought as Pete rolled him onto his back so he could sit up and punch him. *At least things can't possibly get worse than this—*

"Hold that pose."

Mr. P and Eddie both froze, then turned to look in unison. Jacqui Gendron stood there grinning with that little gargoyle cam on her shoulder. She was a bit dusty, and a few strands of hair had blown loose from her bun and were shining like strands of bronze wire in the sun, but it was only beer-commercial dishevelment, not serious down-and-dirty disarray. Both men hated her for it.

"This is a World-Historical event," she said, making you *feel* those capital letters. "The dreary end of the doomed, romantic Red Sands rebellion. The world deserves to see it all. You too, child; don't bother hiding there in that bush. It is not appropriate behavior for a professor."

Shih Tai-Yu stood up. Her face was smudged and bruised. Her black hair was wild and had little bits of dried desert vegetation clinging to it. If Mattel made a Viet Cong Girl Doll, it would look just like her.

"Ed-die," she said, "I wanted to help. But I do not know how." She hung her head. "I am useless after all."

A light came on in the red and black chaos that was

Eddie's head. "That noise back there wouldn't have been you waxing old Buddy, would it?"

Her tongue peeked out and her throat worked as though trying to hold back vomit. *Bingo*.

"I'd say that makes you a hero, babe. If nothing else, it means I can die happy."

And having distracted Mr. P with a bit of happy horseshit, he bucked him into the air and tried to lay a scissors on him.

Pete wasn't Georgie or the Swinging Richard. He was Mr. P. The instant he felt himself going up, he dove clear of Eddie, hit, rolled, came up dusting himself off and laughing.

He raised a hand to ward off Delgado, who had come up close to see if he needed to intervene. "Are you getting good footage of this, telecunt?" he asked Jacqui. "You think your viewers will enjoy the spectacle of this little kike getting hammered to death?"

"It will be good for a four hundred share at least," she said, letting the epithet roll off her like spittle off a mylar dropsheet. "Maybe a clean billion. It's what TV news is all about."

"Well, it's time for the grand finale." Pete advanced on Eddie. On his feet again, Eddie kicked at him. Pete rode the first with his hip, blocked the second, and closed, pistoning punches into Eddie's face and body.

Eddie tried to keep dancing back, maintain *ma'ā*, engagement range. It was hopeless. Mr. P was damned near as good as he was—to save a shred of ego—and he'd had a much better day. Pete kept on him, pounding him, punishing him.

Running was starting to rankle. Eddie put his head down and charged. Anything to keep Pete from picking him to pieces with those precise blows.

Pete caught him, let him slam into his armored chest. He was laughing hugely. He caught Eddie around the small of the back and squeezed.

"I think I'll break your spine, you little shit," he said.

"Yeah?" Eddie said, which was the wittiest rejoinder he

had in him at that moment. He brought up a knee with desperate power. Maybe his earlier nut-shot had hit off true.

Maybe it had. Pete swiveled, took the blow on the point of his hip. It popped Eddie's Glock out of Pete's belt to the sand at their feet.

Both men watched the handgun fall. "Too bad it can't help you," Pete taunted. He locked hand on wrist and squeezed, pulling Eddie's feet clear of the ground. "And *I* don't need it."

Eddie felt his backbone give, felt the awful leg-watering weakness as bone pressed spinal cord with a creak.

He reached his face forward and bit off Mr. Perfect's nose with a single weasel snap.

Mr. P shrieked and shoved him away hard. Blood arced from the middle of his face, like a smooth red elephant trunk.

Eddie fetched up against the grenade-lumpy chest of Delgado, who had sensed things going wrong and lunged forward to help his new boss. Delgado caught Eddie under the arms and just stood there holding him, staring at Mr. P as he reeled around screaming and hosing blood.

Eddie gagged, spat out blood and Mr. P's perfect nose. His fingers, held cruelly tight behind his back, had only pins-and-needle feeling and the responsiveness of a rubber glove filled with sand. He willed them to work, blind and desperate.

The Cat came back to himself. He pushed Eddie down in the dirt, unslung his CAR-203, and started to bring it up.

He wore his vest-o'-grenades for the M-203 launcher. Like the other members of Texas Team he also carried several hand grenades slung to his web harness, for up-close-and-personal work.

The CS hand grenade whose pin Eddie's numb fingers had found blew. Thick white smoke wreathed the Cuban.

Screaming "*Shih! Get down!*" Eddie sprang up and ran away from the Cat as fast as he could. Which wasn't very.

A tear-gas grenade does not explode. But it does *burn*, at

a fairly high temperature, as the Symbionese Liberation Army found out to its terminal dismay one warm May morning in Watts.

The first grenade to cook off was a multiple projectile round. Delgado's armor managed to deflect most of the force of the explosion and the shotgun-spray of pellets away from him, but a spike of hot gas laid open the right side of his face like a razor.

The next grenade to go was good old Willy Peter. It had a lot more powerful bursting charge than the MP round, but the Second Chance armor still preserved Delgado's life. Which was unfortunate, because he was now covered in flakes of metal that clung like soldier ants and burned like hell. He began to shriek and spin around and around like a dervish at the Loud Zikr. Little threads of white smoke trailed from his face and arms and legs and spiraled about him in an intricate pattern. His flesh burned with a pale flame and much greasy smoke.

Then the rest of the grenades cooked off with a rippling thunder crash, tearing his head off, plucking his armored torso to pieces like petulant giant fingers.

Eddie had thrown himself behind a bush when the MP round went. Fortune had sent the Cat spinning away from him in his final fire dance, so the rapidly expanding tentacles of white smoke, each tipped with a flake of hell, did not find him.

Then he was laughing, and weeping, and someone was behind his back, fiddling with his bonds. He jerked away, though he didn't stop laughing.

A Chinese exclamation, and then, "Calm yourself, Eddie. It is I."

He quit trying to squirm free, but bounced up and down on the hot hard earth like a kid who needed to take a whiz. "You always said I was nuts for watching *Raising Arizona* seven times," he screamed at the smoke-shrouded wreckage of the Cat. *"Who's crazy now, you Cuban son of a bitch?"*

Shih finally solved the fasteners on the restraints. As they fell away, she leapt back, as if fearing Eddie's madness was topical, carried by a touch.

Then she grabbed his shoulder. "Ed-die, look. It's that man!''

Mr. Perfect, no longer so, emerged from the swirling stranded white phosphorus smoke at a run. Eddie knew at once where he was going.

He launched himself off the ground with more strength than he thought he had left. Momentum carried him a few steps, and then his knees buckled. He dropped to his knees, pitched forward, caught himself on his hands.

Yes, my hands. My hands are back. Hello, hands.

He knew his arms would never support him, so he kicked his way upright again, slogged forward in a desperate lumbering dash.

Pete passed him on an oblique to the left. The time for this bare-knuckle kung-fu movie shit was past. Man is the tool-using animal.

Pete reached his tool first. He caught his CAR-203 by the sling and whipped it around as Eddie dove for his Glock.

A burst went over Eddie with a sound like a sheet tearing. His left hand closed around the squat black polymer grip of his Glock. A fleck of white phosphorus had fallen on it. He screamed as it stung his hand like a scorpion.

He did not let go, though he felt the searing metal welding his flesh to melted polymer. Inertia carried him on in a long dive as a second burst raked earth where the pistol had lain.

Eddie flew through a wormwood bush, landed; muscle memory kept his shoulder down, guided him through a roll. He came out of it supine, the Glock burning in his palm, braced by the right hand, forefinger locked around the scooped front of the trigger guard. The stink of his own meat cooking inflated his head like a circus balloon.

A life expressed as a fat white dot nestled in a square U. An elongated shape beyond, light winking from its side. Earth fountains about his face, squirting up, feathering at the top, falling away in khaki plumes as the wind had their way with them. Getting closer. It wasn't like Mr. P to keep missing at this range, but then again, his day had gotten worse.

Eddie's every instinct screamed at him to throw the awful burning thing away. Instead he drew a deep breath, let half of it go, and *squeezed*.

The first bullet struck Mr. Perfect a couple of centimeters left and above his navel. The armor stopped it. The second hit just inboard his right nipple. The vest sucked that too. He kept grinning and shooting.

The impact of a .40-caliber bullet is much less than that of even a 5.45. But Pete didn't have Tex's gross strength and body mass. The bullet strikes knocked him back a couple of steps, threw off his aim just as he was ready to nail that little yid cocksucker.

That gave Eddie a second-splinter more to aim his third shot. It met Mr. P right where his nose used to be. It was a safety slug. It exploded, penetrating the skull, and turned everything inside to pulp.

Pete fell into a burning bush.

Eddie kept firing, hitting Pete in the head once more as he went down, cranking shots into his torso. They brought out little puffs of dust.

The weapon emptied. Fast Eddie put his head on his arms and started to cry.

Miraculously, Sher Khan was still alive when they found him. He lay on his back with Tex sprawled across him, Sher Khan's Khyber knife buried beneath his jaw and most of his blood already soaked into the sand.

He smiled when Eddie knelt to take his hand—with his right. Eddie's left hand had a field dressing from Mr. P's belt wrapped around it, and Eddie hoped he'd never be reminded of its existence again.

"I die with my claws in the enemy," the old Pushtun

bandit said. His voice was thready, almost lost beneath the wind. "Is that not a fitting end for the Lord of the Tigers?"

And having delivered the exit line that was all he'd been holding on for, Sher Khan of the Yusufzai let himself go and slipped over to wherever it was you went when you weren't anymore. Eddie hoped there were plenty of babes there, like the Book promised.

The American pilot and his bandaged Brit copilot surrendered readily. This wasn't their fight, and they found the late Mr. P and his late little friends more alarming than the rebels.

Eight Blue-Sky Riders survived, including two stretcher cases and Rahman, with his right arm strapped down and one of those pinned-up grins on his face. Eddie stood by the verti and watched them load the thirteen bodies of their less fortunate comrades and Sher Khan into Kolya's craft, trying not to feel sick that so many lives had been spent to save his.

Kolya's verti leaped into the air and began a slow watchful circling as the survivors filed aboard the other aircraft, where lost Timur lay in dry-ice and plastic state. Eddie was the last one on.

There was still one person standing on the ground. He shot out an arm and barred the door when she tried to climb in.

"What do you think you are doing?" Jacqui Gendron demanded. Her right cheek was an angry red mess where a WP flake had scorched her before she could swat it away.

"Leaving your attractive ass in the sand," Eddie said.

She reared back, for the moment too outraged to speak. "Jacqui Gendron, speechless," he said. "Now *this* is a World-Historical moment."

Shih Tai-Yu laid a hand on his arm. She was doing better now. She was through with the dry heaves, and hardly trembled at all.

"Back at the tent, when . . . when those men came in,"

she said softly. "She told them to let me go. She saved me."

"Was that because she wanted to help you," Eddie asked evenly, "or because she thought you were too damned insignificant to screw around with?"

Shih looked at Jacqui. The Frenchwoman elevated her head a fraction, and her nostrils flared.

"I'll get canteens," Shih said. "We must at least leave her water."

"Fine. Go for it."

Jacqui suddenly jumped at him. He stiff-armed her between her breasts.

"Try that again and I'll kill you, babe," he said softly.

She shook her head wildly. "But you can't leave me—I'll *die*."

Eddie turned to accept a pair of one-liter bottles from Shih, threw them to the ground at Jacqui's feet. "No way. No matter how desolate this place looks, a lot of people live around here. When the smoke dies down, they'll be around looking to see what happened. They won't leave you to the lizards.

"Besides—" A corner of his mouth quirked up in a nasty grin, "your kind always manages to survive."

She looked at him, blank. "My kind—?"

He jutted his chin past her. She turned to see two vultures—high, black crosses wheeling against the Central Asian sun.

EPILOGUE

Howl Like
a Dog

I will have no agreement with you,
I will have no reconciliation,
I will have no equal division,
Nothing will I give back to you.
Come and take them—well and good!
If you cannot—then howl for them like a dog!

—The *Manas*

The T-72s were rolling across what looked like a dry
lakebed, raising clouds of white dust. Horsetails whipped
from their antennas. In the background, faint with distance,
the distinctive inverted-leek shape of a League *Energiya*
heavy-lift booster with a *Progress* orbital-supply craft attached
stood silhouetted at the gantry against a faded blue sky.

"Inspired with fanatical purpose by the martyr's death of
their leader, Timur, the rebel armies continue their sweep
west," the voice of Jacqui Gendron said from the Satman's
speaker. "Here, elements of the Karakoram Brigade, composed
of foreign volunteers driving League tanks captured in last
year's victory in the Red Sands, smash the perimeter of the
enormous Baykonur Space Complex near the Aral Sea."

The scene switched to Teatralnaya Square—now renamed
Timur Square—in downtown Tashkent. A skinny young

man with a struggling beard stood on a dais in front of the
rubbled-out KGB headquarters, wrapped in a green flag,
accepting the adulation of the mob. The crowd was prevented
from loving its idol to death by a cordon of youths one or
two years younger than he, lean and arrogant in sky-blue
skullcaps.

"It is less than twenty-four hours since Free Turkestan
was declared an Islamic Revolutionary Republic. Whether
or not that means it will be dominated by adherents of the
militant Shi'ite wing of Islam, and what role Iran will play,
remains unclear. In fact, few Turkestanis, Shi'ite or Sunni,
seem to care. Their only thought is to unfurl the sky-blue
banner of the New Mongol Horde over the republics of the
disintegrating League.

"And perhaps beyond, under the leadership of the youth
acclaimed as Timur's successor. Youngest of the *orloks* or
field marshals who served the *Khan*, Yilderim was the only
orlok native to Turkestan, and the only one to survive the
upheavals surrounding the death of the great man. . . ."

Yilderim the Tadzhik techie, Eddie thought. *Jesus. Yilderim
Khan, Nerd of All Men. What's the world coming to?*
Well, all luck to the kid. He'll need it.
"Astakhfirullaa!" The horses tossed their heads and
sidestepped as Uncle Lucky's exclamation came bouncing
back at them from the Tien Shans that surrounded the high
valley, looking too immense for earthly mountains. "That's
wrong! The Raging Torrent Daoud the Jew survived, and
he's a Sart born, as sure as I."

"Another *orlok* pulled through too," Eddie said from
Sertikan's saddle. "But cut the babe some slack; one out of
three ain't bad for a reporter. You can telejournalist, but you
can't tell her much."

"Ed-die! That is *awful.*" Dr. Shih Tai-Yu aimed a playful
swipe at him from the saddle of her white-nosed Fergana
pony.

Laughing Eddie leaned away from the blow. "Well,

enough of this.'' He punched off the tiny television and tossed it over his shoulder.

No con lasts forever. However beautiful.

Finances, resentful awareness on the part of the tributary city-states that they'd been had, and mean-ass outsiders—the Macedonians—busted up Athens' Delian League scam. A similar combination did for Russia's.

The league had absorbed the debts outstanding *to* the USSR, along with most of its other assets. When jihad-maddened rebels blasted westward out of the Red Sands like a volcano's glowing cloud, Vietnam renounced all debts to the League. Since the socialist republic had fought its entire war with America on Soviet credit, that came to substantial coin. The other former members of the Communist Economic Community promptly defaulted too. The Japanese and the Germans, biggest lenders to the League since devolution, called in their notes. It was economic Armageddon.

Armenia and Georgia jointly invaded Azerbaijan—to forestall its joining the jihad, they said. The treacherous Caucasus range, with its terrible Soviet-era roads, slowed the advance more than the fierce but disorganized Azeri resistance. When the columns broke through and converged on the city of Kirovabad, they fell upon one another in a savage battle of outmoded tanks. *That* melee was in turn interrupted by the arrival of Iranian Su-25s—formerly the property of Saddam Hussein—rolling in hot with full combat loads. The Frogfeet were fronting a joint *Pasdaran*/Azeri *Hezbollah* offensive that had just pinched off the Armenian Kafan Corridor running through Azerbaijan to the border with Iran.

In Moscow the military junta, having liquidated the dearly hated KGB, fractured into open warfare as the Russian Republican Armed Forces turned on their League comutineers. This was no perfunctory threat display followed by abject collapse, as in 1991. It was Stalingrad, Part II: both sides wanted the whole pie.

If anything was left.

That was unlikely, because the late Arkady Arbatov's nightmare came true: Siberia blew. Russian Republican garrisons in Krasnoyarsk, Khabarovsk, and the vast naval base of Vladivostok mutinied. The bulk of the League's Far Eastern Military District forces were pinned on the frontier by a gigantic Chinese mobilization and could not intervene even if they were minded to. The Buryat Autonomous Republic declared its independence from *Siberia;* the Chukchi Nationality *Okrug* applied for annexation by its big neighbor across the Bering Strait. Showed what *they* knew.

Vladivostok woke to find itself under siege by a PRC army out of Manchuria. Its rebellious garrison squealed for rescue by the League. But the League's Army of the Ussuri stayed where it was, frozen by the enormity of the Chinese end run and uncertainty as to whom they were supposed to fight against—and whom they were supposed to be fighting *for.*

The League shattered like a block of rubber dipped in liquid oxygen and hit with a hammer. It was Humpty Dumpty time.

In the midst of chaos, the commander of a train transporting political detainees to Siberia's Magadan *Oblast* didn't think twice about obeying orders that sent his train way the hell down south along an old spur of the Trans-Siberian line to Karaganda in Kazahkstan. Rival League and Russian Republic Armed Forces death squads were out a-roving, holding drum's-head courts-martial for those who questioned orders. Besides, Karaganda was still in League hands: the League said so.

Unfortunately, outside Karaganda bandits blocked the track with an old semitrailer piled with rocks, and attacked the stalled train on horseback. The brave OMON security detachment either fought to the last man or took a few token casualties and ran like bunnies into the Kazakh Steppe, depending on whose version you bought. It wasn't liable to make the history books anyway.

Victorious, the raiders swept back across the hills and returned their mounts to the enthusiastic local tribesfolk who had lent them. They also distributed a large quantity of arms and ammunition by way of a hostess gift. Then they fled south in three tilt-rotor aircraft of advanced design. Not important enough to register a blip on history's big scope.

Neither was the fact that among the escaped deportees were the wife of a helicopter pilot captured at the Red Sands and suspected of defecting to the rebels, and their ten-year old daughter. History couldn't be bothered.

History—declared DOA just a decade before—was having a busy day.

Catching the motion in her peripheral vision, Sertikan tossed her head. Her black mane whipped in the cool breeze that blew down the valley. Eddie leaned forward in the saddle to pat her neck with his right hand. The caress had an edge, hinting of the slap the mare was going to get if she got out of line.

"It looks bad, Eddie-*bahadur,*" said a worried Yoldash, holding up the Satman, which he had neatly fielded from horseback. All that goat polo did wonders for your coordination. "The *ferenghi* commentators say World War III may come at any minute."

"Then we'll ride the goddam storm out," Eddie said. "Christ, now I'm living an old REO Speedwagon song."

"But what about the fallout?" Shih asked quietly.

"Oh, you know the song too? Never mind. The League or the Russians, fucks that they both are, may drop a few nice, dirty groundpounders along the Yangtze and the Yellow so the fallout will waste the maximum number of people. But we can stay up here in the *Bam-i-Dunya* a few weeks until it dies to background."

"But the accident at Chernobyl proved how widely fallout can disperse."

Eddie shrugged. "So? We catch a plume up here, maybe we die of leukemia in twenty, thirty years. And nuclear winter was bullshit all along. I'm not gonna put a bullet in my ear, hon. Not yet anyway."

She raised her head. Her pointed little chin was firm. "Nor I either."

"That's a babe."

He pointed down the valley with his right arm. His left was still in a black silk sling. "Check this out, everybody," he said, raising his voice so the whole caravan could hear him. "The coast is clear. What'd I tell you?"

On foot, on horseback, holding the lead ropes of shaggy-humped Bactrian camels, the men of Eddie's *minghan* and their families hung back, staring down the valley. Somewhere an invisible line crossed the shallow green depression. On the other side lay China.

"Nobody can get trucks up to this pass," Eddie said, "much less tanks. So the PRC doesn't waste much energy watching for an invasion to come this way."

Mounted on a chestnut mare not far from his *khan*'s side, dignified and beautiful in his Western suit coat and turned-up black and white skullcap, the master singer raised his arm. His white goshawk stirred its wings, glaring angrily at the humans all around.

His apprentice eyed it warily from a litter slung between two horses. His bad back wouldn't let him ride. "I don't see any damned rabbits," he growled.

"Perhaps I fly him for the beauty of watching him fly," the old Kirghiz said. "Now, attend: today we sing of the wedding of Manas to the beauteous Kanykäi."

Nikolay Kuliyev rolled his eyes at his wife, who sat a horse next to his litter with Anya mounted before her. "I sure hope you can adjust to this new line of work I'm in."

Marina laughed.

Still they all hung there, on the downslope of the Celestial Mountains, as if reluctant to take the final step.

Shih sighed. "My father taught me a saying—a prophecy.

He said the . . . the wild Mongols still quote it, out on the steppe.''

"So let's hear it, hon," Eddie said.

She raised her head to the wind. *" 'When that which is harder than the rock and stronger than the storm shall fail,' "* she said, *" 'when the White Tsar is no more and the Son of Heaven has vanished, then the campfires of Chingis Khan will be seen again, and his empire will stretch over the earth.' "*

"Christ, I hope not," Eddie said.

She looked at him. "It won't be easy. My country is even more repressive than yours. Either of yours."

"Then we'll have to goddam liberate *Chinese* Turkestan."

"Xinjiang," Shih corrected.

"Gesundheit," Eddie said.

He raised his head and drew a deep breath of the cold sweet air of freedom. And danger, sure. But the two always went together, that much he'd learned. *And what the fuck, over? You're safe when you're dead. Not before.*

He closed his eyes. *"Good-bye, Dad,"* he whispered to the wind.

Then he opened his eyes wide and sat up straight in the saddle. "Let's ride!"

He circled his right hand above his head and put his heels into Sertikan's sides. She pinned her ears in token protest and broke into a trot. Behind her the motley, hopeful procession began to move.

Like a figure out of dream, the white goshawk exploded from the old man's hand. It drove down the valley with quick beats of its wings, glided, then flapped again, and flew into China.